# THE GOLDEN WIDOWS

# Isolde Martyn

SAPERE
BOOKS

# THE GOLDEN
# WIDOWS

Published by Sapere Books.

24 Trafalgar Road, Ilkley, LS29 8HH

saperebooks.com

ISBN: 978-0-85495-397-4

*For my dear friend and great reader, Margaret Phillips,*
*for Babs Creamer, who inspired me to become interested*
*in the Bonvilles, and in memory of Eileen Larbalestier,*
*who was such fun and is sadly missed.*

*Sweet widow, by my state I swear to thee*
*I speak no more than what my soul intends;*
*And that is to enjoy thee for my love.*
— William Shakespeare, *Henry VI Part III*

# ACKNOWLEDGEMENTS

Thanks are due to friend and fellow Ricardian, Babs Creamer of the Poole Group of the Richard III Society. It was her suggestion that I should write a novel about Kate and her daughter and she kindly took me to Shute and to Ottery St Mary, where the church contains a beautiful ceiling, commissioned by Cecily.

I am also grateful to John Cochrane, former guide at Shute, who was very kind in answering my email questions about the history of the area; Sally and Gerald Martyn who did some sleuthing for me at Chewton Mendip Church; the wonderful Turramurra critique group for their comments on the manuscript; Jenny Savage for her advice and suggestions; Jan Colman for suggested reading on Asperger syndrome; friends Felicity and Don Head for their hospitality when we were researching Grafton Regis; and last but not least, my husband for the family trees. Yes, and (as a Leicestershire lad) for being such a great companion on visits to Groby, Astley, Kirby Muxloe, Ashby-de-la-Zouche and Bradgate Park. Finally a big thank you to the editorial team in Sydney: Sue, Annabel, copy editor Jody Lee and the cover design team. You are a delight to work with, everyone!

# Kate's Family Tree, 1461

## The families of the House of York, the Nevilles and the Bonvilles

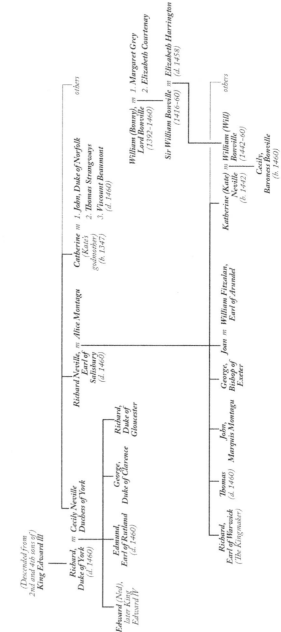

# Elysabeth Woodville's Family Connections, 1461
## The Greys, the Woodvilles and the House of Lancaster

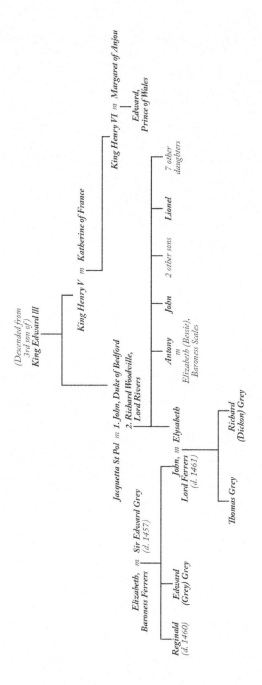

# 1: KATE

## 4th January 1461, The Manor of Shute, Devonshire

Sitting in a splash of winter sunshine on the wall that separated the churchyard from the manor's deer park, Kate Neville tugged off her gloves and took out the letter she had received two days ago from her eighteen-year-old husband, William Bonville, Lord Harrington, and read it for the umpteenth time. This letter of Will's, a long time in coming, had a teasing gallantry that he had never shown her face-to-face.

*Written at Sandal Castle, Wakefield, upon the Feast of St Thomas*
*My entirely beloved lady,*

*I pray God daily for his blessing that you and our child continue in good health. Here is all in readiness to resist the queen's army. I do not doubt that we shall put them to flight else it were great pity.*

*My father is in good heart. The ague he has had a week since is now shent, and this day I was in my lord your father's company too and spoke right merrily with him and your uncle, my lord of York.*

*I beg you remember to feed my birds and I would take it a great kindness if you were to give Cecily kisses each day from her loving father.*

*And, madame, while I shall not be there on the Feast of St Valentine to have you remember your wifely duties, so do I remind you to think upon your lonely husband as I shall think of you in your bed. For you are as ever mine own especial Valentine and true mistress.*

*Your ever loving husband,*
*William Bonville*

A pleasing letter for any young bride, so why did she feel a shivery unease, as though the Devil was opening the door to let in a whole heap of trouble? Guiltily, she read the last sentence of the letter again, wishing she might blush at 'wifely duties' and feel the true heat of love such as the Lady Guinivere had borne for Sir Lancelot, a worldly, muscular knight well past pimples. Of course, better to have a young husband rather than some smelly breathed dotard, she chided herself. Eventually Will would attain the broad shoulders of manhood and not need to crushed madder leaves to cleanse his cheeks.

After being sent to live with his family at the time of her marriage contract when she turned thirteen, she and Will had been friends not sweethearts. The compulsion of intimacy with him once she had begun her monthly flux had estranged them rather than drawing her closer. The wedding night had been so awkward.

Anyway, she thought, tucking the letter back into her sleeve, noble ladies were not supposed to fall in love. Marriage was about family alliances and childbearing. That was the catechism that had been drummed into her and her sisters, and at least being a Neville and of fertile stock, she had given Will a healthy babe within a year of their marriage. A daughter. Not the son he and the Bonvilles wanted (and that was probably her fault for not taking as much pleasure in their awkward coupling as he did). But she was carrying again. A secret that only her bodyservant, Eleanor, was privy to. It would be her gift to Will on his return home, a son that would bring them so much happiness together.

For a moment she sat very still, straining to hear if her tiny daughter might be awake in the nursery but the upper storey of Shute Hall was serene. Smoke rose placidly from the chimneys into the cold blue sky. So much was left to the women at the moment with many of servants and villagers gone to the Duke of York's army. Save for the rattle of a pail being emptied and the comforting conversation of the fowl yard, all was quiet — too quiet. Kate missed the Bonville men, not just Will's company but his father and blustery grandfather. These last weeks there had been no noisy homecomings, shaking of cloaks, scraping of boots, the horses led away, and the dogs muddy and happy seeking the hearth. No swift growl of lost temper between fathers and sons, no male banter, no stories of the hart or fish that got away, no fumings against their rivals, the Courtenays, or complaining about mad King Henry being unfit to rule.

A lone, ragged, offending cloud slid across the sun, and chilled now, Kate wriggled off the wall. Yes, she would walk a little before she went inside; the sunlight would come again. A pity Eleanor could not keep her company but the girl was poorly with a cough and streaming nose.

If Will had been here instead of with her uncle York, they might have taken the horses out. To be honest, that was what she missed most, the freedom that Will's companionship had given her and escapades they had shared before she became great with child.

Getting soaked to the skin — and scared — in a thunderstorm after Axminster Fair; sliding down Steep Meadow on a sledge last winter; and lighting the great beacon to greet the New Year. Will had enjoyed teaching her how to fish for chubb near Whit Ford and given her a falcon of her own to take hawking when they rode out with his father, but best of all he liked to race their horses up the Roman road that cut across the east side of Stockton Hill to the wild, arcane wood that crowned it. Stockton Wood.

And suddenly, staring up at the trees, winter bare and stark upon the hillside, Kate felt again the Devil's whisper of foreboding. Stockton Wood made her afraid of the deep recesses of her soul, afraid that there was a reckoning to be paid.

That first leaf fall after their wedding, Will had spurred his horse through the great rutted puddles left by the woodsmen's carts. She had been riding close behind, but the laughter had left her when he led her on foot deeper into the ancient grove of oaks that tonsured the hill. Everywhere, ivy snaked forth across the fallen logs, clawing upwards, tormenting the barks of the wizened trees. Less obvious, a few venomous greenish-white toadstools, death caps, pierced through the rotting leaves, and the phallus of a single stinkhorn breathed its corrupt miasma out into the shadowy air.

'This oak grove is haunted by the wraiths of pagan victims,' Will had whispered. 'Young virgins sacrificed on a stone altar to the sun god.'

'Then we are trespassing,' she had whispered, pulling free. Their presence seemed a sacrilege. 'Let's go back to the horses.'

He laughed, seeing he had upset her. 'Pah, you are such an innocent, Kate Neville.' His hands reached out to tether her but she guessed his intent and fled.

Whooping, he chased her around the oaks and then he deftly hooked his foot around her ankle, tripping her. She remembered screaming as she fell face down into the mess of ivy. Then he had turned her over, the merriment slipping from his face and she had recognised the silent intensity that always heralded his ardour.

'I don't want to,' she said. 'Not here.'

'Hush, it's your duty to obey me.'

Stifling her protests with kisses, he had fumbled beneath her petticoats, tossed her kirtle back and tumbled her as though she were some common shepherdess. Useless to be angry. Will was quite capable of sulking whenever she said no. Being 'bloggy', his father called it.

'The Druids made love to the virgins before they sacrificed them,' he lied with male authority afterwards, as he stood above her retying the points to his gypon. 'It would have been a waste otherwise.'

'But then they would not have been pure to sacrifice,' she argued, hiding her resentment and tugging her skirts back over her garters and stockings. She pitied the pagan maidens; their ravishment an extra cruelty before slaughter.

He straightened the flap of his hose. 'You are too clever, you Nevilles,' he muttered. 'Anyway, say your prayers, madame wife, that we have made a boy of this moment's work.' But there had been an uneasiness in his eyes, perhaps a fear that he could have provoked the primeval spirits of the grove — a desecration that might require punishment. But then his mood lifted, like a tossed caravel, swinging round to confidence again.

'It looks to rain. I'd better get you home.' He helped her scramble to her feet and then as he plucked away the leaves snared in her boisterous hair, the shadows about them seemed to shrink back, the gnarled trees became less ominous. With his arm about her waist, he had hastened her back to where the horses were contentedly cropping the moss. Maybe it was his new doublet that concerned him, whether the dye of the lining could run and ruin his shirt, or else he was afeared and too much the swaggerer to admit it. Yet they quit the wood with a new spirit planted inside her. It had been there that Cecily had been conceived and although the baby had been born free of any deformities, still Kate feared there was some curse attached to that coupling and that the skein of destiny for Will was tampered with that day. That fear still lay heavy behind her heart although it was fifteen months since the begetting.

'Did you enjoy your walk, my lady?' The wet nurse, Joan Celer, a year older than Kate, sprang to attention from the stool beside Cecily's cradle in the nursery.

Acknowledging the servant's curtsey, Kate picked up a wooden rattle and leaned over her little daughter, delighting in the way the infant's eyes followed the toy. Cecily still had the silvery eyes of a young babe and it was hard to know if they would turn grey like Will's or a Neville blue like hers.

'Fresh swaddling?' she asked, poking an inquisitive finger beneath the cradle blanket.

'Yes, all done, my lady.' Joan curtsied again and Kate nodded gratefully, knowing how hard it must be for her — the Celers' babe had been stillborn. Apart from discussing tiny Cecily's needs, the conversation between them was ever awkward. Only a fool would miss the clench of the girl's jaw now as she stooped to poke the fire into a cheerful mien.

Kate picked up the rabbit toy she had been making and set it down again. How was she going to fill the hours? It seemed a petty dilemma when the Bonville men were likely to face the queen's army any day now. Reread a French romance from Grandfather Bonville's library when Englishmen were riding out to slaughter each other? Music was sometimes her refuge but her lute was unplayable, waiting for new strings.

She sighed. Her own manor house would keep her busy but no chance of that. Not yet. Although Will's mother was dead, Grandmother Bonville, the beloved second wife of Will's exuberant grandsire, had been 'Queen of Shute' for over thirty years and showed no signs of relinquishing her orb and sceptre to an eighteen year old. With ancient Lord Bonville either at court or making mischief harassing the neighbouring Courtenays, charity to the sick, rent-collecting, manorial courts, the upkeep and provisioning of the Bonvilles' many manor houses were all Grandmother Bonville's domain.

At times infuriating, manipulative and stubborn, the old lady (she must be over fifty) had been a formidable challenge for a young bride like Kate, but on the whole they trotted well together. Mind, Grandmother Bonville's grey eyes could pinion a miscreant as well as any schoolmaster's. Kate knew she was in for a scolding if 'Katherine Neville!' was rapped across the chamber.

No babe had ever set within Grandmother Bonville and she was so thin-waisted, one might fear for her safety if she walked the edge of the cliffs at Seyton on a gusty day. Kate, whose body had not lost its thickening since Cecily's birth, felt like a tubby little packhorse beside her. And thinking of horses…

'Joan, is Lady Bonville back from Nalysworth?' Kate asked, wondering if the old lady would be game to ride out with her after noon.

'Aye, my lady came in an hour since. She said Mistress Whittle's leg is still puffed up like some great bladder an' she's a-thinkin' she'll send word to the physician in Axminster.'

Mistress Whittle's husband, one of the free tenants, had gone north with Will and his father, so Lady Bonville felt some duty to help the woman in time of trouble.

'Axminster,' Kate mused. 'Perhaps I could do that.' It had been a statement not a question but Joan shook her head.

'You'd not be back afore dusk, my lady, an' the mist can come down summat awful. Why only last week Dick Geye's granfer got himself lost in the fog an' ended up t'other side of Wyke.'

'That old man would get himself lost between the alehouse and his horse,' Kate muttered. Of course, Joan was right, although it was hardly her place to advise her betters. 'Pray go down and —'

She hesitated as the barking of the dogs and bellow of horn at the front gate spurred her hopes down a different path. Visitors? That would be a welcome distraction. Or could it be Will come home at last? It had been over a week since he had penned the letter. Maybe there had been a peace-making between my lord of York and the queen's grace, God willing!

She was tempted to rush down the stairs and jump the last twist but married women, even eighteen-year-old ones, were supposed to behave with maturity. *You are always in too much haste*, her mother, the Countess of Salisbury, had warned her before her marriage. *Servants expect a lady to be calm; it engenders a peaceful household.* So Kate waited, tapping her foot impatiently.

'It be Peter Haccom, I reckon, wi' spices,' Joan said, smoothing her waistcloth.

Oh, of course, how disappointing. But if it was Haccom, the warty-nosed carter who served the villages and hamlets between Exeter and Axminster, he might have brought her lute strings. Usually if he picked up an extra bargain in spices or some other commodity, he would come to Shute, certain of a sale.

It was him. She could smell cinnamon sticks as she entered the kitchen. A row of spice bags cluttered the end of the kitchen board and a small sack, its stitches ripped open to show the quality of the woody galingale within, leaned tipsily against an earthenware pot of quince paste. But something was wrong. It was like entering a chamber where people who were gossiping suddenly went quiet. Grandmother Bonville, two of their tiring women, the steward, the master cook and three of the young kitchen hands were just standing open-mouthed, staring at lanky old Haccom.

The fellow's expression, though respectful, was almost a smirk. His bony fingers played with the padded brim of his hat. He seemed to be waiting, but it wasn't for payment.

Kate ranged herself by Grandmother Bonville who, with a little shake of her head as though collecting herself, announced huskily, 'Master Haccom has just given us some tidings, Katherine. Pray, repeat yourself to Lady Harrington, sirrah.'

The carter gave Kate a half-bow and the self-gratified smile of someone suddenly important. 'The news in Exeter, my lady, is that the Duke of York is dead, slain on his own doorstep, so to speak. I heard it from one of the sergeants-at-law and he heard it from our mayor.'

But Will's letter, Kate's mind protested illogically, had only arrived a few days ago.

*And today I was in my lord your father's company too and spoke right merrily with him and your uncle, my lord of York.*

Now she, too, stared at the carter open lipped.

'Did he tell you anything more?' demanded Grandmother Bonville. 'When, for instance?'

'A week since, my lady, outside Sandal Castle, near the town of Wakefield. Up north.'

*A week ago!*

Haccom was fidgeting for his usual jack of ale and Lady Bonville nodded to the butler to draw it for him. 'York and his second son both slain, my lady,' Haccom continued, 'an' I know naught else save Queen Margaret had the duke's head lopped off and stuck a paper crown on it. Maybe we'll ha' peace now.'

The cursed knave knew the Bonville men had declared loyalty to the Duke of York, so the remark was offensive, but he escaped a reprimand. Kate's mind was still shaken at the news and Grandmother Bonville, who rarely showed emotion to lesser folk, did not drop her mask of control.

'And the other lords with the duke?' she demanded. 'The Earl of Salisbury, for instance?'

Kate's head jerked up.

'Ah yes, now you remind me, my lady, there was summat.' The carter's gaze swerved to meet Kate's with feigned candour, as if he had forgotten he was in the presence of my lord of Salisbury's daughter. 'Captured and taken to Pomfret Castle. I believe there was mention of one of his sons bein' wi' him.'

Her father and Tom, her second oldest brother, were still alive, thought Kate, breathing out. Prisoners but alive!

Haccom's eyes gleamed. 'I've brought the lute strings for you, my lady. Best qual —'

'Not now. See he is paid,' Grandmother Bonville said calmly to the steward, then she was taking Kate's arm, and the kitchen was left behind.

'No, we don't need the chaplain or anyone else,' she was saying over her shoulder as she hurried Kate through the great hall, but her stern demeanour cracked once they reached the privacy of the great chamber.

'Jesu, Kate!' She let go the latch and leaned back against the door, the gris trim on her bodice heaving and her mouth a downturned horseshoe as though luck had suddenly poured out.

Will's father and Will — O God, had they been slain?

'We should have asked,' Kate said.

'Haccom would have told us,' Lady Bonville muttered. 'Drawn it out like a torment. No, that's all that loathsome wretch knew, I'd swear to it.' Her hands spread as though she was letting hope free into their midst. 'They probably got away. That's why he didn't know. Maybe they've all been taken to Pomfret with your father.' She stared across at Kate with concern. 'Kate?'

'I'm all right — at the moment.' She had sat down upon the window seat, her hands very still in her lap. 'Do you think they will execute Father and Tom?'

She read the possibility in the straight line of Lady Bonville's mouth. 'Oh dear,' she said, swallowing. Her mind began to flick in panic — turning the pages of a book she did not want to read. She imagined the horror of her uncle York's head nailed to the stonework. There were other gates, other walls…

'Oh, my dear.' Will's grandmother crouched before her, her crimson skirt lapping the toes of Kate's shoes as she took her hands with a gentleness that was rare for her. 'Battles are never orderly, child. There is every chance they've survived, and Will has his father to stop him doing anything too hot-headed. Why, we cannot suppose they were still at Sandal when the duke was slain.'

Or they could.

'They'll be back. You'll see.' She rose stiffly and went to stand before the fire. 'Men!' she scoffed, tossing her head in disgust. 'You know the number of times my old fool of a husband gets himself in the thick of things. If it isn't some battle, it's a petty skirmish down the road and he'll come home with a bloody nose, grinning like a dog that had been off rabbiting. Remember Clyston Moor two years ago?'

Kate tried to smile, but it was her family who had talked the Bonvilles into treason.

'Haccom said York's second son was killed, didn't he?' she whispered. 'That must be my cousin Edmund and … and he's

my age and he used to play Robin Hood with us and he'd …
he'd have been better armoured than Will.'

'We need some strong wine.'

Instead of calling for one of the servants, Grandmother
Bonville swept across to the aumery herself. Her words might
have been heartening but Kate glimpsed the telltale, grim line
of her mouth as she let down the board. The chamber was
silent save for the crackling of a log upon the fire. The older
woman set out two mazers and after searching out a flask from
the back, snapped the lead seal that bound the stopper.
'Grandsire's favourite,' she announced, 'but he'll not mind.'
She took a good gulp and ran a cleansing knuckle across her
lips before she carried a generous cup across to Kate. 'To think
that York is suddenly no more. All that rhetoric, all that
posturing, pfft! For sure, Queen Margaret will be in ecstasy to
have her greatest enemy dead. Stupid man, to get himself
killed. Pah, he always was one not to think things through.'

Kate took a mouthful, spluttered and found her eyes
watering at the strength. The liquor certainly kicked her insides.
'There's still my brother Warwick's army,' she reminded Will's
grandmother. 'And my cousin Ned has an army down near
Ludlow.' Ned, who she must think of as Duke of York now.
'Surely if the two of them put their force together, they should
be able to hold London against the queen?' Not encouraged by
the older woman's frown, she added briskly, 'Well, they'll have
to, won't they, or else make peace with her. I hope Will has
escaped to join them.'

'Humpf, I hope to Heaven that brother of yours has his head
screwed on tight,' muttered Grandmother Bonville and then
pressed apologetic fingers to her lips. 'I am sorry, Katherine,
foolish choice of —'

The vigorous banging on the steel platter downstairs summoning them to midday dinner staunched her apology.

'I am not sure I can eat.' Kate announced honestly.

Grandmother straightened her collar and tidied her lawn veil. Even inside the house, she dressed as though she was about to welcome guests. 'We must show our people nothing is of concern, *mustn't we*!' With a spine that generations of her family, the Courtenays, had straightened through adversity — Crécy, Poitiers, Agincourt, not to mention years of armed scuffles with the Bonvilles — she raised the latch, and sallied forth.

'Master Gylle's eldest girl bore a living babe last even — a son.'

Joan's sudden babble next morning made Kate look up at her in wonderment from the blanket where she was playing with Cecily. That was at least one piece of cheerful news after a sleepless night of worrying whether Will would come back safe. Kate watched the girl's nimble fingers spooling the strips of freshly laundered swaddling cloth. The face above carried a knowing smile. Was there some mischief in the telling?

'That's the family over at Cockes' Croft, isn't it, Joan?' she murmured, leaning down to plant a huff of warm breath on her babe's small belly. The tiny legs jerked and two dimples appeared aside the little mouth. 'I didn't think any of their daughters were wed.'

'Lovidia *ain't*.' The snide emphasis on the verb explained why it was gossip to be savoured at the village well.

'Oh, it's Lovidia, is it? I remember her. The one with lovely dark ringlets. She was working here at the hall. I thought she left Shute to wed a farmer north of Axminster?'

'Aye, my lady, but he changed his mind though he was courtin' her nigh twelve month.' A common story. Clearly the farmer had been doing more than squeezing Lovidia's hand, unless, of course, some local fellow had robbed her of her virtue. 'Wed a bailiffs daughter up near Chard,' added Joan. 'More dowry, see.' Kate watched her brush the stray threads from her skirt as though more could be said but wasn't going to be.

Considering how beautiful Lovidia was, Kate had no doubt that most of the young women in the village would be snickering at their rival's ill fortune.

'She be callin' the babe William in the hope the young master may stand godfather, my lady.' Joan was watching her face with such anticipation that Kate wondered if she was either a close friend or else an ardent foe of Lovidia's.

'I think it might be more appropriate if Lovidia's father broaches the matter with my husband on his return,' Kate answered, frowning. She could make no promises on Will's behalf.

'That's as maybe, my lady, but her da, Stephen Gylle, be *with* the young master up north. 'Sides, the babe needs to be shriven.'

'Of course.' Kate crossed herself, remembering how anxious she had been to have Cecily safely baptised. Babies were so vulnerable; only last March the blacksmith's infant son had died in the cradle for no apparent reason, not a mark on him.

Joan took a ball of swaddling from the basket. 'Want me to wrap the little one now, madame, afore she catches her death of cold?'

'Pray do so.' Kate scrambled aside and sat back on her heels watching Joan bind Cecily close. The babe had grown so much since Will had left, but thinking of him, the night's fears rose again like demons to pinch at her heart. How soon would it be before she knew that he was safe? Did Mistress Gylle, cuddling her first grandchild, also fear the worst? Had Joan's tittle-tattle been a hint that the Bonvilles should show some patrimony to the Gylles?

'One of the grooms can take a basket of provisions to the Gylles' cottage,' Kate decreed, wriggling her toes free of her hem. 'Or maybe I shall bear it there myself.' Something to take her mind off listening for a messenger.

'That's right gracious of you, my lady.' Joan, with the babe neatly tucked in the crook of one arm, helped her mistress to her feet. Kate disregarded the satisfied expression lurking in the girl's eyes and knew she had been tugged into the offer as though she was Cecily's wooden duck on a string.

Her mother's voice came back to her. *Always behave like a great lady for the right reasons, Katherine, not merely because of duty or with the selfish hope to have Heaven's door open to you, but because your heart is stirred to compassion by another's need.*

Well, she would show herself 'stirred' and she just prayed that Queen Margaret might be stirred to mercy, too.

Judging by its large barn, capacious byre of wintering cattle and plentiful supply of firewood, the Gylles' farm boasted prosperity as well as hard work, and the last thing the daughter of this prosperous homestead looked to need was a basket of provisions, decided Kate, wishing she had consulted Grandmother Bonville first. Together with Will, she had visited most of their tenant farmers but he had not yet brought her here.

The old gaffer from the stable, who had accompanied her, was clearly thinking the same thing. His hand had hesitated on the straps, which held the pannier and the bed-ale.

'Are you sure you want to take this in, my lady?' he asked, careful to salt his presumption with a straight face.

'Yes, of course.' But Kate's face was burning, not from the lash of cold wind either.

How could Stephen Gylle afford a stained cloth painting on the wall and even a chair, she marvelled, as she was welcomed in. A well-stacked fire burned cheerfully in the central hearth of the crux-beamed hall and there was even a book on a wooden stand before the window.

Mistress Gylle's clean waistcloth and wimple impressed Kate. So did the quality of her gown and the cleanliness of the half-dozen young children who clustered round her. Clearly Master Gylle must be a good husbandman and stand in high favour with Grandfather Bonville. Yet why, Kate wondered, did her arrival (not to mention the hefty goodwill pannier of delicacies) astonish the woman so? Of course, there was no 'we really don't need your bounty,' no hauteur, but too much the reverse; the flustered, tongue-tied housewife bestowed upon her guest more curtsies than even a queen deserved as she backed before Kate towards the sound of squalling.

The room, where the young mother rested, was shuttered and cosy. It was probably Master Gylle's own bedchamber, judging by the excellence of the yellow and green striped bed hangings, and likely had been added onto the older hall for it also boasted a stone chimney. Beeswax candles flickered in the wall brackets. Certainly well-to-do.

The young mother lay upon a featherbed with the babe sucking lustily at a nipple. Dark ringlets streamed across the pillow, and tendrils, lustreless with sweat from yesterday's birthing, framed a vibrant, heart-shaped face. The wench's eyes widened in astonishment at her visitor.

'Why, here's my Lady Harrington come to congratulate you, Lovidia,' cackled the village midwife, rising from the stool on the other side of the bed where she had been nursing a leatherjack of ale.

Kate hid her displeasure at the old woman's tone. She felt out of her depth, as though she was providing some sort of amusement for these underlings. 'Leave us, if you please,' she requested with a dignity her lady mother would have approved, and the midwife withdrew, the puckered cheeks a tad sucked in.

Kate waved aside the offer to bring in Master Gylle's chair and took the vacated stool instead, hoping the midwife had left no lice. As she began the small talk, encouraging Lovidia to share her experience, she found herself increasingly warming to the details of last night's labour. Giving birth made them equals just as the inevitability of death would one day dissolve the difference of rank between them. The girl was euphoric at the tiny miracle that lay within her arms and any mother of a living babe could understand her joy.

Only as Kate rose to leave, did Lovidia set a hand upon her sleeve and revive the fears shared by both families. 'Is there any news, my lady. Your pardon, but you would be telling me, wouldn't you? Word is the Duke of York is slain. Is —' The unasked question hung in the air between them. Had the Bonville retainers survived?

'I don't know, Lovidia. We are still waiting to hear. I'm sure your father will come home safe. I feel for you, believe me. My lord father was also with the duke.'

The farmer's daughter raised her head, fixing her intense blue gaze upon Kate. 'And all the lords from Shute, them as well?'

'Yes. Is…?' Kate faltered, deciding whether to ask if the father of the babe was fighting alongside Will. Of course, Lovidia might not know who the father was. Mind, she did not look like a creature ready to hoick up her skirts at every opportunity.

'Is your child's da with them, Lovidia?'

Long-lashed eyelids shuttered slyly as the girl moved the infant to her other nipple. 'Yes, my lady, I believe so.' So, she was not prepared to name him.

'Then I shall light a candle for his wellbeing.'

'Thank you, my lady.' The pointed chin rose proudly and the glint of something that had been in the midwife's eyes flickered for a second. Perhaps they were all amused at her attempt to behave like a grand lady, thought Kate, a trifle hurt. It was so typical of lesser folk, the exchanged, secretive glances that reminded Kate she was not one of them but something tolerated because they had no choice.

'Ill news travels fast,' she declared, turning at the door. 'I'll send a messenger with good, I trust.'

'God's blessing go with you, my lady, you have a good heart.'

'And remain here with you and yours, Lovidia.'

Another visitor had arrived; the wise woman of Shute. A seer, some said. Neatly wimpled, gloved and gowned, with southerly bosoms bedecked with a rosary, the woman looked incongruous company beside the shrivelled apple-skin midwife.

'Mistress Alice reads fortunes,' piped up one of the children and refused to be hushed. 'Has she read yours, my lady?'

'Not yet,' said Kate, and bravely thrust out her right palm. 'Is he coming home?'

'The young lord?' The woman took her hand and drew her to the candle flame. Because a caul blinded one of her eyes, she bent over Kate's hand like a master goldsmith assaying a piece of jewellery. Then she straightened and, gazing into Kate's eyes, spoke solemnly, as though each word was being weighed out with scrupulous care.

'Your husband will be famous and much loved.'

So Will would live. The reassurance so delighted Kate that she ignored the midwife's snigger. Fumbling in her beltpurse, she pressed a coin into the wise woman's palm. Generosity was her weapon against their conspiratorial winks. 'And here's for your services, too, old ganmer.' She held out a coin to the midwife who bit into it as though Kate was a market-day stranger.

'Thank'ee, I might not be a fine physician, my lady, but I'll warrant I've delivered more livin' babes than any long-gowned dawcock with his fancy scholarship.' Her gaze slid to Kate's belly as though she guessed her condition.

'Hush now, Mab. Perhaps you should leave before the weather sours, my lady.' Mistress Gylle punctuated the suggestion with a further curtsey next to the door. 'Thank you for your kindness, Lady Harrington.' They wanted her gone.

Kate nodded and left the warmth of the farmhouse to face the chill shadows of her own life. The sky was leaden and streaky, and the wind had swung round to the south. The old groom was edgy, anxious to get her home out of the cold. Because of the babe within her, she rode sedately, her knee hooked over the saddle pommel, her rabbit fur-lined cloak and riding skirt shielding her belly.

The rain began as they came within sight of Shute House. Eleanor, her dauncell, was waiting to greet her. Beneath her simple white coif, the girl's normally cheerful face was red-nosed from the ague and full of concern.

'I am pleased you are on your feet again,' Kate called out cheerfully, dragging the soles of her riding boots across the outside scraper. 'By the saints, Lovidia Gylle's babe is a hungry little mite.' Coming in, she heeled off her boots and shrugged off her cloak into the girl's waiting arms. 'I swear it will plummet down before cock cr— Why, you've been crying. Oh Lord! There's been news, hasn't there?'

'My lady desires you to join her straightway.'

Kate clutched her wrists. 'Oh, Eleanor, tell me!'

'No, please, madame, it's best you join her.'

With relief, Kate heard Cecily cooing healthily as she opened the door to the great chamber. That was one concern off her mind. Joan, waiting inside, offered the babe to her in placatory fashion but Kate, her gaze on Will's grandmother, brushed past. The pain in the room was almost tangible. Behind her, she heard Eleanor dismiss Joan and close the door.

Old Lady Bonville sat in the chamber's only chair, her shoulders drooping as though a monstrous weight had been strapped upon her back. Will was standing before the fire, his back turned. He was still cloaked. Waterlets trickled from his rain-soaked hair. His footsteps had trailed mud across the tiles; spatters still clung to his spurs and rimed his boot heels.

Safe. Alive.

*Your husband will be famous and much loved.*

Her heart steadied somewhat. Dear God! It must be Will's father who would not come back and yet...

The young man turned and bowed, and she saw in shock that it was only Rob Newton, servant to Will's grandfather. This ill news must be from London then, not from the north; the Tower of London, where Grandfather Bonville was holding King Henry prisoner. Had the London mob rescued the king? Was Lord Bonville dead?

'Madame?' Kate whispered, approaching in fear that the old lady's world had suddenly shaken into chaos.

Lady Bonville stared unseeing into the fire. An opened letter lay spread upon her lap. Kate recognised the neat flourishes of her oldest brother Richard, the Earl of Warwick's, hand.

Cradled in the centre crease was a small ribboned scroll typical of Grandfather Bonville's 'writ in haste' communications.

'M … may I see, please?'

Resting on her knee, the fingers of Lady Bonville's right hand rose briefly in assent and dropped as if in desperate resignation. Bracing herself, Kate took up the two missives and carried them to the better light in the windowed recess where she usually sat to embroider. Tucking her brother's letter beneath her arm, she pushed back the twin curls of the smaller parchment. Its words began to dance before her vision as she read the opening sentences of Grandfather Bonville's scrawl.

Dead? Her father-in-law, her brother Tom and…

*Will!*

Hurriedly she dashed away the tears distorting her vision and, fumbling, grabbed her brother's letter. It was to Lady Bonville begging her to break the news to Kate that their father had been beheaded in the marketplace at Pontefract on the orders of Queen Margaret.

*Then Father's head must be on a pole somewhere.*

On the gate next to Uncle York's or like a grotesque trophy being brought south in someone's saddlebag to be spiked above London Bridge.

And Will was never coming home. Cecily would never know her father.

'I'm so sorry,' she exclaimed, retreating towards the door. 'Oh God!' Wrenching it open, she ran down the stairs and out in her stockinged feet across the cobbles, heedless of the rain, across the garden and over the steps in the wall that linked the manor grounds to the churchyard.

Blind with tears, she ran between the tombstones and almost pitched headfirst into a newly dug grave. *For Will?* His body to lie forever in the unfeeling, freezing earth? In horror, she stared across the gaping pit at the surprised, uncomprehending faces of two gravediggers and the globs of red soil trickling down their paused shovels.

'My lady, is aught wrong?'

Shuddering, she backed away and grabbing a gravestone for support, retched. Fool, she chided herself once the spasms ceased. Will's body would be put in the Bonville vault. Not alone. He'd have his father...

But her father's body...?

Oh, God! Oh God!

'Lady?'

She fled from the gravediggers' solicitous concern. Stumbling, she reached the church porch and leaned for an instant against its lintel. Her grieving breath made splashes of vapour that bruised the icy air. Grabbing the ring handle, she pushed open the church door. She needed sanctuary, sanctuary against the truth, but here was more pain as she faced the font where she and Will had stood together for Cecily's baptism. And the nave? Numbly she walked the lias flagstones alone, remembering how she and Will had approached the chancel hand in hand after their wedding at the church porch.

Alas, save for the muted sound of the rainwater dribbling from the tongues of the outside gargoyles, the church was silent, lifeless about her. The paltry daylight barely alleviated the dimness; only the oil lamp hanging above the chancel offered a gleam of hope.

Her drenched hem and muddy feet sullied the tiles as she flung herself on her knees before the rood screen. Someone was sobbing. A voice that was hers, and yet not known by her, was whimpering and howling like a snared creature, disdaining the growing whispers at the door.

Hasty footsteps halted at her shoulders. 'Lady Harrington.'

Like a trapped, wild rabbit, she flinched at the rector's touch upon her shoulder.

'Leave me alone, Father! I don't need your help. Go away from me! Go! Go!'

'Daughter!' The admonishment was stern. Did he think she was self-indulgent, wallowing in her misery? Part of her mind heard the annoyance in the retreating rustle of his clothing, the angry creak of shoe leather. Cradling her body, she rocked, her gaze searching about her for answers. She felt guilty, so guilty that she had not loved Will enough. Above her, wearing his crown of thorns, Christ drooped from his cross in his own suffering, but the carved eyes were looking heavenwards.

'Madame, my sweet lady!' A young woman's voice seemed to come from a distance, past the haze of tears. 'Christ's mercy, you are so cold. Come, I beg you, before you take a chill.' Eleanor dropped a fur-lined cloak about her shivering shoulders and with a firm arm, gathered her by the waist and drew her upwards. 'Come back to the house, there's mulled wine for the old mistress and the little one is crying for you.'

'I'll carry my lady!' The youth, Newton, pushed in. Without a by-your-leave, he scooped an arm behind her knees and lifted her against his breast.

Kate's bodily state seeped through her grief, forcing her to recognise that she must still contend with matters earthly; the discomfort of her frozen feet, the damp of her gown between her shoulder blades and the sane, healthy beat of the young man's heart against her cheek as he strode with her through the church gate. This should be Will not some servant, and the fact that Will would never hold her or Cecily ever again shook more sobs from her.

'I can walk,' she protested. Behind them the church's funeral bell began to toll.

'Nay, my lady, not without shoes,' he answered firmly.

'Are *any* of them coming back, Rob?' she heard Eleanor ask.

'The old lord is still hale, remember, an' if Master Gylle and the others survived the battle at Wakefield, they'll be let go. Like as not, there'll be more trouble. Her grace's army is marching south to take London.'

'Jesu! I hope we'll see no change o'masters.' Eleanor's comment needed shaking into meaning but Kate's mind was too burdened to deal with it now, and there was a cluster of servants round the door as though she was a royal barge being met by a group of welcoming courtiers. Robert Newton carried her up the stairs and stood her up like a toppled chess piece. She remembered to thank him and saw he was red with exertion — and perhaps embarrassment for his uncalled-for display of masculine assertion.

Some colour was back in Lady Bonville's complexion as well. 'Chaplain's awaiting us in the chapel — when you've composed yourself, of course.'

Kate flinched inwardly. Masses for the dead. 'Yes, of course,' she said bleakly.

'You are too cold, my lady.' Eleanor was chafing her hands, leading her to the fire.

'Well, get those wet stockings off her!' Grandmother snapped. 'Help her, Joan, you daft ha'ppeth. Are you all breast and no brain?'

Kate gave herself over to their kind hands as they stripped away her sodden kirtle and reclothed her in a sombre gown of mourning with a cap and veil of blue-black lawn.

Freshly kindled logs were burning in the grate but the cold draught from beneath the door wrapped like an invisible icy cloth about her ankles.

The ancient words of the paternoster numbed her mind as they came from her lips. The apparatus of grief had grooves she could follow until they put her to bed.

Later, when there was a posset of valerian warming her insides and hot bricks around her feet, she thought once more about the foolish old soothsayer.

*Your husband will be famous and much loved.*

Will had boasted that one day he would be famous throughout the realm. His plans had included slaying Saracens (he was vague about where), pissing on the Courtenays (his language not hers), knocking some sense into King Henry, invading France (he wanted to be as renowned as his grandsire, one of the few lords still living who had fought at Agincourt) and becoming a Knight of the Garter ('because that's something Grandfather hasn't managed yet!').

*God rest his soul!*

So much for prophecy.

# 2: ELYSABETH

*12<sup>th</sup> February 1461, The City of Leicester*

Alas, not another leering look.

Elysabeth sighed, taking care to keep close behind her husband, Sir John Grey, as they threaded their way out of the Blue Boar. John might complain that she always wore high necklines but it was not merely because of the winter cold that she did so. She hated the way men — whether barons or beggars — fingered her with their stares. This time it had been a greasy apprentice in a leather apron with a ripening boil upon his neck.

'Now, Elysabeth, is there aught we still need to purchase before we leave the city?' John, replete with ale and a dinner of Leicester beef and Tewkesbury mustard, awaited her answer before dispatching their groom to bring their horse.

She shook her head, knowing how much it must have vexed her husband to spend so much time amongst the city wares, especially when he had only been back a day and his family were still in month-mind for his nine-year-old brother, Reginald. But John
had seen how much she craved to escape the gloominess of Groby Hall and his mother's scowls.

'I wish we might return to Astley,' she said wistfully, tucking her arm through his. Astley in Warwickshire had been their home since their wedding, but Groby with its 200-year-old hall and ancient motte had come into the Grey family as part of John's mother's dowry and although John shared the running of it, Elysabeth always felt she was there under sufferance.

'Be content, love. I know you like Groby as much as a cat loves water but I've hardly seen Mother since our brother's death.'

*And I have hardly seen you,* she added silently and, as if he sensed her thoughts, he hugged her against him. 'Thank you for last night,' he murmured. 'You would not believe how many times I imagined holding you once more in my arms.'

Their first bout of lovemaking had been fierce, his hunger urgent. But when he was finally satiated, he had lain beside her with a tight frown creasing his forehead as though his mind was elsewhere, and she could only guess at the ugliness he had seen these last months. Trying to make him unstopper his thoughts had been futile. 'Not now,' he had said. Did he unburden himself to any of his brothers-in-arms? Or were the memories like a poison stoppered in the depth of him, ever to be left untouched?

'Lighten your heart, Elysabeth,' he whispered now, letting go of her as their servant arrived from the inn stable with their bay ambler. 'God has been good to us. Let us not spoil today with ifs and maybes. Live for today not for the morrow.' Yet there was a tensing of his jaw as he spoke as though his thoughts were once more with the queen's army.

She understood. It could not be easy to slough off the preoccupations of the last few months, to rest his mind from packing and unpacking the daily minutiae of soldiering: strategies, supplies, the mustering, the miles, the mud, the wind howling outside the canvas skin of the tent, the arming for battle of both mind and body, and the aftermath, the search for comrades among the dead, the prayers over the mass graves and then the relentless marching on again next day.

All cruel hardships. And no doubt he thought her soft, pampered.

So could he guess the emptiness she had endured these last months and the bliss of being with him now? How wondrous it was to know the joy of being a much-loved wife; the protective, possessive hand between her shoulder blades, the banter between them — sweet heaven, it was so good to laugh again — and his patience. Yes, this morning in Leicester, such patience while she had been deciding on a modestly tasselled girdle for her mourning gown. And later, his indulgence, as she deliberated over gifts for their sons, Tom and Dickon.

'By the way, I've a surprise for you, m'duck,' John murmured playfully, letting his hand stray up her calf after he had helped her onto the pillion, heedless that the groom and half a dozen smirking horse boys were watching.

'St Valentine's Day is two days hence!' She gave him a teasing sideways look from beneath her lashes. Had he purchased some trinket for her?

As they rode up High Street towards North Gate, she snuggled against his back and discreetly adventured her hand beneath the skirt of his doublet to torment him a little. It was amusing to see his respectability under siege. They had been married almost ten years but Elysabeth liked catching him off his guard. She had learned such tricks from her own mother and seen for herself how it kept the love match between her parents vibrant and affectionate. Besides, she was only twenty-four and John still had a year to his thirtieth birthday.

'Wicked wench!' her lord and master growled, shifting her hand back to his belt. 'If you do that again, we'll both end up in the mucky meadow past Walker's Croft, thistles or no.' He chuckled and pulled his cloak firmly across his belly and kneed their ambler to make haste, for the overcast sky was glimmering with the pale rusty hue that betokened snow by evening and it was almost five miles to home.

They were late back to the family house at Groby, carelessly, deliberately so. The penance was enduring his mother's silence through supper. It was one of the baroness's huffy sulks, punctuated by glares and sniffs that quivered the pleats of her widow's wimple beneath her chin. John took no notice. Whenever he returned, his mother's ill temper trickled off him for the first few days, but Elysabeth knew that within a week Lady Ferrers' criticism of her and the boys would start to soak into John's self-esteem and he would grow stricter with the children.

Lady Ferrers had fiercely opposed the marriage, even though Queen Margaret herself had been their matchmaker and Elysabeth had been only fourteen when John brought her home as a bride. After a happy exuberant childhood, she had not been prepared for such animosity.

'By Jesu,' she had overheard John's mother complain to her father-in-law during the first month after her wedding day, 'I cannot believe how you have been so bewitched. You and your son are like two old dotards hastening to please. A pair of winsome eyes and pretty paps...'

'Pah, wife,' interrupted John's father. 'Sounds like the deadly sin of envy to me,' and judging by the small shriek that followed, he goosed her.

That was ten years ago but Lady Ferrers' dislike for Elysabeth had not lessened. Tonight, her mother-in-law was not just angry at their lateness but peeved because they had not taken her with them to Leicester. Tomorrow, verbal crossbolts would be fired at Elysabeth across the mending. Trouble was, to put it bluntly, Lady Ferrers needed a lover. She was two-and-forty and had been a widow for four years now.

'I suppose you did not remember to bring me the ell of black sarcenet I asked for, John.'

*You tell her, Elysabeth*, suggested John's grin as he removed his gloves.

'Of course we did, madame.' Spoken sweetly. '*And* some taffeta for the sleeve lining. *And* the cheeses you asked for.'

'Oh.' Silence and then her mother-in-law said gruffly, 'I see you've bought yourself a new silk girdle, Elysabeth. Must have cost you a fair penny.'

'John bought it for me.' She dashed a smile at her husband.

'Really.' Out of verbal bolts and arrows for the time being, John's mother directed her annoyance to the tearing of an innocent hunk of bread.

John made no comment but the beak of his shoe nudged Elysabeth's beneath the table. His gaze as he raised his goblet told her that they would go early to bed.

There was no linking door between bedchambers to be unlocked, no draughty passageway to be navigated, no negotiations necessary, yet Elysabeth deliberately kept her husband waiting while she went to bid their sons goodnight and give them their gifts from Leicester. For Dickon, who was four, a wooden dragon, which moved its paws when you pulled a string, and for Tom, who was nine, a wooden curiosities box, inlaid with ivory.

The children had been left behind that morning because Tom had been rude to his grandmother and little Dickon was recovering from a cold. Elysabeth was perhaps too careful of Dickon but he had been a frail infant and she did not like to expose him to the miasmas of Leicester's marketplace.

'Were our boys pleased?' John surprised her from behind the bedchamber door, dragging her back against him and stroking her thighs through her skirts.

'Of course. All the more so because the gifts were your choice.'

'Tom is fortunate he's gotten anything.'

Elysabeth leaned her head back against her husband's shoulder but her mind was preoccupied with her children. It was useless to tell John that he should be home more, that the boys longed for his presence like shoots searching for the sunshine, but being a baron, he had spent too much of the last year in Queen Margaret's army or attending parliaments that mouthed much and achieved little.

The wrangling — very lethal at times — had been because of King Henry's health. It was as if God occasionally blew the old king's wits out like a candle and it was happening too often. So often, that the Duke of York had asserted he would make a worthier king and had taken up arms against Queen Margaret, but now he was slain and — please God — the fighting was over. Elysabeth was so weary of sharing her husband with the queen.

'Now his grace of York has gone to Hell, maybe you could spend some more time with the boys and me, my love,' she suggested, primly setting his hands away from her breasts.

'I wish so, too,' he whispered, kissing her naked throat, 'but there's still Warwick who won't crouch down and lick hands, not to mention York's heir, young Edward. Distract me no further, madame wife. I am here at home now and horny as a stag in rut so let us see if we can make a daughter, a daughter as beauteous as you, Elysabeth,' he murmured, deftly loosening the back laces of her gown, a skill he had learned early in their marriage.

She did not tell him it was too late in the month for begetting.

'John,' she murmured, feeling her own desire kindling, as he pushed down her gown to the elbows and turned her in a masterly fashion to face him.

'Look at you, four-and-twenty, and still the most beautiful woman in all of England.'

She wound her arms about his neck. 'No, the most fortunate.' In his presence the world was steady and she was protected from the snags and snares of fortune. Mind, she could have wished his family a thousand leagues away but no matter, she thought, as he laid her down upon the bed and slid his hand up her petticoats, tomorrow was St Valentine's Eve.

Next morning they were slugabeds, making love again, warm within the curtained bed, heedless of the frosty February day dawning outside. John fell into a morning slumber and Elysabeth rose to cleanse herself behind the corner screen and pull on a fresh chemise. Then, clad in her rabbit fur wrap, she fastened back the lower casement shutters.

The voices of the builders' apprentices reached her through the diamond panes. Louder this morning. They were constructing a tower. Newfangled, ugly. Instead of stone, it was being built of small, hand-made bricks. This tower, John swore, would be the first of its kind in England and might indeed set a fashion. If he was pleased with it, he was going to build a new great house entirely of bricks and demolish Groby Hall with its dry rot, draughts and smoke-stained ceilings.

Well, a brick dwelling couldn't be colder than this one! Padding across to the hearth, she lifted off the *couvre-feu*, coaxed the embers into glowing coals and aided by the bellows and some fresh kindling, she persuaded the fire to provide some welcome heat. Satisfied, she sought out her hairbrush but instead of sitting by the hearth, she clambered back into bed, a far warmer place to comb out the tangles that were evidence of last night's embraces. Behind her she heard a yawn.

'Oh lord, is it morning already?' John reached out an exploratory hand but Elysabeth smacked him away. 'I thought you'd be exhausted.'

'For you, never.'

'No,' she said firmly. 'Play my maid?' She held out the brush. When he shook his head, she pointed to the window chest. 'There's a fresh shirt and hose set out for you.'

'They'll keep.' He freed himself from the bedclothes, sauntered over to retrieve his beltpurse and came back to her with a tiny drawstring bag of black velvet, which he set upon her lap. 'Happy St Valentine's! I could not wait. Open it!'

Elysabeth loosened the ties and shook out his gift, a gillyflower of gold set in a fretwork of leaves, fruited with tiny clusters of seed pearls. She had worn a chaplet of such pinks at their wedding and it was her favourite flower. 'This is exquisite.'

'You deserve it, my love. We'll have a goldsmith fix it to the collar I gave you last year. I never liked the pendant that hung upon it.'

Reaching for her hand mirror, she held the heart against the valley of her throat and he slid an arm about her waist, drew aside her long ash-blonde hair and kissed her throat. They laughed together and then, freeing herself, she hunted out the gift she had been saving for the morrow.

It was a broad silken kerchief embroidered with his coat of arms — alternate horizontal bands of silver and azure.

'You are getting better,' he teased, examining the stitching. 'I know full well this was a labour for you. I'll carry it as a token, Elysabeth.' Then he turned his head towards the window lights, frowning. 'The builders are making an infernal to-do this morning. Worse than squabbling rooks.'

She shrugged. 'They're noisiest when they are hoisting a pallet of bricks. Tom's vocabulum of foul oaths has certainly increased, and, by the way, he is hoping you will spend today with him, perhaps ride over to Bradgate Park.'

'No, that's not possible, my love.'

'Why not, John?'

'I have to return to the queen. Today.'

Elysabeth stared at him in disbelief.

'Don't look so mardie.'

'But you said nothing.'

'No, I didn't want to sour matters between us, m'duck. Now say no more! I only came back to please you.' Winding a lock of her hair around his finger, he tugged her face towards his. 'And be pleased that the roads were hard with frost so the riding was easy and...' his breath was like a feather drawn along her lips, '...and that I was hard with desire for you.'

She refused to be appeased. 'Well, I wish all the cursed rivers would rise so I may keep you here with us. Does your mother know you are leaving so soon?'

'Yes, and I asked her not to tell you.' The admission bruised her. 'One last campaign, my love,' he murmured appeasingly, taking up his clean apparel. 'The queen needs to take command of London. We know Warwick will try to block the London road but we'll deal with him. It'll be like swatting a fly with a mallet. And then we'll free King Henry from the Tower. Our numbers are far greater and Warwick knows less about military strategy than the Archbishop of Canterbury does about women. Wipe his force out and then there's only York's lad and he'll soon make peace if he knows what's good for him. Otherwise —' He drew a finger sharply across his throat.

Elysabeth had been suckled on politics. Her mother's first husband had been a royal duke and her father, Lord Rivers, was one of King Henry's councillors.

'But what if London shuts her gates against your army, John? Mother's there and she said in her last letter that many aldermen have lent funds to York.'

'Those fools will soon come to terms when they see which way the wind is blowing. Stop looking so anxious, Elizabeth. I'll be back at Astley within the week, I promise you. And once we have London, I'll ask the queen to take Tom as a page. Think of the golden future ahead for him. Maybe as friend to the Prince, Lord Chamberlain to our future king perhaps?' He tweaked her nose playfully. 'Now, be of good cheer!'

Despite John's optimism, her mind still writhed with misgivings. Queen Margaret might be wearing the laurels of victory at the moment but unless her captains could capture York's son, Edward, there would be more battles ahead. Elysabeth's parents and oldest brother had already fallen foul of Edward — a year ago.

Now he was eighteen.

'Where *is* Edward of York at the moment, John?'

He shrugged dismissively. 'Who cares? In the Welsh Marches somewhere? We'll get to him when we've dealt with Warwick. I'll warrant your father, for one, will be glad to see both their heads stuck on poles at long last.'

Elysabeth grimaced. 'Don't you think…' she began and then fell silent. Best to hold her tongue. Her husband's time was too precious now to spend it arguing about beheadings. 'Well, since you are leaving, I shall, too. Home to Astley.'

His expression hardened. 'No, my love, I desire you to remain here and make sure the masons complete the next floor of the tower. I've ordered the slate for the roof from the quarry at Swithland. It's not the best, harder to split than Welsh slate, but it should suffice.'

'But —'

'No arguments, Elysabeth. You will do that. Besides, Mother may not say so in so many words, but she could still do with your company. Having our sons here takes her mind off poor Reginald's death.'

He was utterly wrong. Tom's presence reminded Lady Ferrers too vividly of her dead child.

'John, I'm not sure that is so,' she began, but an irate knocking instantly silenced her.

Speaking of John's mother must have conjured the woman up. The door timber was shuddering beneath a fierce onslaught.

'John! Elysabeth! Come and deal with your son! He'll not obey me.'

Since Elysabeth was already decent and John's shirt covered him below the thighs, he unbarred the door. 'What's amiss?' he asked calmly.

His mother's sharp eye took in the mussed bed, John's half-nakedness and Elysabeth's unplaited hair. 'Pah, naught, I daresay,' she sneered, 'unless you call climbing the scaffolding and refusing to come down of no consequence.'

'What!' Elysabeth squeaked.

'Oh, do not tell me you could not hear the hubbub? I wash my hands of this! Come and deal with him this instant!'

Having dumped her ill tidings and relegated any decisions to her grandson's irresponsible parents, Lady Ferrers disappeared like a spent tempest before either Elysabeth or John could answer.

With a foul oath, John swiftly stepped into his hose and struggled to lace them up to his gipon. Elysabeth found his boots for him and swiftly tied his points, then grabbing up her own shoes, she hastened after him down the stairs and out across the frosty courtyard to where they were building John's wretched tower.

A wagon of straw with the oxen still in harness was halted between the gates that opened out onto the village's main street. Its progress into the yard was blocked by the array of builder's men, servants and villagers who were gaping up at her husband's cursed, half-built monstrosity as though they were expecting the Second Coming. Only her arrival with her long fair hair unbound loosened their attention from the tower.

'I am sorry, my lady,' wailed Dickon's nurserymaid, wringing her hands in her waistcloth as she waylaid her mistress, but Elysabeth waved her away. 'Not now!'

'What in Hell is amiss here?' snarled John, asserting his lordship.

'The young fellow won't come down, my lord.' The master builder, livid-cheeked from the slapping wind, gestured to the scaffolding flanking the unfinished third storey. 'My apprentice Robin Steynforth's up there trying to make him see sense.'

She could see no one up there. John looked as confused as she was, and with a sigh of impatience he marched across to the doorless opening of the tower and peered up. She followed him in.

The tower was hollow, open to the sky. Joists were in place between the walls but with no flooring as yet. At the top, two bricklayer's platforms, scarce two wide, were linked to the outside scaffolding. A ladder, set horizontally, straddled the drop, and a pair of knees in new woollen hose were showing on the innermost side. Tom's.

'Thomas!' roared John.

The knees wriggled.

On the scaffolding side, a young workman obligingly stuck his head over the gap. He seemed to be on all fours.

'Well, sirrah?' barked John.

'He be not cornin' down, my lord.'

Elysabeth put a hand across her mouth to staunch her laughter. It was not only the Earl of Warwick who could stage a rebellion. John, however, showed no amusement nor did Cowper, the master builder, who had followed them in.

'I fear this is holding up the morning's work, my lord.'

John's answer was brusque and haughty. 'You'll be paid, man, if that is your only concern.' He gazed up again, fists at his waist. 'Listen, Steynforth or whatever your name is, can you not get onto the ladder and haul him across? *Damned child!*'

'Nay, he cannot, my lord,' intervened Cowper. 'It be too risky. Them rungs be slippery as grease, being open to the weather, especially if young Master Grey don't come willing like. I've seen it afore,' he added, with a curl of his lower lip. 'Going up's one thing, but...' His confidence faltered. It was evident he dared not imply that John Grey's son and heir might be a coward.

John's language was blasphemous as he marched back into the courtyard.

Elysabeth gestured to Master Cowper to return outside, and called up to her son, 'Tom, are you not frozen there? Pray stop being an ass and come down. You are holding up the work.'

'Good! I hope it costs Father a great deal of money!'

'Oh, now, that is not —'

'Mother! He did not even ask me why I am up here.'

'But Tom —'

'Go back in the warm, Mama. This will take some time.' That was said with less conviction.

Elysabeth returned outside, back into the icy wind, and touched John's elbow. 'He wants to negotiate, I think.'

John could do indignant huffs. This was one of his finest. She left him to simmer and found a vantage point across from the scaffolding.

'I'm laying this at your door,' Lady Ferrers muttered, arriving well furred and mantled, at Elysabeth's elbow. 'You should have talked John out of building this … this extravagance and … and didn't I warn the children two days ago, when they were trying to build castles with the masons' sand, not to go anywhere near, but do you support me? No,' her voice dropped, 'you tell me I'm a fussy old hag.'

'I never —' But what did it matter?

John joined the women, his face grim.

'Has anyone asked him why's he's up there?' Elysabeth asked, but John's quelling look made her realise miserably that not only was he worried for Tom but the Grey family honour was at stake. Was that what all the people here were thinking? That Tom was too craven to crawl manfully back over the ladder? 'Find out Tom's side of this!' she persisted.

John cursed beneath his breath and, striding forward, shouted up: 'Thomas! Thomas, listen to me! If you crossed the ladder once, you can do it again. Robin Steynforth's there to help you.'

Her son's voice yelled back without an iota of fear. 'Only if you promise to take me fishing tomorrow, sir.' The boy stood up now, his ash-blonde hair bright as he leaned over the unfinished wall and grinned cheekily down at his audience.

Relieved laughter rumbled about the yard. So that was what it was all about. Elysabeth let out a pent-up breath. Of course, Tom was capable of crossing the ladder again, but his father's reaction of smouldering anger boded ill, making her feel guilty that she had stolen John yesterday for her own pleasure especially when he had only been home two days.

'Fishing?' he snarled beneath his breath. 'Devil take it! *In February*?'

'I'd never have let *you* get away with such a jape, John.' Lady Ferrers was stirring up his temper. 'You've raised him to be a milksop.' That poisonous morsel was for Elysabeth, who was gazing up at a boy who was far from cowardly. Could his grandmother not see that?

'Mother, would you ruddy well stop berating us!' growled John. 'It isn't useful.' The Grey family pride was definitely under siege. He stepped forward again. 'Listen, Tom, I'll take you fishing now.'

With a whoop of triumph, his son disappeared and Elysabeth heard him raise his voice in argument. 'Oh, come on,' he was saying, before he reappeared at the wall. 'Dickon's up here, too, but he's afraid now. I am not sure I can get him back.'

'Oh God in Heaven!' Elysabeth exclaimed, clapping her fingers to her lips.

John looked fit to have an apoplexy. 'Why didn't that damned apprentice tell us? Here, take my mantle, Elysabeth! I'm going up.' He discarded his coat into her arms and mounted the scaffolding, leaving her prickly and afraid. Prickly because it was his fault in building this foolish extravagance when normal noblemen had always built in stone, but the fear for her menfolk was greater: some instinctive dread that she might lose all three of them — the human bricks and mortar that held her life together.

'Make way!' John called out as he reached the top and the crowd watched the lad, Robin, edge back at his lord's order.

Shielding her eyes with her hand, Elysabeth saw her husband crouch down. He must be at the edge of the ladder. The murmur of voices reached her. At least he and Tom were speaking to each other. She hastened back into the tower, hoping she might help, and saw Tom crawl across above her. Thank God! But Dickon was another matter.

She heard the cheers and whistles as if she was in a different universe. The most desperate prayers were on her lips and her heart was aching. Climbing up at his brother's heels, little Dickon would not have realised how high Tom was leading him. Perhaps, to be charitable, Tom might have told him not to come but Dickon always followed Tom like a shadow. *A frozen* shadow!

God in Heaven! How long had the children been up there?

John was talking to the child too softly for Elysabeth to hear. She saw him venture his knee precariously onto the nearest rung. Then he reached out a hand, trying to coax the little fellow forwards. No doubt Dickon's mind was dazed with fear not just the cold.

'John, I'm coming up as well,' she shouted.

'No!' he yelled. 'There isn't the room. In God's name, don't distract me!' He edged further forwards.

'Dickon, do what Papa says,' she shouted and hastened out to the foot of the scaffold.

'You go up?' sneered her mother-in-law, swiftly setting a hand upon her sleeve. 'For sure, in your skirts with half of Groby gaping. Leave it to John!'

Whether Lady Ferrers spoke from malice or necessity to stall her, Elysabeth tugged away. 'Do you think that bothers me, madame? My child's life is at stake.' She swung round, facing

51

the cluster of house servants. 'Sutton! Green! Fetch a featherbed from the house! The nearest! Quickly! Quickly!'

'Your pardon, my lady,' called out Cowper, 'but a blanket might be better. We can hold it beneath.'

Elysabeth ignored him. How could a simple blanket best a thick featherbed? Hastening back into the tower she could see John had shifted further forward.

'Wait, my lord! We are putting a mattress below just in case.'

The rungs must have been biting into John's knees for he obeyed her, warning the child not to move.

The servants hauled in a narrow featherbed.

'No, no, fetch a wider one!' Alas, there were two sides to the ladder but if she dragged the bed to lie at right angles …

John was leaning forward again. She could see Dickon's little knees on the nearest rung on his side. He held an arm out to his father's, then jerked it back crying. John coaxed him again. The child let his arm be grabbed. John placed his other hand on the ladder rung and grasped the little boy by the back of his jacket.

Elysabeth jerked her fist to her mouth, her breath held, and then was startled as a thin young body huddled into her. Tom had buried his face in her skirts and was sobbing out an apology. She clutched him to her. He felt so cold. Was Dickon her babe as cold as this?

So slowly, uncomfortably, warily, John was backing as Dickon moved forward. He seemed to have gotten a good grip on the child's jacket but it was hard to be certain from below. Elysabeth, clutching Tom's shoulder warningly, silently urged him back towards the doorway. For an instant, all seemed well above. She watched, not daring to breath.

And then.

Dickon made the mistake of looking down and screamed. He slipped awkwardly, weakening his father's hold, probably forcing the man's wrist against its natural turn and John could not...

Not keep hold!

The wrong side. The wrong side.

She screamed as her child's weight plummeted into her. It was a miracle she thought afterwards. Somehow she sprang sideways as his body filled her arms and the momentum flung them both across the mattress.

Intense pain surged up her forearm in an agonising wave. Dickon was a dead weight across her left arm, his skin ashen, his eyes open, unfocused, and a scarlet stain was spreading beneath his head onto the featherbed.

Was he still alive? O God, O God, be merciful!

'Shall we move him, my lady?' asked Cowper, his face dour.

A canopy of labourers' faces peered down at her.

'Yes, no!' Her voice was frantic. 'Dickon, Dickon, it's Mama. Can you hear me?'

Please, not dead! No, please God, no! The little boy's face was already white as an alabaster tomb monument and still the ugly, vivid insult of scarlet blood beneath him was spreading.

Her maid, Tamsin, was kneeling by her now and then the scaffolding outside rattled fiercely as John, his breath ragged, pushed through the people blocking the doorway.

'*Elysabeth?*'

'I tried to save him.' More pain as she attempted to lift her head.

'Fetch clean cloths and blankets!' Lady Ferrers was behind him giving orders.

Falling on one knee, John lent over Dickon, feeling for the pulse in the boy's neck. 'In God's name, stand back!' he yelled over his shoulder. 'Give us light for pity's sake!'

'*John?*' Elysabeth asked fearfully.

He did not, could not answer yet, too preoccupied with running his hands over Dickon's ribs and limbs seeking for broken bones.

'Alive? Yes, praise be, but…'

Yes, now she saw for herself. A slow tide of pink began to rosy Dickon's cheeks and the boy's eyes opened fleetingly. Just enough for her to glimpse the light rekindled in his eyes as though a forgiving God had once more lit the candle of life within him.

'Thanks be to Our Blessed Lord for the child's deliverance,' boomed the chaplain, falling to his knees, his hands clasped in prayer. *Too soon. Too soon*, Elysabeth thought. But the good news passed. Those in the doorway descended to their knees in a reverent whisper of praise, which flowed out into the yard.

John had no time for reverence.

'Thank you, thank you! *Hell!* Now get out of here, all of you! Mother, see to it! No, do not block the doorway in God's name! We need the light!' His fingers were exploring the back of Dickon's head and puzzled, he eased the boy's head off Elysabeth's arm. 'Well, I'll be cursed, it's you who are bleeding, sweetheart. Let's get him completely off her! Take his ankles. Gently now!'

Relief from Dickon's weight was fleeting. Trying to sit up unleashed nausea and more pain. Squinting sideways, she saw her upper sleeve was bloody.

'Stay still, my duck!' John's fingertips were exploring along her arm for broken bones. 'I can feel a break here, Mother.' Dear God! Elysabeth gritted her teeth, no longer hearing what Lady Ferrers was saying. The faces around her were fading behind a spangled curtain. 'Darling, keep it still!'

She must have fainted. She opened her eyes to find the Groby steward stooping over her, proffering a clean, soft towel. Tamsin stood beside the featherbed, hugging a great bear of blanketing.

'Dickon's belt buckle caught you, I reckon.' John pressed a wad of cloth against the slash on her arm just above the elbow. 'The bleeding will soon stop.'

Lady Ferrers sat beside her now, cradling Dickon in her arms and Tom stood above her. Elysabeth could feel her older son's fear, see the distance people left around him as though he was a leper.

She tried sending him a smile of reassurance. It fell short, like her own hope; why had Dickon neither spoken nor given any sign of recognition?

'Best we carry the lad to bed,' John was saying. 'And you need your arm set.' Letting Tamsin take over the pressure on the cut, he put his arm about Elysabeth, and helped her to her feet. She nearly fainted again.

'See to Dickon, John,' she pleaded, and surrendered to Tamsin's support.

John lifted the child sufficiently so that they might cocoon him in a blanket, then careful as Our Lady would have been with the Christ child in her arms and, with Lady Ferrers holding the tail of the blanket, he carried him out.

'I seen this before,' Elysabeth heard one of the workman mutter, as they passed through the courtyard. 'They be never the same again. Pity, eh?'

John set Dickon down among the cushions of the daybed in the women's solar and Lady Ferrers drew a coverlet up over the cocoon of blankets. Elysabeth sank down on the settle, still feeling dizzy.

Would Dickon recover? Would he speak again? The workman's remark was still echoing. Had the fall turned their son into a village dolthead?

'We all need a strong drink and a dab of it across that cut would be a wise notion,' John's mother said, patting Elysabeth's good shoulder. 'I'll see to it. Oh, out of my way, you wretched creature!' That was to Dickon's nursemaid who had followed them in.

'My lady, my lady, please forgive me!' The wench almost grovelled at Elysabeth's feet, all tears and wailing, like a recanting Lollard fearing the stake. Absolution was unthinkable. Elysabeth exchanged glances with her husband and the fool's future was sealed.

'Send my esquire Weston to me and inform the kitchen we need egg whites, flour, fat and a large ewer,' John commanded. 'And that's your last order from us. We want you gone from here within the hour!' The girl disappeared, sobbing.

John placed his hand on Dickon's forehead. 'My feeling is that he'll mend. He might not know his arse from his elbow for the next hour and he may never remember climbing up the tower, but you saved him from internal injury.'

Had she? She could not stop watching Dickon's breath rising and falling beneath the bedding. Gratitude that her little son could even manage that poured through her. Gratitude combined with a fervent wish that Lady Ferrers would return with a flagon.

'Mind you, that was a cursed foolish thing you did, Elysabeth,' John commented, leaving the bedside. 'Dickon could have damn nigh killed you.'

'He could have killed me in childbirth. The next one might.'

Sitting beside her, John took her good hand in his. 'You know what I'm saying. I thought I'd lost you.'

'Then don't be angry. We need to pray for him, John, not snarl at one another. Why have you called for Weston?'

'You'll need to have your arm set. Would you trust my esquire to do that? If he wasn't born a gentleman, I reckon he'd have made a wondrous good bonesetter. I found him watching the queen's surgeon at work after Wakefield.'

'If you trust him, then so shall I.' Her broken arm needed to be bound to a straight piece of wood by strips of cloth. Saturated in the right blend of egg and flour solution, the swaddling should dry hard as a board. The skill would be in setting the bone so that it would both look and feel wholesome again. She lifted the cloth from her cut. 'It's stopped bleeding.'

'If you were one of my men, I'd cauterise it but we don't want to make an ugly scar. When Mother comes back, we'll daub it with wine and hope that cleanses it. If you start feeling feverish at any time, you must let me know. The sleeve is a ruin. Perhaps you should start a new piebald fashion. Sleeves of different colours.'

It hurt to laugh but it was not the discomfort he read in her face that made John's smile ebb fast.

'Will Dickon get better?' Tom stood round-shouldered in the doorway, like a small pathetic question mark. Behind him, towered his grandmother. Perhaps she had marched him in for retribution. 'Will he, Mama?'

'I do not know, dearest,' whispered Elysabeth.

'Sometimes the damage does not show itself straightway,' remarked Lady Ferrers, half-filling three goblets from the tray on the small table. 'You knocked yourself out once, John, when you and Edward were riding at the quintain but no harm came of it. And, let us be honest, Dickon has always been rather slow-witted for his age.'

*Oh, by the Saints, by all means be honest*, Elysabeth fumed. The woman had the tact of a jester at a funeral.

'Here you are, son John, sup up! Now have you a clean cloth? You'll need to cleanse that wound, Elysabeth.'

John drowned the contents of his goblet and set it down loudly. He was staring at his older son and the colour of his countenance showed white-hot with anger.

'Thomas,' he said, brushing his palms. 'Come with me!'

The boy raised his eyes, his mouth a stubborn arc, defiant as a heretic before the bonfire. Elysabeth wanted to protest: *He didn't think. He didn't mean this to happen.*

John's face was adamantine. With a fierce hand, he seized Tom by the ear.

'No! NO!' Their child writhed and struggled within his grasp like a hooked eel. 'You said you would go fishing with me now. You promised! You promised!'

'John!'

'No, you will *not* interfere! It's time he learned.'

She shuddered, hearing Tom's screams as his father hauled him up to his bedchamber.

Lady Ferrers said nothing as she handed Elysabeth a cleansing cloth yet her upper lip twitched and her eyes gleamed with a triumphant I-told-you-so that presaged a scolding. Thank God, Tamsin knocked at that point to lead in the village healer.

'Lady Ferrers, Lady Grey, I came as soon as I heard. How fares the poor lamb? Such a to-do, eh?'

Sweaty-faced, with a basketful of herbs on her arm, she bobbed them each a curtsey before she went across to the bed and burrowed a clawed hand in to find Dickon's wrist. 'Oh, so cold but his pulse is strong enow.' She scooped back his eyelids. 'A pity he had to be moved but it be biting cold out there.'

She held a tiny silver mirror in front of Dickon's nose. 'Breathing is good. He'll come about, my lady, be sure of that, but...' she swished her mouth sideways, 'it could be his brain's been jarred.'

Elysabeth dragged her good hand across her forehead. 'You mean that his wits may be injured?'

The woman waggled her head. 'I cannot say. If there be any damage, it will show itself soon enow.'

'Time heals, too,' pleaded Elysabeth, and she hoped that God and his saints were listening.


'How's the little lad now? On the mend, I trust.' John sounded blithe but his expression as he strode into the solar later looked stern and strained as St Peter's might have been denying the Blessed Christ.

Elysabeth could not answer him. Another time she might have wished the comfort of his embrace but not now; Weston had set her arm, her shoulder felt like it had been kicked by a score of horses, and John had so misunderstood Tom's behaviour.

Sensing he was in disfavour, he stomped to the hearth and stood chafing his hands. 'Thomas's backside will be sore, but he will remember this lesson. Don't look at me so, my duck. One day there will be men relying on his judgment in battle and if he thinks twice about leading them into danger, today shall have served its purpose.' But he was looking at Dickon's quiet face with a heavy frown.

'Isn't it the intent that's important?' Elysabeth almost screamed at him. 'Tom didn't realise.'

'Grow up, Elysabeth! Of course he knew he was putting Dickon's life at risk. Letting a child so young follow him up there.' He toed the hearthstone moodily and Elysabeth knew she would dislike what he would say next. 'Mother thinks it is high time Tom should be sent to another household. I think so too.'

'No, please, a little longer.'

'I've delayed a year or more to please you, fool that I am. No, my mind is made up. In fact, I shall speak with my lord of Somerset about it tomorrow. Mayhap he will take him as a page, make a man of him before you ruin him.' He straightened. 'Anyway, enough said. I have to make preparation before I ride away.' A farewell bow, as though they were strangers.

Elysabeth stepped into his way. 'Back to the queen? You are still going *to her*? With Dickon still out of his wits! He may die. How can you —'

'Nonsense!' he stepped around her. 'The way you talk anyone would think I'm Margaret's lover. In God's name, can't you see—'

She could have struck him, she was so furious. 'Your little boy fell *hard*, John, and you... Pah, go, then! I care not whether you stay or no.'

With male perversity, he did not head for the door, but folded his arms. 'I suppose you blame me for this,' he said with a sulky expression so like Tom's. 'It's *my* bricks, *my* tower.'

'Yes, perhaps I do!'

'Dear God, I had enough blows to the head as a child, let alone in battle. It is part of being a boy, being a man.'

'Do you think I don't know that,' she acceded, letting the anger ebb from her face. 'My father has taken enough falls in the tourney field but...'

'Aye, and he is never short of an argument just like his daughter. So, let's have an end to this!' He started for the door. 'I've plenty to do.'

'Please John, please, stay until tomorrow.' She flung herself against him but he unfastened her arms.

'Enough! It is your womanish fears that have made a milksop of your children. By heaven, I'll be glad to get back to the army.'

Damn him and his temper! Elysabeth stood staring at the door in shock before she returned to Dickon's bedside. If her own mother had not been in London or her father and brother with the queen's army too, she would have loaded the child into a litter this instant and taken both children to her parents' home except... Except Dickon was so ill and Tom? Lord help her, she would need to use her wits with Tom. Feeling as though God had bound her to a windmill blade, she sank to her knees to pray for her little son to recover.

The disagreement with John set a dampener on their parting. Escorting him to the courtyard an hour later, Elysabeth bade him farewell with a chill countenance, and the rigidity of his body as they formally embraced before the household told her his resentment would simmer yet awhile. She wanted to ask him to carry greetings to her father and brother but the words stayed inside her.

She called out: 'God protect you!' as he turned his horse's head towards the gate but whether he heard, she did not know, for he kept his face forwards and never looked back.

And after supper, as she and the chaplain knelt together in prayer beside Dickon's bed in thanks that he had recovered his wits and was speaking coherently once more, she realised that it was not just St Valentine's Eve, an eve turned sour, but also a Friday, Friday the thirteenth.

# 3: ELYSABETH

*19<sup>th</sup> February 1461, The Feast of Theodulus, Patron*
*Saint of Bellringers,*
*Groby Hall, Leicestershire*

The news of Queen Margaret's victory at the abbey town of St Albans on 17th February was proclaimed loudly through the streets of Leicester. Groby's bailiff, who had been in the city on business for Lady Ferrers (as well as to enjoy the favours of a particular tapster wench), joyfully brought the news back to Groby Hall, where many a keg was opened and Sir John Grey's health was drunk.

Elysabeth, full of forgiveness and relieved that John must return again soon, perhaps laden with rewards for his loyalty (Knight of the Garter, for instance, like her father), rejoiced with the rest of the household, although she had some pity for the townsfolk of St Albans. This was the second battle in five years that had bloodied their doorsteps but at least this time John's side had triumphed.

From what she could piece together, it seemed that the rebel leader, Warwick, had miscalculated badly. Not just the strength of Queen Margaret's army either. He had foolishly wagered all on the assumption that Edward of York would rush to help him hold the London Road. But young Edward's force was protecting his father's lands around Ludlow and had never arrived. And so, lacking the numbers and with his men spread too wide across the town and the surrounding fields, Warwick had stood as much chance of winning as a rooster facing a pack of foxes.

Now the way was open for Queen Margaret to take London, just as John had hoped. What's more, her grace now had King Henry for company again. The proclamations said that he had been found in the town under the guard of old Lord Bonville and Sir Thomas Kyrell and they were now beheaded.

'You are certain the Earl of Warwick wasn't captured?' Elysabeth asked the bailiff.

'Nowt in the proc-*hic*-clamations, Lady Grey. Mind, he could be slain and they may still be a while to discover his-*hic*-body. For instance, if the queen's soldiers have stripped it for armour an' valuables, it could take a while to identify him, see.'

'Probably discover the lily-livered cur drowned in a water butt,' guffawed one of the local aldermen.

'Aye, my lady,' exclaimed the bailiff, wiping pie crumbs from his lips. 'Mayhap he took to his heels the moment he smelled which way the wind was blowing.' He leaned forwards and bestowed a grin on Dickon, who was standing beside her wide-eyed. 'And whose Papa is coming home soon?'

Dickon did not answer, just burrowed his face in the folds of her kirtle. She tousled his hair.

The bailiff, not to be denied an answer, poked the child in the ribs. 'Aye, one day it will be you riding to battle, little man. Having a whack at the Saracens or the froggies.' Receiving no response he bestowed a smile of inebriated pity upon Elysabeth and made his way to the nearest keg.

'Where's Tom?' she asked Dickon. 'He was here a moment ago. Oh, he's not at the motte again, surely? He'll catch his death of cold.'

But when Dickon slid a thumb out of his mouth and nodded, Elysabeth left him in the care of her maidservant and went to berate her older lad.

Tom had taken to keeping his own company in the ruins of the old Norman keep that lay in the grounds of the hall. Today he was perched elfin like — his chin resting on his knees — on one of the ancient wall stones that had evaded being reused.

'There's been a victory, darling. Did you know? The queen's army has defeated Warwick.'

A shrug. 'So?'

'But, Tom, don —'

'Go away, Mother! Leave me alone.'

'It is so cold outside here, Tom.'

'I don't care. Leave me alone!'

'We have to talk, Tom.'

'What is there to say? I wish we were back at Astley. At least there I don't have to put up with Grandmother Ferrers comparing me to stupid old Reginald and wishing I were dead in his stead.'

'She never said that!'

'She did not have to. I can see it in her face every time she bothers to look at me.' He sprang up from the stone. 'We need to go back to Astley, Mama. It's not good for us here.'

'No, but your father asked me to —'

Tom staunched her words with a sneer: 'Mind his cursed bricks for him? He cares more about that damned tower than he does about any of us.'

'That's not true.'

'All right then, about Dickon and I. And *she*...' he jabbed a finger towards the hall. '*She* doesn't want us here. Father may think this tumbling old place is his but it isn't. It's hers and we are not welcome.'

'That's not true.'

'Don't lie to me, Mama. I can see it in your face.' He nodded towards the hall. 'Better go, Mama, it seems you're wanted.'

The Ferrers' chaplain, jowls aquiver, was hastening towards them.

'Ah, my lady, there you are. I've just been informed by the old stable hand, Bart, that one of the horse boys is back with news from St Albans. I haven't seen or spoken with the lad yet myself but I thought —'

She stood up and smoothed her skirts. 'Thank you, I'll come at once. Tom?'

The boy shrugged and stayed where he was.

'I can see your young fellow is still sulking from the beating,' observed the chaplain, puffing somewhat to keep up with her brisk walk. 'It's a difficult age, the transition between being a child and becoming a man. Would you like me to have a word with him?'

Elysabeth pulled a weary face. 'My lord husband blames me for not sending him away. So does Lady Ferrers.'

'Ah, well, I'm sure Lord Grey will soon put matters right. Every lad needs a father to keep him on the straight and narrow.' He bestowed a smug smile upon the clouds as though his paternal connections were more heavenly than most, before he courteously opened the door for her.

The nearest way to the front yard was through the hall and Elysabeth set her hand on her mother-in-law's arm as she passed through the throng. 'There's word come from John, madame.' A revelation she instantly regretted.

'News! News!' exclaimed a happy Lady Ferrers, waving a wine cup. Wobbly and happy, the household lurched out of the hall in the noble ladies' wake only to halt with grunts of astonishment.

Two men were waiting in the courtyard, facing the steps of the hall. Right behind them, still held by its leading rein, was a laden ass.

The grey-haired man — this must be Bart — bobbed in respect and stepped aside. Elysabeth recognised the youth who was with him — one of the stable lads who had left Groby last week as an excited horse boy and returned as…?

The young man bowed and as he raised his head, sorrowful eyes, gritted with weariness and suffering, pierced hers. Elysabeth, confused, skewed her gaze behind him to the pack ass — not one of theirs but a poor bony creature. Its load … was a body.

The corpse was slung across the animal's back. It hung face down, wrists bound to bare ankles to prevent falling. A quilted brigandine, heavily red-stained, had slid downwards to collar the man's head.

Staring at Elysabeth, the lad reached out wordlessly and tugged the garment up so she was able to recognise the tousled, bloodied hair and the hands, ringless and tethered palm to palm.

John.

She screamed and rushed forwards, falling on her knees. The ass, startled, moved forwards. The boy swiftly grabbed the reins.

'How can this be?' Elysabeth shrieked, twisting in anger to face the people behind her.

John's mother's face was as grey as ashes. 'O Jesu,' she whispered crossing herself in horror. 'O Jesu, Jesu, Jesu!'

'But it was a victory,' protested someone.

'What of Grey, my other son?' Lady Ferrers was asking.

'He be recovering from wounds, my lady,' answered the boy. 'That be why he could not come 'imself.'

*Oh, if only John's brother had died instead!* Elysabeth wanted to shriek aloud in her wretchedness. How could God be so cruel? And she and John had parted in such anger!

'No, no!' she protested, her hands fists against the wrath of God.

'My lady?' Exclaiming and muttering, their people were all about them now, the women servants sobbing and the older men blaspheming in shock. And Elysabeth was reaching out in grief and pity to John's brow as if her fingertips needed to assert what her mind refused to believe.

And then the voices halted, as though a knife had been thrust against each throat. She twisted round, dashing her own tears aside. The throng had parted to let Tom through. The chaplain was trying to hold him back but he jerked away from the cleric's hand.

'No, no, don't let him see!' exclaimed Elysabeth. 'Take him in! For the love of God, take him in!' She stumbled to her feet, spreading her arms.

Ignoring her, his face like hewn stone, he came past her and halted, staring wide-eyed at the purple bruises that made his father's profile almost beyond recognition. It was as if he was counting the wounds, forcing himself to register each one. Elysabeth, shaking with shock now, looked, too. There were so many. And the gash. The line of dried blood ribboning John's throat.

'Tom,' she began but her son's face was a mask of defiance.

'This is victory, Mother? I do not think so.'

The servants parted in silence as he walked back through their midst into the house. For a moment no one moved and then his grandmother took charge. 'Why do you stand in such idleness?' Lady Ferrers cried, gesturing the servants towards John's body. 'Carry your master to the chapel at once! And you, sirrah,' she demanded of the youth. 'What of Lady Grey's kinsmen and the rest of our men?'

Elysabeth clutched her fingers to her lips with a painful, guilty gasp. In her anguish, she had forgotten that her father and eldest brother were with the army, too.

'They stay with the queen, my lady. She intends to march on to London. Two of the men from Astley were killed with the master but they're like to be buried at St Albans, and Nicholas Anstey had an arrow in his shoulder but the surgeon got it out and reckons it'll heal an —'

'They will be in our prayers,' cut in Lady Ferrers. 'Come, Elysabeth! Let us to the chapel!' But then rage and sorrow broke through her mask of briskness. 'I'll say this, though, lad, you could have brought your lord home with greater honour, not slung like a traitor!'

'Beggin' your pardon, my lady. It be not my fault nor Master Edward's. Her highness would not spare the horses.'

'No horse?' Elysabeth exclaimed, her voice strange and shrill. 'My lord husband died for the queen and she could not spare a horse?' For an instant, her entire body shook with hatred, welcomed it, but the horror was overwhelming. She was conscious of the chaplain at her side, the murmur of concerned voices.

'Pray go in, my lady,' he was saying. 'Your sons will need you.' And then Lady Ferrers, with an arm about her shoulders, was turning her towards the steps. She could feel the same righteous anger pulsing through the older woman's fingers.

'Ahem! Please you, Lady Grey.' They had forgotten the young messenger who had brought his master home.

Both of them looked back. Elysabeth felt the words stick in her throat, but Lady Ferrers still had a stifler on her grief and nodded. 'We thank you, boy. You shall be rewarded.'

He sniffed dismissively, waggling his lower jaw. 'Not that, my lady.' It seemed he had a speech for both of them but his gaze

69

was for Elysabeth. 'Master's esquire, Andrew Chilvers, wanted me to say to you that the master fought bravely. He led the charge but it was them traps what did it.'

'Traps?' The word tasted raw, bitter as she turned and braced herself to listen.

'Yes, Lady Grey. Lord Warwick hid traps — nets, caltraps and that ilk to wound the horses, see. That's what brought the master down. His horse trod upon the caltraps and he fell upon the field and our enemy's soldiers rushed forward with their halberds.'

'Oh dear God! You saw this?'

'Not I, my lady, but Master Chilvers did. And he bade me give you this.' He thrust his hand inside his jacket and tugged out a crumpled piece of silk.

The St Valentine's gift.

The youth was a blur beyond her tears as he tumbled to his knees at her feet like a penitent waiting for absolution. 'An' I crave your forgivene —'

He broke off. Dickon had burst out of the hall and was pulling at her skirt.

'Mama come, come! Tom is throwing the wooden soldiers that Father made us onto the fire.'

Elysabeth, torn, her heart breaking, caught the child to her side and set a trembling hand upon the messenger's head. 'God's blessing on you for bringing your master home.'

'An' God be wi' you, my lady,' he said.

*With pity.*

# 4: KATE

## *25<sup>th</sup> February 1461, Shute Hall, Devonshire*

Lord Bonville was dead. Unquestionably. By the bloody hand of the queen.

The old man who had been Grandfather Bonville's bodyservant for fifty years wept piteously as he knelt before Lady Bonville and Kate in the great chamber with the saddest of tidings from the battlefield of St Albans. Newton was crouched beside him with his arm about the old fellow's shoulders.

'My master's great age should have saved him, my ladies. He and Sir Thomas Kyriel ought to have stayed at the Tower of London with King Henry in their keeping but my lord of Warwick insisted that King Henry should be carried as prisoner to St Albans, and there we had his highness in a tent, well-guarded. And that night, my lord Warwick came with his brother and my lord of Arundel, and they spoke with my lord on the eve of the battle. They said they had been waiting for York's son, the Lord Edward, to join them but that he had not come and they would have to hold the road without him. They said that the queen's army was great indeed but, for their own part, they had hand gunners and mounted pikemen.

'And my lord king said that whosoever should prove the victor, it would be by God's will, and he would spend the night in prayer for the souls of the men who would die that morrow.

'And many did. We heard the screams of the men and horses even though the king's tent was back amongst the horse boys and the supply carts. No word came, either from my lord of

71

Warwick or any of his captains, so my master and Sir Thomas did not know what to do, but they knew it their duty to safeguard the king and so they waited.

'And then came Queen Margaret with her young son and all her captains, and King Henry asked for mercy for my lord and for Lord Kyriel especially because they were great in years and had been courteous in their keeping of him, but Queen Margaret scorned his plea. "Let our son decide!" she said. "No, madame," protested our lord king once more. "You cannot ask this of him. The child is only eight years old." But the queen laughed scornfully and the boy did, too. "Cut their heads off!" he said, and the order was carried out.'

'Oh, my poor Bonny!' Lady Bonville crossed herself and sank down onto the chair. Kate gestured to Master Newton to fetch aqua vitae from the aumery, then helped the old retainer to his feet.

'God bless you for staying with your master. Tell me now as to my brother Warwick? Was he slain?'

The old man rubbed a hand across his salt-wet lips. 'They were searching the dead for him when I came away. The queen has proclaimed an award for his capture if he is still alive. I fear your brother John was captured, my lady.'

Oh God!

He turned towards Lady Bonville, his aged hands trembling as he clutched his hat. 'It was King Henry who ordered that the master's body be returned to you, my lady. It is —'

'Shall I see to it, my lady?' Newton offered with a bow. 'We'll lay him out in the chapel.'

'Thank you.' Outwardly, Lady Bonville was holding herself together as though God had not yet slapped her face with the reality of her husband's death. 'He always said he should be buried at Chewton where he was born. We shall ... yes, we shall hold a remembrance here at St Michael's on Sunday and then we shall leave for Somerset. Make the arrangements, Newton. It will be your duty.'

The suggestion seemed to surprise the young man but his chin went up as though he appreciated the responsibility. 'As you wish, my lady.' He held out an arm to the ancient manservant. 'Come along, old gaffer.'

Lady Bonville nodded. 'See him looked after, Newton, and send in my amanuensis on your way out. So much to do, Katherine. You must help me make a list. I shall write to inform Lady Margaret, my stepdaughter, at Powderham, although she and Bonny have not spoken for years. There's his bastard, Kirby. I daresay he may come since Bonny provided for him.'

When they were private again, Grandmother Bonville rejected Kate's offer of a comforting hug, 'No, no fuss.' Astonishingly calm, she took a sip of the firewater. Kate poured herself some as well. She felt hollowed out, almost numbed by the horror of it all except...

Except guilt was crawling into her mind like plague rats stealing ashore.

'I expect you blame Richard for insisting King Henry be taken to St Albans, madame?'

'No, child, what's the point in blaming your brother, even if he's still cursed green in strategy. Bonny will have made his own decisions. Stupid old fool.' Her knuckles rose to banish the slow trickle of tears from her cheekbones. Then with a great sigh, she added, 'You know, to have shown mercy would have become Queen Margaret greater than the victory. Maybe it's her being French. Holds grudges. Why are you looking at me like that, Katherine Neville?'

'I don't know what to do, what to say.'

'Pray, girl!' An imperious hand beckoned. 'For your brothers, that they keep their heads and for Bonny's soul this night. I'm for the chapel. The Devil will be sharpening his toasting fork for my old fellow and if prayers can knock off a few years of Purgatory for the lot of 'em, it's the least we can do.'

St Michael's Church in Shute hushed as the two widowed noblewomen walked up the nave in stately single file with their tiring women following. The only sound was the rustle of their mourning robes. Kate felt intensely uncomfortable at being on display. At least the dark lawn veil over her face gave her shelter from the watching eyes, but it also enabled her to notice all the grim faces as household servants, villagers and neighbours touched their foreheads in respect. It wasn't just obligatory courtesy narrowing the men's eyes but something more concerning. Uncertainty? Mistrust? Self-interest? What were they seeing? Two women in charge after fifty years of one strong master and him now beheaded as a traitor?

The news was spreading and so was lawlessness. The thirteen-year-old daughter of one of their tenants had been ravished by three men from Musbury, a manor belonging to Thomas Courtenay, Earl of Devon. Yesternight there had been a brawl in Axminster between men from Colyton and some Whitford farmers, one of the latter had been given a bloody nose and lost several teeth for saying that the earl was a greedy rogue. There was also word that the earl's brother, Henry Courtenay, had come from Yeovil to make trouble. These woes and fears were laden onto the shoulders of villagers who had already lost kinsmen at Wakefield and St Albans.

Kate grimaced. All her fault. It was she who had brought this disaster to Shute. If her father and Richard had not wed her to Will and drawn the Bonville lords into their treason, then…

Oh, so many ifs… So many of her family dead and Richard fleeing for his life with every bounty hunter searching for him.

With relief, she reached the bench reserved for the Bonvilles before the rood screen. Thank Heaven there were some privileges.

'My ladies.' Standing a row behind them, Master Gylle, newly appointed to replace Lady Bonville's steward who had died at Wakefield, bowed with difficulty because of the wound in his shoulder. The poor man had a gash above his eye as well.

Kate acknowledged him, glad of his survival. But there was his daughter, the beautiful Lovidia, brazenly standing between him and her mother with her babe asleep in her arms. She was not even churched, nor like to be with the child unlawfully begotten. The outrageous wench gave a curtsey and a smile that was either shy or… No, *shy*! Shy *and* sly with an annoying pale rose blush that made the men, close by, stare and stay staring.

In ill temper, Kate almost tripped over her hassock. Master Gylle reached out his hale hand to steady her. Embarrassing. *A pox on everything*! Lacking a state of grace, she knelt, crossing herself, suppressing the childish urge to bawl her eyes out because life was not fair.

'…*and we are here to mourn those who are with us no longer*—'

Oh, Will! A broken dream.

Then something rattled her hearing.

Horses. The clink of harness. The west door thrust wide. It was not the Second Coming. The cloaked latecomer, who paused beneath the arch, looked more like the Devil until he swaggered forward and everyone could see he had ginger, curly hair, a nose like Lady Bonville's and no tail.

The priest, Father Gregory, cleared his throat and then faltered, his eyes going wild and round, his mouth like a rock-dove nest hole as armed men in yellow surcoats clanked in around the font. The villagers drew crosses over fearful hearts because — God ha' mercy — the three scarlet rondels on each man's breast roared the Courtenays' presence.

'Jesu!' muttered Kate, jerking her head to the front.

'Move up then!' the newcomer ordered glibly, edging in beside her and ignoring the swift gather of skirts that shrieked a lack of welcome. Darting her gaze sideways confirmed Kate's estimate that the latecomer was at the butt end of his twenties. Old enough to have better manners.

He perched his liripiped hat upon his knee and then leaned across to poke Grandmother Bonville. 'Good morrow, Aunt. And I suppose this is Lady Harrington, eh?'

'Henry, what in Heaven are you doing here?' Grandmother Bonville's nose wrinkled at his tavern breath.

'Henry who?' Kate interrupted crossly.

'Why, Courtenay, sweetheart.' She received a faceful. 'We haven't met before. I've come down all the way from West Coker to join you in your grief.'

'I doubt that very much.' Grandmother Bonville looked fit to clout him. 'He's the middle brother, Katherine. The oldest one is the Earl of Devon and his manners are not much better.'

'Forgiveness, Aunt, I'm here to commiserate for the loss of the old tosspot. And the young one. Ahhh, losing such a young husband.' He drew an impudent gloved finger down Kate's cheek. 'Ah, are these tears for Willy?'

Both women ignored him. 'Oh, for heaven's sake, get on with it!' Grandmother Bonville growled at the priest.

'Poor fool looks fit to piss himself' sniggered Courtenay behind his hand. The next half hour was a torture not just to Kate with a drunken noble next to her misbehaving but to Father Gregory who was trying to ignore the loud yawns, sighs, farts and pretend snores. Kate could hear the rustle of clothing, of fear, from the rest of the congregation.

'Have you no reverence?' Kate snarled beneath her breath.

The interloper was clearly enjoying himself. His repertory held no end of insults. Running a hand salaciously across his stubbled cheek as he leered over his shoulder at Lovidia and sideways at Kate, unhooking the leather jack from his belt, guzzling the contents, and nudging his foot against hers. His breath stank of wine, his armpits stank of sweat and his clothes reeked of horse. He had to stagger out once to relieve himself. Only during the bells and blessings of the most sacred part of the Mass, did he show a modicum of piety. When he belched for the umpteenth time, Kate would have kicked him hard except her feet had gone numb with the cold. Why in Heaven's name had he bothered? To humiliate them or for a purpose more sinister?

'Wish I could excommunicate him, Lady Harrington,' muttered Father Gregory afterwards, bidding Kate farewell at the church door, 'but…'

'But?' prompted Kate.

'I can't complain to your brother the Bishop of Exeter, my lady, because there's a proclamation out for his arrest and, you must pardon my frankness, but apart from being consecrated as bishop, he's hardly set foot in the diocese and —' He smothered an unpriestly oath as Lord Henry emerged from the church and flung an arm about Grandmother Bonville's shoulders.

'You are inviting us in, Aunt?' he asked, with a breath that would have ignited every beacon from Plymouth to Portchester and kept up unsteadily beside them as they swiftly marched towards the church gate, where their horses were waiting. When Grandmother Bonville refused to answer, he repeated his words without the question mark, and rode after them with his retinue. How he managed to stay in the saddle was a credit both to his horse and the nearest man-at-arms.

'Haven't been here for years,' he exclaimed, lurching in to admire the tapestries that adorned the walls of Shute's great hall. An anxious Stephen Gylle hastened in after him. If Courtenay had not been accompanied by his men or the occasion one of grieving, Kate would have dissolved in irrepressible laughter. She made her way to the fire lit in the huge hearth, waiting for Will's formidable grandmother to evict this obnoxious man.

Courtenay joined her, annoyingly grinning and imitating her as he stretched his hands out to the warmth. It was tempting to trip him into the embers but there would be witnesses and... And looking again at his face, her instincts screamed that he was far more sober than he pretended.

'Where's the heiress then? Being burped?'

Why was he interested in her baby?

'Being fed,' Kate muttered.

'Unlike me. *Unlike me*!' Courtenay thumped his chest. 'Where's your hospitality to guests, my fine ladies?' he exclaimed loudly, so his men might hear. 'Where's courtesy these days? Down the jakes?'

Thank God, Grandmother Bonville came back to life. 'You've had enough already, Henry. Why don't you go and burn a few haystacks.'

'But it's February, Aunt.' He gave some sort of signal to his men and they started banging their fists on the trestle tables. 'I've always a thirst on me, Aunt. You know that.'

'Oh, fetch them something, Gylle.' Aunt Bonville took off her winter mantle and slung it over the back of the chair of estate on the dais and then she seated herself. A reminder that it was she who was lording it at Shute? Yes! Kate gleefully waited for the sharp dismissal but Will's grandmother slid a weary hand across her brow. O Jesu forbid! With increasing apprehension, Kate recognised the exhaustion of grief. Never say it was she who must deal with this unpredictable sot and his entourage.

'Am staying over at Colcombe Castle, by the way,' he was saying. Colcombe! Too frighteningly close. God's mercy! For how long? 'Why are you not with the queen's army, my lord?' Kate asked.

'What? Hey, shhhh, you poxy whoresons! What did you say, Lady Harrington?'

She repeated her question in the unexpected silence.

'Not in my interest.' His eyes glittered playfully. It was not cowardice, she realised, but far more threatening. A disrespect for duty? But she was only partly right. 'Brother's heir, you see,' he was explaining. 'It would have been unwise for him to risk all three of us.' Contempt rather than pity lifted the corners of his mouth. 'Three generations of Bonvilles slain, eh. That's bad luck or miscalculation, Lady Harrington.' Then he was looking up at the tapestry behind Kate. Like a dragon flicking a tongue across its lips as it eyes some sheep to carry off, she thought. Then the dragonish smile swerved to confront her. 'My brothers and I will miss the feuding with the old man. Won't be the challenge any more. Can't pick a quarrel with a mewling babe, can we?'

Again that worrying mention of Cecily. Was his real purpose to abduct her child? By Heaven, she'd kill him if she had to.

'And so you are here to convey your grief,' she stated with feigned innocuousness. 'How very gracious.'

'Saw the proclamation about your brother, too, Lady Harr'ton. Where is the noble Dick? Hiding in rabbit burrows?'

'I wish you were,' exclaimed Kate, deliberately beaming. But the remark fell wasted. Courtenay was more interested in watching Gylle ushering in servants with flagons of ale for the soldiers. Why was it men asked questions of women and never listened for answers? If her words fell short, how could she best him? Let him drink again? It looked like she did not have a choice.

It was the new Master of the Horse, Newton, whom she had mistaken for Will, who was carrying a tray of mazers to the dais as though he was suddenly a house servant. The world was going insane. Swiftly she crossed to him.

'Put a guard on the nursery,' she whispered as she took up a mazer for their guest.

'Already done, madame.' Newton bowed.

Astounded, Kate gave a faint approving nod and turned.

'To peace between neighbours, sir!'

Courtenay received the two-handled vessel, drank down the contents and held it out to Newton to be refilled. 'Not a valediction to the dear departed, Lady Harrington? Are you not joining me?'

'Oh, I definitely am,' exclaimed Kate, waiting until Lady Bonville was served before she took a goblet. They clinked metal and again he drank greedily. Was he wed? She pitied his wife if he was. 'Tell me, is boorishness a family characteristic or are all the Courtenays as ill-mannered as you?'

'Oooh, here be dragons!' He swaggered across to the high table. 'Proper Neville, isn't she, Aunt?' he muttered, leaning over Grandmother Bonville's shoulder. Then twisting round with difficulty to face Kate, he came to the point of his visit. 'Listen, Lady Harri-on, we can do this a number of ways. My brother the earl will ask her grace the queen for guardianship of the little heiress.' He giggled, ignoring Kate's horrified face.

The chair shook from the slap of his hand. 'Lordy, Aunt, your old man will turn in his grave at the thought.'

But no one was turning. Not corpses. And not Lady Bonville. No tirade rushed Courtenay to the door. Again, it was up to Kate.

Was he here to snatch her and Cecily for his brother?

'But … *but* I've another suggestion — are you listening, Lady Ha'ton? You can marry me so I become her guardian. What's her name, I forget? Cissie-cely, isn't it?'

'Rot in Hell!' The words shot out before she could stop them.

'Naughty, naughty. I'll be admonishshishing you when we are handfast, but, *but*…' He scowled fiercely. 'Anyway maybe I won't.' He leaned lower over his aunt. 'I like my women sleek, see,' he whispered, undulating his palms through the air.

That was an insult indeed.

'Lord Henry, a private word with you,' Kate purred, with an edge a soberer beast might have recognised as dangerous. The instant the man came across, she tossed her very full goblet into his face. '*Out!*' she snarled, pointing to the great door. 'I don't care if you are a Courtenay. I don't care if you are the Archangel Gabriel, Queen Margaret or the Devil himself, I want you out of here. Go and drink with your little armoured friends somewhere else.' She charged down the steps. 'On your feet!' she shouted at the Courtenay retainers. 'Go! How dare you come mocking us in our sorrow. Have you no respect? Go! And as for you, Henry Noggerhead Courtenay, I'll see you shackled in Hell before I let you have guardianship of my daughter.'

To her amazement and their master's, the soldiers started to shamble out.

'W-wait!' exclaimed their leader.

'You're drunk and you're stupid, nephew,' exclaimed Grandmother Bonville, rising to her feet at last. She jabbed him in the ribs with her finger and jabbed him some more. 'You heard Lady Harrington, Go!'

He jerked his body away. Kate, caught between him and his men, watched him stagger towards her. She held her breath. A whack of his arm would floor her.

'Woman, you are an interfering, bloody Neville. All this,' he lurched and hiccoughed. 'All this is…' he gestured to the tapestries, 'coming to us.'

'I'm not telling you again,' Kate said loudly. 'You insult the dead and the living.'

'Well, I'm taking this! And it's just the beginning.' Henry Courtenay brandished the mazer he was holding, jerked it upwards in final insult and staggered from the hall. His remaining men, with shaky farewell salutes, followed.

Kate collapsed on a bench and started to giggle. She grabbed a fresh goblet, took a swig and her laughter became tears. She wept in relief that the danger was over. For now.

Someone started applauding. It was Newton. Stephen Gylle took off his cap and scratched his head in amazement and the servants crowded into the hall from behind the buttery screen to surround her with praise. Absurd, undeserved, but what a delicious feeling to have stood up to a man like Courtney. It was for her baby, she told herself, she would not have had the courage otherwise, but how reassuring to know that she did have a backbone. The trouble was that Courtney might be like the plague and keep coming back.

Someone else thought so, too.

'I should not rejoice if I were you,' admonished Master Gylle and his eyes met Kate's. 'Henry Courtenay is a lamb when drunk, my lady, but he's a bloody wolf when sober.'

Kate woke in the middle of the night with a rat running across the coverlet and a swarm of fears making nests in her head. She threw a shoe at the rat, wishing it was Henry Courtenay. It vanished under the door but took none of her other dreads with it.

Cecily's future did lie in the queen's hands and if the accursed woman continued being vengeful, a Courtenay could indeed end up as guardian or worse still (and Heaven forbid!) as hers or Cecily's future bridegroom. She would need to keep strong guard about her baby, maybe move her in secret up to Chewton, the Bonvilles' house in Somerset. If matters became desperate, St Mary Magdalene's in Chewton was a sanctuary church.

Having resolved that, she fell into a light sleep, but followed by a nightmare that she was being marched past a row of her family's heads on stakes and before her, waiting by the executioner's block, was Henry Courtenay with an axe, and soldiers were forcing her brother Richard down for beheading.

'No!' she screamed, struggling against her guards to run to him. 'No!'

She awoke to find it was Eleanor's hands trying to restrain her. 'Oh, my lady, you were thrashing summat awful.'

Her heart and breathing still a-galloping, Kate struggled into a sitting position with her knees up beneath the sheets and buried her face in her hands. 'Your pardon, dear friend.'

Eleanor slid an arm about her. 'Can I make you a posset to help you sleep?'

Kate shook her head. 'I dreamed that everything was taken from us. Everything! But, Eleanor, I've been so stupid not to realise. If my brothers have been proclaimed traitors, then all the Neville manors, up and down the kingdom, will be seized for the crown! Mama will be homeless unless they let her have her dower, so will Richard's wife and —' God in Heaven! She straightened her shoulders abruptly as she at last realised the full consequence of Grandfather Bonville's execution.

'If Queen Margaret orders Parliament to attainder Grandfather Bonville as a traitor,' she pointed out to Lady Bonville in the great chamber after Mass — not easy with Cecily's tiny fingers pulling at her earrings. 'Then by law she can send officers to seize this house and, well, everything.'

Standing by the fire, Grandmother Bonville was unpinning the brooch that secured her cloak. 'Ouch! Now see what you've made me do.' She swiftly sucked at her finger lest it bloody her gown.

'It makes sense,' Kate pursued. 'Don't you see, keeping an army in the field all this time must have been very costly for the queen and she will be needing to reward the lords who have fought for her. All these manors could be given to the Courtenays. Your jointure and my dower, too, perhaps! We are the widows of traitors!' She omitted the horrid possibility that the queen might nail Lord Bonville's head up at Exeter's Rougemont Castle. 'And we have to protect Cecily. Vast estates and only this baby girl to inherit them!' She was fearful of telling anyone about the babe inside her. Henry Courtenay might very well shove her down a staircase.

'Of course, we shall take measures, Katherine. Just calm yourself. We must tilt at the enemy when we see them, not at shadows.'

'Henry Courtenay is no shadow.'

'Henry will receive nothing from the queen since he has done her no service. It will be the earl his brother who will prove the greater danger. *Boo!*' She was flapping her veil to distract Cecily.

'I think you are wrong, madame. Did you not hear his threats? And anyway, shouldn't we shift all our valuables from here, before the Sheriff of Exeter receives his orders?' She made play of looking round the solar. 'I am sure if our husbands had lived, they could have bargained, changed allegiance if need be, but as widows we haven't anything to bargain with. In fact, I should not be surprised if the confiscation of Grandfather Bonville's estates up north may have begun already.'

'And where are we supposed to take our moveables, Katherine Neville?'

'I'm not sure,' Kate admitted glumly. 'Somewhere they can be protected easily. There's our manors on Purbeck or what about Padstow? No one would think of —'

'Padstow! That's the end of the earth!' Grandmother Bonville rolled her gaze heavenwards with a groan, and Kate agreed tactfully, 'Yes, you are right and if we send a whole train of sumpters that far it will take days and the sheriff will be sure to get wind of it.'

The faint sound of the vesper bells from the abbey on the other side of the valley filled the impasse between them. 'There's our answer,' exclaimed Kate, bouncing with inspiration. 'Newenham Abbey! Scarce a mile away. Much more manageable!'

The old lady shrugged. She swept her gaze around the chamber, taking in the tapestries, the stained cloth paintings, the costly goblets, especially the silver gilt mazer bestowed on Grandfather Bonville by an abbot of Newenham at his baptism. 'Well, I know the earl my nephew has always coveted that.' She scowled at the lithe young woman dancing for Herod while a brawny John the Baptist, loaded with chains, waited stoically between his guards outside the door. 'Yes, you are not such a young featherhead, after all.' And she wasn't talking to Salome.

'You've been grieving, Grandmother. We all have.'

'No excuse, though. Very well, we shall move everything as fast as we can but in order of worth, eh? Get my secretary in here and tell him an inventory must be made! I'll not go delivering my valuables to any man willy-nilly, even if he has a bell rope to God.'

Within the hour, Grandmother Bonville rode off to negotiate with Abbot Hunteford, an offertory purse heavy on her belt. When she returned without it, the household, already primed by Kate, drew a unison breath and hurtled into action. Shute soon resembled a frenzied, toppled beehive.

Kate was allotted the muniment room because her eyesight was better than Lady Bonville's and she did not get so afflicted by dust. She could hear Grandmother's imperious voice cracking away in the great chamber, overseeing the emptying of the aumeries. Eleanor, the fittest of their tiring women, was on her knees in the best bedchamber, tucking rosemary and lavender into the folds of the coverlets and bed hangings before the servants interned them in boiled-leather chests. Every staircase, wooden or stone, resounded with grunts and shouts as the sweating menservants heaved coffers and chests down to the carts lined up in the courtyard.

There was an added urgency. While Lady Bonville had been negotiating with the abbot, a messenger had arrived from Exeter sent by one of the sheriff's officers, who had been accepting Grandfather Bonville's bribes for years. He confirmed Kate's fear; the queen had issued orders to seize the lands and moveables of any local rebels, and Sheriff Dyneham, whatever his personal loyalties might be, was taking the royal decree seriously. Spiderlike, he was apparently working outwards from the city. It was estimated he would reach Shute Hall within two days. With luck, they might be permitted to live on at Shute as part of their dower rights.

Unless Henry Courtenay attacked it first.

Kate herded up books from all over the house and carried them to join the rent rolls in the muniments room. Two herbals and a bestiary, a *Book of Hours* given to Grandmother Bonville by the queen, several French romances, Will's late mother's *Book of Devotions*, two recipe books, some rather dusty religious treatises, a much-thumbed manual on hunting and several generations of prayer books were all queuing for packing like horses waiting at a mounting block. But the manor rent rolls were the most precious, her children's future, and needed to be dealt with first. Some were on shelves, others stored upright in boxes, many of them over a hundred years old. Each had to be packed swiftly but with care, a task that must be done well away from any candles, and there was no fire in the room to warm her.

Maybe all this effort was in vain, Kate thought frantically, as she placed the last of the Devon rolls carefully in the iron-bound chest. Queen Margaret would hack the Nevilles down, every man jack of them, and the baby boy inside Kate — please God, it must be a boy — would have no strong man to defend his rights. Both her children could be given as wards to any one of the queen's supporters and Kate might be barred from seeing them. Oh, she could just imagine how someone like Henry Courtenay would take great delight in slamming the gates in her face.

No, she resolved as she closed the heavy lid of the last chest and searched through the bunch of heavy keys, she would never let that happen! Will would have expected her to protect his children. And she must remember the good times for their sake and keep his memory burning for them like a well-tended flame. He would have loved them all so much.

With the most valuable parchments secured, she smudged the tears from the corners of her eyes with the back of her hand and hastened down to the courtyard. She informed Newton that the rent chests were ready to be carried down to the carts and sent one of the little serving lads to fetch mulled wine for Lady Bonville, Eleanor and herself, then she returned to deal with the books. She needed to keep busy. What she wouldn't give for relief from the relentless, anxious thoughts hurtling through her head, but they kept her company like horseback demons.

The books needed to be packed with less care than the rolls. Some were already in their own cases. Each was valuable, much-loved by their various owners, and Kate could have wept anew as she ran her fingers across the leather cover of her father-in-law's book on falconry before she placed it in the chest. The pain of all their bloody deaths lashed her anew.

I must bear this child fully to term for all their souls, she told herself, as she finally closed the chest and sat back on her heels for a moment's respite before she strained the leather straps tight. Where was the mulled wine to restore warmth to her cold body? Maybe she should rest now. Common sense was needed.

And caution! There had been some light bleeding in the last few days, nothing of consequence, but this cramped pain in the belly that she was feeling now had come before. She should not keep her secret any longer, she decided. It was time she confided in Lady Bonville. The news would be like a torch in the darkness of the future for both of them.

'Let me help, madame.' Robert Newton had come back in from overseeing the carrying out of the rent chests. He must have heard her deep sigh for he heeled the door closed, strode across and came down on one knee beside her, his callused, capable hands taking over the leather strap. He notched it far tighter round the chest than she was capable of, then he looked sideways at her with one raised eyebrow. 'Begging your pardon but you are driving yourself too hard, my lady.'

They were kneeling like a couple making their trothplight.

She stared at the shadow of stubble on his sun-browned cheeks and let her gaze rise freely to the young man's silvery eyes. The light in them glimmered both hard and kindly at the same time. Idiotically, she glimpsed a fleeting look of Will about him. Imagination! But this was the second time.

'Your pardon, what did you say, Master Newton?'

'I said you are driving yourself too hard, my lady.'

'Keeping busy helps. I am trying to forget the hurt that has been done to us, Master Newton.'

'And if "us" had won, my lady? What then? There are widows aplenty on both sides, to my way of thinking.'

Kate swallowed and stood up. 'I daresay you speak true, sirrah, but you speak out of turn.'

'I beg your pardon, Lady Harrington.' Contrition rimed his voice but he swiftly scrambled to his feet as though he had resented being on his knees before her.

'Oh, it is I who should bite my tongue,' she said wearily. 'Indeed, more than that, Newton. I have to thank you for your care of my daughter yesterday. I understand from Master Gylle that it was your decision to post guards outside the nursery.'

'It seemed sensible, my lady.'

And he had been a subtle presence in the hall, like a guardian angel, a presence that had given her strength to stand up to Henry Courtenay. Remembering the young man's arms about her when he had carried her from the church, Kate's heart began an unspurred, illicit gallop of its own. It was tempting to wish to be held and comforted, but, God's mercy, she chided herself, from where were such wicked thoughts arising? It was because she could see Will in him, that was all.

'*Never show interest in a manservant,*' she remembered her mother lecturing her sister, Alice. '*It is only foreigners who show such ill breeding. The English nobility never accepts and never forgets. Henry V's French queen was never forgiven for marrying her horse-marshal — even if her sons by him are pleasant young men — and as for that disgusting Jacquetta creature marrying her steward, uuugh. Never make that mistake or you will pay for it for the rest of your life.*'

The Neville women did not roll in the hay. She had never betrayed Will nor would she ever.

'Lady Bonville and I are very grateful to you, Master Newton.' She moved across to the chest closest to the door. 'This needs locking then it can go as well. Oh, where's the dratted key? I had it a moment since. Help me find it, I pray you, then they may take both.' Why was she babbling so?

'Madame.' Too perceptive, she thought, recognising a swift glint of understanding in the young man's eyes.

'Try over there,' she suggested, pointing to several bundles of letters. Newton must be a few years older than Will. Broader, taller, protective. Maybe that was why she felt an attraction.

Men's voices echoed in the stairwell and several pairs of heavy feet laboured upon the wooden stairs.

'That Lovidia, darn traper,' scoffed a voice outside the door and there was the sound of a man spitting. 'Nay, she'll not look at me no more. Not now she has a nobleman's brat to suckle her instead.'

'Not much good wi' the young lord dead, though. Only her word for it.'

A third voice joined in. 'Nay, he good as owned she was carrying his babe an' afore witnesses too, including her father. I saw his horse outside their place many a time. 'Sides, have you seen the babe? Has the Bonville chin.'

'Half the shire has the *Bonville* chin,' chuckled the first man.

Kate was aware of Newton taking charge, striding to the door and telling his fellows that the chests were not ready, and that they should sit on the stairs awhile. Having done that, he shut it against the outside draught and leaned back against its timbers, watching her.

She must have looked ill because he said quickly and quietly, 'I hope you made nothing of that, my lady.'

Her voice sounded unfamiliar, bitter. 'Oh no, Master Newton, I gathered that one and one can make one.' She put out a hand to steady herself, waving him back from assisting her.

'The Bonville chin,' she echoed mockingly. How could she have been so blind? 'Tell me, sir, isn't yours a Bonville chin?'

'Yes,' he said, letting out a slow breath as though she was helping him back up a precipice. The comely, roguish grin was almost convincing. 'Indeed it is. So you see, my lady, best not to listen to the gossip of fools nor share their conclusions.' *So you see.* Oh, she *saw* all right. Only a fool would believe his noble attempt to save her feelings.

'Then you are "the young lord's" half-brother?'

'No.' He came forward slowly, as he might approach a wild creature, concern for her writ upon his face. 'No, I'm his uncle. The old man's by-blow.'

'Ha! So the "young lord" is my husband.'

'Oh, Jesu!' Newton smacked his own cheek at his stupidity but it was too late, the truth was spilt like the filthy sediment from a forgotten slop bucket. 'No, my lady, I didn't mean that Will —'

Kate reached the door and wrenched the latch up, holding on to the doorpost for support. 'In here, if you please! Help them, Master Newton!' Somehow she reached the window and gripped the transom to keep herself upright, while the staggers and grunts went on behind her. She could not let go yet or the world would heave beneath her.

A few hours ago she had believed that life could not get much worse but now … Will should have been honest with her!

And the dream, the foolish fancy that all would be well once he returned home, the guilt she had felt at not pleasing him enough, not showing sufficient passion, when *he* …

*He* had been betraying her with Lovidia. Well, there would be no more garlanding his memory as though he were a blessed saint. He could find his own way out of Purgatory; copulate his way out! As for trust, she would never make that mistake again.

Behind her the bedchamber was silent. She was alone, at liberty to turn shakily from her refuge.

'Oh Sweet Mother of God,' she whispered, tears running down her cheeks. She'd been a trusting fool from the start, and everyone, *everyone*, knew it. The old game of master and maidservant and then the family's swift removal of the thickening girl. No wonder the village had smirked at her good works.

It was needful to aim a kick at an innocent cushion. Better than denting a platter or breaking a windowpane. But God Himself could kick as well. A boot force of pain hit and she felt a trickle of blood seep from her womb.

'Help me!' she gasped, but her voice had no power to carry. 'Mercy, God!' she cried, staggering to the door.

St Margaret! Any saint!

'*Newton, help me!*'

# 5: KATE

## 8th March 1461, Shute Hall, Devonshire

Letter in hand, Kate grabbed up her skirts and hurtled upstairs to the nursery. It was the first time she had actually hurtled since losing the baby. The wounds of betrayal and loss had not healed over but at eighteen you could not spend your life miserably huddled in bed with your feet on a petticoated hot brick, not when you had a live, sweet daughter who needed you. Cecily's company had been a constant reminder that she must stay well to safeguard her child. And today, despite the snow that was besetting the inland shires, a party of exuberant clerics on their way to Exeter had interrupted their journey to bring her a missive from her youngest brother George (Bishop of Exeter in his spare moments).

'Richard has crowned my cousin Ned at Westminster!' she shrieked happily, bursting into the nursery where Grandmother Bonville was supervising the spooning of pottage into Cecily, who was more interested in using it either to enhance her complexion or prettify Joan's kirtle.

'King?' exclaimed Grandmother Bonville, Eleanor and Joan Celer in unison. Kate grinned at their open-mouthed astonishment.

The wet nurse recovered first. 'Beggin' yurr pardons, but that be why Sir Henry Courtenay as gone skulkin' 'ome, then. Master Newton 'eard yesterday that 'e waz gone and we wuz all a-wonderin'.'

'Does this mean an end to the wars then?' Eleanor asked.

'Pah, you can crown an ass and call it a king, but it doesn't mean it is one. Not that I'm saying your cousin is an ass,' Lady Bonville added tersely for Joan's benefit lest her words get misconstrued all across the Devon hills. 'Let me read that, Katherine.'

Kate handed her George's letter and turned excitedly to her tiring woman. 'It's all true, Eleanor. London wouldn't open its gates to let in Queen Margaret's army, but instead of attacking, she's withdrawn her army northwards. And the city *has* opened its gates to Richard and my cousin of York — isn't that wondrous? And Richard has crowned — *crowned!* — Ned king in St Peter's Abbey, Westminster! So the attainder of treason will be reversed.

'Oh, I want to ring the bells!' She lifted Cecily into her arms and whirled her about the chamber. 'Who has a clever uncle, poppet! Let us fetch everything back from Newenham and celebrate!'

'Faugh! Enough! You are making the fire smoke.' Grandmother Bonville gave up reading the letter at arm's length and fanned the air with it. 'Out!' she ordered Joan and waited until the woman had gone before she added, 'While I am exceedingly glad to see this news has brought colour back into your cheeks, Katherine, where's the victory?'

'Victory?' Kate echoed in surprise. Heavens, how long was it since Grandmother Bonville had left the West Country? 'If London, Grandmother, and that means our richest merchants, is fully supporting Richard and Ned against the queen, isn't that a victory? By heaven, you cannot say permitting Ned's coronation shows lack of enthusiasm. Wheeee!' She lifted Cecily above her head and blew a kiss on her middle.

'I shall say what I plaguey well please, young woman. King Henry is still God's Anointed!'

'King-Henry-is-not-fit-to-rule,' Kate countered in drumbeat tone, jiggling Cecily up and down.

'Isn't he?' Grandmother Bonville's tone was insulting. Then the old lady was even more infuriating. 'Mad King Henry or young King Ned!' she sneered. 'I'll say it again. Both of 'em are asses! Asses on leading reins even if they've each been sloshed with holy oil by a pack of bishops.' She sucked in her cheeks smugly. 'You'll see, my girl. We'll have no peace until either Queen Margaret is flung into the Tower or your rebel of a brother gets a sword through his heart. And until then, I'm leaving my jewel coffer with Abbot Hunteford. And, pray, don't glare at me like that!'

Kate felt like more than glaring as she put Cecily back on her little wooden settle and grabbed a wet napkin from the bowl on the small table. 'My brother is doing his best,' she exclaimed angrily, swiftly cleansing the little cheeks and fingers. The napkin hit the water with the vehemence of a catapult. 'He has risked *everything* — *everything* — because he believes we should have a king who is in command of his wits not some demented old man.'

A huge wail burst forth from Cecily's little throat.

'Now, see what you've done with your ranting, frightened the poor mite,' snapped Grandmother Bonville. 'Oh, give her here!'

Fuming, Kate passed Cecily to her.

'Is Mama making lots of nasty loud noises, sweetheart? There, there.' She sat the child on her knee, jingled a belled lambkin in front of her and, once Cecily had calmed, dug out a further quarrel from her quiver. 'What I *do* blame you for, Katherine Neville, is losing my great grandson.' For a swift breath, Kate stared at her utterly mystified and then she realised who the old woman meant.

The baby she had lost! Although God alone knew what gender the child had truly been.

This was horrible.

'Aye, you may look daggers at me, girl, but I'll speak my mind. You should have taken more care. Good God! Heaving around those coffers like a young fool and not telling anyone you were carrying the Bonville heir!' She gave a snort and swivelled round to glare at Eleanor, who had been sitting quietly with her sewing, trying to stay unobtrusive. '*We* should have taken better care of her!'

'Madame, I —'

'It's not Eleanor's fault,' Kate exclaimed. 'I desired to keep the news as a surprise for Will. I've told you that, madame.'

Grandmother Bonville shook her head angrily. 'But even when he was dead, Katherine, you never told us. Oh, fie, girl, if something stinks, you air it.'

'*Stinks!*' exploded Kate.

'Very well! I'll allow it was a poor choice of words. However, if we are talking home truths, I'll give you one more, Katherine Neville. Whether it's your cousin and your brothers or Queen Margaret, whoever finally wins control of this wretched kingdom is going to take control of *her*.' She bestowed a kiss on Cecily's cheek. 'And you and I will have no say. *She*'ll be given to some stranger in marriage and all this great inheritance will go to him. Whereas if you'd carried the boy-child full term…'

Kate sprang to her feet in indignation. 'Well, if a boy is so precious, madame, go and fetch Will's boy from Lovidia and make the bastard heir.'

Behind her, Eleanor gasped. 'I didn't know you knew, my lady.'

'Pah, woman,' exclaimed Grandmother Bonville. 'The whole of Shute knew.'

'Wait a moment.' Kate looked from one to the other. 'You *both* knew?'

Eleanor suddenly found her mending to be of great interest. Grandmother Bonville shrugged.

Disgust flamed Kate's indignation. '*You* rant at *me* for not telling you things, madame, when all along you never told me about Will and Lovidia. It's she who killed my babe. I only found out that day, that instant.'

'But, my lady, you can't blame —' began Eleanor, but Grandmother Bonville cut in again.

'Listen to me, Katherine Neville, there will always be Lovidias in this world and Bonville men have always had a reputation. Young men,' she shrugged, 'why, of course they are going to spread themselves around the neighbourhood. They would not be manly if they didn't. A pretty wench only had to stray across old Bonny's path and the foolish old dotard would be knocking on her cottage door in no time. That's the way men are.'

'I am going out for some air,' snarled Kate, '*before* I stab my needle into someone!'

Grumpy, rebellious and feeling five years old instead of a mature widow, Kate changed into her oldest kirtle and mantle, tugged on her riding boots, ignored Eleanor's attempt to stop her and, with Cecily well-wrapped in her arms, marched down to the stables. If Henry Courtenay was gone from the neighbourhood, she was free to ride out without an escort of thousands. Grandmother Bonville would disapprove. Well, good! It was about time that the old woman realised she was a Neville and not on a leash like some brainless lapdog.

Her breath was vapour as she crossed the cobbles and the wind was icy.

'I wish to ride,' she announced, sending the two stableboys on duty rushing to fetch a side-saddle for her mare, Guinivere.

'No! That one.' She pointed to a man's saddle. 'And I need a groom. Where's Newton?' Newton would find her a reliable escort. She could not afford to ride alone, even in high dudgeon, not with a babe in her arms.

'Here, my lady.' Booted, muscular, Robert Newton strode out from one of the stables with a pitchfork still in his hand. Used to exertion, he wore no mantle today, just a sleeveless jerkin, and the cordals of his shirt were untied. There was something about him that was unsettling. Probably his utter masculinity, challenging to her after an excess of women's company. Or maybe because he missed nothing: a wry twist of his lip told her he could read the fury that was tensing her body.

'I need a groom.'

'So I could hear. Well, it had better be me.' Having removed his thick leather gloves, he stroked a clean knuckle down Cecily's cheek. 'How about you take the child back to her nursemaid, my lady?'

Kate gave him a look that could have pinioned him to the stable door with his pitchfork and he stepped back from her, his expression an insulting mask of servitude.

'As my lady wishes.'

So he considered her in the wrong in bringing Cecily, and maybe he was right but she was cursed if she'd be lectured by a Bonville by-blow even if he was comely. And the Bonville by-blow said nothing more when her horse was brought out but he certainly made an unnecessary fuss of checking the ambler's buckles and girths before he led it to the mounting block. She silently handed Cecily to him while she slid across the saddle, and although he gave his full attention to the babe as she adjusted her skirt to a decorous coverage of her legs, she sensed his temptation to behave like a rutting Bonville at war with his rank as a servant.

'Axminster,' she decreed, as she heeled her horse's flanks but they were barely past the gatehouse when Newton impudently kneed his horse to block her and pointed with his riding crop to the lane that ran tamely south along the valley floor. 'Since you're cradling the babe, that way is best. I'll warrant the little one'll be needing the breast in an hour or so.'

Curse it! She should have thought of that before she mentioned Axminster. Why was it men, even servants, always thought they knew better? She stuck her chin up defiantly but, yes, she would need to have Cecily back with her wet nurse and, anyway, the weather would not hold. A scrutiny of the clouds was necessary and having demonstrated that, she nodded condescendingly and, hiding her reluctance, led the way south, keeping her back stiff and haughty. If Newton wanted to smirk behind her, let him.

What the man did not realise was that the ride would take her through the same bland fields and leafless hedgerows that she could see from her bedchamber window. Boring, boring, boring. But what choice did she have? If she were a man, she would gallop down to Seaton and stride along the shingle letting the wind buffet the fury out of her. Instead, with tiny Cecily in her arms, she had to be satisfied with an ambling gait.

Newton tailed behind her with either tact or silence bridling his opinion, but beyond the sight of the last cottage, he spurred up to her. 'If you are wanting a gallop to vent your anger, my lady, you'd have been wise to leave the babe behind.'

'Anger?' she echoed sweetly, hiding her astonishment that he had again penetrated her thoughts. 'I think you overstep your manners, Master Newton.'

'Sorry, *my lady*,' he answered with a politeness as flimsy as a pauper's shroud. 'Your pardon, *my lady*, it's the Bonville blood will out.'

'It isn't only the Bonville *blood*,' muttered Kate crabbily, imagining Will pleasuring Lovidia.

Rob Newton touched his forehead to her with a deference she suspected he didn't feel for an instant, and reined back once more.

Insolent Bonvilles! Betraying bastards, the lot of them. Did men think of nothing but their pricks? Or power? Well, one blessing was she need no longer feel guilty about her lack of contentment as Will's wife. But could it be her own lack of passion that had driven him back into Lovidia's arms? Oh damn everything! It was Will's lying that angered her, not just lying to her that she and Cecily meant all the world to him but the other lying — *with* Lovidia — and the whole world knowing except her. And now to be blamed by Lady Bonville for changing the future by losing the baby. Well, no matter what, she would safeguard her little daughter.

Cecily fell asleep to the rhythm of the hooves. So did her mother's arm but Kate was too proud to turn for home. The even-tempered track with its lack of twists and turns lent no adventure after a surfeit of needlework and nursery songs.

Oh, she so badly needed distracting. It was tempting to beckon Newton to ride alongside and make conversation. Should she? There was a sense of sinfulness in being in his company and it would be amusing to provoke his pride. Amusing but wrong.

'My lady,' he called out eventually. 'We are almost off our land. It isn't wise to ride further. You are carrying an heiress in your arms.'

She slowed Guinivere to a walk. 'Pah, Henry Courtenay is lying low at Powderham Castle, and my lord of Devon will be at the queen's side — wherever she is.'

'My lady, yonder Colyton is theirs, as you know well, and the townsfolk are a pack of smugglers and thieves. Your kinsmen may have wooed London into supporting them but they have no power in Devon with my father gone.'

Arrogant poxy Bonville!

'My lady?'

'We'll ride to there and then turn back!' She pointed ahead to the ford over the Coly River.

Another obedient touch of the hat and the Master of Horse reined in to let her lead.

The ford showed signs of neglect. Neither the Bonvilles nor the Courtenays had bothered with keeping the thick tangle of hawthorn, ivy and brambles on either bank in hand and the slats of the wooden bridge that served travellers on foot were missing in places.

Refusing to ask for Newton's help, Kate had an awkward scramble to the ground. A wonder, but she managed not to drop Cecily. Her tiny daughter was awake now. Even though her baby eyes were too young to look for fish, Kate carried her cautiously onto the footway. The chance of seeing a chubb or a kingfisher was as good as King Henry winning back France but it was all part of being a dutiful mother. Newton did not dismount but waited with a resigned expression on the Bonville side.

It was in mid coo that Kate heard the sinister clink of metal and froze. It was an effort to look cheerful and nonchalant as she slowly turned.

O sweet Christ defend her! Two brawny ruffians, armed with cudgels and knives, were already on the footway. The third, a short, wiry brigand, had grabbed the reins of Guinivere. Unkempt, lousy hair framed greedy faces. Unkind faces. And the sister of the earl, who had just crowned a king, now experienced true fear for the first time in her sheltered life.

And she had no knight-errant. Newton, curse him, was not close at all. She almost had the sense he'd expected this, that he'd let her ride into this ambush.

'Bah Gaw,'ere's a well-fed young piece for the tuppin',' muttered the tallest thief, brandishing a knife blade before her face.

'Girrrl-child, is it?' asked his companion, reaching out a hand to Cecily's shawl. 'We could sell 'em both to one of them Barbary ships. Fair hairr, pale skin'd fetch a fortune.'

Kate recoiled, jerking Cecily away. They were clearly blustering but … if they realised who her child was.

'Lay yurr filthy 'and on this babe,' she growled in the thickest Devon dialect she could muster, 'an' I'll see you 'anged.'

''Er might, too,' Newton called out cheerfully, kneeing his horse a few paces closer. The damned coward was still keeping a safe distance and his dialect had suddenly grown hairy. 'Aye thourrrt you dawcocks 'ad taken to robbin' old besoms in Exeter,' he bantered.

'Well, if it don't be one of old Bonville's by-blows,' guffawed the short fellow. 'Good marning, Marster Newton, and 'ow be service with them scraggy old birrrds in Shute? Bailiff down Dartmouth way's lyin' on 'is bier an' my lord earl'll be lookin' for a new man. Suit you well, I's a-reckonin'.'

'I s'll think about it.' Newton was leaning forward in the saddle, unbothered, amused even, by their presence.

'An' word's out his lorrdship's put a price on the 'Arrington baby's 'ead. Be worth zummat to you, lad. An' speakin' of brats.' Speculation gleamed in the narrow slits of the fellow's eyes and horror clamped like an icy hand around Kate's heart. Why didn't Newton ride forwards, the lily-livered coward? He was wearing a sword. At least he could rescue Cecily. Was he part of this?

*God ha' mercy!*

The bigger ruffian was alongside her, lifting her veil to see if she was wearing earrings. She wasn't. All her jewels were at the abbey. She jerked her head away and the rascal laughed nastily, his hands going to the ties that held his codflap. 'Why we wastin' time? One of you take the youn' zow's piglet. I s'll go first.'

'Says oo?' With a leer, the second man shoved her cloak away from her right breast. 'Soft and plump,' he called over his shoulder to the third fellow. 'Be like fuckin' a pillow.'

*Don't show fear!*

'Get these cursed fools away frrrom me, Rrrob!' Kate snarled through her teeth.

'Rrrob,' they chorused, turning to mock him. 'Rro-ob.'

'Ihn yours then?' asked the leader.

'Of course, ihn's mine,' Newton said with a grin. 'Lordy, I'm not zum nursemaid to be wastin' time on zummon else's spawn.'

'You 'earrd him,' said Kate and she spat.

'Thaas quite fine, though, young Newton,' clucked the ringleader, eyeing the stuff of Kate's gown. 'Been zerrvicin' the young widow 'Arrington, haz you, to afford this?'

The young widow Harrington stiffened. 'Betterr not be,' she growled.

'Now therrre be a challenge.' Wearing a confident grin, Newton at last rode into the ford and up to the footbridge. 'Come on, my birrd, time we 'eaded for 'ome before the li'le darlin' starts bawlin' with hunger.' He held out his arms for Cecily. 'Give ihn 'ere!'

There was no message in his eyes. She had to trust him. He could spur off with Cecily, carry her out of danger. That was best. He couldn't save both of them. She swallowed, trying to hide her terror. Rape would be horrible. But she'd survive, survive and see these curs hanged.

She lifted Cecily up to him, then for a swift breath, hesitated. Would he hand over her baby to the Courtenays? Would he ... O *Mary, Sweet Mother of God*!

Newton took Cecily with a soft cluck of welcome.

'Ahhh,' chorused the villains.

*You're a Neville, damn it! Do not show fear!*

With a flirtatious wriggle of her shoulders, Kate asked, 'Zo, are one of you gormless dafties goin' to help me onto my 'orse or wuz you goin' to stand there like a row of ruddy peasticks?'

Was that brazen enough?

Cecily was mewling as Newton kneed his horse round towards Shute but he did not ride away. Instead, he tarried alongside in the midst of the ford. Why was he delaying? *Give spur! Get-my-child-out-of-here!*

Or was he waiting to see her dishonoured? Kate squcalcd as the largest ruffian shoved her back against the other rogue. A coarse hand swished her skirts up to the thigh. 'Last chance, lads. Woz it gonna be? Err or the 'orse?'

She was praying, praying so hard they would take poor Guinivere.

And then Cecily let out an almighty bawl.

'Changed my mind,' guffawed the ruffian, letting go of Kate's skirt and turning with a grin to Newton. 'We'll take the 'orse! It be prettier.'

Miraculously, they were stepping away. One of them had her horse's bridle. The other two were laughing at her. Was it just a game? Or was she so ugly they did not want her?

'That wurrn't necessary,' she exclaimed primly, thrusting the folds of her kirtle back down.

Stupid thing to say.

She wanted to blurt out: *my brother has just crowned the king of England and you'll pay for this*. But therein lay folly.

Then the air was shocked from her as the largest fellow swung her onto the rump of Newton's horse. It staggered beneath the extra load.

And then, still wailing, Cecily gave a loud and meaningful passing within the swaddling bands. 'High time to head home, I think,' said Newton dryly, wrinkling his nose. His vowels back intact, he raised his hat insolently with his free hand. 'Farewell, lads. Carry my regards to Henry Courtenay.'

They were over half a mile beyond the ford before he slowed the horse.

'Poor babe,' he said, looking down at the real tears on Cecily's little cheeks. 'She'll have a bruise where I pinched her.'

'I should have thought of that.' Kate glanced back fearfully along the track. Like her babe, she needed to be wrapped in someone's arms, assured that this would never happen again. Yes, kissed, and told that she had been brave, that she was prettier than a dun-coloured ambler.

'The tupheads have the horse,' Newton stated matter-of-factly. 'That will suffice. Are you recovered?'

There was no 'my lady'. But he didn't say *I told you so*. And there was respect in his voice that seemed freely given.

'Yes,' she said, swallowing, one hand still holding onto his belt. 'I wanted an adventure but I didn't enjoy that one bit.' She needed to make him promise that he'd say nothing of her shaming to his fellow servants but she sensed it was better to trust him than to ask him. 'And I'm not very comfortable, Master Newton.'

'I don't suppose you are. Nor is this young lady. How about you get down if you can? It's safe now, I promise.'

As soon as Kate slid to the ground, he passed Cecily down to her and dismounted. 'It will repeat in your head all tonight,' he warned her. 'But you will feel better tomorrow.'

That was kind of him. Her face felt hot with embarrassment that she had thought him a betrayer. 'You did it just with words.'

'My lady?' His puzzlement was feigned. Oh he knew. She read it in the smug twist of lip.

'Just words, Master Newton. Three against one and not a blow struck.'

Ah, he could not stop his face turning scarlet. 'Well, we don't want to start a local war again, my lady, even if it means losing a worthy horse. There's always a way out.' Perhaps the scepticism was evident in her face for he added, reddening further: 'The old lord my father was always out for trouble an' it did no one any good. We were just fortunate that them fools had turnips for brains and that the little demoiselle here has very good lungs.' He gestured to the saddle. 'Please you to ride an' I'll walk my lady? We still have one horse to carry you.'

It felt like the road to Bethlehem as he led them back to Shute. He lifted her down in the stable yard with the indifference of a worthy groom, except he said, 'If you decide to do this again, Lady Harrington, I suggest we take an army.'

'Indeed, Master Newton,' she managed with a cheeriness that was only skin-deep. 'I'll order in some French cannon and, yes, we'll load up cradles and an excess of babies — *for pinching*.'

She was in the dumps for two whole days, wanting to see Master Newton and knowing she should not and feeling like a pudding on legs and since incessant rain accompanied her dilemma, she had no excuse to go to the stables nor ask why he was not dining in the hall. That was until Eleanor came excitedly up the stairs with the message that Guinivere was back in her stall. Going to see for herself, Kate also observed that even the saddle was back upon its peg. What's more, there were three extra horses tethered in the other stalls and they all had the Courtenay brand upon their rumps.

Master Newton was no longer in evidence either to thank or to interrogate. That morning Grandmother Bonville had dispatched him to Chewton with a long list of commissions, which was as well since he was still occupying Kate's thoughts in a manner that was not healthy for someone of her rank. Such dreaming was a healthy counter-balance to other less useful conclusions — that she was too plump, too plain and not even worth tupping by a pack of leering louts.

Master Newton might have kept his promise of silence about the details of the encounter on the bridge but it was clear he had suggested to Grandmother Bonville that measures still be enforced to protect Cecily. Once the infant heiress learned to walk, she would not be walking far, not without several attendants, and judging by the number of servants who once more dogged Kate out of doors like favourite mastiffs, nor would Cecily's mother.

There had been a reprimand, not in front of anyone — just her and Grandmother Bonville. It had been degrading to be scolded like some wilful child who had deliberately upended an inkpot on the best coverlet. And so unreasonable. It made Kate defiantly announce she was taking Cecily to visit her widowed mother at Fotheringay.

'Go and comfort Lady Salisbury, if you must, Katherine, but you'll do so alone. Cecily stays here.'

'She's my mother's grandchild, too,' Kate protested, but Grandmother Bonville was unmoved.

'I repeat, the child stays here. If you or your high-strutting brothers cannot keep her safe yet, then by Heaven, I plaguey well shall.'

Hmm, some backbone was definitely needed here.

'Then, speaking on my daughter's behalf, madame, since she is actually the owner of this house and we are her dependents, I am requesting you to come with us as well. You can ride at the front with a primed crossbow and we'll take French cannon and other babies to defend our progress.'

The old lady's tawny eyebrows arched at her boldness but there was a wicked smile on her thin lips as if the provocation had been deliberate. 'You know very well I haven't the faintest understanding of what you're blethering about, Katherine Neville.'

'I'm relieved to hear it! But you'll come, madame?'

'Yes,' exclaimed Cecily's great-grandmother. 'And since you are all puffed-up feathers and a-cackling like some hen that's just laid its first egg, perhaps you'd tell our tiny noble lady that I was only waiting for her to ask.'

# 6: ELYSABETH

## *1<sup>st</sup> April 1461, Groby Hall, Leicestershire*

Grey skies, Grey family, a lonely bed and two children who would barely talk to her. And it was weeks now since John's death and she was still at Groby with little choice in the matter. March had been cruel. The Fosse Way had been smothered with snow, stranding travellers unless they were desperate enough to wade through thigh-high drifts. Although she yearned to return to Astley, she dared not risk her sons' lives to make the journey south, and the promise to finish John's tower felt like a curse, a manacle chaining her in misery to Groby.

The unkind weather also changed England's fortunes. A carrier pigeon belonging to the Mayor of Leicester fluttered home with tidings of a great and bloody victory for Edward of York somewhere in the north. Fought in a snowstorm with hundreds slain. No one knew yet what had become of Queen Margaret but Elysabeth did not care. A woman who could not spare a horse no longer deserved a kingdom.

It was finally a week into April before the black, gritty ice caking the courtyard turned to slush. Elysabeth's bailiff rode up from Astley with sad news of flock losses all over the shires — ewes buried in the snow and newborn lambs dying in the freezing air. She should ride back to oversee matters but the roofless tower waited, mocking her. John Cowper, the master builder, returned with his workmen but several days of rain hindered their labour and the mirey lanes around Groby were pronounced too soft for carts bearing slate. Another week limped by but then the spring winds began to harden the ground.

Sewing, stitching, grieving and too much thinking! She would go crazed if she stayed at Groby any longer.

'I am going to ride over to the slate pits tomorrow morning,' she announced at the supper table and watched several pairs of Grey eyebrows rise.

'Is that not a man's task?' snorted her mother-in-law.

'I shall take Tom with me.'

'Much good that will do,' Lady Ferrers muttered, directing a sniffy glare down the table. Tom was sullenly picking at his salted herring, while Dickon, who had a runny cold, had arranged his fishbones in a line according to size and was counting them.

'See what the weather's like first, eh?' Elysabeth's brother-in-law, nineteen-year-old Edward Grey, gave her foot a supportive nudge. It sounded like Grey might accompany her. He had been dogging her heels ever since he had recovered from his wounds. Fortunate for him, he'd never returned to the queen's army.

Lady Ferrers patted his hand. 'Elysabeth is quite capable of making her own decisions.'

'Yes, truly, Tom and I shall manage well enough.'

*If* they could be saddled up before her brother-in-law was stirring.

But Grey was booted and spurred to accompany her next morning. At least he had put Greek fire under Tom's reluctant arse; the boy was waiting for her in the stable yard already astride his pony. Her son's expression might be indifferent and his 'good morning' was only a grunt but he was out of bed.

Beside him was a laden pack ass. A pack ass she recognised. For an instant, her blood ran cold, and then she saw the strange antennae tethered to the sides of the panniers.

'What's this, then?' It was an effort to speak brightly but she must for his sake.

'Uncle Grey is taking me trout fishing in the Lin, Mother.'

Seeing her surprise, Grey slapped a brotherly arm about her. 'Nowt wrong with that, I hope?'

'Nowt at all,' mimicked Tom, challenging her to argue.

'Aye,' exclaimed his uncle, 'I thought we'd make a day of it as the sun is out at last and ride on to Bradgate. An' stop looking in the dumps, Elysabeth, we'll call at the quarries first. Hurry up with the horses!' he shouted to the grooms. There was a briskness about him this morning as though he, too, needed to escape Groby. 'And, aye, we need to talk.'

Ah, the matter of her dower and Tom's inheritance, Elysabeth guessed, with an inward groan. There were scuffles and skirmishes ahead. Land tenure was so complicated. With his grandfather and father dead, Tom was now Baron Ferrers but he could not fully assert his rights as joint owner of the Grey-Ferrers lands until he came of age. Until then, Lady Ferrers, assisted by Grey, was in full charge, and in any quarrel, Grey, who had no income of his own, would side with his mother.

Well, better to deal with Grey than Lady Ferrers, except his fingers, bereft of gloves, lingered a fraction longer than was brotherly as he helped Elysabeth onto her horse.

'Thank the Lord, it isn't puttering down any more,' he exclaimed, swinging into his own saddle and then he added sheepishly, 'We've ordered the sun to paint some roses on your cheeks, Elysabeth, haven't we, Tom lad?'

She groaned inwardly. Not roses, men.

And the sunlight was a suitor, too. Tardy, but gallant, its warmth like a lover's hand between her shoulder blades as she settled into the saddle.

Around her horse's hooves, morning light blazed upon the ebbing puddles and sheened the winter moss that embroidered the flagstones to a vivid silken green. Even the silver cord edging the cuffs and collar of her dark mourning gown gleamed. Life was opening the doors and casements again.

Along the street, laundered sheets and linen optimistically festooned the brush fences and palings of the wealthier cottagers, but beyond the village, winter still held a relentless grip. Elysabeth swallowed her tears. Last summer when she had ridden this way with John, the trees of Charnwood had been lush with foliage and the warm air drowsy with insects. Today the limbs of the hawthorn hedgerows were bare and the meadow grasses, arched by the months of cold, glittered with melting frost. By now the white blossoms of blackthorn should have been blessing the hedgerows.

*But it will happen.* She knew that. It was inevitable and maybe things would get better, *must* get better.

All this land would be Tom's. No, *is* Tom's, she thought with pride. Charnwood Forest, with its coppiced woods, villages and deer park, was all part of the Groby demesne. Yet, if Tom realised that, it did not show in his face. His shoulders were still a defensive curl of defiance.

Her stratagem to let him speak with the master slater at Swithlands proved a failure, too. Grey could not resist taking charge and Tom wandered around the deep pit holes like a lost soul teetering on the chasm of Hell. Well, not quite that, but the slate men's banter fell on indifferent ears. Oh, by the saints, how was she going to heal him?

Mind, by the time they crossed the planks straddling the ditch that encircled Bradgate deer park, there was colour in Tom's face and enthusiasm in his countenance. Wondrous what the constant talk of fishing could achieve.

'I cannot bring back Tom's father for him but I can give some time to the lad,' Grey told her, behind his glove, as he reined back to ride beside her, their stirrups almost touching.

'That's very good of you, Grey.'

'I'm right glad it pleases you.' His smile — blue eyes like John's — swept over more than her face before he called out loudly: 'Race you, nephew!'

Tossing a grin over his shoulder at her, Tom gave spur.

Elysabeth followed with the grooms and dogs. Above the hill, a lonely kestrel hovered. Below his wings, upon a sweet-smelling bower of summer grass, Dickon had been conceived. She remembered other times, too. John riding through the winter buckled bracken with a fine hawk upon his gauntlet, but today there was no horseman in green to gladden her heart, only a herd of deer, heads down, neatly feeding. Stoking the embers of memory hurt so much but the future looked even bleaker, no strong male hand clasping hers, no laughter with the wine. Oh, St Valentine, St Valentine.

When she joined them at the fishing hole, she tried to busy herself but the grooms did not need help or supervision in the unpacking of the cheeses, pastes and bread or the worms and the maggots. Tom was stamping and laughing. The ground at Bradgate always had a hollow sound. John had taught him that. She stamped too but she could not laugh or smile. 'Go and unpot the worms,' she said. 'Your grandmother is expecting trout for supper.'

'Elysabeth,' Grey called to her across the rim of his ale jack, 'I'll fish with Tom awhile and then after our repast, happen you'd like to ride to the top of the hill?'

She nodded, hiding her reluctance. Now the remembrances of John's embrace would be overlain with Grey's talk of money.

Defended by a palisade of grass from the fishes' view, and with a trout already flapping in the basket, Tom was happily lobbing his line upstream as his uncle set aside his tackle and cleansed his fingers in the water. Now would come the bargaining.

Grey dried his hands on his thighs, whistled the dogs away from the water and they left Bart to keep an eye on Tom and the younger grooms and rode past the young oaks and up the deer cropped turf towards the jagged, dark grey crags that surveyed the land like ancient creatures. The dogs, with rabbit scent in their nostrils, crashed delightedly through the dead bracken.

Halfway to the summit, a lone stag, mayhap dreaming about rutting, sprang up in panic. Grey thrust out a hand to control Elysabeth's horse but she was a skilled horsewoman. His concern was pleasing but... Oh Devil take it! Stockier, darker, like his mother, yet so like John when he did that — John when they were first wed. It was the small mannerisms as well, just a toss of head or the way he blew on his soup before he supped that pricked her to fresh sorrow.

'Your arm's healed well, Elysabeth. I noticed you didn't favour it at all as we rode here, or is it you're just puttin' up with it?'

'It still aches.' *Like her heart.*

'I've been thinkin' about you and the boys a great deal,' he added as the steep hillside compelled them to ride more cautiously. 'It can't be very easy for you at Groby now.'

'Nor for you either, with two brothers to mourn,' she replied carefully, guessing where this was leading.

'If you and Mother dealt better together…'

'*If*! It is a decade now, Grey, and nothing has changed.'

'Fire 'n' water, that's what you two are. What I wanted to tell you, Elysabeth, is —' He hesitated, chewing his lower lip. 'Thing is, see —'

'Spit it out, Grey. That's the best way.'

'Ay up, then — Mother is about to marry again.'

'What!' Her horse jerked up its head with a rattle of bridle at her sudden grip on the rein. This was the last thing she had expected to hear. 'When was this decided?'

'Aye, well, it's not exactly writ in stone yet, but she received a letter yesterday from my lord of Warwick. Seems he's found a husband for her.'

Ah, so the reward giving had begun. She could wager the queue of Yorkist supporters for heiresses and wealthy widows was a mile long. If Tom's inheritance had been a clean issue, she might have been one of the prizes. Warwick was a man who left no stone unturned.

'And who is the fortunate man, Grey? Did the letter say?'

'One of the Earl of Essex's younger sons.' Another revelation.

'I didn't know there *was* an "Earl of Essex".'

'Well, there is now, m'duck — Sir Henry Bourchier, husband to one of King Edward's aunts. And it seems our shiny new sovereign, or should I say, Warwick, is handing out favours to those who fought for him. Chose the wrong side, didn' I? Ah well, nowt I can do about that 'cept lick hands and grovel to the new boots at Westminster like everyone else.'

Elysabeth sighed. 'And which fortunate Bourchier has drawn your mother?'

He chuckled at her tone, relaxing more now his news was out of the way. 'John Bourchier. Third or fourth son. About your age.'

Elysabeth blew another gasp of amazement and began to laugh. 'And what says your mother? A husband almost half her years! I knew there was something different about her last night. A fizz through the blood perhaps.'

'Don't be unkind now. Mother's still capable of bearing even if she is getting a mite croffly at times.'

Capable of bearing! This had implications. Her merriment ebbed instantly. 'But if she marries, Tom will not get the baronetcy. Oh Heavens, this John Bourchier will become Baron Ferrers, won't he?'

His mother had kept that hushed, and more besides, judging from Grey's shadowed expression. 'Aye, that's the truth of it. Always see straight to the crux, don't you, Elysabeth, an' I've always admired you for that. Anyhow, I'm also warning you that Tom will most like be given to him as a ward.'

'I see,' she answered gravely. It was as if the reins of life were falling from her fingers leaving her without direction, powerless, and she did not like it

Grey was in full flow now. 'I'd hoped maybe I'd have the guardianship of him. I haven't spoken of this to you before but I promise you I'm not without ambition. I've abandoned the old king's cause. That was why I never fought at Towton. We need to move with the times. I'm right glad we now have Englishmen at the helm, instead of that old French bitch.' When she did not answer, he blustered on. 'I daresay my brother would turn in his grave to hear me speak so, but I see no future otherwise. Promise me, you understand.'

She stared at him sadly. 'You want absolution from me, Grey. Here.' She drew a cross in the air and let her mare move ahead. Yes, she understood. *As long as it is not Warwick's boot caps that you will lick.*

A promise followed her. 'If I can gain the new king's trust, Elysabeth, I'll help you get John's attainder reversed. I'm hoping the Bourchiers will give me a leg-up once I've gained their trust. An' we've already had word that John Bourchier is arriving here the day after morrow.'

'Jesu! That soon?' She felt so betrayed.

Grey was saying no more, letting her ride ahead and chew the matter over. But as they reached the top of the hill, she sensed there was another reason for this private conversation and dismounted swiftly before he could help her.

'Is there more you wanted to tell me?' she asked.

'Aye, if you are wanting to return to Astley, Elysabeth, I'll take over your promise to John and oversee the rest of the roofing. The tower shall be finished, I promise you.'

His kindness was another surprise.

'Why, Grey, I should be more than happy to hand that responsibility to you, really grateful, but why have you not made this offer before, since you know that I have been anxious to go home? What else does your mother want me to hear?'

'By Jesu, you weren't born yesterday!' Relief mingled with embarrassment lit his eyes. Now would come the unwelcome ifs and buts about her dower. 'To be blunt, Elysabeth, my mother thinks it might be a good thing if you left for Astley before Bourchier arrives. He is coming to look her over, so to speak, and if he sees you, he'll be so dazzled, he won't see her.'

When she did not answer straightaway, he blurted out, 'You do not realise how wondrously beautiful you are.' She felt his gaze sliding down her body, tearing open her dark kirtle. 'Compared to you, all other women are —'

'Enough,' she said with deliberate lightness. Frustrating his hot stare, she moved apart, making pretence of staring out over the valley. Other women might revel in their beauty but she could not. It was a curse. Men became so stupid in her presence. Was coming here a stratagem — the bronze hillside, the shadows of the soaring clouds caressing the fields, a place for confidences that should never be uttered?

'Elysabeth.' There was a lot a man could put into just one word.

The winter grass crunched beneath his boots as he stepped closer. Oh Lord, must she deal with this when the memory of John was still so raw?

*Whisper John's name over and over like an incantation.* Toeing the tufts of grass, she searched for a portcullis of words to keep Edward at bay without giving offence. 'John and I loved this place. We could be private here, escape from Groby. Your mother could be so difficult. Perhaps you don't remember, but she always opposed our marriage because I brought no land in my dowry. I think she might have been jealous because we were so much in love.'

John, a young esquire in the queen's household, she, a maid-of-honour. By Heaven, she realised sadly, she had shared him with the queen even back then.

Grey's arm wrapped awkwardly about her shoulders. He drew her against his side. 'I do understand.' Except his fingers against her defensive body were splayed, adventurous, anxious to offer more than comfort. 'With you, I…' he began.

Was he being deliberately dense? By heaven, she must strangle this wretched infatuation before it grew and grew.

'What is it, Grey?' She tried to sound patient as she drew away and swung round to face him.

'With you at Groby, the other women are like drab chickens beside a swan. You are a swan, Elysabeth. The whole world knows it.'

'Then I had better hide away in the rushes at Astley.' God pardon her triteness.

'God forbid!' Hurt flickered in his eyes. More, too. Desire. His hands seized her shoulders. 'Do you not realise how I feel about you?'

She unfastened his fingers. 'It was a mistake to bring me here, Grey. I am too much in grief to think of any man but John. Everything…' The golden hillside sloping away from where they stood. 'Everything brings back memories of him.'

Grey's jaw was tense with anger. Anger and entitlement. And a young man's lust-hunger. If he tried to take her here, this would be sacrilege.

'Dickon was conceived at Bradgate, Grey. Almost this very spot.'

That seemed to impel him more. 'Imagine John is here in me.'

Now it was she who was angry. 'Oh, in God's name, stop it!' Palming the air as though to brace against his feelings, she strode away to stand shaking in fury where the bracken lapped the grass.

'Why in hell should I?' he snarled. 'I have always loved you, Elysabeth. Ever since John brought you home.'

She looked round at him coldly. 'You were nine, Grey. It's infatuation.'

'Hell, no, it's not. You're treating me like a child.'

'No, I'm preventing you from having a broken heart, Grey. Like mine. It's broken beyond belief at the moment.' She made pretence of searching her beltpurse and her clever horse instantly left off cropping and trotted over to her for a titbit. Grabbing the bridle, she swiftly used the nearby rock as a mount and slid onto the side-saddle. 'And I'm not weak, Grey. I shall be both sword and buckler for my children, you'll see.'

'Elysabeth.' His hand fastened round her ankle. 'Listen, it's going to be hard for you. You and I can stand up against Mother. You won't manage things alone. Marry me, I'll run Astley for you. It is my birthplace, damn it!'

*Marry?*

Grey?

Generous, or was it? She was not going to dash into some reckless handfasting. Yes, she should consider another husband when her year of mourning was over, a mature man who could safeguard her children.

And she did not like the slur that she could not manage Astley. She had done so whenever John was away. By Heaven, she could run a palace if she had to.

'What's your answer, Elysabeth?'

'Grey,' she began patiently. 'I owe you thanks, but your mother would never consent. Nor would she forgive either of us. She wants to match you with Elizabeth Talbot.'

'Who is ten years old! What am I supposed to do, take cold baths for the next six years?'

'No, yes, I don't know.'

'Elysabeth.' His fingers slid up her calf and his voice grew silky. 'I can give love and protection to you and your sons. I want you now, Elysabeth. Lie with me, m'duck. Please. I'm desperate for you.'

A nineteen-year-old husband like Grey, even if he was her sons' uncle, would expect her to put his needs first. But she was nearly five years older than him, ten years a wife, with children who needed her full love.

'I cannot betray John. Nor should you. Dear God, he's only been dead a few months.'

Grey let go of her, his mouth a sullen arc of disappointment. He had always wanted what John had, she suspected. The title. The lands. Her. Now, she was the only possibility — consolation for losing the rest.

'Tell me, John's wife,' he exclaimed, 'which one of us *is* his betrayer? The brother who is offering to care for his sons or the foolish wife spurning protection for them? Think about it, Elysabeth. Think hard! You came with no land and you may find yourself leaving with none if Mother has her way.' He slapped her horse's rump, knowing it would carry her roughly, and shouted after her, 'You'll keep your beloved Astley if you marry me. I'll make certain of it.'

And if she did not marry him?

# 7: ELYSABETH

## 24th April 1461, Astley Hall, Warwickshire

'*My lady!*'

Elysabeth dragged her attention from the lamb carcass in the dewy grass at her feet. Why was Tamsin beckoning her so urgently across the meadow? Nodding to her shepherd to deal with the poor mauled beast, she picked up her skirts and, avoiding the dew-spangled spider webs, started briskly back across the field. She felt sad, angry, vulnerable. After the loss of so many lambs in the snow, she could ill afford losing any of her flock to a village dog pack or a hungry fox; the dark side of the manor ledger bore too few entries.

Tamsin was urging Dickon over the stile. 'Men, Mama!' he was shouting as he ran towards her.

Visitors! Well, even though her larder was meagre, it would be good to share a flagon of wine with somebody. The neighbours had not come near her since her return and running Astley had left her no moments for any pastime. Her domain was neither large nor remarkable, just a fortified manor house and farm, surrounded by fields and woods, barely close to anywhere save the small town of Nuneaton, but the land was flat and easy for the plough. For Elysabeth, it was heaven after the purgatory of Groby. But this heaven required labour and servants needed wages and ... losing a lamb ... St Jude, that poor creature did not need to die.

'Now, what's all this lather, sweetheart?' Elysabeth sighed, putting an arm around Dickon's shoulders.

'No lather, see.' He blinked up at her with his owl's eyes and lifted his forearms. 'I always rinse all the soap off when I wash. Every morning. Always.'

A deeper sigh escaped her. Soap was soon going to be something she could not afford and Dickon seemed to take people's words at their most basic meaning.

'Mistress Tamsin says hurry!' he announced, striding ahead.

She followed him over the stile. For a glorious moment, she wondered if the visitor could be her eldest brother, Anthony, who had vaguely promised a visit on his way home if the new Yorkist king freed him with a pardon.

'Is it one of your uncles who has come?'

'No, men!' In Dickon's concise vocabulary that might mean anyone — from knight to itinerant peddler. Times were still hurly-burly; it was not unknown for some swaggering bully of a knight to come pestering a young widow. Hand in hand, she and Dickon scrambled down across the dry moat and up to the postern gate. Tense now, she untied her waistcloth and smoothed her skirts, wishing she were not so plainly arrayed.

The courtyard was full of horses. No brother of hers could afford an entourage like this.

'Go to your bedchamber, Dickon, and stay there. Go!'

Pausing beside the hall's carved screen that hid the entrance to the buttery, her eyes went wide with shock. A dozen or more men-at-arms in kettle helms and brigandines were ranged around her hall. Their commander, a man in his fifties, was seated on John's chair of estate with her best flagon at his elbow, and her steward seemed to be undergoing an interrogation. The stranger, noting her arrival, flicked her servant away and rose to his feet. He was clad in a long, murrey coat which scarcely met across his dove grey stomacher, and upon his immense fur collar lay a clanky chain of office. His buttonhole eyes and patrician cheekbones reminded her of the celibate tyrant who had once been her brothers' tutor. Some men seemed born irritable and this was clearly one of them.

Tamsin materialised at her elbow from the shadows. 'The Sheriff of Coventry, John Savage,' she warned, her hand lifted to mask a false cough. 'We've given him refreshment.'

What in God's name did this old cur want at Astley? With a creak of leather boots, a jingle of spurs and an assessing eye, he was sauntering across to inspect her.

Elysabeth gave him a mid-curtsey and received a lift of peppery eyebrows at her simple dress. He was having a good stare at her bosom as well.

'Good day to you, my lord.'

Her visitor was also well practised in disdain. 'I am seeking the relict of Sir John Grey. Who might you be, mistress?'

'The relict,' she answered with equal frostiness as she rose to face him.

His eye slits broadened. At least he removed his liripiped hat and dipped his balding head at her.

'What, pray you, sir, is your business with me?'

'The King's business, madame. I am the new sheriff. I understand you have Sir John Grey's sons here with you?' The inquiry, unexpected, puzzling, drew blood.

'Yes,' she replied, trying to stay calm while her anxious thoughts were running amok. Christ forbid, the king would take them from her.

'Let them be summoned hither, madame.' The sheriff looked round at her steward, 'And you, sirrah, assemble the servants forthwith!'

'My lord, surely —' she began, but he ignored her.

'Some fine arras you have here.' The jerk of a sharp chin towards the 'Hunting of the Hart' tapestry rang alarm bells in her head.

'A wedding gift from my grandmother, the daughter of the Duke of Andria,' she informed him, and watched the man's thumbs waggle behind his back as he stood in front of it.

'Not Flemish then?'

'Italian.'

'Not worth so much then.' Christ's Mercy, he was assessing her possessions as though she was not the widow but the deceased. 'Your family are not born here, then?'

'My mother is Jacquetta, Duchess of Bedford.' As soon as she said it, she knew she had been set up like a quintain to tilt at. The sheriff's mouth serifed into a smirk.

'Ah yes, the foreign woman who married her servant.' The shaft of the insult cut in deeper still as he added: 'And here I take it is her grace's grandson.' He looked past Elysabeth with a sneer. 'Master Grey, is it?'

Tom had arrived. There was no mistaking him in the proud tilt of head as he halted in the doorway behind his father's chair and stared at the sheriff as an equal. After the round-shouldered, keep-away-from-me misery of the last two months, this stance was a surprise to Elysabeth, but to her shame, he was not even wearing a doublet over his gipon. He met her appalled glance with a defiant quirk of mouth as he led his small brother across to salute their visitor. Mind, he made his bow to the sheriff with sufficient grace. Poor Dickon, however, mimicked his older brother to such perfection, even down to the tight smile, that the men-at-arms broke into laughter.

Embarrassed, Elysabeth gestured the boys across to join her and unhappily watched the last of her household being sheep-dogged into line.

'All here?' Stretching his neck with the importance of a rooster surveying the henhouse, the sheriff perched his spectacles on his nose and drew a thick parchment from his belt. The servants hushed their muttering. Only Tom stood with his arms defiantly folded and one heel turned nonchalantly in, just like John in a testy humour.

'In the name of the King, by the powers invested in me by his highness, I am here to proclaim that "*the property of the attainted traitor, John Grey, Knight, late styling himself Lord Ferrers, is confiscate to the crown.*"'

Christ in Heaven! Elysabeth's first thought was for Tom. He was still holding his head proudly but she could see his jaw was clenched. God give us strength, she prayed, as the pompous voice droned on:

'"*All manors belonging to the said traitor are to be seized and any coin, plate and other moveable are to be yielded to the cro —*"'

'Excuse me!' Tom cut in. The sheriff turned his head so sharply, the spectacles skewed. 'Your pardon, Sheriff,' her son persisted haughtily, ignoring the man's outrage, 'but there is a part I find confusing.'

'Which part, boy?' Sarcasm underscored each word. 'I should have thought it was plain to anyone of intelligence.'

'The part about the king, sir. There are two kings in England. Which one sent you?'

Two of the young grooms in the back row of servants sniggered. The nearest men-at-arms clapped hands to their sword hilts and, Elysabeth, although she loved Tom for this show of courage, wished he had held his tongue.

'Then maybe this next part will make it clearer since it is addressed to you, boy.'

'And I have no wish to hear it, Master Sheriff. Mother, tell these men to leave Astley at once.' Oh, he sounded so like his father.

'Seems we have a traitor's nest of fledglings as well.' The sheriff opened the second folded parchment and glared at Tom. 'I hope the following is clear to you, Master Grey.

'"*Let the traitor's sons be held excluded from the inheritance. Let them forever be paupers, and let their father's infamy attend them always. Let them never attain to any honours nor be permitted to take any oath. Let them be forever in such poverty and squalor that death will be a comfort to them and life a torture.*"' He cast an eye at the shocked faces of the servants. '"*And we hereby command also that whoever shall be so rash as to intercede with us in their favour shall be infamous and without pardon.*"' He looked across at Tom as though inviting some witty comment but it never came.

Her son was white with shock.

'Right, back to your work, all of you!' The sheriff swung round to Elysabeth. 'I was, of course, merely extemporising on the political treatise by John of Salisbury. Never hurts to put a young gentleman like this in his place.' He turned back to her sons. 'You'd have been imprisoned for your father's sins in ancient times, Thomas Grey. Treachery is the most heinous of sins.' Directing a stern stare down at the boy, he added, 'Your father would have had his insides yanked out on Tower Hill if he hadn't been slain on the battlefield. You *do not* rebel against the lord's anointed, ever! I'll be watching from now on to make sure you behave!

'As for you, madame,' he declared, handing her the writ, 'by the end of this day you will remove yourself and your children from this house. You may carry away your clothes and personal items but no bed hangings, coverlets and napery. I am allowing you two sumpters, an ambler, and a pony for the boys, or is there an ass that would suit you better, Master Grey? The rest of the horses remain with the property.'

'You expect us to leave Astley?' Elysabeth exclaimed, her hand warningly on Tom's forearm. 'But this is my dower house, sir.'

'Not any more, Lady Grey.'

'Speak to my brother-in-law, Sir Edward Grey, my lord. He was witness to my husband's promise at the church door. By law a widow is entitled to a third of her husband's property and goods.'

'None of my business. Matter for the courts. Begin, lads, take that for a start.' He pointed his riding crop at the silver salt.

'But that was part of my dowry from my parents,' Elysabeth protested, barring the soldiers' way.

'Oh, I'm sure every blessed thing in this house was,' he countered cynically. 'Prove it, ma'am. Come and visit me with the evidence and I'll have your property returned. Now step aside if you please or I'll order my men to carry you to the courtyard while we finish our business. How about you make haste to your bedchamber and start packing? I'm sure you don't want my men rifling through your underlinen.'

'This is most unjust!' Oh God, she felt like a lamb bleating at a pack of wolves. She stared down at the words of the writ, searching for a clause that might exonerate her.

Tom was slack-jawed in disbelief beside her as the soldiers dragged a trestle across to the wall so they might dislodge the Hart tapestry. 'Don't let them do this, Mother! Send someone for Uncle Grey. At once, Mother!' He tugged hard at her arm but Elysabeth could only shake her head, too choked to find her voice. 'Then what about Grandfather Woodville? Can he not help us? Mother! *Mama*!'

'Grandfather is still a prisoner, Tom. There's nothing we can do. *Read it*!' She unhappily handed him the copy of his father's attainder. He scanned it down to the signature of Richard, Earl of Warwick, and a half-dozen other knights of Parliament.

'If I was a man already, they would not dare.'

'Oh, Tom,' she whispered, turning to him and holding him by the forearms, 'you were man enough today, I assure you, but we cannot gainsay the law. I'll apply to Chancery for my dower rights and, meantime, we shall go straight to Groby.'

'A pox on this bloody Earl of Warwick!' Tom spat upon Richard Neville's signature. 'We all know it's him who has done this to us. It's him who rules the kingdom not the —'

'Thomas! Hold your tongue! Shall you make matters worse for us?' Tears misting her eyes, she stared at her son, so old for his years, with loving sadness. She and John had failed the boy. All his inheritance gone. Yet at least this disaster had jerked Tom out of the dark silence that had dogged him since the day that Dickon had been injured.

'Bad man. Can't take that!' Dickon was tugging the back of the sergeant's surcoat as he unloaded the aumery.

'Get away from me you, little runt!'

'Don't hit him!' Elysabeth grabbed her son away.

'Ha, bit gormless, is he, mistress?'

'He injured his head in a fall,' she stated, disliking the fellow's lewd stare.

'Jesu, your problems don't come by halves, do they, lady? Listen,' he drew so close, she could smell garlic and rotting teeth. 'Seems a shame to take everything from a pretty widow like you. How about you say what you want and we can stow it for you. Come out to the stable for a few minutes and seal the bargain.' He jutted his hips forward in case she was simple as well.

'You mistake your quarry, sirrah. I'm too proud to beg.'

# 8: ELYSABETH

## 24th April 1461, Groby Hall, Leicestershire

But she was coming close to beggary, she realised, as she rode into the courtyard at Groby at dusk and relinquished the reins of the ambler to one of the grooms.

'Elizabeth? Boys? This is a surprise.' Was it? Grey's voice was too cool, too empty of astonishment, as he strode out from the front door and gave her a half-bow. They did not embrace. Clearly, her rejection of him at Bradgate still rankled. He stared at the packhorses. 'Why are you back here so soon? Mother's wedding is not until next month. Is there illness at Astley?'

'Astley is perfect, Grey, except that the Sheriff of Coventry has seized possession and taken everything I own except the upstairs floorboards.'

'Already? We sent a messenger off yestermorn to warn you.'

'We passed no one from you on the road, Uncle.' Tom shook Grey's proffered hand with no enthusiasm.

Ignoring the boy's comment, Grey gave orders to the grooms to bring in their baggage. 'Go in to the fire!' he said sternly, pushing Dickon towards the house.

'You knew this might happen, Grey?'

'We had a visit from the Sheriff of Leicester because of John's attainder. Mother was able to produce her dower deeds and prove her right to the barony.'

'Well, I wish I'd had mine. They even took the Hart hanging that my grandmother gave me.'

'Have you no copy of your pre-marriage contract?' He halted and turned, frowning. 'I went through all the family deeds last week and there was nowt here of yours. Are you certain John did not keep it at Astley?'

'Yes, of course, Grey.'

'Aye up, I must have missed it, then,' he replied smoothly, 'though there's a chest of John's in the guest bedchamber that I haven't been through yet.'

An ill feeling began to build in her belly. 'No matter, I'll look for myself in the morning. In any case, you can testify that you heard John promise me a third of his lands on our wedding day.'

He did not answer but opened the door of the solar for her. 'Mother! Elysabeth and the boys are back with us. The Sheriff of Coventry has taken Astley on Warwick's orders.'

Lady Ferrers rose to usher the boys to the fire. Her pleated coif of widowhood was gone. Instead, her brown hair was gathered up beneath a cap of dark blue velvet and the square neck of her blue damask kirtle framed a dainty undergown and permitted a generous summer cleavage.

'You are looking very well, madame,' Elysabeth told her sincerely.

'Yes, you look different, Grandmama,' exclaimed Tom. 'Not so old.'

'How can people look older or younger than they are?' asked Dickon. 'Grandmama is two score years and two, and twenty-seven days.'

'Thank you so much, Dickon.' The teeth on a crocodilus would have looked friendlier. 'Has your mother told you I am marrying again, boys?'

Tom did not meet her eyes. 'I suppose so. Maybe I wasn't listening.'

Another strained smile. 'Well, Thomas, in a week you will be meeting Sir John Bourchier, the new Baron Ferrers.'

Tom's gaze was on her face now. 'But I'm Lord Ferrers, Grandmother.'

'No, Thomas, not anymore, you are not.'

This would be as futile as hunting for dragons' eggs, Elysabeth warned herself, as she opened the door to John's old bedchamber next morning. She might have accepted Tom's help but there was none on offer. Taking Dickon, he had disappeared across the fields, resentment still curdling. It was she, not his grandmother, who had borne the bedtime accusations of betrayal.

Barring the door of the bedchamber so none might disturb her, she paused alone with her memories, wondering if John's ghost watched her from the shadows, shaking his head at the mess she seemed to have made of things. For a few minutes she wept softly, leaning her cheek against the bedpost and trying to muffle her sobs in her kerchief, and then shakily she returned to her purpose and knelt before the oak chest that stood at the foot of the bed.

Grey and his mother had not touched anything, or so they claimed, but the chest was unlocked and the doublets and stomachers that John had kept in the upper tray of the chest had been removed. She was grateful for that, and staring round her, she was aware of the other changes. New wall hangings had been put up. Above the pillows, the painted cloth of St John experiencing revelations had been replaced with a besotted Tristan and Iseult plighting their troth. These differences helped exorcise the pain in her heart but the bedcurtains were the same and so were the towels of Coventry blue hanging on a wall rail by the ewer stand where John's razor and her combs had lain.

*I must not waste time.* She fed another log to the fire in the hearth and then started on her task, planning to lift out all the ribboned bundles of papers in the chest onto the floor and then replace them one by one, after she had checked the contents. A painful business indeed. Each bundle was wrapped with a label in John's Italian hand, and at the bottom of the chest nestled on the folds of an old cloak were treasures from his childhood: a cloth bag of marbles, knucklebones, a toy dagger with a blunt blade that rattled back into the hilt, an old copy book in a spindly script and a painstakingly whittled knight, its sword broken. There were no loose papers. The smallest packet — bearing her name — contained the few letters she had sent him in the early part of their courtship. She never knew that he had saved them. One even held a daisy chain she had made playfully to garland him, but where was the leather sheath in which he had kept their pre-marriage contract? She retied the ribbon and then she went through the next bundle and the rest. Had someone removed the contract?

Outside it had begun to rain and plump drops of water cascaded down the panes like tears. Elysabeth found a candle stub, spiked it onto an empty candlestick, lit it and carefully lowered it into the darkness of the chest in case she had missed something.

Flakes of paint from the little knight argued that the cloth on which it had lain had not been disturbed for a long time. Setting aside the candle, she lifted out what appeared to be a child's cloak. Beneath it was a rolled vellum document. With relief, she discovered it was the document drawn up six years earlier confirming the trust that John's father had set up for them before he died: a hundred marks a year derived from two manors in Northamptonshire and one in Essex. Relieved that her quest had not been fruitless, she replaced everything else except her love letters and John's treasures, then she closed the lid and sat for a moment, running her finger pensively over the clasp of the lock before she rose with a smile.

Grey was in the accounting room.

'Found nowt, I suppose?'

'Not the dower deeds, but I came across the trust document your father set up for John and I.'

'What, in the old chest? Well, plague take me!' This time his surprise seemed genuine. Suspiciously so.

'And have you found my pre-contract, Grey?' she asked, wondering if he'd tell her if he had.

He sucked in his cheeks. 'Found Mother's but not John's. The sheriff's officers went through our muniments, maybe they took it.' That was possible after her experience at Astley, but why did Grey no longer look her in the face? He unhooked the keys from his belt and held them out. 'Here, you are welcome to search for yourself, Elysabeth, but Mother and I are invited to dine at Mayor Sheringham's in Leicester and must make shift. I'll see you at supper.' He grabbed up his hat and gloves.

'Grey?'

He looked round, his eyes meeting hers at last. 'Yes?'

'I hope there is still friendship and trust between us.'

'Aye,' he said. An abrupt, why-would-you-ask 'aye'. Then he looked away like a child caught out. There was no green suitor in him now.

'I am pleased, Grey.' *Though I don't believe it.*

'Good, then. Lock everything when you've had enough.'

She spent the next half hour searching through the rolls and documents to no avail and her heart only lightened when Dickon wandered in. Mud buttered his boots but she was so pleased to have his company, she could not rebuke him.

'Where is Tom, love?'

'With the dogs.' The child picked up a manor roll and a cushion, wriggled into a cross-legged position, spread the parchment out and stared at the columns of figures. Three heartbeats and she wagered he'd cast it aside.

Twenty heartbeats.

'Mama, the numbers do not add up properly.'

Elysabeth set down the trust document she had been reading for the umpteenth time. 'Show me.'

'This side,' he pointed to the left column, 'adds up correctly. But this does not.' Laziness in Lady Ferrers' steward? She wondered. But that did not matter. Her five-year-old son had just added up over a score of numbers.

'Dickon, if I have 576 horses and 89 cows, how many animals do I have?'

'But you don't, Mama. Astley doesn't have the pasture for that many. We have sixty sheep if you do not count the lambs that died.'

'If I *did* have those horses and cows, Dickon. How many beasts?'

'Six hundred, three score and five.'

Marvelling, she picked up a quill and dipping it in the inkwell, wrote down six numbers. Dickon added them up in an instant, faster than she did. When she handed him one of John's receipts for bricks, the child was interested in the numbers but not the words.

'Your tutor schooled you well in arithmetic,' she exclaimed, giving him a hug. Since his fall, he had never hugged her back. Nor did he now.

'I am far better at numbers than Master Anstey was,' he stated. 'You are not very good at cuddles, though.'

'Do I need to be?'

Dining with a closed order of nuns would have been more exciting than breakfast at the Greys, Elysabeth decided, as she finished her breakfast of pottage next morning. It was time to pursue John's mother to the solar and mention money. A deep breath was necessary as she ventured in. Not because the chamber was scented like a mercer's shop from the bales — amber velvet, green satin and a moonlight gauze — cluttering the broad window seat, but because she was desperate.

'Madame,' she exclaimed, edging the twirls of embroidered ribbons along the settle so she could sit down, 'we need to talk about the future.'

Lady Ferrers gave a flick of her fingers and her tiring women rose, curtsied and, clutching their unfinished sewing, quietly left the room.

'Mine or yours?' The green eyes above the needle glittered sharply.

'Mine, madame. Until I regain my right to Astley, we need to make some other arrangement for my dower entitlement, if you please.'

Thimbling the needle through the layers of fur and velvet looked conveniently difficult; it not only required Lady Ferrers' concentration but made the cruel answer easier to deliver.

'Out of the question at the moment, I'm afraid, Elizabeth. Your father still owes a hundred and twenty-five marks of your dowry and my lawyer tells me there can be no settlement until that is dealt with. And since your sire is still in the king's custody, I'm sure that will take some time.'

Knowing how stretched Father always was with money, and that the new king might extract a hefty fine before the shackles were unlocked, Elysabeth could believe it. Or was her mother-in-law lying about the dowry payment?

'John never told me there was any problem.' Perhaps she had been foolish not to ask him but then she had never imagined he would be dead by the age of twenty-nine.

'Ah well, he wouldn't, I daresay, but there have been letters back and forth and I'm afraid your father can only show receipts for the first two hundred marks.'

Elysabeth tried to keep her temper. 'In the meantime, there is the trust that John's father arranged for us. One hundred marks a year, the income from Newbottle, Brington and Woodham Ferrers.' She unrolled the document to show Lady Ferrers but she did not let it leave her hands.

'Hmm, I remember that being drawn up and a great deal of fuss it was too. We had to sort matters out in the Court of Common Pleas. It was to avoid John having to pay any duties on the lands on his father's death. Those manors belonged originally to my grandfather but the cleric William Walesby holds the title and fee simple now. He granted it to several men for their usage but we paid them to pass that use to John.'

'It seems very complicated.'

Lady Ferrers read it through. 'Well, there you are then, consider that your dower instead until you can find your deeds.'

*Instead!*

'However, Elysabeth, a word to the wise. You will need to confirm the matter once more with William Walesby and apply to each of these other men to reconfirm the enfeoffment. I daresay they will need depositions from witnesses to say that you and John were lawfully wed.'

*Lawfully* wed? Never say that this infernal family were going to dispute the legality of her marriage!

Her mother-in-law had yet another warning. 'The deed mentions John and the heirs of his body, and these men may have concerns that if income from these properties is granted to you, you may dispose of these manors at some future date.'

'But I wouldn't if it's for my sons.'

'True, but, as you say, any matters concerning land are complicated. Perhaps you need to ask your father to commission a diligent lawyer to sort matters out.'

'I am quite capable of finding a lawyer but all this could take weeks, madame.' Let alone be expensive!

She vaguely remembered John's verdict after he had spoken with Walesby and met with the trustees. Sir Thomas Fynderne, Isham and Bolden, he considered to be upright, worthy gentlemen but the mercer, William Fyldyng of Lutterworth, had an oilier rub to him. 'Not the sort of fellow I would buy a horse from, but Father seems to trust him.' What if this Fyldyng proved difficult? Where could she find money to grease his palm?

'It has to be done according to precedent and procedure,' her mother-in-law was saying.

'Yes, I realise that,' Elysabeth answered tersely, appalled that there seemed to be no iota of sympathy in Lady Ferrers' demeanour. Unhelpful answers tripped too readily from the woman's lips.

'I recall that Sir Thomas Fynderne was made Lieutenant of Guisnes. Whether my lord of Warwick has reappointed him is another matter. Anyway, Elysabeth, you will have plenty of time to gather any depositions. The annual payment is not due until All Saints Day.'

November! Six months hence? How could she manage until then? She needed to find a new tutor for the boys as well as support Tamsin and the few servants she had left. And Tom had almost outgrown his boots. It was pathetic to cry penniless when there were poor peasants who scarce had a crumb to assuage their hunger, she would just have to find a way.

'Surely there must be some funds to carry us through?'

'No, Elysabeth, to my knowledge there's naught to hand. I daresay you'll find that John put most of what was spare into building that ridiculous tower of his. Which reminds me. I must give you these.' She reached out to the pile of papers on the small table next to her sewing basket and handed them across.

Bills. Mostly from the master mason for bricks and labour, but the timber merchant was overdue for the cost of the joists and scaffolding, and then there was the roofing slate and the transport thereof.

'John never settled them,' her mother-in-law informed her, 'and I'm certainly not doing so.'

Elysabeth stared at her with narrowed eyes, and panic churning her insides. 'But it's on your property, madame. You agreed that the adjoining lodging would be useful.'

'No, I certainly did not. Where did you get that notion? This was John's enterprise from the beginning. Don't badger me to share the cost, Elysabeth. It is entirely due to you. And in any case, I have no ready coin. All my income is bound up in the estate.'

There *was* money. Ever since Lady Ferrers had brought her rich inheritance into the family, the Greys had never been poor.

'But the Groby fleeces sold well, so surely...' Her gaze took in the costly wedding fabrics and she had her answer. Or part of it. It was not John's mother's wealth but her goodwill that was lacking.

'Oh, by the Blessed Christ!' she exclaimed, her hands fisting the air. 'It's not for myself I ask, madame, but for Tom and

Dickon. Surely you do not want to see your grandsons penniless?'

Lady Ferrers set down her sewing. 'Heed me, Elysabeth, if I was in my dotage I should make over some of my inheritance to Tom, but these are uncertain times, two of my sons are dead, and I have my own future to consider. I cannot go to my new husband empty handed. Come, be understanding, Elysabeth. What choice do I have? Bourchier will not be wanting to wed a pauper, especially as he is a younger son.'

*Understanding!* The selfish shrew. What was she expecting her to do? Grovel?

'I know we have had our disagreements, madame, and that you were displeased that John married me but, I beg you, Tom and Dickon are your family. Surely you could cede *something* to Tom in the meantime?' She paused. Lady Ferrers' attention was on threading her needle. Was she even listening? If Tom had not been so sullen and silent since his father's death, then maybe his grandmother would have been showing compassion.

'A small annuity perhaps,' Elysabeth pleaded. 'Just a little amount that will keep him until he is a man and may find his own way in the world.'

Her mother-in-law moistened the thread and tried again. 'You are years late with that idea, my duck. If you'd have taken my advice when he was seven, he'd be high in a great lord's favour by now and not a worry to you. Quite frankly, there's little of the Ferrers family between Tom's ears and nothing at all between Dickon's.'

'That's a despicable thing to say of your own flesh and blood.' Elysabeth was tempted to grab the cursed woman's needlework and fling it in the fire. 'John's children and you do not care a jot. Must I take your family to court for my dower?'

Lady Ferrers knotted the thread and jabbed the needle up through the collar. 'With scarce two pennies to rub together for a lawyer? Let's not mince words any longer, shall we, Elysabeth? You are welcome here for a week longer but after that you must fend for yourself. I don't want Bourchier to see you drooping around, all mardie-faced.'

*Not mince words.* Very well, then. 'Why is that, madame? Are you afraid I might rob you of your suitor?'

The older woman drew a ragged breath and the envy that had been suppressed since Elysabeth had first come to Groby was plain now in her narrowed eyes. 'I thought my son's death left you inconsolable.'

Wincing inside at the wicked, heartless remark, Elysabeth clapped a hand to her forehead. Was there no way she could thwart this woman? 'I'm sorry,' she said, falling back on politeness. 'That was ungracious of me. You must see I am fighting for my sons with every weapon left to me.'

Nothing softened in Lady Ferrers' eyes. 'Then ask your family for help. Your mother is a duchess, after all.' Oh yes? Aunt by marriage to a lunatic king, who was in hiding somewhere up in Northumberland and more likely to gain a heavenly crown than regain his earthly one.

'Madame, you know very well that my family does not stand well with the new king. My father and brother have yet to be pardoned for fighting for Queen Margaret.'

'A wonder then that they *stand* at all.' Lady Ferrers crossed herself mockingly. 'And God forbid that they should be attainted, too.' She set her handiwork aside and stood up, like a queen weary of some tedious entertainment, and swept over to the door, where she paused and turned. 'Sue me for your dower in Chancery if you feel yourself unfairly treated by us. But be of good cheer, Elysabeth. With your fair looks, I'm sure you'll not go hungry. There'll be some old knight who'll take you penniless so he can paw you before his younger friends.' Elysabeth's shock had been guaranteed. 'And if you feel accepting charity from this family does not suit you any longer, I think you'd be happier if you return to yours.'

'Why are we not eating in the hall, Mama?' Dickon asked Elysabeth as Tamsin served their evening repast in the boys' bedchamber.

Tom bit into a capon leg. 'Because Mother is not on speaking terms with Grandmother Ferrers. The old skinflint won't give us any money.'

'Tom! Mind your manners and your language!'

'Why won't she?' persisted Dickon.

Tom charged in again. 'Because, Knucklehead, Grandmother wants a new husband and no one will marry her unless she is rich.' Before Elysabeth could reprimand him further, he added, looking hard at her, 'And she must be keeping her money all to herself because I heard Uncle Grey say to her that he was going to ask for Warwick's good lordship because it was his only chance of rising in the world.'

Grey was going to Warwick, cap in hand? Not the new king but *Warwick*!

'Warwick killed Father,' Dickon stated mundanely as though he was talking about the weather.

'Yes,' Elysabeth muttered, 'he did.' Both children were watching her face as she exchanged glances with Tamsin. 'Excuse me,' she said. 'I seem to have lost my appetite.'

She fled. Not to the Norman ruins that had been Tom's refuge but to John's tower, up the inner wooden steps, round and round to the upmost floor, where sawdust still flaked the boards and the smell of fresh timber hung in the air. There she fisted the wall and cursed the slate that had arrived from Swithland on her request. If only she had known. Oh stupid, stupid of her. She had not thought to ask.

'John, help me! *Help me*!' she cried out in desperation and fell to her knees on the floor. 'O Sweet Mother of God, you had a son you loved who died to save the world. Please intercede for me. Give me the strength I'll need.' But the dim air around her was silent. With bowed head, she wept and afterwards, when all tears were wrung from her, she rose, leaned her head against the wooden frame and stared out across the fields and the woods, lit to gold and burnished green by the beams of the dying day. Somewhere lay the answer, she knew that, sensed it in the depths of her soul. But where? And how?

'O Blessed St Jude, hold my hand and those of my children in the years to come. Help us find our way.'

'Madame,' she declared at breakfast next morning, pushing away the platter she had shared with the boys, for she had little appetite anymore. 'I promise we shall leave well before your wedding but I need just a few days more.'

'Indeed? Why?' *Haughty crone*! 'Dickon, stop behaving like a lackwit and bring the ewer for your mother's hands!'

Elysabeth dabbled her fingers in the lavender water held unsteadily by her serious little son, then she set the napkin back over his arm and turned him to perform the same duty for his grandmother and his brother. 'It is so I can pay some of the bills you gave me yesterday, madame. I am riding to Leicester this morning to sell some of my jewellery.' Her fingers rose to the collar she was wearing. Her precious pendant was in her jewel coffer still unworn.

Lady Ferrers wiped her hands upon the towel. 'Are you now? Very well, Elysabeth, but take care you are not fleeced. John must have been out of his wits to give you baubles when he owed so much on the tower but there's no accounting for people's whims. Enough, Dickon! You can take it away now, child! Don't just stand there.'

'It was out of love, madame, as you well know,' Elysabeth retorted, rising from the table. 'Indeed, I sincerely wish you joy in your new marriage for I know you never enjoyed it in your last.'

She gave John's mother an ambiguous curtsey and received a cold stare that told her that remark would be stashed away for kindling.

'I trust you are taking that nuisance with you this morning,' Lady Ferrers muttered, scowling at Dickon's precarious passage. He perched the basin back on the sideboard and to Elysabeth's astonishment, turned wearing his grandmother's arch expression and announcing with exactly her tone: 'Tom and I are going to Leicester, because Mama says you don't want us here anymore.'

Along the table, Tom muffled a giggle.

'Thomas!' Elysabeth growled reprovingly.

Lady Ferrers recoiled at the unexpected mockery. 'We could all do without your brother's vile manners that's for sure,' she exclaimed, with a sideways glare at her older grandson. 'As for you, little Master Grey.' A scrape of chair, fingers coiled, she swept fiercely down the steps. Elysabeth followed swiftly to intervene. Dickon's brains were shaken enough already.

'Tom is not vile, madame,' Dickon asserted, fists on hips like his father. The 'madame' sounded just like John on his high horse.

His grandmother stopped before him. 'Yes, he is. Thomas Grey is a lazy good-for-nothing with a tongue like a razor.'

'No! He's! Not!' To Elysabeth's horror, Dickon launched himself forward, all kicks and punches. He was still flailing as she dragged him back.

'The little devil bit me,' exclaimed his grandmother. 'Look, you can see the damned teeth marks.' Behind her back, Elysabeth met Tom's eyes and he was laughing.

But she wasn't. Baubles! Dear God, maybe she needed to sell her gillyflower pendant not the lesser jewels. Leicester might not be prosperous enough to boast a goldsmiths' row since the city's livelihood came from wool, cloth and leather, but its wealthiest citizen, a merchant of the Staple, Roger Wigston, was an old friend of John's. Maybe he would buy it from her.

Leaving Tamsin to buy hot pies for the children at their favourite cookshop (although she could ill afford the cost), Elysabeth made her way down past Newark College to where Roger Wigston's three-storeyed house lay in the shadow of the castle.

Christ be thanked, John's friend was at home.

'Lady Grey,' he exclaimed, as his steward showed her into his modest hall. 'I am most happy to see you but I was just on my way out.'

'Please, just a few moments,' Elysabeth begged. 'My business is urgent and I am desperate for help.'

'Be brief, then, my lady, and I shall assist you if I may.'

Perhaps because he was in haste or else moved by her circumstances, he agreed without hesitation to buy her precious pendant and went further, generously offering to lend her funds so she might journey to London to see the trustees as well as settle some of John's tower costs.

'Are the Greys not bidden to the reception at the Mayor's Hall this morning to welcome our steward of the city?' he asked, as he hurriedly counted out the money for her onto his table in his strong room.

Steward of Leicester! Another newly created office. That could have been John's if he had chosen the winning side.

'Reception, Master Wigston?' No wonder her host was wearing his best livery and looking so well shaven. 'So that's why the city is unusually busy for a Tuesday. No, I received no invitation, sir.' The wife of an attainted traitor would not be on the morning's list of handshakers.

As though he realised his tactlessness, Wigston added, 'Actually, it's more a guild banquet this morning. I daresay the Leicester nobility will find their own way to Sir William Hastings' door.' He turned to a shelf behind him and took a pre-written receipt to be filled in and signed.

'Hastings, did you say, Master Wigston?' she murmured as she added her signature. 'I have heard of a Sir Leonard Hastings, a northerner, who served the Duke of York.'

He passed across the bag of coins. 'This man is Sir Leonard's eldest son, knighted at Towton. He's already the king's chamberlain and likely a baron, too, before the summer is out. The reception is in his honour. There'll be plenty of forelocks pulled this morning, but such is the way of the world. Now I fear I must escort you out, Lady Grey, and, as I said earlier, I'm right sorry about John, God keep him. Although I never shared his allegiance, I regret his passing with all my heart.'

He must have seen the tears glistening in her eyes for he set a comforting hand upon her arm. 'Any road, come and have supper with us some time soon and if there is aught more I can do for you, do not hesitate to ask.' But the lift of eyebrows suggested much more than a hospitable smile and a mazer of wine was on offer. Just before the door, he bent and kissed her on the mouth, as was customary between good friends. 'Aught!' he reiterated.

'Thank you, Master Wigston, I'm very grateful and John would be, too. You have been more than generous, and I will repay your loan, I promise, as soon as I may.'

*But I shall not lie with you.*

'Take care in the streets now, there'll be cutpurses in plenty today.'

Stuffing the drawstring bag down her front (even though it make her look as though she had three bosoms) and drawing her light cloak tightly about her, she walked northwards along High Street past the backs of the gathering crowd to the corner of Blue Boar Lane where Tamsin and the children were to meet her. The thoroughfare had been cleared for the procession and she saw them standing behind the crossed halberds of the civic guards.

'How fare you, my lady?' whispered Tamsin, straightening up from wiping the crumbs from Dickon's chin.

'Well enough, considering. He gave me a fair price.' She lifted a finger to her lips but Tom was distracted, talking with one of the soldiers.

'Looks like we've no chance of getting back to Bart and the horses at Master Gaddsby's, ma'am. There is some great lord arriving at the Mayor's Hall yonder.'

'No matter,' murmured Elysabeth, curious to set eyes on the shiny new official. 'Let's see this wonder. Leicester would welcome a rooster if it crowed loud enough.'

They waited almost till the next o'clock before the fanfares and procession of guildsmen, accompanied by shawms and tabors, confirmed the Yorkist cockerel had squawked in from the dung heap.

Mayor Robert Sheringham in his fur-trimmed scarlet mantle and civic chain was easily recognisable. The richly clad stranger riding heel to heel beside him on a fine white stallion must be the royal usurper's arse wiper (a term she'd better not use in front of the children).

One of Warwick's newly blessed, perhaps? Oh, angelic indeed! His hair, battle-short like John's had been, was passing fair, and his face, impressively handsome and grave, was freshly barbered and devoid of beard or stubble. Plentiful jewels gleamed on this rooster's apparel: in the brooch pinned to the scarlet rolled brim of his hat, on his black-gloved fingers and the garter on his thigh. A fulsome chain of interlocked S's, roses and suns lay across the lapels of his scarlet brocade robe. He would have looked better in blue but maybe he had 'acquired' the horse and its expensive scarlet leather saddle from some dead enemy after Towton and was dressing to match.

At the Mayor's Hall, not far from the corner where Elysabeth was watching, he dismounted, and Sheringham began introducing him to the green caterpillar of waiting worthies. The fawning of the city aldermen made Elysabeth yearn for a basin to retch in, but this was the way of the world, as Wigston put it.

It was no surprise. The city was already in favour with the new king because Mayor Sheringham had sent men to fight for him at Towton, but there were city charters to be reconfirmed, not to mention permission for the annual fairs. This Hastings could rely on being wined, dined, oozed over and ogled. He certainly had the Leicester market wives hallooing, and a cheerful trio of cherrylips, who had illegally broken into an empty messuage next to the Blue Boar Inn, were leaning out of the casement, waggling their scarce-covered breasts at him.

'A comely bird, ain't 'e?' cackled the housewife next to Tamsin, with a dig of elbow. 'An' unwed as yet. Goin' to be rentin' at Kirby Muxloe whenever he's up our way.'

No wonder the buttering up ceremony was fulsome.

*I daresay the Leicester nobility will find their own way to his door.*

Elysabeth bit her lip. Kirby Muxloe! Oh, St Jude, you've been listening to my prayers.

'Tom,' she said, laying her hand on her son's arm. 'I think we shall be paying Sir William Hastings a visit if he's at Kirby tomorrow.'

# 9: ELYSABETH

## *29 April 1461, Kirby Muxloe, Leicestershire*

This newly acquired castle seemed more at home to weeds and weevils than a shiny knight with lordly prospects, Elysabeth decided sourly, as she and Tom, with Bart as their escort, crossed the repaired drawbridge of the Greys' new neighbour. She was hoping that Sir William Hastings might agree to take Tom as a page but the boy's compliance was as likely as an icicle's survival in Hell and, judging by her surroundings, maybe she was asking the wrong man; the planks beneath her horse's hooves might be freshly hewn but not much else was. The hall within the bailey was even worse than Groby's — no new windows in its south wall and a roof louvre instead of a chimney. Even John's bricks would be an improvement.

Why would Sir William in his gems and velvet bother with this ruin? Gossip of buried treasure within its walls? Cheap rent from a relative? Ah, maybe military strategy!

Perhaps Hastings wasn't a bucket short of a well, after all. Kirby Muxloe was in the centre of the kingdom, within spitting distance of the Fosse Way or Watling Street. The plethora of wattle and daub buildings within the walls, despite shrieking for a re-thatch, could probably house a hundred soldiers at a squeeze. With repairs made, the curtain wall could be easily defended, and the moat, flowing in from the local stream, looked deep enough to drown in. Lordy, but it would take a huge amount of riches to wallop away the spiders, let alone make this worthy of a royal visit.

The king's new chamberlain already had his pennons up flapping above the crumbly battlements and the ancient keep. Sable maunche — a black sleeve. Not a clenched fist but it still looked threatening and she had best not underestimate him. He might prove to be the Pole Star of the Yorkist constellation until Queen Margaret's boy came of age.

Apparently most of the kingdom thought so, too. The smoky bailey was as crammed as Leicester's May Day Fair and could have out prized the Tower of Babel in hubbub. Dialects from every shire shouted and swore. Snapping at Tom to keep up, Elysabeth tried to direct her horse behind an abbot and his retinue who were attempting to nose their mules through the chaos to the stables but she ended up triangled between a carter trying to prod protesting livestock from his wagon into a pen, the hot fire of a spit roast and a string of tubby pack ponies laden with panniers of cheeses. In the end, she surrendered the horses to Bart and wriggled her way through to the steps of Hastings' hall, trying to avoid being goosed by the men-at-arms. There were too many of them for her peace of mind, fellows not just with Hastings' maunche embroidered on their brigandines, but soldiers in the royal livery and couriers with Warwick's bear-and-ragged-staff. Men who might have slain John.

It was hard seeing the scars; here, a stump instead of a hand, or there, a patch over a missing eye, and not remember John's hacked body. Hastings had not been at St Albans, thank the saints, otherwise she would not be here to ask for his good lordship.

But she and Tom were just two of many seeking his favour. Since this knight was now a conduit to the new royal water butt, the hall was bursting with people: church, trade and tillers, the greedy, the desperate, widows like her, mothers with babes mewling hungrily, whole families, all crowding the trestles, leaning against the walls, fidgeting, stamping, mouthing and complaining. Some of them smelled of perfume and many of them just smelled.

'Have you a written petition, mistress?' demanded a tabarded usher, blocking their way. 'No? Then, that line there!' He spread his arms to herd her and Tom into one of the four long tails of people stretching down from the dais.

'You mistake us, sir!' Tom argued, folding his arms and squaring up to the fellow like some brave little lapdog with a temporary truth: 'I'm — I'm Lord Ferrers and my grandmother is a duchess.'

'And mine's married to the Pope,' guffawed Hastings' man, his sneering gaze observing that Tom's russet doublet was too short in the sleeves and barely fastened over his shirt.

'Mother, say something!' But she had seen the fellow's thumb and fingers rub together hopefully. Only a bribe would speed them to the front and she had none to spare.

'Remember Aesop's tale of the tortoise and the hare, Tom.'

'But if we keep our heads stuck in like a pair of tortoises, no one will bother with us.'

'Tom! Be patient.'

*But for how long?*

Officers sat at trestles at the top of each queue questioning each petitioner. The fast moving line was for written petitions, the other three were for commoners to briefly state their purpose.

'*Briefly!*' the ushers and sergeants-at-arms repeated loudly at intervals.

No one took any notice. Only a fortunate selected few appeared to be ushered behind the dais to the sacred tabernacle containing Lord Hastings, and each person seemed to take an infernal time with his lordship before they reappeared. After two hours of standing, Elysabeth cursed herself for not setting out her request in writing but even had she done so, how long would Hastings take to answer? Would he even read it?

She tried mentioning that she was his lordship's neighbour and a woman of rank to one of the soldiers keeping order but, like the usher, the man had a swift answer.

'Then I am sure his lordship will entertain a beautiful widow like you to dinner some day soon, my lady, but if you've a cause to plead like the rest of 'em, then think of it like Judgment Day, all are equal and the officers at the front'll decide whether you're a sheep or a nanny goat and which pen you go in.'

Insolent cur! Damn him! If this wasn't for Tom's future, she would storm from the hall this instant.

And she should have brought some food and ale with her. People around the hall were unwrapping kerchiefs of provisions. Her head was aching from her best headdress, she needed air, and more besides. Assured by Tom that he would stay in the line, she went outside to find a chamber of ease. There was a queue there, too, all women. The men were pissing wherever they could find a wall.

There was no room in the gatehouse's reeking garderobe to fiddle with her headdress and she was likely to lose the pins. As a traitor's widow, her honour was already smirched, but surely there was somewhere she could reset her cap without inviting lewd comments? She tried behind the chapel only to find the ground stank with urine and then she spied the open postern in the wall. Wandering through, she found herself alone facing the moat on a narrow path that soon disappeared round the corner of the outer wall. There was no one on the opposite bank. Here was her chance. She put the pins for safekeeping between her lips and eased the crespinette off. Released from its tight confine, her thick plait of hair tumbled free. Now she would have to pin that back up that as well. Hands full and unable to curse, she was struggling to stuff her headdress under her arm and clear her lips when someone grabbed the cap from behind her.

'You need another pair of hands?'

Elysabeth nearly swallowed the pins. She spun round and discovered her helper was a tall youth and, judging by his thigh-high boots, the wooden box slung from his shoulder and the cered sleeveless doublet hanging loose over his open shirt, he had just returned from fishing.

Elysabeth's glance darted from the couple of plump grey chub tails flopping over the edge of the pail up the willow rod leaning against his broad chest to the cheerful, glowing face gazing down at her. She was aware that there was a lot of him in between and found herself blushing. A long while since she had done that. The grin that was neither a man's nor a boy's dimpled further and it was irresistible not to smile back.

One had to be practical. She blew the pins out into her hand first.

'Hope I'm not giving your cap a fishy smell.' He spoke before she could. Dear God, he might be only a stripling but he was giving her a thorough lookover as though she was his age, or was she imagining it? 'Take your time. I'll hold it while you finish.' There was no 'shall I?'

'Thank you,' she said gravely, trying to prove she had some decorum left. 'It's not very comfortable. Why we women put ourselves through such torment, I'll never know.' Why was she prattling so? He must be several years younger than her. Grey's age more like. 'It rubs around the ears,' she added.

He set down the pail and leaned the rod against the stone wall. 'Glad I don't have to wear such a thing,' he assured her heartily. 'Perhaps I can hold the pins for you as well, mistress?' He wiped his hand on his thigh before offering her its service. The river water had rendered his ample palm soft as a gentleman's and the tiny chains of his life and heart lines were not threaded with dirt, as with most fellows his age. Did he realise how charming his thoughtfulness was? How it restored a vigour to her life. Made her wish she was a milkmaid instead of a widow with a bale of worries. Goodness, she was even noticing this fellow's freckles and his hazel eyes were thickly lashed, with a glint of gold in the sunlight.

She tried to concentrate, twist the braid once more around the crown of her head and take the ivory pins, one by one. 'It's easier with a maid.'

'You want me to try?'

'Goodness, no,' she laughed, imagining those large fingers trying to be nimble in such a feminine task. For sure he would be good at unlacing, she almost said, and was conscious of a rosy flush spreading yet again over her face and shoulders. He handed her the crespinette and she dragged it down over the coronet of hair and straightened it over her ears. 'There,' she sighed, tethering it with the last of the pins. 'That will have to suffice. Are you —' she began just as he said the same words. They laughed together.

'A friend of the family and you, mistress?'

'A neighbour but I've not met Sir William Hastings yet. I came on a matter of business and, well, to be neighbourly, but since he is now so high in the king's regard, I see I stand no chance. Have you seen the number of petitioners, sir?' He shook his head. 'Believe me, they would take up the length of Westminster Hall.' She hadn't meant to say that. These days

157

mentioning she had served the fugitive queen would be like admitting she had slept a week with the Devil.

'You have been to Westminster Palace, mistress?'

'N-yes, I did not say that to impress, sir. I have been fortunate to see inside, that is all.' She lingered, not wanting to leave that sunlit spot and his cheerful company. 'I hope those fish were not from the moat.'

He grinned. 'Lord, no, just been scaling them. Caught these at Heathe Brook, well above Kirby. Wouldn't fish here. Mind, Sir William is desirous of putting vaults below the latrines instead of letting the waste into the moat. Not a bad notion but expensive and I wouldn't want to be mucking them out.'

'Nor me,' she laughed. 'Well, I'd better return to the line. Thank you for your help.'

'My pleasure, mistress. Mistress...?'

'Elysabeth, Lady Grey.'

'Oh, your pardon.' He inclined his head sweetly.

'I know,' she apologised ruefully. 'Barons' wives do not pin their hair behind the stables.'

'Evidently some do,' he quipped but it was not said lasciviously.

'Adieu, then.' She made a curtsey that was respectful; his bow was neither fulsome nor stiff.


'You've been a long time, my dear,' said the draper's widow ahead of her. 'If it wasn't for the boy here, we'd have thought you'd given up.'

She felt like doing just that. Thrice more, she heard a bell from Kirby Church strike the quarter. Every time the door behind the dais opened, there was a rustle of anticipation. This time, instead of taking the next in the queue, Hastings' steward was striding down the hall.

'Is there a Lady Grey among you still?'

'Yes,' she replied, astonished. Had the young 'friend of the family' put in a word for her?

'Follow me.'

'By Heaven!' exclaimed the draper's widow. Her tongue stalled between her teeth in outrage.

'Wish I had a pair of lovely duckies to shake at his lordship,' snarled an elderly chapman, as Elysabeth passed him.

'Hold your foul tongue, master, or go to the back,' ordered the steward with an indifferent expression. 'This way,' he barked and led Elysabeth and Tom up the dais steps, past two men-at-arms and into an accounting chamber.

They were ordered to wait before a trestle table, draped in dark green baize. The steward left by a side door and a soldier in a brigandine with Hastings' maunche embroidered on his shoulder took up position behind her making her feel more like a prisoner than a supplicant. Two clerks were seated at one end of the trestle, hedged in by a row of inkpots and a bristle of goose quills. One of the men was busy finishing off a letter.

The chair behind the table was empty. Its owner was standing by the open lower lights as though he longed to be outside. He was once more wearing the chunkish collar of suns and roses across his shoulders but he had abandoned his mantle over the back of his chair. The short brown velvet doublet panelled with gilt-threaded brocade did not displease her. It glinted as he turned reluctantly to observe her. A tallish, well-made man.

'The widow Grey?' How drab it sounded. How demeaning. No acknowledgment that she was Lady Grey.

*St Jude, I hope you are with me*, she prayed as she spread her skirts in a deep curtsey. Tom at least had the manners to remove his cap and bow.

'Sir William,' she acknowledged.

Her host did not affirm so or gallantly assist her to rise. Rather, he was assessing her, perhaps playing his own guessing game.

'Thank you for seeing me.' She kept her voice lower than usual.

'What is the matter you wish to discuss with me?' He did not sit down.

'I greet you as a neighbour, sir.' He inclined his head in thanks. 'From Groby but...' Oh Christ's Mercy! She floundered at the lack of response in the patrician features. 'That is, I wondered...' Struggling for the arguments she had rehearsed, her mind went blank. 'Please, is there a stool here? Do you mind if I sit down? I have been standing a long time.'

No apology was offered, merely the flick of command. The soldier brought her a three-legged stool. Tom was looking at her with concern as she loosened the cordels of her cloak. Sir William was, too. Realising her gown was gaping somewhat, she corrected it primly. She had become thinner since John's death.

'Are you with child, Lady Grey?' this new lord chamberlain asked. His hand moved towards a small handbell. 'Do you require some ale?'

She shook her head. 'No, my lord, I am not but ... but since my husband's death —'

'That would be Sir John Grey, Baron Ferrers of Groby?' he interrupted. 'Slain at St Albans?'

On his right, one of the secretaries lifted his head. '*Attainted*, my lord.'

Beside her Tom stiffened.

'It was no treason back in February, sir,' she retorted swiftly to the clerk and then took a sharp breath. O Jesu! She should have held her tongue. At least Tom had held his.

'But now you want my help, Lady Grey?' Hastings asked, with a lift of forefinger to forestall another comment from his scrivener. His stare took in the embroidered edge of her bodice neckline and its persistent attempt to bare her shoulder before returning to her face.

'Yes, Sir William. I should like to offer you the wardship of my son, Thomas.'

'Oh, you would.' If there was dry humour in Hastings' tone, it was piquant with arrogance. 'With an attainder on his estates?'

She darted a swift warning at Tom to hold his tongue. 'If that were to be reversed through your good offices, my lord,' she suggested, 'the income due to you as my son's guardian would not be negligible.'

He sat back in his chair, his right thumb stroking the edge of the table. 'I met your husband's family two days ago at Sir Robert Sheringham's and they gave me to understand the Ferrers lordship is about to pass to Sir John Bourchier. Is that correct?'

Did he read the astonishment in her face, the hurt of more betrayal? Why hadn't they told her they had met Sir William?

'Yes, that is so,' she admitted miserably. Did this stranger suppose she had deliberately withheld that truth? 'But if there is no issue from the marriage between my mother-in-law and Sir John, then Thomas will inherit the title.'

He nodded and then gestured to his secretary to write down the request. She waited for his verdict as the scratch of the quill filled the silence. Meanwhile, the other clerk sanded the letter he had been writing, rose and set it in front of his master.

Hastings signed and she was forced to watch and wait as the process of dripping wax upon the folds and handing it back for his lordship to jab his seal ring down was carried out. It was done as though she and Tom were no longer visible.

Damn them all!

She cleared her throat. 'Sir William.'

Oh, how those in authority could tug down a protective visor of courteous gravity. People said power in a man could be attractive. Well, Hastings, for all his fair looks, left her unmoved, frigid. If it wasn't for Tom, she should have enjoyed slapping the arrogance from this neighbour's face. Instead she said, 'Sir, my son will be in need of good lordship as he grows to manhood. Truly, I should wish to see him given wise counsel.'

Hastings' gaze flicked Tom's face then came back to her. 'Make him into a good little Yorkist, you mean, Lady Grey?' The blue eyes gave no quarter. The soul behind his stare offered no friendship.

'Yes, my lord.' How she hated herself for sounding so compliant; God forbid that John's soul would ever learn her treason or that his family were belly up to the victors.

Tom was clenching his jaw. She had reminded him on the way here that William Hastings had not been at St Albans, that he had had no hand in his father's slaying.

'And what have you to say for yourself, Thomas Grey? Do you desire to become my ward?'

Her boy could be charming when he chose. Or scornful. Elysabeth held her breath and propelled another prayer to St Jude.

'I think, my lord, that I must cut my cloth to clothe my arm.' Unsmiling, her son looked meaningfully at his ebbed sleeve.

'Well, that is one way of putting it.' Sir William's gaze strayed back to Elysabeth. 'I feel immensely flattered by this, Lady Grey,' he remarked. She realised her neckline was slipping again. 'Was that the only matter you wished to raise?'

*I hope the Devil carries you and your precious king to hell,* she thought. Aloud she said, 'Yes, my lord. I … I do not expect — I mean, I hope you will think further about Thomas. Maybe if not as a ward, perhaps you might consider him as a page?'

Hastings' mouth tightened and he looked back at Tom. 'How old are you, Thomas?'

'Nine, sir.'

'Two years older than most pages. That could make life rather difficult for you.'

'Yes, sir, I suppose it could.' No more words followed.

That was it then?

She rose before he could dismiss her, shaking her skirts and straightening her collar. 'If you would kindly send word to me at Grafton, my lord, when you have reached a decision and my family will forward your answer to me.'

'Grafton? Grafton Woodville?'

'My mother is the Duchess of Bedford.'

'Oh.' She doubted his surprise was genuine. Of course, he knew. 'So your father would be Richard Woodville. Didn't he and your brother, Lord Scales, oppose King Edward at Towton?'

'Yes, Sir William, but they are hopeful of a pardon.' It was needful to swiftly spur the conversation onto a different path. 'Unfortunately, my circumstances may compel me to return to my family home, sir, a situation I hope to avoid with your good lordship.'

Hastings' eyes widened slightly.

*His good lordship*! Curse it! Had she implied she was looking to be his mistress? Embarrassed, she had no resort but to incline her head in cold, stately fashion and turn away, expecting the guard to open the door for her. It had all been a waste of effort. But the guard, curse him, was awaiting his master's nod.

Hastings, still unsmiling — he probably could be devastating if he bothered — came round the table, courteously offering his wrist to lead her to the door. She felt no alchemy at his touch.

'Farewell, Lady Grey.' She hated the amused glint in his eyes, the flick of a glance at her breasts but what insulted her most of all was that if he assumed she had just propositioned him — which she hadn't — he certainly was not keen to take advantage.

'Good day, my lady.' *And good riddance*, he probably added as a postscript.

# 10: KATE

## 10th May 1461, The road to Bisham, Berkshire

Arranging a visit to Kate's mother had taken a week or so and the Countess had suggested a compromise. Instead of expecting her youngest to journey with a baby all the way north to Fotheringay, she had bestirred herself to meet Kate at Bisham Priory, northeast of Reading.

Flanked by armed outriders, the Bonville retinue finally managed to trundle out of Shute and trot towards Berkshire. For Kate, it was a pleasure to travel again especially since the promise of summer was in the stillness of the morning. Bright green foliage dappled with flowerlets fringed the ditches either side of the Devon lanes and the hollow ways were shady now, vaulted by newly leafed branches. Bluebells and violets had burst through the ivy and wild garlic in the woods, and the cow meadows were sprinkled with yellow-glazed buttercups and white marguerites.

It probably felt like this to go on pilgrimage, Kate decided, glad to be quit of Devon for a few weeks and to behave like a dutiful daughter, but it was timely to depart: since French supporters of Queen Margaret had seized the Channel Islands, there had been rumours of invasion on the south coast and moving inland seemed very sensible if you believed such nonsense. But there was another reason Grandmother Bonville had been so easily persuaded: the garderobes and latrines of Shute Hall needed a good airing.

South of Chard, the procession of carts and riders crossed paths with a lone horseman — Robert Newton, returning to

Shute. Old Lady Bonville had been moving him like a chess knight always out of reach. Well, be damned to that! Kate halted the party by the gate to a farm track, fetched Cecily from Eleanor's arms and carried her over to the patch of grass to make water.

After he had dismounted and greeted Lady Bonville, Newton came across to make his bow to her.

She offered her hand. 'I haven't been able to thank you for rescuing Guinivere until now.'

'No matter, my lady. I am pleased to see you ride her still. And now how's this little demoiselle?' he asked, going down on his haunches in front of Cecily. The child clutched hold of Kate's skirts and peeped a head of yellow curls warily round at him.

'Your great niece is thriving, Master Newton.'

Her way of putting it clearly touched him. The young man's grin, as he rose to his feet, could have matched Noah's, when at last he saw the rainbow. 'I miss playing your groom, my lady,' he said softly, his fingers stroking the coiled brim of his hat as he looked down at her. 'If ever I can do aught for you, send for me.' Then he blushed beneath his tan. 'No, that came out amiss. I meant if ever you need my help, my lady.'

Now she was blushing. 'Likewise, Master Newton. I mean it truly. God be with you.'

'And you, my lady. I wish you a safe journey.' He bowed over her hand and then mounted up and gave spur. Kate did not dare watch him ride away.

That flutter of interest deep inside her was momentarily reassuring. Of course, she felt secure in flirting a little because Newton was a servant and could not gainsay her but (a really large, illuminated 'but') her hope was to find true love amongst her own rank. Was that likely? Oh yes, indeed, she scoffed at herself, and if she slept in a toadstool ring, the King of Elfland would come riding by, become enamoured at first sight and carry her off. An inner voice, like some nasty demon, warned her that despite being eighteen and in her prime, she had already failed. If her lack of passion had driven Will to continue tumbling Lovidia, how could she possibly excite love — and loyalty — in some other lord who could tup the whole neighbourhood if he chose. Oh, if only there was a butterfly cocooned inside her skin and ripening to emerge!

No, wait on! She argued with herself. Newton was attracted to her, so maybe there was a man of higher rank who would be. She would find him somehow.

'Who likes butter?' Grandmother Bonville joined her, holding out a buttercup to Cecily. 'Hold it here, poppet!' The infant giggled. Grabbing it in her fat little fist, she jabbed it under her chin. 'That young man thinks he is a full Bonville sometimes.'

'He's your unlawful stepson,' murmured Kate, straightening her daughter's petticoats. Cecily must always come first, she told herself. 'Anyway, you don't have to move him out of my way like an unwanted cushion, Grandmother. I'm not about to clamber into the next hayloft with him.'

'If I was your age I'd be tempted. I'm tempted now.'

'*Madame*!'

'I may be over thirty years older than you but I can still admire a fine-looking lad. Bonny was always … shall we say … very attentive. Never lost his ardour. I miss him.'

'*Grandmother*!'

'Newton has his father's looks. You're assuming I was moving him out of *your* way but what about *mine*, girl? And if you exclaim "Grandmother" one more time…'

'Were you?'

167

'Moving him? Maybe. Wait until you reach my years, young woman, and then you'll know the answer.' She gestured to Master Gylle to give the order to move on.

Kate hoisted Cecily onto her arm. 'You could marry again.'

Grandmother sighed and put her foot in the clasped hands of a waiting groom. 'No,' she said, settling herself on the saddle. 'Bonny was my great love.'

'Despite his infidelity?'

'Yes, Kate. Life or God, what you will, raps us on the knuckles as a reminder that there is no heaven on earth. No husband is perfect.' She lowered her voice. 'That's why the Almighty created a woman in Paradise. He got things wrong on the first endeavour.'


'I shall lie here soon.'

Alice, Kate's mother, shrouded stoutly in a black fine wool kirtle with a missal in her hand and a golden lozenge reliquary dangling against her bosom, stood in the church of Bisham Priory, the mausoleum of the Earls of Salisbury. Sorrowful lines seemed permanently chiselled into her skin and perpetual grief was rotting her from within.

As far as Kate knew, no one had consulted God. The proclamation of an imminent shuffle from life was purposed only in her mother's mind; any dolt could observe that Lady Salisbury's lungs, limbs, sight and hearing were sound.

It was possible to blame the Bisham prior and canons for encouraging such morbidity. Perhaps they were thinking of the endowment of another chantry or that the tombs of the earl and countess might draw illustrious visitors. Richard had promised to bring her father and Thomas to rest here, once he and their kinsmen had calmed the north. However, to be charitable, her mother must have been thinking of cered shrouds and other similar cheerful items long before she left Fotheringay. She had no grief to spare for the Bonville lords and showed not the least interest in being cheered up or developing a deeper friendship with her youngest now they were both widows. No confidences shared, no playing with her granddaughter or happier reminiscences washed down with a flagon of sweet wine and cinnamon wafers.

Indeed, there had been so much talk of death since the Bonville entourage had arrived at Bisham, that Kate almost expected to encounter a hooded figure carrying a sickle around the next corner.

Yes, a surfeit of masses for the dead and too much kneeling for the living!

A murrain on it! Bisham was proving another instance in her life that she had rather drop in the slot of the poor box and forget about. Her sister Joan had been more a mother to her, she realised now. Curse it, they should have journeyed to Arundel to see her instead. It would have been a plaguey lot jollier.

Aware of Kate's exasperation, Grandmother Bonville maintained a grave face as she asked, 'Have you decided on alabaster, Lady Salisbury? I'd rather have Purbeck marble myself but of course I am biased since my great-granddaughter here...' she blew a kiss at Cecily, who was crawling up the steps of the chancel, 'is owner of one of the quarries near Corfe.'

'Excuse me!' Biting her lip, Kate scooped Cecily into her arms and fled the mausoleum. Only the gravestones outside heard her laugh but she could not help herself. Sinful, disrespectful. Yes, all those things! It was either that or have a thoroughly good weep.

She carried Cecily down to the river's edge and kept a good hold on the leather reins as Cecily tottered forward and chattered incomprehensibly at the moorhens.

Down river lay Windsor Castle and further still, Westminster Palace, though no one of consequence was at either yet. Maybe...

'Katherine!'

Seeing the two older widows waiting for her at the abbey door, she definitely felt the wriggle of something that was possibly rebellion, the temptation to rip off her dismal black apparel, but she still had four months of mourning to complete and Richard would expect her to behave like a Neville.

'Mama,' cooed Cecily.

At least her little girl had an adoring mother and great-grandmother and knew the warmth of an embrace.

'We'll go home to Shute,' Kate whispered, saving Cecily from muddy feet and kissing her on the nose.

'Shoo.'

'Shoo, yes, Shoo.'

# 11: ELYSABETH

*3rd July 1461, three days after the Feast of St Peter and*
*St Paul,*
*The Great North Road from London*

It was an ignominious thing to return to your parents' home
with scarce two groats to jingle. Shame rode pillion behind
Elysabeth as her little party crossed London Bridge and passed
through Bishopsgate to begin their three-day journey up
Watling Street. With luck, they might reach Grafton by the
evening of the second day but they had sixty-four miles to
cover. They would have to ask for accommodation at religious
houses; they could not afford to stay at any inn.

She was out of temper with the Almighty and St Jude, not to
mention the rest of the heavenly establishment, for a whole
basketful of reasons. Hastings, a lord now, had not consented
to become Tom's guardian. Added to that disappointment,
finding the enfeoffees of the three manors had taken time.
Two of them, Boulden and Ischam, had been accommodating
but the others... The priest, William Walesby, had passed
away, which had necessitated establishing he had no heirs with
claim to the three
manors; Sir Thomas Fynderne had been dismissed from his
post as Lieutenant of Guisnes and was with the queen's rebel
army in the north, but since he had been attainted a traitor and
lost all rights to any land, his consent was no longer needed;
and Master Fyldyng, a cunning creature (probably in
Bourchier's pocket), had refused to enfeoffe the trust and so
Elysabeth had been forced to take her case to the Chancery

court. Her father, mercifully freed after the Battle of Towton, had scraped up some money for her to find a lawyer and agreed to be her fellow plaintiff, and Master Fyldyng had been subpoenaed to appear before the Chancellor, Warwick's brother. However, there was a great queue of cases to be heard and only a fool would expect to have good news before the next Yuletide. And during all this, London (lawyers and lodgings) had sucked money from her like some monstrous leech.

The high-stepping cost of staying in the city was mainly the usurper Edward's fault because of his decision (or Warwick's) to return to Westminster that month for the ladling of more holy oil, fulsome flaunting and a great dollop of pageantry — in other words, a second, less hurried coronation. Consequently, rents instantly soared higher than the carrion kites circling over the city shambles, and the Goldsmiths' Guild, which owned the messuage by Oldbourne Hall in Shoe Lane, where Elysabeth and the boys had been living throughout May, was no less greedy.

With her purse as exhausted as she was, Elysabeth moved her little family across to stay at the abbey of Bermondsey. She did not join the hordes of Kentish men crossing London Bridge to watch Warwick and his braggart cousin in procession, nor were her prayers that rain would soak their finery acknowledged by Heaven. God was still a Yorkist; a cloudless day had cheered Edward's sunnes-in-splendour.

And the treasonous sun had shone hotly all the following week burning bared flesh to lobster scarlet. Londoners and the cheeses in their cupboards sweated. Noses peeling, housewives lingered by the conduits, dabbing their throats and necks with water before they carried home their pails; beggars fought for places in the shade; and the venal trustee, Fyldyng, irritable, overdressed and sweaty, demanded a higher price for his consent. Only the London flies were euphoric, breeding in the dung and the filth and swarming round the fish and meat stalls like a crowd come for a hanging.

The miasma of disease from the north bank's stinking ditches and Southwark's filthy tenements had begun to concern Elysabeth. Plague had not witnessed the coronation but its fellows were arriving in the city with gifts of runny flux and vomiting. And since her sons were the only precious possession Elysabeth still owned, it was time to take her boys to healthier air.

The day they left the city, the unobliging sky was leaden towards the west. By the time her little party passed through Stony Stratford and reached the more familiar countryside of Pottersbury on the afternoon of the third day, Elysabeth and her maidservant were damp from the morning drizzle and weary from Dickon's 'Are we there yet?' The rain clouds shifted fortuitously as they took the rutted track that led east from Plumpton End but the mire from last night's downpour slowed them and sometimes the horses sank in to their fetlocks. Elysabeth finally drew rein with a sigh of relief at the Grafton alehouse and the old hermitage in the field opposite. She was almost home. Almost. Some of the village — mostly cottages belonging to tenants of her father, Lord Rivers — had darned itself over the Northampton Road but most of the dwellings, the church and her parents' manor house lay further to the east. A woman's call hailed her from the meadow flanking the crossroads. Grateful she was still recognised here, Elysabeth waved back.

Turning off into the village street, she noticed changes that would have been less obvious to a stranger: fences repaired instead of renewed, a shutter hanging by a breath, proud oak trees gone, the wild wood edged by stumps, less cattle in the fields; and the straggle of tenants' cottages shabbier than she remembered.

The usual Friday odour of fish was seeping from the kitchen of the religious house next to St Mary's Church and there were fresh gravestones in the churchyard. Elysabeth crossed herself with a prayer for the dead, hoping it was none from her parents' household.

Her family home lay beyond a thick hedgerow on a small rise where the track dog-legged and dipped away through pasture. As a manor house, it was less modest than Groby Hall, but considering Elysabeth's mother was a duchess and had once been sister-in-law to King Henry V, victor of Agincourt, it should have been a palace. Yet it did have a great hall large enough to seat thirty and a little gem of a chapel.

Memories of a rumbustious childhood tumbled back into her head. It was useless to expect to recreate those carefree days. Her oldest brother, Anthony, was married and two of her sisters were in other households about to be wed, Lionel was studying canon law in Oxford yet that still left eight siblings, some she hardly knew.

As her ambler led the others wearily into the hall courtyard, four children halted their noisy game of Touch and stared at her like curious sheep. Three had her father's gilt hair and lithe frame and one of the girls had Duchess Jacquetta's alabaster complexion and brown hair. These must be her younger siblings: Eleanor, Mary, Cat and Edward, strangers to her now. Outside the stable, the head groom, who had been with the family all his life, paused on his rake and peered at them.

'Master Burcote,' she called out and waved.

In an instant, his face changed from puzzlement to delight and he was at her stirrup, grabbing the bridle. 'Shake the bell,

174

lad!' he bawled at one of his underlings, and beckoned to the children. 'Here's my Lady Grey, your sister, come to visit. And see here! How are our fine gentlemen?' Of course, he reached out to take Dickon from her but the boy went rigid. Since the ransacking of Astley, the child had shown a fear of strangers. Maybe the exuberance of these little aunts and uncle would batter through his shield.

Tom slid down from his pony unsmiling and shook the small hands with such an adult air that tears prickled behind Elysabeth's eyes. Lord Hastings' rejection had ripped open the wounds of his father's death and disgrace.

Grafton, God willing, would be good for both boys.

'Elysabeth!' A chorus of male exclamations greeted her as four young men ran down the stone steps from the hall. Anthony, Lord Scales, blessedly released from captivity, gaunter but elegant as ever, even if there was a dark rub to the pleats of his mustard doublet; John, the jester of the family, bean-lean and straggling for the light, his sleeves short of his wrists; Dick, the quietest of her brothers, looking more like a stable hand in his leather sleeveless coat; and 'Bishop' Lionel (whether he would attain that ecclesiastical height remained to be seen), on the cusp of manhood, all blackheads and a voice that did not know whether to go high or low. Why was he home from Oxford? Was there no more money to pay for his studies?

'This is a wondrous surprise, Anthony,' she squealed as her oldest brother swung her into the air. 'God be praised that the king has pardoned you.'

But then an ill thought struck her. If they were all here … and she had just glimpsed Anthony's wife coming down too. 'Christ's Mercy!' she whispered. 'Is aught wrong? There's no funeral, is there?' She pummelled his shoulders with the privilege of being eldest born. 'Tell me!'

'Nothing's wrong, Lyssie,' he whispered, lowering her. 'Just holes in my purse at the moment. The new king fined me mercilessly. Give Bessie an embrace. She was not pleased at me bringing her here so soon after I was set at liberty.'

Elysabeth swung round to greet Bessie, Lady Scales, a woman of her own age. However, hugging the young baroness was like wrapping her arms about a sackful of trowels and it was a relief to turn to her other brothers.

'You have grown thinner, Mistress Tamsin,' John was chortling as he shouldered the young woman's saddle pack. 'You too, Lyssie.' The words stung. She had. Scraggy, she thought herself now.

'John,' she caught his arm before he turned to greet her sons. 'Do not tease them yet.' He stared at her and then looked round at Tom and Dickon, standing together and gave them a wink.

'Stitches and mending needed, eh? They'll keep. And here's our creaky Papa, at last. Toppled from the saddle at Towton.'

She knew her father had been injured, either during the battle or beaten afterwards by the new king's ruffians, but he had made light of it in his letters, yet it was still a shock to see him hobbling down the steps using a stick.

'Elysabeth, sweetheart!' Age spots dappled his cheeks and the lines of his handsome face were hewn deeper now but there were still pale gold strands in his hair and power in his arms as he embraced her.

'Thank God, sir!' she exclaimed, tears spilling as she nestled against his broad chest.

'Aye, my love, netted but thrown back into the pond again, and I'm to receive a pardon from the king!'

'Wondrous, wondrous news! When did you hear, Papa?'

'After the coronation.' He frowned, 'Aye, last month. No misericord in the heavenly choir yet, my dear, not like your poor husband, eh, God rest his soul!' He swept her towards the uppermost step where her mother waited. 'Is this not splendid, Jacq, darling? See, who has come a-visiting!'

He made it sound like her choice, Elysabeth thought sadly. What would her parents say when they learned she had nowhere else to go?

'Darling!' After kissing her on each cheek, her mother's dark eyes explored her face. 'But you are looking so fatigued, *mignonne*. It eez not good.' Even after twenty-five years of living in England, her grace of Bedford's vowels still marked her as an outsider. Young John had delighted in mimicking her behind her back until he was caught for it and locked in the cellar for the night. 'Elysabeth?'

'Saddle sore, Mama ... worn out with lawyers fleecing me.'

'Well, you are 'ome now.'

Yes, she was. Arm in arm, they walked inside together, and she breathed in the familiar scents of the house: the rosewater, orris and ambergris perfume her mother wore, the meadowsweet rushes on the floor, the detestable smell of scalded milk from the nursery upstairs and the kitchen aromas of onions, dried herbs, yeast and home-brewed ale.

There had been no stripping of furnishings by the sheriff's bailiffs here. Elysabeth trailed her darned gloved fingertips along the great oak table, relieved the hall still boasted the sumptuous Flemish tapestries and an exquisite illuminated book that had belonged to her mother's first husband, the Duke of Bedford. All the good pieces of furniture were reassuringly in the usual places in the withdrawing chamber: the cross-legged chairs that had been imported from Florence, the carved cupboard that had once belonged to Henry Bolingbroke before he deposed King Richard, one of the Burgundian linen chests that had contained her mother's bride clothes and on the wall hung the sword that Bedford had worn at the Battle of Verneuil.

Her mother's favourite room was the south-facing solar and here a goblet of malmsey was set in Elysabeth's hand and honey-and-oatmeal cakes were brought in for the children. Six-year-old Cat clambered onto her knee and Mary made funny faces at Dickon, who showed no reaction until John got down on his hands and knees and played at being a lion, trying to maul their ankles.

'Why is Uncle John doing that, Mama?' he asked.

Elysabeth reached out an arm and drew him to her side. 'He is trying to make you laugh, Dickon.'

'Why, Mama?'

Elysabeth made a face at John. 'You know, Dickon, I don't know either.'

Over on the window seat, her mother was attempting to winkle some conversation out of Tom. A curly feat. At least Tom was answering and he actually said something that made the duchess his grandmother give one of her husky laughs — or was she only pretending to be amused?

Mary gave up on Dickon, bossily grabbed Cat's hand and whisked her from the room without a courteous by-your-leave. Elysabeth disapproved. That would never have happened at Astley or Groby, nor had it been permitted when she had been in charge of her brothers and sisters. At least, because of the Yorkist victory, her parents were forced to be at home now for the younger ones and she must resist interfering. That might be hard. The love was here yet she sensed within days she would be yearning desperately for Astley, in charge of her own little patch of Christendom.

But the wine was relaxing her now, seeping through to her toes and she caught Anthony watching her fondly. She nodded back, glad the depth of understanding that had always been between them was fresh as ever. Anthony was not just her brother but her oldest friend.

In truth, she had shouldered more burdens than him, accepting responsibility as the oldest child whenever her parents had been at court. There had been little leisure time, especially when her mother had another babe due or was not yet churched, except perhaps a snatched walk in the meadows when Anthony would tell her about the book he had been reading or a summer twilight gallop together after tiny John and Jacquetta had been put to bed. Becoming a royal maid-of-honour at twelve had been like stepping into Paradise, no milk to warm, no tiny bottoms to be washed, nothing to be mended. But now here she was — at home again.

Anthony must have observed the sudden release of her shoulders. With a grin, he languidly drew a cross of absolution in the air and Elysabeth laughed. However, Bessie, like a child in the middle trying to catch the leather ball, witnessed the rapport between them and tightened her lips.

Clearly, Anthony was very much in the doghouse. Although the couple were sitting side by side on the second-best settle, they might have been England and France with the Channel between them. Bessie looked as though God's hand had stuffed a poker down her spine while he was lounging back, utterly self-contained, his finely muscled legs crossed at the ankles and clearly unaware the worn-through soles of his beaked shoes were on display.

'May I help myself?' Elysabeth let go of Dickon and rose to her feet to replenish her goblet but she found the flagon empty. Turning, she met her mother's shake of head and sensed Bessie's raised eyebrows.

Hard times for all of them, then, even a duchess. She sat down again noting the freshly turned cuffs that lengthened her mother's sleeves, the snags in her veil that betrayed its age and the threadbare hem of her velvet gown.

'Aye, lean times,' began her father.

There had been other less obvious defeats than Towton, he explained: her sisters sent home unwed, the betrothal about to be arranged for young John called off by the bride's kinsmen; neighbouring gentlewomen refusing to acknowledge her mother on the street in Stony Stratford, and Lionel's tutors in Oxford turning brusque and short of time. Elysabeth commiserated, sorry that relating her boys' misfortunes was piling more dung on the Woodville midden.

It was a relief to go into supper but the helpings of squab, rabbit and preserved pork were not generous and there were fewer house servants being fed at the lower tables and only three grooms, which meant that her father must have sold off some of the horses.

After the meal there were serious signs of an ensuing family conference. The duchess shooed all the children outside and lured the older family members back into the solar with the promise of the sweetmeats she had been saving. 'Sent from Uncle St Pol in Burgundy!' Only three of Elysabeth's siblings escaped their mother's scoop net.

Elysabeth helped her mother carry in the platters and sat down beside Bessie on the window seat.

Idly thumbing through a book of romances that one of his sisters had left on the small table, Anthony was wearing his most morose expression. John was sitting with his elbows on his knees, resting his chin on his knuckles and Lionel was perched before a small sloping writing table in the corner. Had he been older, he could have been mistaken for a notary at a manor meeting, for he was ignoring the Latin text open before him, humming as he sharpened a goose feather quill and watching everyone.

'Are we about to have an entertainment?' Bessie asked sarcastically.

'You could call it that,' muttered Elysabeth.

'Out in the cold, that's where we are,' her father exclaimed. 'And high time we stopped sitting on our hands.' He usually took up a stance before the chimney mantle when he was in a haranguing mood, legs astride like a sword master holding a post-mortem on combat practice, but since the settle had its back turned to the summer hearth and his hip was paining him, he stood beside the settle, one arm resting on its back, the other leaning on his stick.

Elysabeth could have answered but the trick was to let the men think they held the field.

'Lost your tongue at Towton, did you, Anthony?' Her father's fingers tapped impatiently on the settle.

Elysabeth's oldest brother sighed. 'It's a fact that with the Yorkist sunne likely to blaze over England for several years to come, no one wants to show preferment to a family connected to mad old Henry.' He raised an eyebrow meaningfully at his mother.

'Or a marriage alliance,' John added, provoking a quiet snort from Bessie. Easy to see that she regretted being married to a courtier who was out of favour even if he had the athletic physique that made most husbands look like scarecrows and…

Of course! Bessie's first husband had been a Bourchier. No wonder she was looking like a dog whose bone had been snatched.

Papa, who had sat at King Henry's council table, warmed to the argument. 'Exactly, and if the Yorkists are yoked in for a long haul, we must shift with the times and find some means of acquiring our new sovereign's favour, and raise our fortunes again. It's a cursed nuisance that I haven't been able to get to Westminster. Nominally, I'm still a royal councillor, you know,' he informed Elysabeth, 'even if I haven't been summoned to the table.'

'But which ruler of England are you talking about, Papa?' she asked.

'Yes, Father, the new king or the new *ruler* of England?' Anthony tapped his fingers on the table with irritation. Elysabeth threw him a sympathetic look. At twenty-two, he must be frustrated — blocked from achieving high office by the change of dynasty.

'Don't misunderstand me,' muttered their father, tossing aside someone's embroidery practice and seating himself. 'I'm not for ingratiating myself with Warwick. Pox take him! Not after the shameful way he paraded us as prisoners at Calais behind his horse like some trumped-up Julius Caesar. Making your mother walk with us and —'

Her brothers groaned.

'Do not forget my husband's death at St Albans, Father, and him being branded a traitor!' Elysabeth said sharply.

John palmed the air. '*Doucement, doucement*! If we are going to get into bed with the new masters of the realm — no, I did not mean that literally, Lionel, go back to your book! If we are to accommodate ourselves to the status quo, isn't it wise to forget what happened at Calais? It's over a year ago.'

Anthony was ready with a put down: 'You weren't there, John.'

Elysabeth had not been either but she now understood humiliation. Her father had been at the port of Sandwich on the south coast mustering a force to protect the ships that had been captured from the Yorkists. The Earl of Warwick had mounted a successful, surprise attack. Not only were the ships retaken but her parents and Anthony were manacled and taken to Calais, where they were displayed as captives. She could imagine the ignominy of the torchlight procession and the public sneers of Warwick, Salisbury and seventeen-year-old Edward, the young braggart who had now acquired the crown. The three lords had harangued her father and Anthony as upstarts — lowly esquires not fit for the company of noblemen.

John, irrepressible, shattered the brief silence. 'My hypothesis, Father,' he exclaimed, with a wink at their mother, 'is that Warwick envied your Adonis-like appearance. That's why he marched you both in at night.' His brother and father's scowls merely fuelled his irreverence. 'What's wrong with that, Anthony?' he persisted.

'It was you who reckoned Warwick got the dumpy Montagu looks from his mother's side. Never fought in a tournament, has he, Papa? Some Julius Caesar!'

'Ha!' snorted their father, a former jousting demi-god, almost appeased.

'Come, sir,' John teased further, 'Mama always said she married you for your calves.'

'Well, it certainly wasn't for my money, eh, Jacq?' He met his wife's superior smile and turned back to his sons. 'Let's keep to the path, John. Yes, Warwick may be the brains behind the new king but you can't tell me the royal lad is going to behave like a nursery babe on leading strings for the rest of his reign.'

'Is it true King Ned's already had more harlots than King Solomon had concubines?' Lionel asked. His answer was a clip on the ear from Anthony.

Grabbing the bowl of cherries from the table, John tumbled to his knees, holding the vessel on his head like a crown. '"Beloved Cousin Warwick, may I have another pretty nurse to rock me to dreamland, so I can sleep through tomorrow's royal council meeting and you'll be able to do anything you please?".' He scrambled to his feet, preening at his mother's laughter. Bessie ignored him and Elysabeth felt like giving him a clip on the ear as well. 'Ah, I'm a genius,' he exclaimed and lobbed a cherry at Anthony.

The fruit hit the book. Anthony fastidiously examined the cover for a stain and then ate the offending projectile. 'A pity the fool of the family has never experienced a battle otherwise he would not be so damned trite.' He glared at John over the binding.

Elysabeth winced inwardly, remembering past wrangles, and much as she loved the exuberance of her family, John's high spirits jangled her nerves. Part of her felt like fleeing, seeking out some stile to lean upon where the wind in the leaves and the evensong of a robin might anthem her weary soul. A walk across the summer fields at Astley with her husband's arm about her waist. Sadly, she brought her mind back to the present.

'Why not aim lower first?' she suggested. 'Seek out the rising stars on the horizon, look where the favours are being handed out. These men will be the ones whom the new government must depend upon.'

Across the chamber, her father drew his lips together digesting her idea but Anthony forestalled any comment. 'Yes, forget about the king! And Hell will freeze over before I lick the Nevilles' boot soles.'

'Shall we make a list?' piped up Lionel, pen poised above his writing board. 'Give me some names.'

'There's the new Earl of Essex,' muttered her father. 'Bah! Be damned to him! I'll not go grovelling to such a whoreson. O Jesu! Your pardon, Bessie, I forget that Essex was your former father-in-law but he's still a... Anyway, think, lads. Someone with growing power but still hungry to win friends.'

Elysabeth gritted her teeth. *Lads*? She exchanged glances with Bessie.

'There's Sir William Blount and Sir William Herbert,' suggested Anthony and rippled off a rollcall of lesser barons. He strolled over to peruse the list over Lionel's shoulder. 'Devil take it, I've left out William Hastings.' He looked round at his father. 'That's our man! The new lord chamberlain.'

'Yes,' agreed her father, chewing that further. 'An affable fellow — apart from being a Yorkist. Nothing personal against us to my knowledge. No squabbles or skirmishes over any land. Yes, Hastings might be just the man.'

'And he'll be in charge of any tournaments,' jeered John. He prodded his brother in the belly. 'Anthony wants to joust again.'

'What if I do,' retorted Anthony loftily. 'For me, the tiltyard may be the road back to favour and prize money, too. People forgive your sins if you give them a good afternoon's entertainment. Didn't your reputation increase when you won that tournament against the Spaniard, Father?'

'Consider a pilgrimage to Jerusalem, brother.' Still being tiresome, John flung a cushion with the family's cockleshell coat of arms at him. 'They may have forgotten that you fought on the wrong side by the time you come back. Sorry, Bessie, I thought you'd like the idea.'

'You could always be a jester, John,' suggested Elysabeth sweetly. 'Warwick needs someone who can make him laugh.'

John shrugged and retreated past the women's skirts to the open window.

'But what can *we* offer Hastings?' muttered her father, cutting to the bone.

'You can offer him nothing,' Elysabeth informed them but her menfolk gave no appearance of having listened; the Woodville cart rattled off again.

'How about a bride?' John turned from the casement where he had been making faces at his young sisters in the garden below.

'Isn't Lord Hastings long in the tooth?' Lionel asked. From his young perspective, nearly everyone was. 'Surely he's married already.'

'He's not,' Anthony informed them authoritatively. 'But that is nothing significant. He's probably been waiting to see how things turned out.'

'There you are then,' smirked John. 'So if he's not gotten any unnatural leanings…'

'He'd still marry,' corrected Anthony, and broke off at the noise from outside. 'Oh, Lord, Cat's found that whistle again. Shut the lower lights, Bessie!' His wife ignored him.

'Just listen to those girls shrieking,' spluttered their father, fisting his side. 'You think Hastings would put up with one of them? If he's past thirty, he'll be wanting an heir and none of ours are old enough to breed. Besides, we haven't sufficient for their dowries. John, close the poxy window! All that female pig squeal is giving me a megrim.'

John fastened the lower light and leaned back against the stone transom but the squabble could still be heard.

'Have we a cousin of marriageable age?' Anthony mused. 'A Haute or one of the Fogges?'

Elysabeth rose to her feet. 'I think Towton certainly affected your hearing, Anthony. I've told you Hastings needs nothing from us. *Nothing*! And you know why? I have already pursued the matter.'

The masculine silence. Were they going to listen?

Now it was she who stood before the fireplace.

'I've had audience with Hastings, requested him to take Tom into his household but he refused because there's no profit in it for him.'

'Maybe you should 'ave worn a lower neckline.' That absurd firecracker was from her mother. Was it Gallic humour or utter crassness?

Elysabeth managed to keep her temper firmly chained. 'Your pardon, Mama, I don't think a low neckline looks becoming on a mourning gown, especially one so recently put on. And I also think low necklines are inappropriate for the daughters of duchesses who loved their husbands, don't you? Now, if you will excuse me for a moment, I am going to see if my children are behaving themselves. Would you like me to check on yours as well?'

She left the solar, dispensed justice in the garden, checked on Dickon, who was making mud pies with his young Uncle Edward, and returned to the stairs, wondering why she had bothered to return to Grafton. Perhaps she should reopen the hermitage up the street to find some peace!

Bessie was on her way down, looking distraught.

'Are you not feeling well, Bessie?'

'I came away. To be frank, your family's talk is so … so mercenary. It makes me wonder if I was chosen in such a manner.'

Elysabeth shook her head. 'No, by my faith, no. Mama always wanted you and Anthony to wed because she loves your mother so and Anthony always thought upon your father as a hero.' Realising what she had just said, she quickly reached out to Bessie. 'No, listen, of course he wanted you.'

'Ha!' Her sister-in-law pulled away. 'Well, whether he did or not, I'm a disappointment. No children still and I cannot dissect the works of Boethius or … or St Augustine like —'

'Bessie, Bessie, no one I know can. Come, walk with me in the garden and you'll feel better.' Today, it seemed, she must play so many roles, traveller, mother, daughter and now comforter.

There were more sniffs behind her as they went out to the garden.

'Here's my refuge.' Elysabeth's favourite seat was sheltered by a northern wall and blessed by a hedge upon its eastern side. The stone slab needed scraping free of lichen but she sat down and patted it for Bessie to join her. There had been many times when she had been asked for counsel on this same bench. It had been her brothers mostly who had come to her. Her sister Anne was more the favourite with her mother or young Jacquetta.

Tightly strung Bessie Scales certainly needed an ally. Every muscle looked taut. She did not evoke the offer of a comforting arm; only words might offer warmth between them. Well, at least it was not some fruitless conversation about plucking eyebrows.

'It's not easy being a new wife, Bessie, especially here at Grafton where everybody knows your husband better than you do.'

The woman's upper lip swished sideways. 'You are very shrewd.' Was that praise or a needle jab? Lady Ferrers had left her on her guard in noblewomen's company. Men were much more readable.

Bessie gave another sigh and some of the icy edges thawed. The crevasses began to show.

'Sometimes I think I should have stayed a widow or taken the veil. Your brother has been so moody and irritable since he came back. He thinks of no one but himself. Can he not rejoice that he is alive, unlike your poor husband, God save him!' She crossed herself.

A thrush sang descant to their mutual sadness until curiosity prompted Elysabeth to ask, 'How long were you betwixt husbands?'

'Three years, Elysabeth, I grieved more for my father than Hal. And … and if you want to know why I am further out of temper with Anthony … it is because it is almost a year to my father's murder and I need to be with my mother not here.'

'Oh, Bessie.'

Lord Scales' death in the July of last year had shocked everyone. He had been serving as one of King Henry's captains at the Tower of London, when it had been under siege from the Thames by Warwick's ships and cut off from supplies. There had been negotiations and surrender but no trust. Scales had been savagely killed out on the Thames as he tried to flee to Westminster Sanctuary, and his body had been dumped naked outside a city church. Warwick claimed he had naught to do with the killing and that might be true, for the city had been full of panic, lawlessness and violence, but how many great lords turn a blind eye when it suits them? Another reason for her to loathe the man.

'I'm sorry, Bessie.' Jesu! Anthony needed a lance up his backside. 'I'll talk to him about it, I promise you.'

'He's so stubborn.'

'I'll make him think it's his decision.' She set her hand upon Bessie's. 'Shall we go back in?'

Bessie shook her head. 'I'll stay a while longer, and Elysabeth —'

What, another complaint? To show courtesy, she turned, hiding her weariness.

'I just wanted to say I'm not surprised you had trouble from John Bourchier over your dower rights. I hope you get fair judgment. They're an ambitious pack, the Bourchiers. Mind, your family are no angels.'


The unangelic Woodvilles were still in session. Elysabeth, hesitating outside the solar door, could hear John in full flight. 'Who better?' he was saying. 'Fair hair, dark eyes, a figure the mirror of Venus would recognise.'

There was a finger-in-mouth sort of gagging that sounded like Lionel.

'You've forgotten her teeth,' added Anthony sourly. 'She has all her teeth.'

'Indeed, sweet-breathed. *Ow!* You cur! I'm only trying to help.'

'Oaf! You know nothing about women,' sneered Anthony's voice. 'And from the utter nonsense you're spewing, you don't know her.'

Elysabeth sprang back with a squeal as the door was flung open.

'Eavesdropping, sister?' Anthony pulled it swiftly shut behind him.

'I was on my way in.'

'Yes, and your nose will get longer with the next lie.' He whirled his finger in the air, directing her to go back down the stairs. 'Out!' There was no argument. Even though she was tall for a woman, he topped her by a head and he seemed to have grown broader.

'Let go!' she said good-humouredly, tugging her elbow free. 'And if we are heading for the peace of the garden, your wife's out there waiting to bang you on the head with a shovel. I'd have used a dibber myself.'

'Tell me later. Let's go to the withdrawing chamber, then, if Anne and Jacquetta aren't winding wool there or playing with kittens.'

The servants were tidying the hall for breakfast but the great chamber beyond was empty of giggles or livestock.

Elysabeth did not feel like sitting. 'So what has John decided for me?' she asked, tugging off her cap and veil. 'Prodding to market with the cows?'

'Vain cat! You think it was you being talked about.'

She pushed back her hair. 'Ears burning, see.'

He peered close. 'Bah, that's where the linen's been rubbing. Now I know where Papa has a secret flask of aqua vitae. Want some?'

She nodded. 'It will help me sleep. Strange bed.'

'Aye, and the girls will keep you up all night whispering.'

A curse escaped her. Thin wooden boards or worse still, just curtains. With so many offspring, Grafton was a warren of humans.

Her brother lifted a small carpet off the wooden chest behind the door and flung the lid back. The smell of lavender was strong. Some rustling ensued before he hoisted up a stoppered flask like a huntsman displaying a snared rabbit. 'Voila!' He pointed to the aumery. 'Well, move, wench! Not the mazers. On the left. The left! Lord love us, let me!' He tipped a dead ant out of one of them and blew the dust out of a second. 'Your health, Lyssie!'

'Hmm,' she said, savouring the golden brew. 'Where did this come from?'

'One of the monks at St Albans trades from the postern. Good, eh?' He sat down, stretched out his legs. 'Now, I'll tell you what John was wittering on about. He and our duchess, Lord love her, reckon you should have another tilt at Hastings, since he's a neighbour at Groby et cetera. Ha! Thought you'd like the notion.' His grin might have resembled the Devil's when he heard of St Peter's denial.

She deliberately played dense. 'Badger him about Tom, they mean?'

'No, you dafty, as a diversion for Sir William Hastings when he's not holding the royal piss pot.'

'Become his whore?'

'Well, you can't marry the plaguey knave. He'll want a broad hipped, virgin heiress.' He jabbed a finger at her annoyed expression and laughed. 'I told them it wouldn't work. Anyway, you said he wasn't interested. I'm right, he didn't make an offer, did he?'

'No.' She shook her head.

He pulled a face. 'More a fool than I thought.'

'Him or me?'

'The pair of you.' He leaned forward, rolling the little goblet between his palms. 'So what's to be done, Lyssie? You're stuck here, aren't you?'

She nodded. 'Have they guessed yet? Will they mind?'

'Our wrinkling parents? It's whether *you* have staying power. You can always come and malinger at our house if you need some air.'

'Maybe. Thank you.' Come November, she hoped to have the case settled and receive the trust money.

'You'll be looking for a husband sometime, though, when the twelve months are up. It'll be hard to replace John Grey. He was a good fellow.'

'Enough, Anthony!' Her grief might never truly heal. 'It's my turn.' Time she mentioned Bessie's wish to leave, loathe as she was to lose her brother's company so soon. But the door behind her crashed open and Bessie charged into the chamber as though the Devil Himself was after her but it was only Mama who was following.

For once there was colour in the young woman's cheeks. Something white and pasty had been spattered down her dark red skirt. 'I have had enough!' she shrieked at Anthony.

'Which of zer girls was it, Bessie?' pleaded the duchess, although she was shrugging her shoulders at the tantrum. 'Why do you not tell me, *hein*?' Her daughter-in-law ignored her; the tirade was levelled at her husband.

'They run amok, my lord. They have no respect and...'

'I'll deal with it!' An outsider might have seen Anthony's purposeful departure as magnificent avenging rage but Elisabeth recognised it as a male dash for safety.

'My dear Bessie,' persisted the duchess. 'You will get your death of cold, so I order you a hot bath, *oui*, and you may use some of my bath perfume, *hein*?'

Bessie rolled her gaze at Elysabeth before she permitted herself to be ushered from the room.

'Welcome to Grafton.' John was leaning against the lintel, his arms folded. 'When I marry, I shall choose a woman who appreciates me, not a whey-faced misery.'

'Then you'll be fortunate. At the moment I see nothing to attract a wife.'

'Whoo-hoo.'

She walked across to the cupboard and poured herself another swig. 'John,' she said calmly, swinging round to face him. 'My husband was brought home dead across a pack ass, my children have been disinherited and I've been fighting in the courts for my widow's dower. My older son feels he's worthless and my younger son doesn't know how to laugh anymore. I'm not sure I do, John. And now you would like me to be a whore. How would you feel if it was asked of you? And you, Anthony,' his older brother had returned from playing magistrate, 'you should poxy well take your wife and her mother to London so they may lay flowers on her father's grave!' She marched across to the settle, sat down and took a gulp. 'Well, I'm waiting, John. Come on, *grovel*!'

'Your pardon, Elysabeth.' He hung his head.

'Lyssie.' Anthony sat down beside her; his long fingers curled over hers; her pain was like a mirror in his eyes. A childhood memory came creeping back. Him taking a beating for her when she had failed to latch the pigsty. No end of adventures and him always loyal. Dependable.

'Tell us about John Grey,' he said. 'Really tell us.'

She told them how Queen Margaret had sent him back to her. And with the telling came tears, like raindrops trickling down the panes of her face, and then a torrent that darkened the pleats of Anthony's doublet.

Afterwards there were no quips, no foolish comments and the three of them sat silent.

'If the queen had taken London,' Anthony said eventually, 'none of us would be in this bind.'

'No, and nor would she,' muttered Elysabeth.

'But she has managed to keep the old king out of Warwick's clutches and there are plenty still fighting for her in the north.' John prowled to the window and back. 'By my faith, were I a stranger coming to England this very day and given the choice of supporting a woman, a madman and a child or Edward of York, a soldier who never lost a battle, well...' He made a questioning face at them, his hands splayed.

'Yes, John,' Anthony muttered, 'but Margaret has too much spine to give up, and one day when he's a man, "the child" may come back to claim his throne. If we change sides now, we have to be certain King Edward's future is sure.'

'Or maybe all the people like us have to *make* it sure,' Elysabeth murmured. 'If I were in your shoes, Anthony, I should join the king's forces in Wales or the north, putting down any uprisings.

It will take time to prove yourself again but if you've the stomach for it, it can be done. John or Dick could go with you. They've no proven allegiance except being a Woodville.'

Anthony rubbed a hand across his stubble. 'I'd already considered doing so but it will mean fighting against some who were my friends but, yes, if a man like Pembroke will accept us, we can only try.'

'And I daresay we could cart Papa off to London for the next parliament,' suggested John. 'Dick could take over here.'

'You need a strategy, too, Lyssie.' Anthony shook her knee. 'Not to mention a bed soon. We can talk again in the morning.'

'I have thought of something,' she said slowly. 'Instead of seeking the patronage of Yorkist lords, perhaps we should look to the women. Use the backstairs, so to speak.'

'Mama's a liability now,' Anthony pointed out quietly. 'She has no more influence. You could try petitioning one of the new king's sisters. It won't help your case in Chancery but it might assist with regaining Tom's inheritance. Pity there's no new queen to influence the king.'

'Well,' declared Elysabeth, 'there's bound to be one shipped in soon and if all else fails, I'll plead that I'm half a foreigner and fling myself on her mercy. She perhaps can melt King Edward's heart.'

# 12: KATE

*28th October 1461, The Church of St Mary Magdalene,*
*Chewton Mendip, Somerset*

Leaves were falling fast. Only the St Michael's Mass flowers, pale mauve petals fluffed around deep gold centres, were lingering in the manor house garden at Chewton Mendip, old Lord Bonville's birthplace in Somerset. The household had been here through the late summer, mostly cloudy, irresolute weather that made Kate leave her straw hat on a peg and tuck a gauzy scarf into the neck of her gown when she went outside.

It had been the season for braving the bramble thorns for the most luscious of the blackberries, brewing cider, perry and elderflower wine, weaving corn dolls and holding a feast in the great barn for the harvest labourers.

Every day, as well as carrying out the manorial duties she now shared with Grandmother Bonville, such as speaking with the bailiffs, hearing disputes and receiving petitions, Kate either took Cecily out on horseback across the fields or walked her to the church. The child's Papa was in some unmarked grave in Wakefield but at least Grandfather Bonville's tomb was there (he had grandified the building with a tower in anticipation) and Cecily liked being lifted up to put a clutch of wildflowers on his monument, or, to be correct, on top of Lady FitzRoger. It was too early to explain to Cecily why her great-grandfather looked like a woman.

For sure, the Bonville crests were on his tomb but as yet no marble likeness so Lady Bonville, being of tidy mind, had insisted the effigies of the FitzRogers, a lord and lady who had once owned the manor, be shifted across for the time being.

'It looks better,' she decreed.

Today, instead of flowers, Cecily had scattered some leaves on the lady's stone bosom. Kate had kept a few back — beech, oak and hazel with gorgeous liveries of red, copper and gold — and she sat down beside Cecily on the steps of the preaching cross in the churchyard and, like any diligent mother, arranged the leaves in a row upon her dark woollen skirt and tried to point out their different shapes and hues. Cecily, at sixteen months, was more interested in the rabbit droppings. Yesterday it had been cow dung.

Kate had tried to compensate the child for having no father, grandfathers or great grandsires. Will would have scoffed at any timidity so she had let the precious infant totter through the long meadow grass even though she could not help thinking about vipers or ticks. Nor did she fuss when Cecily leaned precariously over the large fishpond or held out her plump palm to feed apples to the grumpiest of the stallions.

'Pah, she'll turn into a wench who cares more for horses than she does for men, if you're not careful,' warned Grandmother Bonville, but she was proud of the tiny one's fearlessness.

Cecily's eyes were no longer the ambiguous colour of a newborn but grey as the stones of Shute Hall. The colour and tilt came from the Bonvilles, too, and sometimes, Kate felt she was looking into Will's eyes, and her heart ached for Cecily's sake that the child's father would never know the joy of hearing her chatter and watching her blossom.

It was possible to recognise features of Cecily's grandparents in her little face: eyebrows from Lady Bess, Will's mother, and the Neville corn-coloured hair from Kate's father. It was fairer than Kate's, with a will that matched its owner. And the freckles? Well, too much time in the sun perhaps, teaching Cecily to love each tree and gather the wildflowers. That was how the world should be for a child.

And the world beyond the walls of the manor had thankfully grown safer. There was still anxiety: rumours that although my lord of Somerset had paid homage to the king, he had plans to ferment an uprising for King Henry in the southern shires, and more fears that the French might come before the winter, but with the passing of the Bonville lords and their feuding neighbours, lawlessness had abated. Thomas Courtenay, Earl of Devon, had been executed for treason and word was that Henry Courtenay had been summoned to the king. Presumably that was partly Richard's doing. He had read Kate's complaints and taken it on himself to become Cecily's guardian 'as a temporary measure'.

'Richard must be carrying so many honours now that you can probably hear his chains of office rattling from a league away,' Kate had commented to Eleanor but she observed how the gentry round about spoke of her brothers now with awe. Both her brothers! Bishop George had been appointed Lord Chancellor of England.

The incense of power had even wafted in her direction. Caps came off and forelocks were tugged in Shepton Mallet and Midsomer Norton; there was a formal reception every time she visited Wells (which was rather a nuisance when she just wanted to shop); innkeepers jostled to provide my Lady Harrington with refreshment; peddlers and chapmen, lawyers and clerics, masons and merchants called at Chewton or inquired for her at Shute. It was a wonder Somerset woodlice weren't coming out from under the flagstones to beg her to intercede with her brothers; certainly gentry who had supported the queen or sat upon the fence were now eager for her friendship. Even the Bishop of Bath and Wells had called at Chewton on his way back from Ned's coronation in London (the proper coronation not the swift business back in February), and he was full of praise for my lord of Warwick.

And 'my lord of Warwick' was becoming rather a nuisance, too. As head of the family and 'temporary guardian', he was trying to rule Kate as well, demanding that he approve the appointment of any new steward or bailiff and meddling in all sorts of tiresome ways as though she and Lady Bonville had the brains of snails. True, his letters always inquired how Cecily fared, not because of an uncle's fondness, Kate suspected, but an anxiety to make sure that her child stayed healthy and the vast inheritance did not pass outside the family. Lately, his letters had been more personal.

'Flou-ers,' said Cecily, and louder, '*flou-ers, Mama*!'

'Leaves, darling,' Kate corrected, swishing her thoughts back to the moment. 'One, two, three, f —'

A horseman's horn sounded up near the hall gate.

'Time to go, dumpling!'

Whisking Cecily up into her arms, she walked briskly through the garden postern, past the vanguard of house leeks and beans along by the pelotons of marjoram and chamomile and the spikes of lavender.

'A messenger. From the king this time, Kate.' Lady Bonville, with a couple of the hall dogs at her heels and Eleanor in attendance, had come out to find her. 'He is waiting in the hall. The new steward has seen he is given refreshment.'

'Hell take it,' muttered Kate and, remembering Cecily, clapped a hand across her lips.

Her twelve months of mourning would be over by the end of January. What would be in this letter? Richard's missives had become increasingly demanding. At first it had been:

'*Cousin Ned would welcome you to Westminster for Yuletide, dearest sister.*'

Followed by: '*Come at Yuletide and see what a fine king I have made of Ned.*'

But she could read between the lines. Her sister Joan had warned her. Richard was husband hunting.

Today's letter, signed with royal aplomb by Ned, invited her yet again. There was an enclosure from Richard as well.

'*I desire you to come to Westminster Palace for Yuletide, for the eyes of the world are watching and it behoveth all our kinsmen to show loyaltie to our new king and cousin, and unitee thereof.*

*Diverse times have I desired you to assure me that you will present yourself at court this Christmastide but you have hitherto not obeyed and accomplished the same, much to our lord's the king's displeasure and to mine also.*'

Before the final flourish of a signature, he wrote:

'*Mine own offices are so heavy and much multiplied, so that I desire to pass the guardianship of my niece's demesne as soon as I may.*'

The head of the Nevilles was slamming his fist on the table.

'I shall give you a letter of thanks to carry back to his highness,' Kate informed the messenger when she received him in the hall. He did not salute and bow. Instead, he asked, 'My lady, is your answer likely to be "no"?'

That was an impertinent question.

'What of it, sirrah?' Her stare rose from the yellow leopards stitched across his blood-red surcoat to canny old eyes surmounted by spiky, silver eyebrows.

'Such a message will be more than my life is worth, my lady. "You bring back an 'aye' from my lady Harrington", says my lord the king, "an' you take no excuses."'

'Was my lord of Warwick present when the king said that?'

'Aye, madame.'

She laughed. 'Good sir, I shall give you my answer tomorrow morning. You may stay at Shute this night.' She watched him bow and leave the hall, then she went to have a storm and a rant in the solar.

'But maybe you should go to Westminster, my lady,' Eleanor suggested, bending down to play tickle-spiders on Cecily's dirty palm. 'You have your whole life ahead of you.'

*As a milk cow?* she thought grumpily. But yes she would like to go. 'I suppose Richard imagines if he doesn't shove me into lawful wedlock with someone post-haste, I'll run away with some penniless Devon nobody.' *Like Robert Newton.*

Lady Bonville snorted. 'Ha, after all the slaying that's been going on, it's a wonder there are any noblemen left for marrying save hoary-headed widowers and hot-headed codlings.' Then the old lady bit her lip and crossed herself, remembering Will. 'I may be wrong but if your brother wants to give away Cecily's wardship, Katherine, mayhap someone's leaning on him for favours.'

'I don't think anyone ever leans on the kingmaker, madame. He writes that he is overloaded with lands, offices and trusts.'

'Then maybe he wants to *bestow* favour on some fortunate retainer. Let us be practical, Kate. You have received a summons from the king himself and while kings are two a penny these days, unless you, my dear, are past breeding and there's no land involved, you have as much choice in defying his will as catching the moon in a pail of water.'

'But we are still in mourning. Richard and Ned are being quite unreasonable.'

'Pooh, as if that makes a difference. Men with power are stubborn pigheads who always *think* they are right, are being told they *are* right by other men, and *won't* be gainsayed.'

'You should address the House of Lords on the matter,' muttered Kate, but there was truth in Grandmother Bonville's argument. 'However, my brother cannot marry me to anyone if I am not there, don't you see? Not *habeas corpus* but *habeo corpus*!'

'Yes, I realise that's your stratagem, my girl, but maybe your brother or the king will send his soldiers to make sure he shall have your *corpus*!'

Kate gathered her little daughter into her arms. 'But Grandmother, I don't want to have Christmas without Cecily. This will be the first time she's old enough to enjoy it.'

Lady Bonville blew the little girl a kiss, and Cecily giggled and blew one back. 'I believe this little poppet's future is more important than her first Yuletide, Katherine. If you want a say in her guardianship, you won't achieve it by staying out of reach.'

Kate paced the rushes. 'What if there is a rising?'

'Pah, I'll believe that when I see it,' muttered Grandmother Bonville. 'Kate, you can sit on your hands here until kingdom come or you can go and have a say in your child's future. Clearly your brother is too beset with other duties and wants to unshoulder his duty to Cecily. If he can appoint a powerful lord to oversee her lands, then it will bring stability back to these parts. You and I have done our best, God knows, but our people will feel more secure with a man in permanent charge and you need to give your opinion on the matter. And with Henry Courtenay hobbled, I know I can keep Cecily safe while you are in London if that is what concerns you. You'll only be gone a few weeks.'

The restless yearning for change had been growing inside Kate. It was time.

Eleanor added the last pinch of gold dust to tip the balance.

'Consider also, my lady, you've never been to court.'

Dancing beneath a hundred candles, flirting over the wine and sweetmeats? Westminster shimmered in her imagination and beckoned.

Beckoned like a lover.

# 13: KATE

*23rd December 1461, two days before the Feast of the Nativity,*
*Westminster Palace*

Crinkled, pink and restored after a steaming bath that had deliciously lapped her collarbones, Kate almost felt that the gruelling four-day ride from Chewton to London in freezing weather had been worthwhile. *Almost...* She cast a critical eye over her Sunday kirtle set out on the bed, and sighed because it was a mourning gown and out of style for court.

Just riding through the courtyard at Westminster Palace and seeing her sisters arriving had been enough to choke her confidence; her best headdress was inches lower than anyone else's and with her short stature, even if she wore one of the latest Burgundian caps, she would probably look like a chicken coop with a steeple.

She groaned and shuffled across the chamber in her towel. 'I was content with this until today,' she said ruefully, picking up her best headdress and plucking at the cowardly gauze. Eleanor had restarched it at Chewton but the packing and the London damp had made it limp again.

'Don't you fret, my lady. Give me leave to seek Paris lawn and stiffener down at Cheapside this morning, an' I'm sure I could copy the new styles by tomorrow.'

'And it would take you all night. Thank you, Eleanor, I appreciate your offer but I should still end up looking more like a strutting pinnacle than a person.'

'My lady, that's not true. Besides, since you are cousin to his royal grace and —'

'No one will dare snigger? No, it's all done with raised eyebrows.' Kate picked up the hand mirror and exercised her eyebrows. Only the left worked. 'They'll pick me to pieces like crows on a corpse.' She shrugged and tossed the mirror onto the bed. 'Nothing to be done but paste on a smi —'

The imperative knock at the chamber door silenced her and she quickly pulled across one of the bedcurtains and took refuge behind it. Probably one of the Lord Chamberlain's men inquiring if she needed more hot water. Peeping round she watched as Eleanor warily opened the door. There was a brief, low-voiced argument and a momentary tussle over the door's opening ability before a stocky, richly dressed man in his thirties limped in. For an instant, indignation swamped Kate's reasoning. It was not until he unwound the liripipe that scarfed his throat and removed the crimson, rolled-brim hat that she recognised him; candlelight and fading daylight glinted on thick brown hair, far less ginger than hers, but familiar nonetheless.

'My lord of Warwick,' announced Eleanor, addressing the curtain with a roll of eyes.

'Richard!' Kate exclaimed, emerging from concealment. It was impossible to curtsey dutifully in a tightly wrapped towel, but she managed a deferential nod and a slight knee bend. After all, he was the head of the family and the foremost earl of the realm.

'Oh,' he exclaimed, studying the cocoon wrapping his second youngest sister from breasts to calves, but if he felt a momentary embarrassment, there was no apology. 'Find something to do, girl!' That was to a disapproving Eleanor, who looked to be still reeling from his insensitive refusal to return later; she darted a curtsey and retired to a corner.

Kate had not seen Richard since her marriage day. The limp astonished her more than the deep vertical frown line, scoured above the bridge of his nose, or his flamboyant embroidered long coat, glinting with gold thread. He had not started wearing short doublets, she noted. Just as well, he did not have the legs.

'Have you sprained something?' She punctuated the question with a concerned smile, extending her free hand in welcome. Expensive musk assailed her as he kissed her on either cheek. His garments were cold and smelled of the outside air — a blend of frost and wood smoke.

'This? A memento from the skirmish at Ferrybridge — the day before Towton,' he explained, taking off his gloves and setting them on the chest at the end of the bed. 'Do not get cold.' Drawing her with him, he led her to the fire, where they each took up position either side like Gog and Magog. 'The surgeon says it will dissipate with time.'

'Before or after you slew your warhorse?' The story was he had put a blade through his destrier, announcing he would fight on foot with the common soldiers. Was it true?

The lordly nose wrinkled. 'Let's not talk about that, Kate. Sometimes it's necessary to make a gesture.'

'Very Roman, though rather a sacrifice for your poor horse. Well, it seems to have worked and put heart into your soldiers. Here we are.' She gestured to include the palace's tapestried walls and painted panelled ceiling. It was tactful not to mention their father or brother, or three generations of Bonvilles.

'Yes, here we are.' Gratitude for her forbearance gleamed in his eyes. Warmer now, he moved away from the heat and paused, staring at her supine black gown. 'You are not wearing that tonight?' He sounded like a husband rather than a brother.

'I am a widow, in case you have forgotten,' she replied gently, tempted at last to allot blame. 'And I thought we were following the fashions from Bruges. Didn't Phillip, Duke of Burgundy, make black acceptable?' Her jibe slid beneath his guard; Richard had never had much time for the Burgundians.

'Kate,' he began, turning back to face her. 'I am not sure how to couch this but the king is trying to put the past behind him. If he no longer outwardly mourns his father, nor should we. It *is* a year ago.'

'*Almost.*'

For an instant, an accusation of insensitivity quivered on her bow but she could not shoot that at him. Had he personally unhooked Father's head from the gate at York, or had the mayor of York quickly ordered a discreet change of decoration before the victors arrived? Richard must have detected some hurt in her for he took a deep breath and tried again.

'Mourning clothes might suit life at Shute but the eyes of the world are upon us now.' Ah yes, the words in his letter. She gave him stare for stare. Why make it easy for him?

'Lambkin,' he persisted, digging out a name she had forgotten, 'we are not trying to diminish those we lost but … for Lord's sake, this is the first breathing space Ned has had since he was proclaimed king.'

She did catch his meaning. Flaunting extravagance at this Westminster Christmas was like waving the banner of success at anyone still doubtful as to who the victors were. She looked away, suddenly finding the flames needed inspection.

'Kate, are you hearing me? I promise you when I have the time, I shall arrange for Father to have a proper funeral at Bisham and we'll all attend. Not a groat spared.'

'That will please our mother.'

Perhaps her tone was too sarcastic. She watched him prowl in the awkward silence, clasped fingers twitching behind his back, the gold chain of Yorkist sunnes and roses across his shoulders clinking as he moved. She had forgotten how he hated not to be taken seriously. If anything, that fault had been strengthened. Observing his splendour now, the great fur collar, sitting high at his nape, and the crimson long gown trimmed with gris at his ankles, she recalled that even as a boy he had chosen clothes that gave him dignity among the older lords.

'By God, I hope it will please you, too, Katherine, and the rest of the family.'

'Then you must let me know how I can help you when the time comes, Richard.' A verbal kiss of peace. *Compiesse et joy*, comfort and joy, like the new king's motto.

'Thank you, Kate.' He must have been seeking safer ground too, for he asked, 'I take it you are all happy with the steward I appointed at Chewton?'

That unsettled her as well. 'You are not thinking of shifting him somewhere else, I hope, brother, for he is very efficient and extremely good at dealing with Grandmother Bonville.'

'Excellent, then.' Another awkward pause. 'And my niece thrives?' A safe subject.

'She is a darling.' Then suspecting it was mainly Richard's tenacity that had kept the House of York at war, Kate plunged her own truth into him like a blade. 'I ... I was with child when your letter about Will arrived, Richard, but I miscarried not long after.'

He did not answer. Pain showed, followed by a compassion that softened his face, and she knew it was sincere, guessing he too must still long for a son.

'I try not to be *too* protective of Cecily,' she confided, feeling somewhat contrite now. 'I think ... I think about how Will would chide me for being foolish but sometimes I'm afraid ... when you only have one.' Dear God, she was missing the little mite dreadfully and now she was probably being womanly enough to bore Richard. 'I wish your girls might meet her. They are well?' He nodded. 'And is Nan to be with you this Yuletide?'

'No, she stays at Warwick.' He ran a finger down the twisted carving of the bedpost. The bell in the gatehouse of the courtyard sounded the hour. 'I had better go, let you get clothed.'

'Yes.' She looked down at her towel and pleated her lips.

For a moment, her brother's gaze lingered on her as a stranger's might meeting her for the first time. She supposed he was trying to see the little girl he had carried on his shoulders, to reconcile the child with the woman. She watched him collect his beaver hat, and tuck it beneath his arm. Concentrating on drawing on his gloves, he asked, 'Would you be offended if I ordered some tailors for you so you have something more suitable to wear tomorrow and at the Yuletide banquet?'

He must have misread the astonishment on her face for he came across to her now and said softly so that only she could hear. 'It can be done. *Anything* can be done from now on.'

Ah, so it *would* be letting him down for her plumage to be at fault. Suddenly she could almost breathe the power and pride that emanated from him. Here stood the real ruler of the realm, not Cousin Ned in a diadem that only caught the sunlight when Richard's shadow moved from off him. The cogs and wheels of the kingdom ran with the stream of energy that issued from her brother like a saint's aura.

'That would be most kind.' *What else could she answer?*

He inclined his head in acknowledgment. 'Very well, then. Farewell for the moment.' He drew her to him and kissed her forehead. 'It is good to have you here, little sister.' But his parting remark left her instincts rough-edged: 'There will be rewards, I promise you.'

It was joyous to be reunited with her brothers and sisters though Kate did not know many of them well. She had been sent to live with the Bonvilles from the age of thirteen and her older siblings had left long before that. But Joan, wife to Thomas, Lord Arundel, she remembered like a second mother and was much drawn to confide in her. Mind, Lord Arundel, a rather ill-tempered man, seemed mighty put out on Christmas Eve that the two sisters spent several hours together. Kate often caught him watching them that evening. She hoped he would not be called upon to be her darling's guardian for Joan looked wan and hollow-eyed and it was an easy wager that theirs was not a happy marriage, which made her even more on guard about her brother's scheming for her own future.

But if Richard was thinking about her usefulness, he was keeping the matter shelved as though he guessed that his little sister was a tangle that needed patient unwinding.

Kate found herself marvellously distracted by the festivities. On Christmas Eve, a great Yule log was hauled into Westminster Hall and set alight. After that, St George came a-knocking at the great doors with his fellow mummers, then Ned and his sister Meg led the carol dancing. At midnight, a rather inebriated court attended the Angel Mass in St Stephen's Chapel, and at dawn, with bleary eyes, they met again for the Shepherds' Mass. Later in the morning before the wassailing and the Christmas Banquet, the court followed the king in procession to a service in St Peter's Abbey, then everyone returned to feast on boar's head, goose and swan. There were tumblers, fire jugglers, who almost set the tablecloths ablaze, storytellers who kept everyone doubled in laughter, and much minstrelsy.

In the evening when the candles were refreshed and the trestles had been set back against the walls, the pipers and tabor players returned and the lords and ladies danced, their satins and velvets like the rich hues of jewels as they moved with such grace about the hall.

Not all the dancing was stately. Kate, whirled by her royal cousin up the line of clapping nobles, arrived breathless and happier than she could remember. Dancing with a king, even if he was a newly minted one and almost twice her height, was very flattering. Ned, with two battlefield victories behind him and no doubt, a trail of lovelorn girls — was truly the King of Hearts, a cheerful, comely young giant. There was gossip that he had once been overfond of the Earl of Shrewsbury's daughter but no matter, soon Richard would be finding him a princess. That was a very levelling thought! It was not only any unwed Nevilles who might be pushed into marriage beds by Richard but the king as well!

*Rewards, I promise you.*

Well, she was not going to be pushed.

The flowerdelice in the next dance with the two little royal dukes, Clarence and Gloucester, holding her hands, was less amusing. The older boy kept gleefully prancing the wrong way to confuse everyone. That was until the royal chamberlain, Lord Hastings, at a nod from Ned, removed him and poached his place. A well-favoured youngish man, Hastings did not make conversation, but since the threading beneath arches of arms required some concentration and he was probably worn out by organising the entertainments, Kate forgave him.

By the time the candles were down to stubs once more and she had kicked her heels in a salterello, glided in a sedate pavane, threaded, hayed, skipped, spun and clapped, the number of noblemen and knights she had touched hands with was beyond her sane reckoning. When she finally kicked off her leather dancing slippers and collapsed back spreadeagled on her bed, with the four posts spinning from too much wassailing, her self-esteem was nicely shined.

The rest of the week passed blithely with no potential husbands shoved in her direction, but behind the lilting melody of the viols and flutes, the sweet anthems of the choirs of St Stephen's Chapel and St Peter's Westminster, the cries of the children being spanked on Holy Innocents' Day and the shouts of the lords and commons hurling snowballs, the discerning could hear the continual drumbeat of rebellion. Ned might sit in the royal audience chamber beneath his canopy with a collar of expensive ermine and a jewelled sceptre across his knees but his power, stretching out like a thin web to all the corners of the kingdom, was by no means secure. There were still skirmishes with Queen Margaret's supporters in the Welsh and Northern Marches and the deposed king and queen had taken refuge at the Scots court and were enjoying the hospitality of the Dowager Queen of Scotland and attracting the interest of the King of France.

Kate did not like to criticise her royal cousin, but attending in the audience chamber with the other members of the court, she saw clearly that it was Richard who was ruling the realm. Ned might have more to say in the council chamber but here in the common eye, he seemed too languid.

As each matter was brought before him, Ned invariably had a whispered exchange with Richard, who always stood behind his chair of estate, before making a decision. Even when he seemed about to draw breath and make an answer straightaway, Richard would touch him on the sleeve and offer a suggestion. Ned seemed not to mind neither the interruption or the instruction, although occasionally Kate glimpsed a frown before he nodded and made a public reply to the matter before him. Sometimes he even directed Richard to step down and make a direct answer to a messenger or embassy without any consultation. Mind, Richard always couched his words with tact. He might begin with: 'His grace has decided...' or 'His highness wishes me to say ...' but it was clear who was making the decisions. Or was it?

Of course, she could see that the two men needed each other. The royal blood and military laurels belonged indisputably to Ned; the political skills belonged to Richard. To the less observant, it might seem a satisfactory situation but if she was sitting on Ned's cushions, she would be wanting to stretch her kingly wings, wave the royal sceptre with a lot more decisiveness and tell her brother to pipe down.

Was Richard expecting Ned to be meek and mild like old King Henry had been? If so, he was being really stupid. Surely he realised that the youth who had won the battles of Mortimer's Cross and Towton wasn't going to be fobbed off forever on a diet of crown wearings in the mornings and pretty girls in the evenings? And if she was thinking this, Heavens, what on earth was going on in Ned's head?

Lordy! Her royal cousin had caught her staring at him but she didn't dip her gaze. She was a Neville and she felt safe and mischievous enough to send him a commiserative grin. In return, she glimpsed the shrewd glint in Ned's eyes and it confirmed her suspicion that he knew exactly what he was doing. So who was manipulating who? And where would it leave her and Cecily?

Was the Queen Dowager of Scotland as deft at diplomacy as Richard?

He was clearly determined that the Scots lords would carry back a message to her that no invasion could topple Ned and he surprised everyone by declaring that there would be a great supper at Erber, his London house in Downegate, on the feast of the Epiphany. Kate was delighted. It would give Richard plenty more to think about other than husbands for her and she had no doubt it would be splendid. Another chance to wear one of her new gowns and maybe flirt a little.

Richard spared no expense. He invited Ned and all their kinsmen, the foreign emissaries and the leading dignitaries of London, who were still hopeful of seeing a return on the money they had lent to Ned's campaign earlier in the year, and anyone else worth bothering with. It would be two fingers up at any fool who thought to back Queen Margaret.

Thames Street, Downegate Street and all the lanes and alleys near Erber were already clogged with dismounting dignitaries when the king and his retinue arrived. Kate was pleased to be part of his company rather than making her own way there. It took a great amount of blowing on horns and ripe invectives to clear a path through the chaos. In her robe of mulberry velvet over a rose-hued underskirt, Kate had to step carefully to keep her hem unmired by the steaming clumps of horse dung as she accompanied the king's young brothers across from the stables.

Inside Richard's house, the benches lining the great hall on either side were so packed that only starving fleas could have squeezed in. The seating at the high table proved a tight peapod as well; the unfortunates at each end had to lean forward to let the pages with the ewers of perfumed water inch past to serve the guests of honour.

Richard was generous with his hospitality. Nothing was stinted. Malmsey, claret and bastard wines, mead, hypocras, perries, cider and the best of ales washed down the slabs of beef riall, the slithers of peacock, crane and partridge, the morsels of fishes *à folie* and Yuletide rosetts, fritters of crispy sweet batter.

From her privileged position on the dais, Kate watched the mercers and goldsmiths below the salt growing rosy with wine while their wives cooed with painted smiles at each other's finery. As the hubbub increased and pages kept refilling the goblets and tankards, so the more brazen among the wives bit their lips and ogled the nearest nobleman.

On the high table, the Nevilles outnumbered the Plantagenets and even most of those were half-Nevilles. Had any of the foreign dignitaries noticed? Kate tried counting all her relations between courses of flampayene royal and subtleties of almond-flavoured roses and saffron-tinted sunnes. Apart from Richard and Bishop George, there was her older sister Joan, and her husband, Arundel; John and his wife, Isabel; Eleanor and her husband, Lord Stanley; Thomas's widow, Lady Willoughby; Kate's aunt and godmother, Catherine Neville, Dowager Duchess of Norfolk; Ned's mother, the Duchess of York; Uncle William, the new Earl of Kent and ... well, a lot. She wondered if Cousin Ned had done his sums in that direction, too, for her siblings seemed to have married into every wealthy noble family in the realm, but the king seemed unbothered, listening attentively to a story that her brother George was telling him.

Richard had been busy squiring the king through the Twelve Days of Christmas but tonight Kate trapped him looking down the table at her and he was wearing his 'I must remember to do that' expression. Suddenly the comfits on the plate she was sharing with Lady Willoughby lost their appeal and she unwittingly splayed her hand across the low triangle of embroidered silk that drawbridged her cleavage.

O Jesu, surely he wasn't going to offer her in marriage to one of the Scots or give Cecily's wardship as a reward to 'Black William', the new Earl of Pembroke, who was galloping around Wales besieging castles of Queen Margaret's allies? She should not have mentioned the Courtenays either, he might give her as a peace offering to Henry in return for a change of loyalty.

Damnation! She would need to outwit him somehow.

Richard had always been a chess player. Even her happiest memory of him carrying her on his shoulders at Bisham Fair had been tainted some years later when one of her sisters told her he had only done it to evade being recognised by his tutor.

'It was this big.' Ned's voice carried along the table, crashing through her thoughts. He was stretching out his hands.

Next to Lady Willoughby, the Duke of Clarence giggled dirtily.

'Ned is talking about fishing, my lady.' Nine-year-old Gloucester, on the other side of Clarence, twitched his mouth disapprovingly at his brother's manners.

'Didn't you catch a perch bigger than that in the Axe, Katherine?' Richard called out to her. Fancy him remembering their fishing trip on his brief visit to Shute two years before! The row of faces jerked round in her direction like folk watching the ball at tenez. She felt her skin scorching but she was not going to be embarrassed. This time at court had already strengthened her spine and she was the mother of a very wealthy heiress.

'Yes, brother,' she answered, her mind trying to outguess his strategy.

'Truly, cousin?' prompted Ned, looking genuinely impressed, but male obsession for proof made him add, 'Did you weigh it?'

'A three pounder, your grace.'

'I think,' exclaimed King Ned, sucking in his cheeks and sending her a delicious smile, 'that we need to have a fishing contest. Would you be party to that, cousin?'

'On the Thames in January!' exclaimed her godmother, Aunt Catherine.

'No, Kate, you can't possibly consider such a thing,' agreed her sister, Joan.

But Kate could. She was nineteen now, the same age as Ned. Hardly in her dotage. 'Of course, I accept your challenge, your grace.'

'Bravo!' He leaned out to address his new chamberlain down the table. 'Arrange it, my lord!'

# 14: KATE

## *7th January 1462, Westminster Palace*

Insane, thought Kate, rugged up in so many layers that she felt like a she-bear as she followed a torchbearer across the wet cobbles of the palace courtyard towards the Watergate. Her cloak, lined with rabbit fur had sensible slits for her arms. Beneath it, for further warmth, she was wearing a stomacher of budge — a lamb's wool fleece laced tight from neck to thigh — extra petticoats under her gown, and scarfing her throat (on Joan's insistence) a veil rolled thick as an eel. She did not have fishing gloves, so for now she was wearing her riding gauntlets.

It was a moisty morning. A light fog obscured the beacons of Lambeth Palace across the river and wreathed misty auras around the flambeaux that burned above the walls behind her. Somewhere a dog barked and men's voices, sharing some jest, reached her from the royal barge, which was waiting for her at the wooden quay below the steps. A lantern dangled on the vessel's ornate prow, and on tall poles along its sides spluttered torches, each sending reflections dancing out in a set across the black water, constantly fragmenting into glittering shards and melding until they vanished where night and river were indistinguishable.

One of the bargemen hastened up to welcome her. 'Good morrow, my lady. His grace has not yet arrived.'

But it seemed he just had. The sentries at the gate were stamping their halberds to alert and she heard several heavy footsteps approaching. Aboard the barge there was a sudden, swift rattling of oars as the rowers scrambled into their places.

There was no mistaking Ned because of his height. He was flanked by two companions (no doubt, dragged forth from their beds out of duty) and two young torchbearers. Four servants were at his heels carrying an assortment of baskets and fishing rods.

'Here she is! Well done!' Damp fur and strong cousinly arms embraced Kate and swept her onto the cleated plank bridge ahead of the rest.

'Up river, then, lads,' Ned ordered, once the last pannier was safe aboard. Within the instant, the tethering rope, freed from the capstan by one of the linkboys, was flung on deck, and at the helmsman's shout, the oars rose in precision and dipped. The barge surged smoothly forwards but the royal hand beneath Kate's elbow made sure she was steady as he urged her towards the curtained heart of the barge.

There was a whiff of vomit from the planking but the small pavilion — cered cloth on the outside and silken stripes within — was fragrant with freshly strewn herbs. Kate had never been in one of these before. Hmm, rather like being within a giant four-poster bed, she decided, save that the two oil lamps suspended on a rail beneath the canopy revealed an unlit brazier, a low fixed trestle and two benches set at right angles to a luxurious settle large enough for two. The Yorkist insignia of sunnes-in-splendour and falcons-in-fetterlock glinted upon the plump bolsters arranged along the wooden back but the seat cushions, worn and shiny at the edges, still bore Queen Margaret's crown-necked swan device. She wasn't sure what lay beyond the scarlet curtain behind the settle, a close-stool for a queenly bladder?

'Make yourself comfortable, cousin,' Ned exclaimed, gesturing towards the royal seat. 'And these are for you.' He plucked a pair of gloves from his belt.

'Why, thank you, your grace,' she exclaimed, discovering they were proper winter fishing gloves, the sort that ended at the joints and freed the fingertips for delicate work.

'Your pardon but it will take a while to reach my favourite spot and I didn't order the brazier to be lit yet but say if you want it. Hey, here's the rest of the competition, Kate. She's here, Tom.'

'Brave lady.' The Irish lilt to Thomas, Earl of Desmond's voice was a delight. 'Mind now, in Ireland this is nothing. We send out the colleens every morning to blow away the clouds before the break o' fast.' He kissed her gloved hand with great charm. She had met him during the feasting, a short, lithe and boyish nobleman, with dark, fey curls escaping from beneath his fur hat.

The other man, a good deal taller, drew the curtains before he turned. Now his face was lit, Kate recognised Ned's chamberlain, Lord Hastings.

'Lady Harrington.' He removed his hat and bowed with the serious grace that he had shown when he had danced with her. If he was supposed to accompany Ned everywhere as part of his duties in organising the royal leisure, she felt rather sorry for him.

'We had the rods prepared last night, my lady,' he was saying. 'They each have a four-fold horse-hair line, so I'm told, but if you prefer to set up your own…?'

'No, that sounds excellent.' She sank against cushions meant for royal backs, feeling very privileged.

'Do not get too comfortable, sleepyhead,' grinned Ned, flicking her nose.

'Your pardon, your grace,' she laughed, rising to her feet again. 'So what bait did you plan for us to use?'

For some reason, Ned glanced silkily at his chamberlain and she sensed her question had raised some old jest between them. 'Red worms, Kate. Worms of Lancaster.' He pushed out through the curtains and Desmond followed.

She relaxed somewhat, admitting to the thrill of being in such illustrious company, but deep down her sense of propriety was rampant, censoring her for being the only woman out here with a handsome king who was unmarried, not to mention two other good-looking men whose marital status was unknown to her. Don't worry, her reason counselled, you are no unwed virgin. Besides, you are clothed like an apple dumpling and you do have two rows of oarsmen to chaperone you. And even if the king were to be interested in you, which would be as miraculous as a woman becoming Holy Roman Emperor, your brother would put a dampener on it instantly. Anyway, what can you do about anything? Ask the king for the barge to be turned around?

'Are you hungry, Lady Harrington?' The lord chamberlain summoned in the servants. Kate watched the activity with growing delight. They clothed the table, brought in squat candles floating in small ewers of water, unswathed several flasks of mulled wine and set out covered platters. She leaned across and peeped under the lids. Cheeses, viands and fresh, warm bread rolls.

'Hmm,' she sighed, breathing in the yeasty smell with a smile.

'Help yourself, my lady.' Hastings waved the servants out. 'Mead or wine?' He took up the flask of her choice, poured them both spiced wine and sat down on the left bench, nursing the warm mazer between his palms.

Kate ripped up a roll and helped herself to the repast. Noblewomen were supposed to eat like sparrows but her appetite was definitely owl-size. 'This is excellent,' she told him, assuming that he had been responsible.

His half-smile was a courtesy. He lifted off the mazer lid and sat staring pensively at the wine's surface. Perhaps it was just the lamplight which made him look weary or maybe he disliked early rising.

'I don't fish,' he said by way of conversation. 'This is something new for me. The king's passionate about it so I imagine I shall have to learn fast.'

'Well, there must be a copy of Dame Juliana Berner's treatise on fishing in the royal library, sir.' Then she added mischievously, 'You can learn all about whether to use cankerworms, cow dung grubs or...' she added, eyeing the table, 'cheese, tallow and honey.'

'Thank you, my lady,' he replied dryly. 'I can see I've been missing out on an entire new world.' He downed the rest of his wine and set the vessel back on the table. 'Truth to tell, there hasn't been much time to sport this year, what with the Scots and French funding Queen Margaret against us. I have no doubt she'll create more havoc, come the spring. I believe you lost your husband at Wakefield?'

For a moment, Will's face was a blur in her memory. She must have frowned for he said swiftly, 'Your pardon, my lady, I should not have mentioned it.'

'Sir, there are many widows in England and —'

'And bachelors!' exclaimed Ned, breezing in and collapsing on the seat beside her. 'What, no ale?' Having thwatted their conversation in a different direction, he helped himself to the mead and a pie. 'For sure your brothers would like to have a say in finding me a wife, Kate,' he added, knuckling away the pastry crumbs from his lower lip, 'but *they* haven't got to bed her.' He downed the mead, grimaced, and refilled his cup with the spiced wine. 'Well, to the Devil with that. Come on, William! If you are going to learn this art, it won't be hanging in here quaffing with a pretty girl.'

*Pretty?* Kind of Ned but fulsome. She was here because she could reel in perch. Glad of the warm drink inside her belly, she followed them out. Ned seemed to know the river very well, for he commanded the helmsman to steer closer to the bank and then some fifty paces later, ordered a halt. In her estimation, they were not far beyond the village of Chelsea but it was too misty to be sure.

There was a neat splash as they made anchor. The rowers set their oars to rest and sat in silence so as not to disturb the fish. The only sound was the lap of water bothering the sides and a single, grebe-like honk from the reeds.

'Bring the boat alongside,' ordered Desmond quietly.

Oh Lord! So they were not fishing from the barge. Kate found it irksome having to kick her petticoats out behind her as she descended the rope ladder at the rear of the boat, but Ned steadied her in and seated her next to Hastings.

'We'll be the ones rowing back, I suppose,' she quipped softly to Hastings as the King of England and my lord of Desmond took charge of the oars.

'Oh, he's too old,' chortled Ned, swiping at his chamberlain's knee and received a swat in retaliation.

'Behave, Englishmen! Such horseplay, tsk, tsk!' Desmond waited with raised oar to achieve unison again.

The current carried them upriver. Now it was possible to see the reeds not far away and back beyond the dark hulk of the barge Kate glimpsed the beginnings of the dawn. She had not been so truly happy for months. There had been very few times like this with Will and certainly not when they had fished at Whitford or taken his father's flat-bottomed boat out on the Axe.

'Whoa!' Ned ordered and lowered his dripping oar alongside Kate. As she shifted closer in, so did Hastings.

Desmond dealt out the equipment. 'Do you want some help with your rod, my lord chamberlain?' he asked Hastings.

'Surely it will be easier if I help him,' exclaimed Kate and when Ned gave a snort of laughter, she realised the Irish lord had been wicked.

'Thank you, my lady.' Dry amusement laced Hastings' voice.

'I should have warned you that Desmond's a cursed rattle at this ungodly hour,' chuckled Ned. 'But Kate will forgive you, won't you, cousin?'

Her answer was a soft laugh.

The fishing rods were well made. Kate's was shorter than the others. Very flexible, she approved, testing it.

'In Ireland,' prattled Desmond, 'they say a fishing rod should have four, no, I lie, t'ree things: the satin texture of a colleen's thigh, the suppleness of a young rabbit and the resilience of a harlot.'

'In Ireland they say too much,' replied Hastings, but he laughed nonetheless.

'I don't quite understand the last one, my lord Desmond,' Kate admitted, both shocked and amused still at the earl's careless wit.

'Why, *leannán*, a harlot will bear any weight and bend as you please.'

'Oh.' Kate felt her cheeks burning but she managed to laugh at her own innocence.

'Can we attend to the business in hand?' muttered Ned.

'Have you heard of the flying fish of Limerick,' began Desmond, 'that leapt int —'

'Don't —' cut in Hastings, and then, so as not to create a rift in Yorkist-Irish relations, he added quickly, 'Don't bold jests frighten the fish?'

'Yes, Desmond, keep a still tongue for once!' That was from Ned. He was busy. Kate heard the flick of line and a plop of bait followed by the gentle splash as his cork float hit the water.

'To be sure, I was forgetting,' chortled the Irish nobleman. 'Serious business, eh?'

'It *is* when you've never fished before,' complained Hastings. 'Ouch! God d —'

'Save the hooks for the fish, friend.' Desmond's cast landed neatly.

'Let me,' Kate offered, propping her fishing rod between her knees after she had set her line. 'Pray pass it to me.' Diving her hand into the little box of red worms that was set between four pairs of feet, she baited it for Hastings and deftly flicked the line out on his side of the boat.

They sat in companionable quiet waiting for the fish to bite. Kate's bared fingers were chilled, but she did not care. In summer the midges and mosquitoes would have plagued her and she was simply grateful there was no stiff, freezing wind.

'Ah, come to me, my sweet.' Ned was at last playing a fish. Finally he drew it to the side and rocked the boat, bringing it aboard in a small scoop net. A goodly perch.

'You call that a decent size, your royal highness of England,' said Desmond. 'We didn't come along for minnows.'

Ned made a face. Save for the flapping of the catch in the wooden bucket, the boat lapsed into a businesslike silence once again.

Kate felt the gentle investigation of the bait. 'Oh sorry,' she muttered, knocking back into Hastings' shoulder as she whipped the line back and lost it. No, there it came again.

'Is yours bigger?' asked Desmond, leaning forward, ready to help with a net. 'Because I'm wagered on a win for the fairer sex.'

'Isn't your money on yourself?' panted Kate, landing the fighting, flashing silver creature.

'Ah, that's no fun,' wailed Desmond. 'I'd always win, see. A beauty! *Maith thú*!'

'Excellently done! Hey, we should have a wager, too, Kate.' This was from Ned. 'If I win, you kiss all three of us.'

That created more blushes inside her fur hood.

'Pah!' she protested good-naturedly. 'And what if *I* win?'

Ned laughed. 'You kiss us all out of sheer triumph, of course. And then, my sweet dove, you shall have a ring for your finger and a silver rattle for Cecily.' Kind of him, though Cecily was past rattles.

'I can feel something,' exclaimed Hastings. 'I can feel a lot.'

'Ah, that would be Lady Kate's doing, Hastings,' Desmond quipped. 'No, slowly, slowly! Tease it, man!'

Hastings almost landed his catch in the royal face. With Ned's help, they got it in. A modest bream.

'Huzzah!' exclaimed the ruler of the realm. 'See, William, it's not that hard.'

'I can think of better things to do at this hour, your grace.'

'So can I,' concurred the Irish lord. It surely was deliberate when the toe of his boot nudged Kate's for the sky was light enough to show his irrepressible grin, but pulling in his line a few minutes later, he discovered his bait had gone, and as she had withdrawn her toes well beneath her skirts, from then on he concentrated on proper angling.

By the turn of the tide, she could feel her blood had chilled. A quarter of an hour more and she would have been shivering. The weak sun was hiding behind a depressingly grey sky. The men, fortunately, were also weary, and Ned and Desmond took the oars again. Rowing would have warmed her, she reflected ruefully. Could she and Hastings have done it as well, though?

'King Edward of Caernarvon was much criticised for rowing on the river,' observed Ned, lifting his oar so the boat drifted sweetly to the side of the barge.

'And more besides,' murmured Hastings.

'Ah, so I was only asked along to save your reputation, your grace,' Kate teased, knowing his namesake had been too fond of men.

'Not just that, sweetheart. Hey, I'm famished. For Heaven's sake, let's have some repast.'

On board the royal barge, the servants had lit the brazier and were waiting with hot broth, and the oarsmen gathered round as the catch was weighed and measured. To her astonishment, Kate's perch was deemed the largest.

'The lady wins,' whooped Ned, grabbing Kate's arm and thrusting it aloft. 'You know what that means,' he teased, hugging her to him as the four of them returned to the pavilion.

'Oh dear,' she said, and holding Desmond's shoulders, she reached up and pecked him chastely. 'My mother would not approve of any of this.'

'Oh come on, Kate,' coaxed Ned. 'Hey, I want something decent.'

It wasn't decent but indecent. Her mouth felt assaulted and he did not let her go straightaway. Will had tried kissing like that but she had not encouraged him. Clearly Ned was far more experienced but, well, she felt like drawing her hand across her lips. At least this would all be over in a moment.

'My lord chamberlain?' A sudden shyness claimed her. She reached out but Hastings stayed apart, arms folded. A sapphire finger ring glinted on his left hand as his breath moved within his body. Perhaps he shared Edward II's tastes. Gathering her courage, she looked up reluctantly, expecting coldness. He was feigning disapproval. Or was he? There was a slight curl at the corners of his mouth. A fish to be played? No, dear God, why should she even think that? Swallowing with embarrassment, she lowered her arms, but before she could mend the silence, she had her answer.

'With your permission, madame, later. Unlike these two rascals, I prefer not to embrace a woman smelling of fish.'

'*Sir!*' she exclaimed.

'No,' he protested laughing as Ned and Desmond grabbed his arms, threatening to force him to his knees before her. 'No, madame, I meant me.'

Well-furred and booted, Richard Neville was waiting for them on the quay like a true courtier. Kate silently applauded him; he always remembered his duty to Ned as king.

'Lady Katherine angled with brilliance.' Ned almost clapped her brother on the shoulder but remembering his glove smelled of bait, he buffeted the air instead.

'But did she catch anything, your grace?' Oh, the family pride again!

'Hey, yes, she's won a ring for her finger,' the king answered simply, with a grin over his shoulder at Desmond and Hastings. 'And a silver rattle for Cecily. Meantime, we lords are for the bathhouse, and our dear chamberlain, Lord love him, has arranged a hot bath for you as well, my lady, in the queen's quarters.'

'Have you, Lord Hastings?' Kate swung round to him in great delight. 'How very kind.' She could not fathom this man. Was his excuse not to kiss her genuine?

He inclined his handsome head. 'Let me know if it is satisfactory, Lady Katherine. God willing, we shall have a new queen soon and it would be good to know that the apparatus works efficiently. A servant will conduct you there.' He bowed and hastened after the king.

'Well, I mustn't let the water cool,' murmured Kate. 'The queen's bath. How gratifying.'

'Wait.' Richard delayed her before she could follow the waiting servant and asked in a whisper, 'Did Ned behave?'

'Of course, although I learned some new curses when he lost the bait.'

'You know very well what I mean, Katherine. If I had a castle for every widow he's seduced since he discovered girls…'

'Oh to be sure, Richard, we had a Druid orgy with piles of mistletoe and fish guts. Honestly, brother, do I look dressed for committing adultery on the river in mid-winter at dawn with two married men and a bachelor king?'

'*Two* bachelors.'

'*What?*'


It was not quite the thing to have done. Finding herself neighboured at dinner by her second eldest brother, Bishop George, who was in a holier-than-thou temper, she tried not to yawn through his stern lecture on behaving herself. It helped that they were also watching two make-believe ships being trundled into the hall in honour of the king's guest, my lord

Earl of Desmond. Lines of servants on either side the hall billowed waves of azure fabric sewn with silvery fish in between the vessels and, to Kate's delight, a mock naval battle commenced.

George's peroration on her morals was drowned out by firecrackers and a great deal of smoke, which irritated his throat and set most of the spectators a-coughing. The carnage ended with sea dragons and a giant frog rising to devour the bodies of those who were struggling amidst the waves.

'Enough!' guffawed Ned, mopping his eyes, and the victorious captain sketched a hasty bow and was born off aloft by his triumphant henchman. Kate escaped while the defeated were being tidied away, and at the king's whooping encouragement, Hastings, who had been responsible for the entertainment, wearily rose to take his bow.

Kate waited until the crowd around the lord chamberlain had dispersed before she made her way round the side of the hall to present her congratulations. 'And the sea dragons were so enthusiastic,' she added, 'especially the baby ones.'

'You liked the dragons.' He smiled at last, a quiet devastating smile that might easily wobble the knees of any woman from Cornwall to Northumberland.

'I adored the dragons, my lord, and the frog, even if the back legs got left behind.'

'You must agree it was a pity that Sir Tristan's sword broke.'

'Ah but winning the combat against Sir Marhaus with half a hilt merely proved Sir Tristan was a champion, my lord.'

'Yes, there is that.' They stood side by side watching the dancers who had now taken charge of the floor. 'Was the bath to your liking?'

'Bath? Oh, your pardon. Yes, indeed, thank you, although the taps could do with greasing and I noticed a lot of cobwebs in the rafters.'

'All easily remedied.' He must have noticed her foot was tapping to the music for he added, 'And since my task in the revels is over, maybe I can cast off my office for a little space. Would you care to dance, Lady Harrington?'

She cocked her head on one side. 'Are you sure, my lord? You look dead on your feet, if I may say so, and it will be rather shameful for me if you swoon at my feet in the middle of a *volte tonda*, let alone a basse dance.'

An appreciative smile lit his face. 'Then I shall endeavour not to.'

It was a lively Italian tune requiring so much whirling and skipping that partners only linked their little fingers and the gliding steps required the ladies to keep their heads up but their eyes modestly downcast. Just as well, for she needed to watch her footwork. Twice she went the wrong way and had to be twirled back, but she only trod on Lord Hastings' shoe once.

Will had not enjoyed dancing. Lord Hastings clearly did and in the second slower dance, which required more intimacy, looked her in the face with attentive gallantry every time their hands met, as a gentleman should. More than the last time they had danced together.

'Do you think you will ever go fishing again, my lord?' she asked as they took steps forward in stately fashion. The feel of his skin beneath her fingertips was exciting.

'I daresay I shall.' His glance flicked forwards to where the king and Desmond stood quaffing. 'How long do you remain at Westminster, my lady?'

'Only until we have a hard frost and the roads back to Devon are passable. To be honest, I am concerned my little daughter will be fretting.' Now Lord Hastings would probably think less of her for being too doting. 'I do not suppose you have much chance to be at home, my lord?' she asked, diverting the conversation back to him.

'No, nor a true home as such and little enticement at the moment. Last time I had to endure three hellish days of petitions. The entire district descended upon me with their grievances. It seems I am looked upon as a royal ear. They think if they shout loud enough, their words will reach the king.'

'You need a dragon then to guard your door.'

'My door and my honour, Lady Harrington. The number of nubile daughters hauled into my vision by their soliciting fathers not to mention widows with loosened garters and gaping bodices.'

For such a handsome accomplished man, his expression was so woe begone that Kate laughed wholeheartedly. 'You don't need a dragon then, you need a wife.' Idly spoken but suddenly the air between them seemed taut. She felt breathless and foolish. 'I am sorry. I spoke out of turn,' she said awkwardly. 'I was but jesting.'

'Of course, Lady Katherine.' The answer was diplomatic.

'Hey, one of the delights of being king,' said a familiar voice behind her, 'is that no one may gainsay us. Let us dance, cousin. It's a royal command.'

'What happens if I say no?' Kate asked mischievously, folding her arms.

'You get thrown in with the ravens at the Tower for the night.' He dug out her wrist and she had to hurry to keep pace with his great stride. 'You and old Hastings seem to be trotting well together,' he observed.

'I think he needs a wife.'

'Excellent. What a good notion. You will do him to a nicety.'

Kate halted, shocked. 'Me?'

'Hey, surely dear old brother Richard told you what he had in mind — with my blessing, of course? Remember, I promised you a ring for your finger.' Instantly, she dropped his hand and stood staring up at him as if her feet had been pasted to the flagstones.

'Not with a man attached, you didn't.'

Ned managed to look sheepish and annoyed at the same time.

'Kate, we are attracting a lot of attention.'

'I do not care, your grace. Please don't gull me.'

'Kate, I'm the king, my sweet, and I think it's a match made in Heaven. Unless you want to pay a hefty fine to stay unmarried… Do you?'

'I am considering kicking you in the royal groin.' She clapped a hand to her lips realising the enormity of what she had just said. It had to be the Earl of Desmond's influence. Fortunately, Ned nearly doubled over with laughter while she stood red-faced, not daring to run away.

'Your grace?' Richard materialised, doglike, at Kate's elbow.

'What are the penalties for treason, my lord? Your sister just threatened to —'

Delivering a don't-you-dare-say-it look, she sank into a placatory curtsey and Ned spluttered even more and then he wiped his eyes with his knuckle, drew himself up to full regal height which made her feel like David crouched before Goliath. 'You Nevilles have a very high opinion of yourselves.' Those nearby froze with interest. 'And quite deserved,' he added pricking the bubble of dangerous tension surrounding them. 'Good night to you, my lord cousin. Lady Harrington, you have leave.'

She set her hand on Richard's wrist and let him lead her to the side of the hall.

'What in God's name was that about?'

'Nothing of importance.'

'He must have said something to annoy you.' She gave him her best scowl but he was out to interrogate the truth out of her. 'Kate?'

'Well, he asked me if I'd consider being queen of England since I was already using the royal bath.'

'Jesu!' For a moment Richard believed her. The look on his face was priceless.

'No, my lord brother, of course he didn't. Ned is not a fool and neither am I. Did I mention I am leaving for Shute tomorrow, Richard? No? Well, I am.'

But her brother was too clever for her 'Not without royal permission, little sister. It would be seen as an insult and your horse will get bogged to its hocks before you reach Kingston.'

She opened her mouth and shut it again and then she asked: 'Do you remember when you carried me on your shoulders at Bisham Fair, Richard?'

'Yes, what of it?'

'Did I nearly strangle you at the time?'

'No, Kate.'

'Pity!' she muttered under her breath as she walked away.


Surely Ned had been teasing her, she told herself as she snuggled against Eleanor's back in the bed that night to keep warm. A match with Lord Hastings? No, out of the question. She wanted a husband who would be faithful. Lord Hastings' fine feathers attracted women, *beautiful* women. Kate had noticed the heads turn, the swish of maiden mane that betokened interest, the biting of lips, the side glances in seductive fashion. No, she was too much of a sparrow, a plump sparrow, for such a well-plumed hawk and she would tell her brother so. She might agree that he should become Cecily's guardian but without the conjugal strings attached. But then that too had consequences. Oh, curse everything, she needed to think this through! Joan, her older sister, might prove a willing confidante, but when Kate knocked on her sister's bedchamber door after Mass next morning, Arundel told her gruffly that her sister was indisposed and seeing no one.

That was concerning. There had been strange bruises on her sister's face. She must mention that to Richard since he was head of the family. Mind, he was so busy, she stood more chance of entertaining St Peter to sweet wafers and a beaker of cider.

She awoke next morning to an excess of minstrelsy and tugged back the bedcurtains. 'Eleanor? What in heaven…'

A giggle reached her from the open window. 'Come and look, my lady. Poor things, they are all red-nosed. A wonder their fingers can manage the strings in the cold.'

Kate wriggled out of bed and padded over. 'No, Eleanor, stay where you are,' she murmured, setting a hand upon her handmaid's shoulder so she could stand on tiptoe. 'Oh, my goodness. There's three of them.'

'I think you're being wooed, my lady.'

'By a castrato. Oh, this is ridiculous.'

'The piper is very winsome and … oh lordy!' Eleanor clasped a hand to her mouth and ducked back. 'They've woken my lord of Arundel.'

Weighted by insults, a gruff voice belonging to Kate's brother-in-law, Fitzalan, Earl of Arundel, rumbled forth from the next chamber's window. The singer persisted. Someone who was not a castrato swore back at the earl and then there was a splash as my lord hurled the contents of his piss pot at the entertainment. Ripe expletives rose upward and the trio retreated, huffy, angry and spattered, across the puddled courtyard.

Kate jammed a fist into her mouth and laughed until the tears came. 'Poor fellows,' she spluttered. 'How unfair.'

'I daresay they were paid well by your suitor, my lady. Do you think it is my lord of Desmond? He made a meal of kissing your hand yester eve.'

'Perhaps. Go after them, Eleanor, and give them a silver penny each for their trouble and inquire who sent them.'

A woman's pleading and shrill cry of 'No' came from the bedchamber next to them and Kate's grin froze. Eleanor hesitated for an instant and then said softly, 'Pardon me for saying so, my lady, but it's not the first time.'

'No,' said Kate grimly. 'But if I have anything to do with it, it's going to be the last!'


She waited until her brother-in-law had left her sister's chamber before she knocked gently on the door and let herself in. Joan Neville was still abed. There were fresh bruises on her cheeks and bared arms and her freckled skin was the hue of a death monument.

'I came to see if you had breakfasted, sister,' Kate declared brightly, coming further into the chamber. 'Ah.' A wooden tray of pottage stood unwanted on the uppermost bed step.

'I tried to persuade her, my lady,' muttered the aged maidservant, smoothing her skirts with a sniff. 'The master is so quick to find fault.'

'Is there anything I can do?' asked Kate, reaching out to clasp her sister's hand upon the coverlet. Joan might be in her late-thirties but her suffering made her look far older.

'I am not well but Fitzalan will have everything his way,' she murmured weakly.

Kate pulled a face. 'He should know better at his age. How old is he now?'

'F-five-and-forty.'

'Hmm, I think I shall definitely speak to Richard about this.'

The bleakness in her sister's pale blue eyes was pitiful. 'You think Richard can fix *this*?' she muttered bleakly, shaking her head.

'Richard *is* the law or so everyone tells me. Consider it done, Joan.'

'You are very kind ... and very young.' *And happily a widow at the moment*, thought Kate. There was too translucent a quality about her sister's skin. 'You were named for Aunt Catherine, weren't you?' Her sister's fingertips reached out to touch Kate's cheek. 'You have her zest for life.' Her breast rose unhappily with a deep breath. 'Enjoy the music while you can, dearest. It was for you, this morning, wasn't it?'

'Unless they chose the wrong window.' Kate gave a little gurgle of self-conscious laughter. 'Maybe it was for Aunt Catherine!' She clapped a hand to her mouth and grinned at her sister. Dimples appeared in Joan's cheeks.

'Ah, you are a philtre for my woes, Kate. I wish we could have seen more of one another these last years.'

'Unfortunately, that is the way of things.' Kate picked up the tray, wishing Arundel was there so she might crash the whole lot across his head. 'Now how about we warm this pottage?'

And if Richard would not listen, she would go to Ned.

She found the King's Painted Chamber empty save for Ned's servants putting new sheets on the royal bed and swabbing mud off the floorboards. The royal council must still be in session. The councillors usually met before attending Mass with Ned in the royal chapel and then they would disperse to fulfil their various duties. Kate hastened down and waited outside for the session to end. They came out early and as Richard was not in conversation with Ned, she was able to draw him aside in the Little Hall. Lord Hastings overtook them, doffing his hat to her as he strode past but he did not linger. She did not know whether to be disappointed or much relieved.

'Be brief, I've much work to do,' growled her brother, striding across to stand with his back to the fireplace. He hitched up his fine woollen robe to warm his calves before the glowing embers.

'I have a very important favour to ask. That you will tell Lord Arundel to stop hitting poor Joan. It does not take a village idiot to see she is ailing and needs kindness.'

Richard looked down at her. 'Are your wits gone?'

'Can't you … can't you strip him of some lucrative office if he refuses?'

'By Heaven, you are such a bird-brain, Kate. He adores your sister.'

'*What*? But I heard her cry out and he was so horrible.'

'Because she won't eat. He's trying to save her life. She's very ill.'

She swallowed. 'I thought that he had been hitting her. The bruises —'

'Well, you're mistaken. The bruising is coming from within, God help her. She has not long for this world. Oh God, Kate, you are such an innocent.'

He left her standing by the fire, feeling stunned, blind and incredibly stupid. A murrain on innocence! And there had she been thinking she was now such a woman of the world. Justly rebuked, she returned to Joan's bedchamber and spent the rest of the morning with her and even discussed with Lord Arundel what repasts might tempt her poor sister's flimsy appetite.

Later, in great sadness, she left her sister to sleep and went down to St Stephen's Chapel where she lit a candle for Joan and, kneeling before the altar, prayed for her sister's recovery, for Cecily and Grandmother Bonville's wellbeing, and her mother's health, then having been cornered by Thomas Rotherham, Ned's chaplain, she made confession.

She received the usual sentence of aves and a reminder to use her rosary beads more often but his advice stayed with her as she left the chapel.

'To make an error of judgment is not a sin, my daughter, especially when you were only thinking of my lady your sister's wellbeing, but maybe, being young, you are still somewhat hasty in your conclusions. Observe and consider before you speak, for you are a noblewoman of great standing, and people will look to you for wisdom and desire to respect you for your knowledge. There will be many times in this world when you will be called upon to make judgments that affect others and you should always be prepared to hear both sides. Meditate upon King Solomon's wisdom and pray to our dear Lord for his love and guidance.'

So she was of 'great standing'. Kate halted on the steps down to the great hall and felt like she had just been knighted. Was that how everyone in Westminster truly thought of her? Father Rotherham's words were like a sort of juicy munch from the apple of the Tree of Knowledge. A munch that implied, yes, duty, but a greater purpose than just being the mother of an heiress, a sense of being herself. As for listening to other people's side of things, of course she did. Just because she had misunderstood Joan's situation...

A passing esquire doffed his hat to her and winked. It reminded her she was nineteen and for a little space she had the leisure to frolic before she returned to being 'grand' again. Absolved, advised and definitely replenished, she decided that after dinner she would ride to Cheapside with Eleanor and find a gift to cheer Joan.

Heaven decreed otherwise. By noon, God's angels, or whatever whimsical celestial beings lived above the clouds, were hurling down sufficient rain to turn every highway out of London into a hoof swallowing muddy dough, especially the much-travelled road through Charing to Ludgate. Truly England's weather was as unpredictable as a flock of sozzled friars.

Nor was she the only one who felt thwarted; the men of the court who had had their hearts set on more strenuous pursuits had been reduced to inside pastimes; *boules* or board games such as fox and geese, merrills, tables, or the newly introduced playing cards from France. And for some gentlemen, like the Earl of Desmond, flirting was on the agendum.

Eleanor had discovered that he was behind the music beneath their window and no doubt still hopeful of an affair with Kate before he returned to his wife in Ireland.

He was waiting to take his turn at *boules* as she stopped to watch the game.

Ned was howling with laughter as Lord Stanley's ball went wide of the jack. 'Are you going to join us, my lady?'

'Maybe, your highness.'

'*Boules*, pah!' Thomas whispered, stealing his arm around her high waist. 'I could teach you to make love like the Irish do.'

'How do you know I don't know already, my lord?' she teased back, pushing his fingers away from where they were adventuring.

'Shall I test you then, sweet Katherine?'

'Go on!' She raised her chin in challenge.

'Oh no, not here,' he laughed, stroking his other fingertips down her cheek. 'We'd need to be private somewhere.'

She gave him a playful flick in the chest with the back of her hand. 'Then you'll never know my repertoire, my lord. Ah, it's your turn. They're waiting for you.'

'And I'm waiting for you,' he said with mock sorrow.

'Thank you for the minstrels,' she murmured, wondering if he'd had to pay for their ruined clothes, and with her virtue still intact she left him and wandered across to watch the chess game between Clarence and Gloucester.

'Oh, cousin, what timing on your part!' the older boy exclaimed and she found herself talked into taking his place while he stalked off to the latrines. He didn't return.

Her small opponent, Gloucester, proved inconsistent in his play. Sometimes he would risk a valuable piece.

'Checkmate! You did not watch my bishop, your grace.' She removed his queen.

'I forgot they moved diagonally.' He glanced over at Archbishop Bourchier as though he was imagining the prelate crossing between corners with mincing steps.

'Some of them move obliquely,' Kate agreed dryly, 'and some don't move much at all.' She indicated her brother, the lord chancellor, who was helping himself to a sweet tart as he stood deep in discussion with Joan's husband, Fitzalan. 'And, my lord of Gloucester, since I'm feeling merciful, I'll let you have your last move again.' She handed him back the queen. 'I suspect you had your thoughts on something else. I don't mind but it makes for a poor game.'

'There's no need, my lady.' He did not set the piece back but rubbed a thumb pensively over its wooden skirt. 'I am to become a page to my lord your brother at Middleham.'

Ah, so dealing with Richard was bothering him. Although there was little chance of Richard spending much time at home.

'Well, that's all to the good,' she commented cheerfully. 'Most young noblemen see service in another lord's household and my brother will teach you well.'

Gloucester looked up. 'Yes, I know.' It was not a peevish answer.

'Then why so glum, little lord?'

'It's just that I wanted to take Verity — she's the falcon that Ned gave me when I became a duke — but Cousin Richard says we will ride hard because there is much trouble he must attend to and it were best that Verity stays with my brother Clarence. I don't trust him to take care of her.'

'I see. Then, how about I speak to my brother?'

'Would you? Oh, Cousin Kate, if you can persuade him, I will grant you any favour within my power.'

She laughed. 'I'll try. Now save your king!'

Together they worked out the chess moves that would give him the game.

'This little rascal,' exclaimed Ned, looming up and seizing his small brother by the waist, 'should learn by making mistakes.'

His grace of Gloucester was lifted high in the air. 'No, I've done that already. Ask Cousin Kate!' he squealed, upside down, red-faced and clearly delighted by his royal brother's attention.

'Has he?'

'Yes, your grace.' Kate rose from her curtsey and slid back onto the stool.

'*Par Dieu*, Dick lad, then you shall come and see the new pony that shall bear you to Yorkshire.'

There was a whoop from behind the dangling hair. With a grin at Kate, Ned tossed his brother over his back. 'Shall you come, too, Cousin Kate?' he asked with mock gravitas. 'I can put you over my other shoulder.'

'A dizzying elevation that I shall thankfully forego, your grace.'

She was left contentedly setting the chess pieces out again as a courtesy for other players when a shadow fell across her and Lord Hastings sat down on the empty seat opposite.

*You will do him to a nicety!*

Nerves, heart, breath, all suddenly seemed to accelerate.

Had Ned been jesting? She was suddenly wondering what it would be like to have this man for her husband and she felt her face grow warm at the thought.

Hastings was wearing his slightly harassed look. Did he know of the king's scheming? Had the fishing trip been devised to make them more acquainted? Maybe Ned could be just as calculating as Richard. There was a thought!

'This matter of a silver rattle, Lady Katherine.' Of course, that was Hastings' task as well. The man had the bluest eyes, a true Saxon blue like Our Lady's robe.

'Rattle?' Oh dear God, she was staring and her heart seemed to be doing the rattling.

'You see, I don't know much about rattles, my lady.'

'No, I don't suppose you do, my lord, nor it seems does his highness. Cecily is eighteen months old.'

'Ah, then she would prefer...' Kate with amusement let him flounder. At his age, he probably did have some love children somewhere. After all, Ned did. But the man opposite her had her measure. The earnest look had fled as though he had tucked away his mental notebook for the present. 'I cry you mercy. Tell me.'

'A silver beaker might suffice, my lord.' She was trying to keep it simple for him.

The gleam in his eyes told her he was not to be appeased. 'I doubt Cecily would think so, my lady. Would she not consider it boring? And surely silver beakers can be easily dented if thrown against the wall. I speak from experience. My mother tells me I ruined a christening cup.' He stood up and somehow his right hand had curled round one of hers, drawing her to her feet. 'Come!'

To where? Truth to tell, she was too curious to refuse and fast realising that the path of the conversation had been anticipated. He led her out into a torchlit passageway that birthed into a gallery behind the royal apartments. Their destination proved to be a spacious business chamber, heated by a cheerful fire. This must be his demesne, she realised, noting the trestles orderly with piles of correspondence. Beneath several shelves of rolled documents was a wooden rail where parchment and vellum documents hung like drying napkins with balls of red tape perched between them. The air smelled of sealing wax and ink. Straddling the far corner was a leather daybed scarce visible beneath costumes from last night's interlude. Along the window were several desks for scriveners and amanuenses but only one of these was in use and its occupant, a secretary, judging by his *cor-du-roi* tabard, rose and bowed as they entered.

Hastings seemed to communicate with the lift of an eyebrow and the man nodded. 'All is ready, madame. If you please…'

Intrigued, Kate followed Hastings into a smaller, unfurnished chamber where to her astonishment three peddlers stood waiting with a multitude of children's toys set out around their feet.

'Oh, my goodness,' she exclaimed, kneeling down to examine such a treasury. Cecily would be in paradise.

'Choose whatever you will. It is the king's gift.' Hastings folded his arms and waited.

There were rattles, fustian rabbits and hedgehogs, cloth dolls with embroidered smiles, sweetly carved wooden horses, some with detachable saddles, others drawing wains and coaches; ducks and geese on wheels (Cecily had been given one of those already); and a plate of wooden chickens standing in a circle with a ball and strings attached below so that when Kate swung it, the chickens pecked.

'Here is such skill and excellence of craft,' she exclaimed, sending the peddlers into a flurry of inner preening. 'By Heaven, you have given me a hard task, my lord.' She could only marvel at the forethought and trouble he had gone to; the sort of man who might prove an excellent father.

'You are not choosing a doll, then?' Hastings' tone held surprise as she finally selected a horse on wheels drawing a little wooden cart. Its doweling sides were so smoothly planed that there was no danger of little fingers getting splinters. 'This will please Cecily, I'm sure. She can put bricks into the cart.' Seeing one of the peddlers' faces break into a smile, she asked, 'Did you carve this yourself, sirrah?'

'My father does 'em, mistress.' He smirked at his fellows.

'Settled then.' Lord Hastings offered Kate his hand and she clambered to her feet, clutching the plaything to her heart.

'Thanks to each one of you, sirs,' she said graciously to the peddlers. Lord Hastings paid for the cart and gave the others coin for their trouble and left his secretary to see them out.

'That was so kind of you, my lord.' Kate turned to him in the passageway. 'Especially when you have so much to occupy you.'

'My pleasure. You made a decision right speedily. Unusual in a woman.'

She gave him her best smile. 'All this is most thoughtful of you, my lord. Not every man would have…' She subsided with a gesture. Goodness, she was babbling out of nervousness; maybe because there was no one else in the passageway and he was standing looking down at her with that faint smile that was hard to read and yet becoming rather endearing. 'I had better get back,' she murmured, suddenly finding it easier to study her toes than his expression. 'I-I promised I would write to my mother this morning and Richard says there is a courier leaving at noon.'

'My lady, a moment. Can you not sense it?'

'Sense what, my lord?'

'A delectable perfume and it is not fish.' A male arm, entirely clad in silk, slid deftly past her cheekbone. Turning her head, she saw his other arm swiftly bolt her in against the wall. She was a woman of the world, a widow with a child not some timid virgin. Yes, she must be mature about this.

'My lord?' She would not have been surprised if her voice had emerged as an undignified squeak but it came out more breathy. The fine eyebrows above her lifted in amusement; his lips curled into that devastating smile. Oh heaven, it would be pathetic if she could not deal with this … this situation.

'I am calling in your promise, Lady Katherine. The fishing wager that hasn't been paid.'

He wanted her to kiss him?

'I see.' Her heart was dancing frantically.

'I thought you might not prefer an audience.'

And how was she to take that remark?

'Of course it also would help if you could look just slightly eager, my lady.'

That made her laugh, but she felt an honesty towards him. She wanted to say *I am afraid of you* and then realised, *no, I am afraid of myself*. No use explaining that.

His face was closer now, his eyes only for her, as though she filled his entire universe.

'I'm…' *I'm afraid to lose myself to you*. 'I'm not,' she asserted.

'Not eager?' He drew back.

'I didn't mean…'

'Good,' he answered, 'then do you mind if we move this?'

'Oh.' The height of worldliness! Clutching the toy cart to her bosom like a shield! It was still tempting to confess she was out of practice, or had never been practised. Instead she reached up a hand to Hastings' shoulder curling her fingers round the top of his pouched sleeve. 'I hope you can kiss better than the king, my lord.'

Her lips touched his with a feather's caress.

'I hope you will find out, Lady Katherine.' His voice was a deep purr.

'What, my lord?'

248

'That I can kiss better than his grace.'

'Then let's…' She parted her lips, ran her hand to the back of his neck, feeling the neat cut of his hair touching the back of her fingers, and kissed him, astounding herself.

His lips were firm, responsive, playful. He kissed her back, his hands stealing round her shoulders. Curious, compelled, she sighed, let him deepen the kiss. She had never done that with Will. It had been physical domination by consent but this man's lips aroused an exquisite hunger that almost melted her.

Then she came to her senses. A door had edged open and a ring handle was being rattled most tactfully. Lord Hastings straightened and stepped back, his arms no longer enclosing her in a sensual prison.

'My lord?' The secretary advanced to hover a few yards away, and behind him waited a courier. The spell was broken, the wager fulfilled.


Richard found her at breakfast in Westminster Hall next morning.

'George tells me you have another favour to ask me. I hope it's less stupid this time.' He straddled the trestle opposite.

'Ah yes,' Kate swallowed her spoonful of frumenty, and wondered if she could accidentally kick him. 'Little Gloucester desires to take his hawk to Middleham but you have told him no. He says Clarence will neglect the bird if it remains here. I am his herald with fanfares and authority to negotiate.'

Her brother laughed. 'If it is that precious to the boy, let him bring it, then.'

'Thank you, Richard.' She blew a kiss on her fingers, leaned across and touched his cheek. Well, that was one set of victory trumpets blaring.

He idly scuffed a scatter of trencher crumbs into a pile with his forefinger and said smoothly, 'So what do you reckon about Lord Hastings, Kate? He's a good match for you, no green wood there. Good teeth, healthy, competent, affable to boot.'

He had misjudged. *She* was the green wood.

'And he'll make a fine profit from administering Cecily's inheritance,' she muttered, pushing aside her bowl.

'Of course, he will. The wealthiest heiress in the land. We have to give him *some* reward.' Seeing her bristle, he added swiftly, 'You are too damn spiky, Kate. I didn't mean it that way. Jesu, dealing with you is like dealing with a ruddy hedgehog.' He beckoned a servant to bring him a jack of ale. 'No, I meant *he* wants to be part of the family.'

Oh, *the family*. The ubiquitous, ambitious Nevilles! So that's what Hastings really wanted. Not her at all. She untangled herself from the bench and strode up to fume in front of the great fireplace.

Richard followed her there. 'God's sakes, stop behaving like a spoilt little fool. Can you not see how much Ned trusts the man? Think how useful that will be to us!'

'Ha!' Kate reiterated over her shoulder.

'Be damned to your contrariness. Joan warned me you were being too cursed skittish. Our family has been to Hell and back to set England to rights and, well, now it is your turn.' He ignored her glare and swung round to stare into the fire, which, newly topped with logs, was dull and dark now. She watched his thumbs twisting behind his back, a sure sign of ill temper in Richard but she was not going to be browbeaten.

'Oh, so now I am to do this for the sake of England?' With an angry sigh, she observed the painstaking progress of a brown cockroach that had just arrived with the firewood. It was running up and down a log surrounded by smoke and just when she thought it was doomed to choke or burn, it opened its back, sprang into the air and landed on the hearth. Richard set a boot heel upon it.

'I am truly disappointed in your attitude,' he muttered, his face hardening. 'Curse it, girl, have you no sense of duty? How can you suppose that we would leave you unwed when there are desirable alliances to be made?' He turned his head, waiting for a white pennon to show in her expression but Kate gave him stubborn look for look. She hoped it was a face any Neville would recognise. With a deep, angry breath, he abandoned further diplomacy and turning his back on the hearth, folded his arms. 'Stow your plaguey rebelliousness! Just be grateful the man finds you pleasing or by God I'll match you up with old Lord Wenlock next time he loses a wife.'

He let that sink in to the haft, and added, 'Christ Almighty, Katherine, if Hastings can protect your child's inheritance, what else would you ask of him?'

Kate stared at him in utter amazement. Maybe Richard was the innocent, not her! Had he never been besotted enough to write a love poem? How could he ask if she wanted more? Of course, she did! Marriage for her must be more than a land contract or how many retainers her prospective husband could bring to the Neville banners.

Further annoyed, he barked, 'Devil take it, you're not smitten with some low-bred Devonshire squireling, are you?'

'Well, yes,' she replied, trying to keep a straight face, and provoked by his outraged expression, added wickedly, 'It's one of the Courtenays. What's more, my friend reckons the Nevilles are a rabble of north country upstarts who breed like rabbits.' In delight, she watched Richard bristle at the insult to his lineage. Had he been a dog, every hackle would have been showing, and it would have needed an iron chain to hold him. 'My friend also says,' Kate purred, 'that there is no great family left without some Neville worming their way into the marriage bed.'

His arms instantly unfolded. 'Who is this false-tongued jack? I'll deal with him, by God! Why are you laughing? Katherine? *Katherine*! Are you gulling me?'

'Yes, my lord brother. It is great sport, too.'

His teeth no longer showed. He sheathed his temper, but famous for tenacity, he could not resist saying in gentler tone, 'Let us not quarrel further. Come, tell me truly what colours your opinion so? Why can't you like poor Hastings?'

Sometimes she forgot her brother was the ultimate strategist. She did so now.

'I do like him, Richard, but I am not quite ready to wed again.' *Prodded to the church door at sword point to 'please' her brothers? No!*

'Not ready? Not ready and you're a nineteen-year-old widow? What kind of reason is that?'

'A valid one.'

Pointing out to him she wanted love and loyalty for her and Cecily would be trying to thread a bodkin with an anchor rope. Demanding words like 'marital fidelity' probably did not exist in his glossarium; he already had one bastard daughter. Besides, how could she clarify anything when her feelings were already so confused?

Maybe if Will had been more like Newton or... And this was where her body was trying to rule her judgment. 'Forget the fumblings with Will,' it told her head, 'and imagine Lord Hastings running his hands across my skin and kissing me awake, hmmm...' But the demon in her head growled back, 'If you couldn't satisfy Will, how could you hope to pleasure a man like Hastings?'

'Oh, do spit it out, Katherine.' Richard's fingers tilted her chin up. 'Maybe I can understand.'

She disliked the scrutiny, fearing he might prise out her sinful reverie. It was needful to draw back from him. 'I am sorry, Richard, you're not a woman. It is hard to expl...' Her palms rose in apology.

'Try!' He suddenly looked disgustingly smug. 'For my part, Katherine, I am attempting to understand why a man and a woman practically devour each other outside an accounting room and then only one of them will admit to desire.'

The *coup de grâce* — and she had not seen it coming. The kiss with Hastings had been reported!

She bit back an angry curse. Did Richard have informers all over the palace or had some weasel of a clerk borne the morsel back for payment? Could she take anything at face value in this court? Was Hastings spying on Richard, too, and Ned on both of them?

'I think you place too much weight on such reports,' she retorted, 'no doubt it was the aroma of money in the nearby coffers that enflamed the foolish couple's senses. I am sure if the lady dangles the deeds of her daughter's manors in the gentleman's face, they may achieve the same heat of lust once again.' She displayed her most cattish smile and hoped it annoyed him. It did.

'For such a young woman,' he countered, 'you are prodigiously cynical and too sharp-tongued for your own good. You definitely need a husband.'

'What, to pull me into line?' It was a pity Richard's wife had never stood up to him for he badly needed toppling from his saddle. If nobody else in the family would dare gainsay him, someone had to. Kate drew a deep breath that lifted her shoulders and said firmly, 'Enough! I think I have made myself clear, Richard. I *am* returning to Devon as soon as the roads are passable. You and Ned may ring the wedding bells for all you are worth but I am not yet in a marrying mind.'

The gauntlet was picked up. Teeth clenched, her brother met her disobedience with typical Neville hauteur, 'Gainsay me all you like, *little* sister, but William Hastings shall have you. *By God, he shall!*'

She was not some paynim slave up on a block for sale, Kate thought angrily, as she marched out of the hall and made her way to St Stephen's Chapel for Mass.

Even as she knelt in the chapel, staring at the painting of the *Adoration of the Magi*, she began wondering why there could not have also been a wise princess led by the star to bring a gift to the Baby Jesus. True that Our Lady was depicted in a palace enthroned in robes of rose and azure, with the Magi laying their precious gifts at her feet but she was important only as the mother of Christ. Only as a mother, a carrying vessel. Kate crossed herself with a shudder, horrified at her blasphemy, but it brought home her own circumstances. Noble wives were nothing but bondswomen decked in silk. Ignored by common law, disdained by Holy Church, continually risking childbirth and constantly impregnated. No, not bondwomen but milk cows with pasture attached.

And milk cow Kate Neville was only marketable for wifehood as the Earl of Warwick's sister and Cecily's mother, and even if she fell in love with someone like her mythical Courtenay, her brothers would prevent the marriage.

She shut her eyes as Ned and his lords strode past her skirts but she knew Lord Hastings was among them. The Devil was tempting her to gaze upon him, setting flint to the fire of lust that was smouldering down below in her body, and finally she could resist no more but looked to where he knelt behind his king's heels. He appeared moral enough with his fingertips pointing devoutly towards the rood screen and his head tilted forward in prayer yet even now her insides shivered longingly as though her body, breaking free of her mind's control, acknowledged his presence.

Chaplain Rotherham, standing on the step above Ned, trapped her staring and embarrassed, Kate ducked her head down and sent a grovelling apology to God.

Afterwards, instead of following the royal party through to the Painted Chamber, she hastened outside. At Shute or Chewton, she could have called for her mare to be saddled; here, the open water of the Thames drew her. She would tolerate the wind thrusting its breath in her face or numbing her fingertips, providing it was free of incense or heavy perfumes.

The rain had eased but a miserable, damp fog, heavy with the smoke of the palace chimneys, mantled the colourless river. Tugged low, the tide exposed a dark gritty shoreline and scab lines of debris that invited no close inspection. Stark of leaves, with no squirrels streaking up their trunks like tiny flames, the oaks and beeches loomed like sinister mourners, brooding and hunched in their dark ivy wrappings.

A man might have been permitted to idle, to stare across to the Lambeth marshes or watch the cluster of little boats off King's Bridge jostling for passengers to Queenshithe or observe the bargemen unloading bales of hay and straw for the palace stables, but she felt exposed to the curiosity of the sentries, even though she made sure to keep her gaze modest.

She was being observed from the water, too. It was not just the ducks who paddled hopefully in the wavelets.

'Take you anywhere, lady?' called out one of the watermen, swiftly rowing in.

'Queenshithe, my lady?' shouted another.

'Find you a fine lad in Southwark, darlin'?'

Although that earned the impudent fellow a ripe reprimand from the household officer who was supervising the bargemen, the wherry boats still followed her. She turned; the cogs and ducks turned. Defeated she followed the trail of hay in beneath the Watergate.

'Freezin', ain't it, my lady? You go in, eh?'

'Yes,' she answered the fatherly sentry, but her smile faded. Beyond the handcarts of horse fodder bumping across the cobbles, she glimpsed Lord Hastings escorting a slender, well-dressed lady in a velvet, fur-edged hood — indeed, a married woman, for her hair was utterly concealed by her headdress. Tasselling the respectable cap veil brightly against the darkness of the woman's cloak were locks of golden hair. Was Hastings procuring the lady? For his king or himself?

As they disappeared beneath the opposite archway, perversity drove Kate across the yard, and she halted hidden in the dark of the inner archway, determined to confirm her belief that Hastings was no more to be trusted than Will had been. Her quarry had reached the stables and now they stood close to each other, deep in conversation. Conversation? No, more than that. Kate could tell from Hastings' stance that he was listening and looking at the woman with the same intense expression he had been wearing yesterday when he had kissed her. Had Will Bonville looked so meeting Lovidia on the stairs at Shute?

The lady's gloved hands rose and he caught them as though in reassurance. Then as a groom led a saddled mare forth and halted at a respectful distance, the lady seemed to recollect herself, glanced over her shoulder towards her servant, and then withdrew one of her hands. Hastings embraced her and they parted; she mounting with the help of her servant's cupped hand and he began walking towards the very archway where Kate stood, with a smile on his face, like a man utterly sure of his charm.

Panicking, Kate looked for a bolthole but Heaven was merciful. Halloed respectfully by the chief groom, Hastings turned back.

Still she lingered, watching Ned's friend like some infatuated young maid, beguiled by the confidence of his stride, the way his cloak descended from his shoulders and fluttered at the spurs on his heels. Velvet, leather and steel. She crossed herself, grateful to God that her suspicions had been confirmed before it was too late. How could she hold a man like him? He was made to break hearts just like Ned. She imagined a fraught future, were she joined with him, bucklering herself against the gossip, showing a wifely calm demeanour while she ached with jealousy imagining him selecting his concubine for the night from among the eager London wives. No, he was not for her nor a mirror of morality for Cecily.

'Isn't this rather draughty for an assignation, young Katherine?'

Kate started, blushing. 'By my faith! Godmother!'

Aunt Catherine Neville, Dowager Duchess of Norfolk, warmly wrapped to her chin and gloved to her elbows, was standing behind her. 'Not one of the grooms surely, my dear?'

'No, one of the horses,' Kate retaliated with a skin-deep smile as she made a hasty obeisance. 'What about you,

Godmama?' It was an effort to sound pert and cheerful when she was hurting inside.

Her godmother stared across her shoulder. 'Hmm, the young man yonder with the large handcart would suit me perfectly. The muscularity of a fist fighter and the face of a scholarly angel. Trouble is he'll stink of the stable but that's sometimes a welcome change.'

Kate giggled. Not only because her godmother was in her sixties, but she resembled a tall, austere abbess if you discounted the dyed black hair showing beneath her pointed cap and the redrawn eyebrows. 'But if that is a piquant sauce for you,' continued the dowager dryly, 'you can ask young Hastings to splash on a bit of *attar de cheval.*'

'I believe you've have been listening to too much gossip, dear Godmama.'

'Have I? Your brother is hearing wedding bells for sure. Didn't you know you're one of the prizes for loyalty and fidelity?'

Kate's good humour fled. 'I think Cecily's inheritance is the prize. For my acquiescence, I win a lord who has an eye for every passing wench.'

'Does he?' queried Aunt Catherine pensively, peering at the stable entrance for a sighting. 'I've a mind for a walk. Shall you come with me or have you had enough?' She was observing Kate's mud-spattered boots. 'How about as far as the Sanctuary?'

'I should be glad to keep you company.' Perhaps her aunt had skills in bandaging aching hearts or rescuing self-worth. Yet a suspicion struck her as they circumambulated the laden barrows. 'Richard has not sent you to drive sense into me, has he?'

'Like a battering ram? I fancy I look more like an assault tower on wheels. No, your brother has said nothing to me but your mother will ask me how you fare when next I see her. So, is it true then?'

'Maybe everyone knows except Lord Hastings.' Kate sighed. 'I don't know either. That is, I mean my consent has not been requested. My brothers can't make me, not unless they hold a dagger to my throat. It's just that I am not ready to marry again.' Then she confided sadly, 'I suppose I'm still wound licking. Will Bonville cuckolded me.'

'Ah.' They walked on in companionable silence. 'You're still very innocent, poppet, at least from my ancient perspective.'

Oh, not another accusation of innocence! Kate halted, rebellious at her aunt's patronising tone. 'I intend to bring up Cecily to be a decent Christian in a loving family, Godmama, and … well, I don't see it is wrong to wish for a loyal and loving stepfather for her.' Having provoked a sheepish expression from her godmother, they resumed walking.

'To my observation,' muttered Aunt Catherine, 'and I have been married for over fifty years, on and off, most husbands do some dilly-dallying. Not all but most, especially when they're not at home. Weak as nestlings, can't resist temptation, the naughty lads.' She nodded graciously at a pair of Richard's retainers as they winked and doffed their hats to her. 'My third, Beaumont, didn't. We trotted gloriously together, but then, with a third husband, one usually does. I still miss him, particularly on cold nights. Now with my second, we *both* used to have a bit of dalliance on the side.'

'And you my godmother!' Kate chided but she had dismounted the high horse of morality. 'So you are advising me to accept Lord Hastings?'

'Not exactly.' Her godmother waggled a gloved hand in the air.

'Not exactly? And pray what do you mean by that, Godmama?'

'Instinct will out, poppet. Like … like a haystack suddenly bursting into flame.'

'I see,' replied Kate politely. 'But don't haystacks in those circumstances burn down to nothing?'

The old lady raised her palms in exasperation. 'Behold the white cloth of surrender, Katherine, take all my weaponry. I give up, defeated by your youth and experience.'

It would be discourteous to scowl. A grind of teeth was tempting. 'Perhaps we should turn back now?' Kate suggested.

'As you wish. I am invited to Aunt York's for dinner. I hope she has a decent fire in the hall. Baynard's can be disgustingly damp this time of year. Mind, so can Fotheringay. I'll save visiting your mother until the spring. Maybe she'll be more cheerful than last time.'

'So, what shall you tell her when you see her?' Kate asked, when they drew near the steps leading up to the eastern door of the Painted Chamber.

'That she has a daughter who is a good mother.'

Kate was able to smile; it would make a good epitaph, if nothing else. 'Then give her a daughter's love from me, Godmama.'

'That is a promise.' They passed the guards and halted in the antechamber. One of the royal greyhounds came out to investigate their soles. Beyond the great doors, a counter-tenor was singing.

'I cannot stand castrati,' sighed Aunt Catherine. 'Poor knaves. Such a waste.' Then she held out her arms to embrace Kate. 'Adieu, my poppet. I shall be leaving tomorrow morning, rain or shine. My chaplain says the weather will turn cold and it already feels as though the wind is shifting.' She kissed Kate's cheek and straightened. 'Why, by the Saints, I think there is a young man waiting for you. And a duke, no less. Farewell.'

Surprised, Kate turned round and found young Gloucester petting the greyhound, clearly biding his time to waylay her.

'Madame cousin,' he said, rising to his feet and giving her a formal bow. 'I ... I saw you talking earlier with Cousin Richard.' Kate must have looked blank for the boy's face crumpled. 'He doesn't want me to take Verity, does he?'

'V-Verity?' Her memory returned and with it, a slow smile. 'Yes, of course, you may take Verity. He agreed with no trouble.'

'Oh!' Not only did the child fling his arms about her waist but the greyhound scampered over to join in. 'Thank you, thank you.' The little duke beamed up at her with such joy. 'Yet he looked so angry, I thought...'

She hugged him with one arm and managed to caress the hound as well. 'With me, not you, cousin. So, do not worry any more.'

Gloucester scrambled back. 'I'll tell the falconers that she's allowed.' In delight, he took to his heels and then halted abruptly on the outside step as though invisible fingers had grabbed hold of him. He turned so solemnly that Kate put her fingers to her lips to stifle her laughter. 'Your pardon, cousin!' Once more the little courtier, he bowed and said gravely, 'I made you a promise. Maybe one day when I am grown, I can repay you. Please do not forget.' He bowed again.

Kate curtsied demurely and was licked on the cheek by the amicable dog.

'As your grace pleases.'

Brown eyes examined her face as though he suspected she might not be taking this matter with equal seriousness and then satisfied, he raced off towards the mews.

Kate straightened and shook her skirts. It was time to feel irritable again. Why did everyone keep calling her an innocent. If she was, then she was *definitely* not a match for a man of the world like Hastings. She wanted a husband who would love her, not betray her.

She was spared meeting Lord Hastings at the midday repast next day. Lord Arundel mentioned that my Lord Chamberlain was gone to the Tower of London. Wearing his Master of the Royal Mint hat? Or maybe he had refused Ned's suggestion that he marry a Neville and had been sent to the dungeons in manacles — wearing his worried expression, of course.

'I hear you are in the market for a husband again.' Meg, Ned's thirteen-year-old sister, leaned over Kate's shoulders following the last course, still sucking one of the almond paste mice that had been served with the wafers and quince paste.

Kate jerked the girl's auburn tresses. 'Go away, gossip. There's no truth to it at all.'

'Then you won't be interested in coming to Cheapside with me this afternoon. There's a new shipment of cloth come in from Bruges and Ned has granted me forty pounds a year so I can well afford a new gown.' Her voice sank to a whisper. 'Please, Kate, I need a married lady with me and I'll be hanged if I'll take any of Mother's crones else they'll make me choose some old-fangled weave and...'

'Enough. I'll come with you right happily. It's something I planned to do anyway. Ughh, Meg, must you?' she protested as the girl bestowed a sticky kiss upon her cheek.

London always had a touchy edge to it. Compared to Fore Street, Exeter, Cheapside with its shops and stalls was exuberant, deafening and full of thieves. Kate, riding pillion behind her groom, both relished and disliked the press of people, the stink and scents, the raucous voices of the touting apprentices as they caught at sleeves and stirrups. Babble and Babel! She caught the guttural snatch of Flemish and German among the crowd.

Meg was not a whit fazed by any of it, for she had spent almost the last year at Baynard's Castle and the Londoners knew her. With her brother's soldiers keeping any braggarts at pikestaff distance, the girl could enjoy the whistles. Let London indulge her, thought Kate benevolently. Before long she would be shipped out of England to seal an alliance with her maidenhead. By comparison, Kate could refuse; Meg would be given no choice.

The display chamber of the warehouse that her cousin sought was already crowded with wealthy wives, clothiers from the shires and noblemen's agents but the crowd obsequiously made way for the king's sister. Kate's womanly heart thumped in delight. Bales of glistening Italian and Syrian silks, tisshews, gauzes and finest English wool, re-imported as cloth from Bruges, were stacked to the ceiling and Kate was soon utterly distracted by the rivers of fabric that were rippled out across the counter for consideration. She had a shopping list. Lady Bonville would make a pincushion of her if she went back to Shute without a sumpter loaded with cloth.

She made her selection and then sat down happily on a bench while the fabric was being measured out.

'An' I saw him go in. No lie.' Behind her, a woman's voice — London, by the dialect — spoken softly, leaving a question.

'My Lord Chamberlain, no, truly?' The second voice was younger, astonished.

Kate stopped counting the measures of cloth and sat still as a rock.

'An' I asked her, she standing there with her raven hair all loose beneath her cap. "I saw you had a fine visitor to dinner," I said. An' she said, "Oh, yes, he was here to order gold for the Royal Mint from my husband." "A pity your husband was not here to greet him, then," I said, "for didn't I see him riding to the Goldsmiths' Hall this morning at nine o' the clock?" "Aye, mayhap, you did," she said blushing withal. "But I think he went away satisfied nonetheless."'

It hurt Kate as much as a vicious box on the ear. Not just a fleeting hurt though; this pain would eat away inside her head like a canker.

'My lady, shall you take this still?' The apprentice was poised with the scissors in his hand over the lustrous fabric she had chosen for herself but now it seemed too gaudy and extravagant, fit for flaunting a harlot's body, not for quiet dinners with Devon neighbours. Or did she have a harlot's heart, putting her arms round Hastings' neck and drawing him close? She, a respectable widow and mother!

'Madame?'

'Yes, of course, she'll take it.' Meg was back, flinging an arm round her. 'What's amiss? You look pale as ashes. Have I exhausted you?'

'I'm not six foot under yet,' growled Kate. Except that life had just barrelled a great cart of dung across her path.

*A pox on men!* she thought angrily riding back towards Ludgate, the Westminster Garden of Paradise had been exquisite at times but the daydream was over. *Primus*, she was not going to permit a gallivanting whoreson to become stepfather and guardian to Cecily; *secundus*, she was not going to marry any nobleman who was going to be absent most of the time nursemaiding and procuring for Ned; *tertius*, Lord Hastings was far too handsome for a plain looking creature like her; and *quartus*, he had not even stated he wished to marry her and it was probably just some bee of an idea buzzing around in Ned's skull at the moment.

As though the Devil was determined to tempt her further, a party of riders caught up with them as they were leaving the city and Lord Hastings cheerfully doffed his high-brimmed hat and seemed intent on riding alongside her, his boots almost brushing her skirts.

'You're looking weary, my lord,' she observed. 'A tiring day?' *An unattiring morning with a goldsmith's wife perhaps?*

He was looking her over with a jaunty eye. 'No, but perhaps you have. Are your Devon ponies strong enough to carry home all your purchases?'

'Oh, you should see the cloth she has chosen, Lord Hastings,' chimed in Meg, watching them from her pillion on the horse in front. 'She'll make some suitor's mouth water in that, I can tell you.'

'My lady!' snapped Kate, with a look that told the maiden to mind her language.

'What colour have you chosen, tell me.' Hastings sounded genuinely interested and maybe he was. All the garments she had seen him in enhanced his colouring and flattered his body. The dye of his doublet now was a stormy blue that echoed the silver-blue starbursts of his eyes and ... Jesu! He was bewitching her again, this sorcerer, and repeating his question.

'Green.'

'Emerald, chrysolite, peapod, apple, fir?' he prompted.

'Like the hue of blemished copper, my lord, shot with gilt and silver thread.'

'You will look well in it if your hair is the same colour as your brothers'. Of course, he had never seen her hair.

Meg had to interfere. 'Kate's is cinnamon. "Neville Ginger", Mother calls it.'

Lord Hastings' gaze locked with Kate's. The message that he would like to see her cinnamon hair unbound passed between them sure as Doomsday.

'I have heard…' started Kate, trying to rescue her integrity and instead scuffing the mire of tittle-tattle, 'I have heard that the woman with the loveliest hair in London is a goldsmith's wife.'

The man's eyes narrowed when they should have widened. 'It could be true. Juliana Shaa, perhaps, or Mistress Rede.' Perhaps? Had he not savoured the perfume in the woman's hair, parted it to set kisses upon her, touched her below? *It could be true.* A wreath of carefully woven words adorning the grave of any future between them.

'She probably uses henna.' Meg was trying to sound knowledgeable.

'No, hers is raven, I believe,' Kate said. 'Does that ring any bells, Lord Hastings?' He did not answer but directed a sidelong glance from beneath his own fair lashes; an almost imperceptible annoyance tightened his mouth.

The narrowness of the bridge that divided Westminster from the hiatus of Charing forced the riders to ride two by two. Two of the outriders closed in behind Meg and with her out of earshot, Lord Hastings seized his opportunity.

'May I desire a favour of you, Lady Katherine? There's another troupe of players petitioning me to let them present an entertainment for the court but I would have your opinion of them.'

'Mine, my lord?' An innocuous request, flattering one might say. It was needful to inspect his expression for some illicit motive. After all, she had not anticipated that the selection of a toy for Cecily would lead to kisses.

'I have given them leave to practise the day after tomorrow in the tenez court. If you would care to come as well? See if there is aught in their piece that might offend the older noblewomen.'

'Are you implying that I am old for my years, my lord?' she asked with a hint of tartness.

'If I value my life, no, Lady Katherine.'

He reached the stables ahead of her groom, dismounted easily and came across to assist her down. To resist would have been impolite.

'God as my witness, I should truly value your opinion on the piece, my lady.' Here was no lingering touch about her waist as she sprang down from the seat, not with Meg and a score of retainers to observe them. She should have said no to this philanderer.

'I suppose I can but surely…'

'Done, then.' He took her hand with a brief bow. 'My thanks. May I advise you to wrap yourself warmly. Buskins if you have any. It will be almost as cold as fishing. If you could be in the great hall after dinner, I shall send a page to fetch you.' He smiled, touched his hat in salute to her and even though she was protectively scaled with caution and spined with knowledge, she still felt that somehow or other, she was on a hook and a man's clever hand was reeling her slowly in.

# 15: ELYSABETH

## *12th January 1462, Stony Stratford, Buckinghamshire*

The snow that had fallen briefly on St Stephen's Day returned several days after Epiphany, at first falling delicately like loose feathers shaken from an upstairs coverlet. Any man with weather lore would have observed the pale marigold tinge to the heavy clouds and not ventured far, but for Elysabeth and her brother, John, setting out from Stony Stratford, there was no choice. They could not afford to stay overnight in the town, even though they had just sold the Duke of Bedford's sword to a London merchant who traded in such mementoes. The money, not as much as they had hoped, was needed to pay for Lionel to return to Oxford (once he finished his studies, Holy Church would take care of him), to repay some of her parents' many debts, provide John with better armour and maintain a lawyer on her Chancery case.

Elysabeth felt laden with guilt and shame to see the sword lost but powerless to help. She had sheathed her pride and written to Lady Ferrers again before Christmastide but the answer had come from Bourchier: 'Pay what is owing on your dowry!' The responses to her petitions from the king's sisters had not been so frosty, merely 'no' couched with formal indifference. Papa had been disappointed but gracious.

'By Heaven, my darling, where else would you stay but with those who love you? And we've always been in debt, haven't we, Jacq? It's been a way of life.'

'Snowballs!' exclaimed John, crashing through Elysabeth's thoughts as usual. His recent service as a soldier had not dulled his exuberance. 'I'll wager the children will be waiting to ambush us.'

'As long as it's just the children.' Not for the first time, she looked round to see if they were being followed. Thankfully, apart from Master Burcote, two armed menservants and the two donkeys bearing John's new breastplate and the sacks of oats in which the gold coins were hidden, no one was following in their wake. Thieves had more sense; the mantling across the fields was already deeper than rabbit nose height and any fool could see it would thicken.

They preferred to keep to the lanes, avoiding the churned main roads. Each of their party knew the track well but Elysabeth could not drop her guard. The initial beauty of snowfall usually thrilled her but today she saw it as a white veil concealing a pox-scarred harridan — all those hazardous ruts and holes hidden from wayfarers. The horses disliked it, too, planting their hooves carefully, and several times John and the lads dismounted when they remembered there might be a pothole ahead, preferring to test the way on foot rather than have the precious beasts risk broken limbs.

By the time they joined the Northampton road for the last mile to Grafton, it must have been past four o' the clock and the wick of day was burning low. Copious steaming horse dung sullying the snow suggested a large company had recently passed. All to the good, but even though the preceding hooves had compacted the loose snow into useful dints, the rising cold was freezing the ruts into slippery ice. Fresh snow crystals began to flutter down, settling with uncertainty on the hats and shoulders of the men and melting into the horses' manes.

Scarcely half a mile from the village, the nonchalant snowflakes became right evil as though some malicious hand had sliced a featherbed with a sword blade and emptied the entire contents over an upstairs windowsill. Even keeping the hedges in their sight without stumbling into the roadside ditch on either side the road was an effort, especially when both humans and horses had their heads bowed to avoid the blinding snow.

'Listen, John!' Elysabeth exclaimed, interrupting a further grumble from her brother. 'I think I heard voices.'

'So did Joan of Arc.' But he understood the reflex of fear underscoring her voice. 'Thieves don't make such a hubbub, Elysabeth.'

'Aye, my lady,' agreed Burcote, shaking the garnish of snow from his hat, 'probably some other poor fools trying to get home.'

They passed a line of loaded, miserable-eyed sumpters halted on the road. At the front blocking anyone else's progress was an untidy group of horsemen. The raised voices clearly concerned a chariot that had tumbled into the ditch. It lay almost upside down, its uppermost door thrust back. Grooms were struggling to unharness the frightened draw-horses, and several menservants were struggling to heave a large wooden travelling chest that must have been strapped to the chariot's rear up the bank. A portly man was up to his boot calves down behind them bawling instructions. The Woodvilles' sudden muffled arrival surprised the nearest gentlemen and they started apart, gloved hands hovering at their scabbards.

'Good day to you, sirs!' exclaimed John, saluting them. He dismounted and strode forwards, his hands held clear of his sword belt. 'I see you've had bad fortune.'

Elysabeth, edging her horse forwards, was better able to see that in their midst sat a woman, hunched in the snow, with her arms wrapped around one bent knee. No doubt she was the occupant of the coach because servants were holding a cloth above her as a man in a dark robe crouched beside her, examining her outstretched leg.

'God be thanked, perhaps this youth can tell us where we are,' exclaimed an authoritative female voice and one of the people beside the injured woman unfolded into a tall, elderly lady. Her skin was like the palest white leather within her pleated, widow's coif and her upper lip betrayed the sunray lines bestowed by living long. Discerning eyes, the colour of speedwells passed over John and inspected Elysabeth who inclined her head with obligatory politeness, before the demanding stare snapped back on John.

'Where would you like to be, mistress?' he asked roguishly, lifting his hat to her.

'A pox on your manners, you young varmint! Answer my lady!' It was the large man who had been supervising from the ditch. Elysabeth heard the metal clink of a chain of authority beneath his mantle as he ranged himself at the woman's side.

Her impertinent young brother ignored him. 'Then, where would you like to be, *my lady*?'

'On the road to Towcester, lad, not this God forsaken byway. Well, where are we, for the love of God?'

'About half a mile south of Grafton, my lady.'

'*Grafton*! There,' she snapped at her servants, 'I told you we took the wrong road from Stony Stratford. All these years and they haven't put up a decent fingerpost. Plaguey blizzard. Where's the nearest religious house?' She turned before he could answer, announcing to her entourage, 'We'll put up there.'

'There isn't one, my lady,' John intervened. He included the chamberlain with the farmer's complexion as he added, 'You could take a track westwards at Grafton and that will bring you once more to Watling Street, but you are probably looking at eight miles to Towcester from here and with this depth of snow already, I warn you, you'll never make the town by nightfall. You are welcome to stay the night at our house.'

Instantly, the ancient dame looked him and up and down, assessing now what he might be worth.

'That might be wise, madame.' The advice came from the man who had been tending to the injured woman. He rose, brushing the snow from his black hose.

'John!' Elysabeth murmured, indicating that they should leave the strangers to discuss the matter. He had the wit to pay heed and drew rein where she halted her mare at sufficient distance to give him a dressing down.

'Mother will skin you, John! And Father won't return from Northampton tonight with this snow. How could you make such an offer? There must be at least twenty of them.'

'Exactly, but the old dragon is someone import —'

'Young man! We'll accept your offer.' The old dragon came in person, standing at the apex of her entourage rather like a besieged Frankish princess agreeing to surrender her citadel to the Saracens. Yet Elysabeth detected a relief in the announcement; the accident must have badly shaken those old bones.

John plunged back through the snow. 'Mind, my lady, there could be reasons you might not want to stay the night with us.' His cheekiest smile accompanied his bow.

'Why, are there more fleas in Northamptonshire or don't you wash your sheets at Grafm —'

'Grafton, madame, and I think we might manage clean bedding. Some of your party might like to put up at the village inn or else sleep by the hearth in our hall.'

'*I* will sleep by the hearth in your hall if need be.' She drew breath, no doubt to give orders, but the large man who made himself known as old woman's chamberlain wanted his two penneth. His mistress would not be allowed to suffer any indignity.

'Are you aware, boy, that this is the Lady Catherine Neville, Dowager Duchess of Norfolk?' His tone implied that a modest Northamptonshire dwelling might be utterly inadequate for a Neville, let alone a duchess.

'No.' John gave not the slightest indication of awe although his bow and smile respectfully deepened. 'Madame, your humble servant.'

'I don't think humble applies,' murmured her grace with an ambiguity that was hard to interpret. 'And your name, sirrah?'

He had one eye on the irritable chamberlain as he bowed yet again. 'John Woodville, son of the Lady Jacquetta of Luxembourg, Duchess of Bedford.' Like her brother, Elysabeth relished the inbreath of astonishment from the dowager's servants although the lady seemed unruffled.

'Permit me to introduce my eldest sister, Lady Grey of Groby.'

Elysabeth had already dismounted, ready to curtsey. 'I wholeheartedly endorse my brother's offer, madame.' Even if they never heard the last of it from Mother.

'Yes, well, Jacquetta, eh.' The duchess tasted their mother's name as though it was some exotic food once tried and found unappealing. 'Hmmpf!' With a little shrug and a mutter beneath her breath, she turned for further discussion with her officers. Elysabeth, remounting with the help of Burcote, wondered if her high and mightiness had changed her mind but she was wrong.

'Could you lead me there straightway and could your man remain here to escort the remainder of my people?'

'Our pleasure.' Another bow. Smirking, John returned to wait by Elysabeth's stirrup while their prospective guest gave further orders. Elysabeth raised her gloved hand to mask the scolding she had ready.

'Heaven's mercy upon us, you idiot! You realise we could be snowbound with her come morning?'

He grinned. 'Elysabeth, I told you before, we need new friends. This ancient duck is not only the king's aunt but Warwick's as well.'

'John, I remember her now. She used to terrify the maids-of-honour. Her second husband was one of the Greys of Codner.'

'So she's a distant in-law of yours. Be sweet to her.'

'But the woman is a veritable battle-axe!'

'Then,' chuckled her younger brother, 'there'll be two of them at the board tonight.'

The torches to guide them in were spitting above the gatehouse in the last gasp of light. Elysabeth expected a berating from their mother for causing the maternal heart such severe anxiety and she was not disappointed. But Jacquetta had drawn breath now, blinking in astonishment at the half dozen strangers who were dismounting in her courtyard and clearly expecting to come in.

'*Mon Dieu*? Who are zeese?' she hissed at Elysabeth, and setting her to one side, exclaimed in her best English, 'But why did you not send ahead to warn me, my dears?' The sweet tone was deceptive.

'Good evening to you, Jacquetta,' said their noble visitor with a discernible hint of cattishness. 'I am afraid I am your guest for the night.'

'Mother, permit me to present Lady Catherine, Dowager Duchess of Norfolk.'

'I know who she is,' Jacquetta snapped at her son. Then, rearranging her features in a smile that resembled John's at his most manipulative, she added, 'Well, you 'ad better come in, Lady Catherine. Where on earth did my children find you?'

'In a ditch, Jacquetta. I expect you wish they'd left me there.'

Seeing the two older noblewomen standing together in the solar was like comparing an English broomstick to a Burgundian shovel. Changing before supper, Jacquetta had chosen to brandish her comparative youthfulness by wearing a jewelled collar that required a low bodice and creamy, unblemished cleavage to lend perspective. Her English counterpart wore a pectoral cross of amethysts that cleverly drew attention to itself rather than to the drooped bosom of its owner.

Her grace of Norfolk had abandoned the widow's garb for the evening. Upon her temple, Elysabeth could see a bruise that would yellow by the morrow, but a splendid cone cap covered in red brocade shot with gold thread covered her hair. Pleats of scarlet silk scarfed the old lady's shoulders and throat and tucked in beneath a collar of gris, safeguarding her against the cold, and the font of brocade beneath the dangling cross matched her headdress. The rest of the ducal person was swathed in an exuberant blood-red velvet.

'This is priceless, Elysabeth,' chuckled John, like an exuberant puppy pushing past her to peer in at the doorway. If he had possessed a tail, he'd have wagged it. 'I've never led two duchesses in to supper before.'

'It's not a dance, John. You only need escort our guest,' sighed Elysabeth. She had just come from tweaking the table linen into perfection. She was weary and famished. The delay while the kitchen servants struggled to create a supper worthy of Lady Catherine had nettled her temper and appetite even further.

'Tally-ho, then. My money's on this Norfolk bird. What say you? There'll be enough feathers flying to stuff a cushion by bedtime.'

'Behave!' She shoved him in. Her mind was obsessed as to whether the capons would be sufficiently roasted by the time they had finished the onion tartlets, but she managed a sensible exchange with Lady Catherine's steward and then an even more sensible one with the man in the black gown, who introduced himself as my lady's physician. She learned that the injured woman, Lady Catherine's bodyservant, had suffered shock to the nerves rather than injuries to her person and was now seeing to her mistress's clothing chests. Nothing and no one had been left at the roadside.

One of the knights in the retinue joined her, touching his wine cup to hers. 'Your health, madame, and thank you for rescuing us.'

She nodded graciously, estimating that in a few heartbeats he would be ladling flattery. The look in his eyes was warmer than the mulled wine between her fingers. He was an attractive fellow though proved to be nobody she had ever heard of.

'Did you lose your husband recently, Lady Grey?' His spatula fingers rose and uncurled, indicating her sober robe of green-black.

'At St Albans in battle a year ago, sir.'

'I'm sorry to hear that, madame. It must pain you to travel through there whenever you ride to London.'

She nodded. 'Indeed, it does, sir. Thankfully, I have little cause to journey south these days.'

'But surely a lady as beautiful as you would be welcome at the court?'

She could not be bothered to inform him she had attended *other courts*, Chancery, for instance, and she had not been welcome there either. A shake of her head did not deter the gentleman.

'I was at Westminster a few days since and believe me, madame, I saw no lady who could light a candle to your beauty. What's more, my lady, I find it impossible to believe that you are here like … like a violet hiding in the undergrowth. You, the daughter of a lady, whose husband once ruled France.'

'You flatter me, sir. Unfortunately, our family took the old king's part in the civil strife so you see we are definitely not welcome at Westminster. If truth be told, I doubt her grace of Norfolk is happy to spend a night beneath our roof. No doubt she will be amused to tell others of our reduced estate.'

'My lady is no gossip, I assure you. These are difficult times but the new king is determined to reconcile York and Lancaster so, if you will forgive my counsel, Lady Grey, stay proud of who you are.'

She smiled. 'Pride, sir, is about all I have left.'

Well, that put a stifler upon the conversation. A sure test of seeing whether his interest had been merely a feeler to her wealth.

'Dinner awaits us, sir.' It was a relief to see her mother's steward signalling that all was in readiness.

'Excellent,' murmured the knight, bowing for her to precede him through to the high table. 'I find myself a very hungry man tonight.'

In their father's absence, Elysabeth was both amused and perturbed that it fell to seventeen-year-old John to play the host. Like a King of Misrule, he escorted their ancient visitor to the high board and seated her in his father's chair with such uncharacteristic solemnity that his younger siblings began to giggle. Behind Lady Catherine's gaunt shoulder, Jacquetta sent her brood a glare calculated to reduce them to bread and water for a week.

Tom was more subtle than his younger uncles and aunts but several times during the repast, Elysabeth noticed him aping their noble guest's way of craning her neck when she was listening and several times she observed him whispering behind his hand, making the others laugh unkindly.

The knight, who had escorted her from the solar and was seated next to her, observed her concern. 'Perhaps you should consider seeking her grace's patronage for your sons, Lady Grey, or if you'd prefer, I could mention the matter for you,' he offered smoothly.

His breath played upon her ear; beneath the cloth, his hand ventured onto her left knee.

'Thank you, sir, but I honestly would trust neither my oldest son's manners nor my younger son's wits at present,' she replied, lifting his fingers aside.

'How so?'

'My older son is still affected by his father's death.'

'Hmm, yet there are plenty of cures for melancholy.' The teasing lift of the man's eyebrow suggested that she too might find his services useful. 'Perhaps the boy needs to be bled.' She imagined what Tom would say to that.

'As for my other child over there.' While Cat and Mary poked each other behind his back, Dickon was contentedly arranging the plum stones from his tart into precise formation. 'He has not been the same since he had a bad fall a year ago.' Mind, even before that, Dickon had never showed very much emotion and he had always counted the toy soldiers, the ones

Tom had later destroyed, back into the chest when he'd finished playing with them.

'Would you like her grace's physician to examine your children? His fees are affordable. For you, my lady, a special price.' The knight's foot nudged hers meaningfully.

For an instant, Elysabeth was tempted. Not just to have the physician's opinion but to feel a man's arms round her once again and this knight for all his silvery tongue was very personable. No, honour was more important. Besides, she saw Tom watching. He pulled a wry face and had her smiling.

'I regret I cannot afford your price, sir,' she answered demurely, 'although I appreciate your offer. Pray excuse me.' She should not neglect her right-hand neighbour, the duchess's chamberlain, but the conversation with the latter proved donkey-like at first, full of starts and little progress, and she knew the knight was listening with amusement. Not only listening but sliding looks down her profile from beneath his ebony lashes, fingering her in his imagination, permitting his gaze to linger where her nipples disturbed the sleek drape of the woollen fabric over her breasts.

'Her grace shows no ill from the day's adventure.' Another attempt at conversation.

The chamberlain finished chewing his mouthful. 'My lady's left forearm is bruised and tender but she is fortunate.'

'Some women of her years break limbs very easily. I assume she's three score years and more.'

'Aye, but sharp as an arrowhead,' asserted the chamberlain, holding out his tankard for more ale. 'It would take one of these new-fangled cannon balls at close range to knock her grace over and then she'd probably blow out the flame before you lit the powder.'

Elysabeth bit her lips not to laugh. The knight leaned closer. 'She's had three husbands already and is looking for a fourth.'

Patches the hue of summer poppies had bloomed upon their noble guest's countenance, clashing with the rosy powder already brushed there. The lady's heartiness owed much to her young host's persistent wickedness in replenishing her wine. Elysabeth could see the king's aunt was purring, and John was taking care not to be fulsome. He was too clever for that but their mother looked like she was aching to smash the ornate salt across his head.

'Oh dear me, you have so ... so many children, Jacquetta,' declared Lady Catherine loudly, peering once more at the row of young Woodvilles on the lower table. Elysabeth suspected that it was a lazy spite rather than inebriation that was giving the old lady a confused estimate of her hostess's progeny. 'It must be very —' a polite hiccough and she continued, '— hard to find marriage partners for them these days.' Here, the dowager sniffed and pale-lashed eyes watered in maudlin fashion. 'We have lost so many of our young men in this unfortunate civil strife.'

Elysabeth found she was holding her breath as she watched her mother's face but Jacquetta made no treasonous retort, merely she shrugged in Gallic fashion.

'Ah, zere is plenty of time since most of our children are still in ze nursery. Our belle Elysabeth she is the exception. All she requires is a new lord to protect 'er rights.'

As their guest of honour craned forwards, as if making a further assessment, Elysabeth's admiring neighbour slid his hand further up her leg, intent on a more erotic destination.

'I need a husband to protect my *sons*' rights, Maman,' Elysabeth corrected, fiercely preventing the opportunist fingers from delving into the woollen folds between her thighs.

Undaunted, the knight beamed attentively at the conversation and curled his thumb round to stroke her palm.

'You have no … er … suitors at present, Lady Grey?'

'No, madame.' It came out somewhat breathily as she tried to shift further from her lascivious neighbour. Such a tactic brought her up against the chamberlain's thigh and slapped a sudden foolish grin upon his face. Now he too put a hand on her knee.

'Nonsense, my daughter is just being modest.' Jacquetta paused to lick the quince paste from her fingers. 'We are 'oping she may make a match with the king's chamberlain. They are neighbours and acquainted, you know.'

'Mother, I don't think —' Elysabeth began.

Lady Catherine flicked a crumb from the corner of her thin mouth.

'I think you have missed the courier on that one, Jacquetta. The king, my nephew, has already arranged for Lord Hastings to marry my niece, Lady Harrington. Her daughter Cecily is a considerable heiress, you know, estates all over the West Country. Could I trouble you to pass me another wafer, if you please?'

Jacquetta took the rebuff on the chin. 'Would that be Katherine Neville? Ah, I think I met her once. A rather plain little demoiselle?'

Katherine's aunt and namesake drew a deep breath. 'One has to face the fact that noblemen have always had to look to their purses when they choose their brides. Mind, your daughter still has her looks. I know one or two elderly wealthy widowers who might be interested if you would like me to raise the matter.'

'Thank you, Lady Catherine, we have other irons in the fire.'

'But, Mother,' began John and received a quelling look from Jacquetta.

'Never mind, Lady Grey,' murmured the knight beside Elysabeth. 'There are consolations, "a bird in the hand…"'

The chamberlain was equally solicitous. 'I am sure that with your beauty, Lady Grey, you will soon find a suitable husband but in the meantime…' Each man was stroking her through her skirt. The steward, the tardy tortoise of the two, conveyed a hard-shelled tenacity.

Despairing of male vanity, Elysabeth considered slamming her sole back into the knight's shin. Instead, she slid her fingers caressingly over each of the men's soft hands, and joined them together!

For a moment nothing happened. The two fools wore daft, triumphant expressions until Elysabeth pointedly lifted both her hands to straighten her coif, and darted a sweet smile at each of them, waiting for the hammer to hit the anvil.

It was priceless. It took one scarlet mutual glare between the men to ensure that any further fishing expeditions remained in harbour. There was no more conversation and mercifully no more courses; the sweet wafers and quince paste were finished. Elysabeth rose thankfully to her feet with the rest of the company as John led Lady Catherine to the solar. He deposited her on a settle by the fire and drew up a cross-fold chair for Jacquetta. Elysabeth sat down beside their guest and had her hands patted.

'Yes, you certainly are a pretty creature. Hmm.' The old lady's mind retreated from the present for a few moments, as she stared into the flames. 'At least at my age,' she giggled suddenly, her insides now laced with goodly wine, 'I can wed to please myself' and then turning to Elysabeth, she declared, 'The first time is for your family, the second time is for the security of your children — if you have any — and the third time is to please yourself.'

'And the fourth?' quipped John.

'The fourth?' It was uttered with amusement and almost a little astonishment as if at her advanced years she had not considered the possibility.

'Why not, madame? A lady is surely as old as she feels and judging by your lively disposition, you must be as young as I at heart.'

Colour once more suffused the dowager's pale countenance 'Well, yes, a pr … pretty speech, young man, but I should be an old fool to believe you. How old are you, nineteen?'

'Seventeen, madame.'

'Indeed? So young.' More sadness moistened Lady Catherine's eyes.

'If you will permit me to catechise you, madame?' John persisted with a sinful glint, and when the old lady acquiesced with a nod, he asked, 'Do you feel your age?'

As intent as him, she too leaned forward. 'No, Master Woodville.'

'Do you forswear the marriage bed?'

An angry frown flicked across her face but it was gone in an instant. 'No.'

'Do you enjoy the company of younger people?'

'Since I am older than all my acquaintances, young man…'

'But do you, your grace?'

'Yes, very much so.'

He opened his hands as if his point was made and she sat back smiling. 'You have an agile tongue, John Woodville.'

'And you have an agile mind, Lady Norfolk.'

They eyed each other with mutual approval.

Elysabeth would have rolled her eyes at John's behaviour but the old lady was lapping up the attention like a famished old tabby, except that John was right, her straight demeanour meant that 'old' was not the word to describe her.

'Please forgive me if I seek my bed now. I must rise early to resume my journey.'

John drew breath and for a moment, Elysabeth thought he might make some unfortunate play on 'rise'. Instead, he murmured, 'Of course,' and helped her grace to her feet.

'I shall speak to my royal nephew on your behalf when I see him again. Maybe he can find a place for you in his household.'

'That would be most gracious of you, madame.'

'Lady Grey, I hope your circumstances improve. Speak with the abbot at St Albans about educating your sons for the monastic order! It will certainly suit the younger boy.' All loftily suggested and before Elysabeth could even say 'no' and 'no!', the ancient bitch was giving another order. 'Jacquetta, oh, there you are. Pray see me to my chamber! I cannot remember my way in this coney warren of yours.'

'Do not lift your hopes, little brother,' warned Elysabeth as they carried candles to the stairs later. 'As if she'll mention you to the king.'

John shrugged. 'Thought it was you who was all for buttering up the high and mighty. So, the old lady goes to bed happy.'

'Yes, but tomorrow with a soberer head, she may think you false and fulsome.'

'And Hastings, in his cups, may remember your beauty and wish he had not turned you aw —' He cut off his words at the telltale rustle from the landing above, but to Elysabeth's relief it was only Tom who loitered.

'You excelled yourself tonight, uncle,' he sneered. 'A wonder you did not suck the mud off the old crone's shoe beaks.'

'*Tom!*' Elysabeth hissed angrily.

His eyes glittered like orbs of white. 'Uncle John's no better than that ragged whore who does her business with the old men in the laneway by the inn in Stony Stratford.'

'Tom!' Horrified at her son's ingratitude and astonished at his worldliness, she grabbed her brother's arm to stay his fist.

'Don't you call me a whore, you ungrateful, landless lump of Groby sh —'

Elysabeth flung up her hands between them. 'Be quiet both of you! Will you shame us?' In the tense silence, she could hear conversation beyond the door of the guest chamber up the stairs but thank God no latch was raised.

Tom was still blocking their way. 'Oh, truth will out. At last I know what you really think, dear uncle.'

'Go to your chamber this instant, child!'

'A pity Lord Hastings would not take you in and teach you manners, Thomas Grey,' growled John. 'You need a good thrashing and I shall be very pleased to give you one.'

'No!'

'Why not, Mother?' sneered her son. 'It's all that I'm good for. Groby shit, eh, Uncle?'

Beside her, John's breath became even. 'Then you can muck out the stables in the morning.'

She did not argue with that.

'Go, Tom, now!' Amazingly he obeyed.

John stormed off angrily to his sleeping chamber and Elysabeth, with a deep sigh, sat down wearily on the stairs waiting for Tom to cool his temper before she went to the cramped bedchamber to speak with him.

Dickon was asleep but Tom was an angry hunched-up bundle beneath the sheet.

'I cannot tolerate such behaviour, Tom. If your uncle punishes you in the morning you have only yourself to blame.'

'I don't care!' he muttered, as she sat down beside him. 'How long are we going to stay here like beggars? I thought it was only to be a few weeks but it's almost half a year. When are we going to get Astley back?'

'I don't know,' she said. 'Until there's a verdict on the three manors your grandfather settled on us.'

'Then we'll go and live on one of them?'

'No, they are just farms, I'm afraid.'

'Are you going to marry again? I saw the way those men you were sitting with tonight were looking at you.'

'No, darling, only if I met someone who would be a good stepfather to you and Dickon.'

*And who was wealthy enough to love a landless bride.*

'You loved Father, didn't you?'

'You know I did, and I love you and Dickon. We'll get your lands back, Tom, but it may take a while and it doesn't help you being rude to your uncle.'

'Why not, Mama? Uncle John's only fought in skirmishes and he's never had anyone he loves die, or been shamed like I was at Astley in front of all those soldiers.'

'No, he hasn't, so do not blame him for being merry-hearted. And you must remember that he hasn't any land either. Your grandparents have eight manors, that is all, and when they pass away, everything will go to Uncle Anthony because he's the oldest.'

Tom sniffed. 'At least *his* father's been pardoned.'

'And so shall yours be. I'll get the attainder reversed, I promise. But listen, my darling, we all have choices. You can go around with woes strapped on your shoulders for the rest of your life, or you can outwardly make the best of things, even if you are hurting on the inside. Everyone has a cross to bear. Perhaps God is trying to temper you into a better person.'

He shrugged and then he looked round at her again. 'Do not marry anyone just to provide for us, will you, Mama? It must be someone you truly love.'

She smiled, ran her fingers through his hair, touched deeply by his understanding, and remembered another tousled head back in the summer — the only man she had found truly tempting since her husband's death.

The young man she had met at Kirby Muxloe.

# 16: KATE

*12th January 1462, Westminster Palace*

The tenez court where Lord Hastings had arranged for the actors to rehearse was narrow with a lofty, pitched ceiling, a sloping gallery of seats on one side and some very odd masonry protrusions, presumably pertinent to the game. Kate had never actually played tenez or *jeu de paume* as it was also known, but she knew that the parallel lines marked in whitewash across the floor were called chases. The massive net, rolled-up and lying alongside the gallery wall, was serving a new purpose, strewn with garments like a Cheapside slopseller's stall.

Most of the players, already masked and costumed, were huddled at the hazard end of the court. One young man stood apart while a kneeling young woman sewed his sleeves tight in at the wrists. Their breath was vapour and one of the older men clad only in hose and a sleeveless leather jerkin must have been feeling chilled.

Sitting at the service end on Neptune's throne — now lined with furs instead of mock seaweed — Kate felt very cosseted. At Lord Hastings' insistence, she now had a hot brick beneath her feet and a brazier of glowing coals behind her chair. His concern was almost enough to exorcise the dismay of two days ago from her thoughts. Almost. And when he drew up a mock throne beside hers, taking his seat like a king to her queen, it was hard not to feel flattered. It was equally hard to be prepared to say no to this man; should he outmanoeuvre her. However, with some twelve players to play gooseberry and her attendant, Eleanor, sitting on a cushion next to the footstool, the king's handsome chamberlain was unlikely to get adventurous.

Still, even with him scarcely beyond touching distance, she could barely draw her gaze from him. She liked the power and authority that he wore, not like some newly acquired rich mantle to be flaunted, but as though born to it. The way he took his ease, an elbow nonchalant on the arm of the throne, his hand supporting his chin, the cabochon amethyst that adorned his third finger, lavender and gold against the mulberry hue of his glove. He could be hers for the taking, but at too great a price.

'Whitfield, the portly knave wearing the crown, is their master player.'

'He looks greatly afeared of you, my lord.' Kate smiled graciously at Master Whitfield as the fellow looked their way. 'For players, they seem quite timorous.'

'And no wonder. With all the lords in England thumping the hell out of each other, and the old king not liking pageantry unless it had a religious theme, these poor wretches have had it hard these last years. I beg you to look entertained even if you are not.'

'Oh, I am sure I shall be, my lord,' she murmured contentedly.

'I hope they live up to your expectations.'

'They wanted to perform *Sir Gawaine and the Green Knight*, but that was out of the question.'

'Indeed? Surely the playfulness between the Green Knight's Lady and Sir Gawaine would have provided much humour?'

He drew a deep breath. 'I am sure you are right, my lady, but it was the first part when the Green Man asks Sir Gawaine to strike his head off that concerned me.'

'Oh dear, I suppose that would be quite difficult although they might manage something with a sheet and a lant —' She broke off as the stone of realisation hit the bottom of the well. 'Oh, Jesu!' Shameful blood flushed her skin. She had just spoken like some insensitive fishwife back from a disembowelling at Tower Hill.

'Exactly,' he agreed grimly. 'Like yourself, there would hardly be a noble watching who has not had a kinsman beheaded by the old queen or been afraid for his own life. It is only through God's good grace that Ned and the rest of us survived such a fate.'

A worldly dame might have passed off the mistake but Kate was mortified. How crass and utterly stupid of her not to have grasped his reasons to begin with. He must think her such a young fool.

'I crave your forgiveness, my lord. B-But the tale is so ... so well known that I truly did not link the make-believe with...' *My father's death.* The words hung in the air between them.

'And I am right glad you did not, Lady Katherine,' he cut in. 'May you keep such innocence.' Oh, not again! The comment stung although his voice lacked irony. She might have struggled to defend herself except suddenly, despite the fur lining to his cloak, he shuddered, not at the cold fingers of the frosty air, but involuntarily as though an angel passed across his grave. 'By Christ's Blessed Mercy! It's such an ugly way to die.'

She drew a cross between her forehead and heart. 'God grant that it was swift for my father.' But the wry twist of his lips denied even that certainty.

Clenching her gloved hands in her lap, she realised that Hastings had been scarred by the recent war, whereas Richard seemed hardened, if anything. Hmm, there was an unexpected vulnerability in the man beside her that did him credit and was unquestionably appealing. It was to her shame that she had spoken so crassly.

'Madame?' Eleanor rose, her dauncell's antennae alerted to her mistress's discomfort.

Kate forced herself to look up. The players were watching her and Lord Hastings like grazing rabbits ready to scatter. She shook her head at her servant and, clearing her throat, asked huskily, 'So what piece is it to be, my lord? Not Salome and John the Baptist, that's for sure.' Pray God that shaft had not flown amiss. She turned her head, fearful at his silence and found to her relief that his face was creased with amusement.

'So humour is your sword and buckler, Lady Katherine. I must remember that in our dealings.' It was spoken with the satisfaction of a hunter who has a hind in his sight. *Our dealings.* Well, she would pick up her skirts and outrun him if she had to.

He seemed to expect some further wit from her but she had no answer, and with a tight smile, he rose to his feet. The players instantly fell silent. 'Shall we begin?' The authority in his voice resonated in the rafters.

Master Whitfield stepped forward and after much ahemming began:

> *We bid you, gentles all, to gather now*
> *Whether ye rule this land or guide the plough.*
> *For herewith we shall play, come sun, come rain,*
> *The tale of the Lion and the Knight Erwayne.*
> *I am King Arthur, come to narrate this story,*
> *Of how a brave youth rose to fame and glory.*

King Arthur then introduced each character and when it came to the Lion, who burst out with a roar from behind the screen and tripped, Lord Hastings, who had been watching with sucked-in cheeks, buried his head in his hands. She thought it was with despair at the poor player's ineptitude but his shoulders were shaking with laughter.

'Good man! Keep that in!' he called out, then muttered beneath his breath, 'Devil take it, I've seen statues with more life than these fellows.'

Kate watched on stoically. The players had to mime while King Arthur narrated the story in hapless verse. Each man was so desperately earnest, and it would have increased their courage if my lord chamberlain could have leaned back and looked less like a fraught merchant watching his cargo-laden ship sink to the seabed. True, any bumblings in a performance before the court would be laid at his door but King Arthur, noting my lord's frown, began to stumble his lines.

Something had to be done. When Sir Erwayne defeated Sir Kay in combat, Kate clapped her hands in seeming delight. The stratagem worked. The players, reassured by her pleasure, budded confidence and by the time the Lion broke down the portcullis and bounded in to savage the evil Sir Salados, Lord Hastings looked to be actually enjoying the performance. Finally, when King Arthur's narration ended with a blessing on his descendant, King Edward IV, the true and rightful King of England, begotten through the line of Mortimer and Plantagenet, Kate sprang to her feet applauding heartily! Although she could not see the players' faces behind the masks, if rosy necks were an indication, they were gratified by her enthusiasm.

'I do not think you should be concerned, my lord,' she exclaimed, whirling round excitedly to face her companion. 'A little more practice is needed, that's all.'

'You do not think there was too much gore? Some of the older ladies might not have the stomach for it.'

'Well, Aunt Catherine has gone home and Aunt Cecily doesn't usually object to anything except blasphemy. I do have some suggestions, though, that you might wish to pass on to Master Whitfield.'

'Ah, I knew it.' He reached out and took her gloved hand. 'Then, come and tell him yourself. Attention, Master Whitfield and good friends all! My lady wishes to speak with you.' The players halted in clearing their properties to the side.

'No, my lord,' laughed Kate, hanging back. 'I do not think they would...'

'A third of their audience will be noblewomen, Lady Katherine. Have confidence! Come!' He led her forward and stood back, allowing her the pulpit. The entertainers fanned out around her, the young men showing quills of arrogance and suspicion, the rest anxious to please, except for the seamstress who was preoccupied with moistening her lips at Lord Hastings in a come-hither fashion. What bothered Kate was that Hastings had noticed.

'F-Firstly, it was most excellent.' Kate beamed at them and swept them a curtsey, calculated to disarm their nervousness and they actually broke into cheers. 'However, with my lord's permission...' At least Hastings' attention was once more on her. 'I should like to make one or two suggestions. There are ways you could provoke even more merriment.' Their crestfallen looks were back again except for the ambitious seamstress.

'Sir Lion,' she addressed the eyeholes in the huge mask. 'Why not behave more like a real lion? Find a flea, roll on your back to scratch it, snap at a horsefly. Purr sometimes. Play the lion for laughter. I am sure my lord here would pay for you to see the real ones at the Tower.'

'Of course,' he agreed, although Kate was suspicious there was indulgence rather than agreement in the twitch of his lips.

'You, Damsel in the Wood, instead of waggling those … those false breasts, sirrah, why not use your eyes like this.' She gave the boy a slow seductive stare and ended up blushing and self-conscious, laughing with them. 'Or ask this young mistress here how she would do it.' Guffaws of laughter broke out when the seamstress realised she had been caught out.

'Sir Erwayne,' Kate purred. 'We all know the damsel is really a youth, but do try and look more genuinely tempted. Yes, share the jest with us and raise an eyebrow, but you must appear serious when you are gazing into "her" eyes. Perhaps you gentlemen are not aware how intense you look when you are about to melt a woman's heart with your kisses.'

Lord Hastings suddenly found an interest in the beamed ceiling, his mouth tightly seamed shut, except at the corners. When Sir Erwayne, whose golden curls were not a wig, opened his conceited, full-lipped mouth for argument, Kate forestalled him. 'How did you do the gore in the combat, Master Whitfield?' she exclaimed, whirling round to face King Arthur, suspecting that he would be delighted to explain. She let him take her across to the bloodied shield but Hastings stayed with the others.

'Well thought out,' she agreed sincerely as Master Whitfield explained the concealed bag of chicken blood in Sir Salados' wig. She was trying not to mind that on the other side of the court, the seamstress had pushed her bodice lower and was actually conversing with Lord Hastings in simpering fashion. Sweeping back across to join them, Kate bestowed a generous smile on my lord chamberlain's worshipper before she beamed at him.

'So you were not interested in how the lance pierced Sir Salados, my lord?'

'Towton was enough for me.'

By the Saints, she had done it again, overstepped the mark with such utter tactlessness. The bloodiest battle on English soil, fought in a snowstorm, with thousands slain. He had been part of that killing while she —

Swallowing, she managed to keep her smile. The instant she could, she would escape his company. They just did not understand each other.

'Gentlemen,' Lord Hastings was saying, 'make the changes and if it pleases me, you shall play before King Edward.'

As the players whooped and jubilantly slapped backs, Hastings held out his wrist to receive Kate's hand and they farewelled the troupe and walked out into the watery green light of the ebbing sun.

'Thank you for inviting me to participate, my lord. I enjoyed that very much.' Spoken in formal manner and punctuated by a curtsey. Where was her maidservant? If only Eleanor would come out, she could retreat as fast as possible but Lord Hastings framed her shoulders with his hands as though he was calming a distressed child.

'Sometimes I think you judge yourself too harshly, Lady Katherine. Any fool could see you were just giving Whitfield a chance to boast. Think no more on it!'

'Boast, no! I thought if Master Whitfield felt appreciated, his enthusiasm and confidence would flow into the rest of his troupe.'

'I'm impressed. Do you also deal with your household with such care for their feelings?'

'I haven't ever had a household of my own,' Kate answered with a sniff. Her nose was running with the cold air and she fumbled in her girdle purse for a kerchief. 'I am gradually taking over from Grandmother Bonville although she'd never admit it.' Looking up, she snared him studying her. 'Are we finished here?'

'Yes.' He held out his hand to her again. 'Come, let's forget about bloody mawed lions, shall we? Katherine?'

'I-I'm not sure I can, my lord, because I just saw one in the bushes?'

'*What?*'

He turned his head and glimpsed the man in the lion apparel fumbling with his codpiece. An arc of water spattered the outside wall of the tenez court.

'Not there, curse you!' Hastings shouted, raising a fist. 'Piss there again and I'll stick your head up your —' He remembered Kate's presence. 'Ignorant cur,' he muttered. 'Give them an inch and they take a plaguey yard.'

With a further glare and an assertive flex of shoulders, he turned back to usher Kate down the path. Pleating her lips to staunch her giggles, she kept up with him for some paces until she remembered he might start talking about marriage. Darting a glance behind her, she saw with relief that Eleanor was discreetly following them.

'You do not mind a walk, Katherine?'

'No,' she lied, and it would have been discourteous not to tuck her arm through his, when offered.

'Would you like to see my barge? Hey, why are you laughing?' But he was smiling, too, now. 'I do have one.'

'Yes,' she giggled.

'Stop laughing at me.' Grinning, he reached up and flicked her cheek.

They walked on companionably. It was needful to lift her skirts to keep the mire at the edges of the long puddles away from the furred trim of her over-gown. The path soon became more ruly, but then it divided.

'Are you warm enough?'

'Yes, thank you.' She wasn't but she did not want his arm about her. It would feel too comfortable and … well, best not. She did find him attractive and she respected him for admitting he had been affected by Towton. Not a milksop squeamishness but sorrow, revulsion. Would Will have returned feeling that way? Would he have been honest enough to say so?

Peeking up, she saw that Hastings' frown was back, making her wonder whether the memory of Towton was haunting him like some dismembered foe? Did he dream at night that he was back in the midst of battle and wake sweating and afraid? Maybe if he had a wife to hug him, make him laugh, the scars would heal quicker. Could she do that?

But then she remembered the seamstress. Would his wife be able to tolerate that? Could she?

Anyway, no one had mentioned the 'wife' word, thank goodness! Hastings would not want a plain 'innocent' like her anyway. Had Richard or the king even asked him?

He chose the left-hand path. It meandered through a natural thicket of hawthorn, ivy and alder that had been tamed into a hedge and, judging by the lack of footprints, seldom used. Only a cock robin in scarlet and brown livery eyed them from beneath an arch of briar. Surely, a few minutes would bring them safely within sight of the Queen's Bridge Wharf and as a contingency Eleanor had instructions about when to make her presence obvious.

Suspicious, Kate glanced sideways but her lordly companion seemed more mindful of their surroundings than he was of her so she just breathed in the peace of the moment. The hedgerow mercifully thinned to a scatter of oaks and ash along the reedy tributary, and at the wooden bridge that could have taken them across to Millbank, Kate made pretence of looking at the water, wondering if Eleanor needed time to catch up. A few paces on they joined the bridleway along the Thames and turned towards the palace.

Already the tired sun was failing, gilding the edges of the clouds and changing the walls of the abbey to a dusty, mellow gold against the smoky sky. Ahead, high above the glinting weathervanes that tipped the pinnacles and turrets of Ned's palace, Kate could see a solitary red kite soaring imperiously, his feathers like fiery copper. Below him, the lozenged, grisailled window of the great hall was transfigured into a hundred tiny mirrors of dazzling vermillion. The sight stole Kate's breath like a lover might.

Her companion was keeping his own thoughts close. Maybe he often came this way; perhaps his office forced him to observe that one of the palace chimneys was not drawing like the rest or that the nearest gable had a missing tile. No, she was wrong.

'I mean to live life to the full, every damnable instant.'

The sudden, uninvited outburst from him sounded like some angry vow, as though he felt it his obligation, a duty owed to the dead beneath the battlefields of Mortimer's Cross and Towton.

'God keep you in his grace, my lord.' The blessing bounced out too tritely. She must have sounded like his chaplain. 'I meant may He give you many years, my lord,' she corrected swiftly and then guessed she had offended him because he violently thrust aside the wands of willow and plunged down a makeshift way of jutting grass to where the land embraced the end of the wharf. Kate grabbed her skirts and followed, halting a little way off.

For a moment he stared up at the glowing clouds as though they were two great hosts assembling for battle and then he looked round at Kate as if she were a little girl who had asked a profound question.

'Come the spring, we'll deal with the northern rebels once and for all, God willing. I just hope to Heaven we can snare Queen Margaret and the boy. If we don't, he'll forever be a thorn in our flesh.' He looked back down at her. 'I want to see Ned establish a dynasty, Lady Katherine, so we can sleep safe in our beds. We don't want a world where your Cecily will lose her young husband in battle just like you did.'

'I share your sentiments, my lord, but the Lancastrian prince is only a little fellow.'

'Give him ten years more, and he will want the kingdom, and then we may need to sharpen our sword blades again and grease our rusting armour.'

'God forfend!' Kate looked up at him unhappily. This was not the conversation she had expected. Ten years from now she would be twenty-nine and he in his early forties, still young enough to fight, especially if he remained in high office. But anything might happen between now and then. She could not let him scythe away her peace of mind. She wanted a rosy future for her daughter.

'Oh, come now, my lord,' she exclaimed, in the hope of lightening his humour. 'The boy, if he lives that long, will need more than envy to conquer England.' She grabbed the thumb of her left hand. 'To start with, there has to be some silly foreign fool willing to lend him the money for an invasion;

what's more, he'll need sufficient misguided traitors to follow his banner, not to mention that he has an obnoxious mother whom nobody likes. Besides...' She floundered, tapping her fourth finger. 'Besides, Ned has you and my brothers to...'

Lord Hastings' hand fastened round both of hers and he was laughing at her vehemence. 'Why, you little dragon fighter.'

'If you can be serious, so can I, Lord Hastings!' she informed him, pulling free. 'Ten years is surely long enough for Ned to entrench himself in the people's hearts. He'll be as hard to shift as ... as this tree, don't you agree?' She toed the nearest root for emphasis and then skittishly swung round the other side of the tree.

'If Heaven wills it so, Lady Katherine,' he agreed, leaning his shoulder against the bark and watching her. 'But, by God's truth, sweet lady, it doesn't take much to create a grievance. So long as there is a leader, there are always the dissatisfied who will follow, alienated because of a lost court case, or indeed an unkind look or —'

She should have moved out of arm's reach for it was wondrous how a man could suddenly forget the hurly-burly of statecraft. His fingers reached out to touch her cheek and with such gentleness drew his thumb along her cheekbone.

'Katherine,' he began.

Someone coughed.

He turned his head and beheld Eleanor standing up on the path. It took only an instant for his slack-jawed look to vanish. 'Devil take it, madame!' he cursed, swinging away from Kate.

'It's only my maidservant.'

'Really?' This was a lord chamberlain suddenly on his high horse. 'She reminds me of your brother George at his most sanctimonious. And why is she watching me as though I am about to throw you on your back? Is the Lord Chamberlain and Master of the Coinage deemed untrustworthy with anyone in skirts?' He was so thoroughly indignant that Kate seeing the humour of it all could not resist stirring him further.

'Well, you do have a reputation, my lord,' she pointed out demurely.

'Do I indeed?' he snapped. 'Who would you prefer to walk with, Lady Katherine? Her or me?'

It was definitely time to smooth honey on his wounded pride before it festered. Kate gathered up her skirts and swept back to Eleanor, asking her to return to their bedchamber but when she turned round, her touchy companion had misconstrued her choice and disappeared. She found him along on the wharf moodily staring out across the river with his arms folded and a foot set on a capstan. There was nobody else within an arrow's shot but any thought of being endangered by his company had fled; her only thought was to restore the cordiality between them.

Standing behind him, she found herself quoting a verse, learned in childhood, from *Sir Gawaine and the Green Knight*.

'For, see here, I believe you are Sir Gawaine.
Whom alle the worlde worships wher'ere you ride.
Your honour, your courteous manner, is worldwide known
By lordes, by ladyes, by alle that live.
And now you are here, y-wiss, and we but on our own.'

Beneath the velvet cloak, the pouched tops of his sleeves rose in a shrug. How could there be such a vulnerability about him? And yet there was, although the man's shoulders were thrust back in defiance and his mouth was as thin as an angry pen stroke.

'Lord Hastings, please, my servant meant you no offence.'

The Adam's apple in Hastings' throat moved awkwardly as though it pained him to swallow and then he quoted back to her:

'*Though I be not now he you speke therof.*'

'Yes,' she answered, heartened that he was at least answering her.

'*Nor,*' he added, '*do I reach the reverence as you here rehearse.*'

'I am right glad of that, my lord, for Sir Gawaine sounds an unctuous bore.' She ventured a gentle hand upon his sleeve. 'Therefore sheath your anger, my lord. I know my royal cousin is lucky in those that serve him.' Then, giving his honour time to cool, she drew back and seated herself upon a fallen tree that had been crudely hacked to form a bench. Eventually, he turned his face towards her as though it was she whose trustworthiness was now on trial.

'Why are you afraid of marrying again?'

Kate did not answer. She stared down at her gloves.

'What happened to you, Katherine?'

Compelled to reply, she looked up at him and even though her hands were clenched, she said indifferently, 'I find trust a challenge, my lord.'

'*Trust!*' He came across and stood staring down at her. It did not seem to be the answer he had expected. Then his face lightened. 'Maybe you haven't been kissed enough.'

'It's only because I'm Warwick's sister I've been kissed at all!'

'You're wrong, you know.'

'It seems I am wrong about a great deal, my lord. It's my "innocence", you see. It attracts errors like a dung heap attracts flies.'

'Ouff!' He pulled a face and blew on his fingers as though her words were scorching. 'Have you considered that dung makes plants grow?' he asked teasingly.

'I truly believe what *I* consider is likely of no real interest to you, Lord Hastings, or my brothers,' she said sadly.

He chewed that over for a moment and then his voice lost its playfulness. 'Since the king wishes me to take you for my wife, you'll have to admit it might be.'

A murrain on him! So the matter was beaten into the open at last. Had he expected she would fall in beside him like an obedient chariot horse? Or that a stolen kiss in the counting house was eternally binding like a betrothal vow?

'*Take* implies that a person or property is seized without consent.'

The wince was almost imperceptible but he rallied with masculine stubbornness.

'Without consent. I see. That also is the problem?'

'My lord, it is getting chill.' She gathered her skirts to stand and then saw in his face that he would prevent her. With a sigh, she decided on outright honesty. 'I don't like sharing.'

He took that on the chin and then pointed out, 'But you shared your child.'

'Pardon?'

'You shared your babe with a wet nurse. You trusted her, I'm sure.'

'Yes,' she said and added gravely, 'And I can see that breasts are involved in both instances. But sharing a husband is another matter.'

For an instant, she thought he was trying to keep a straight face. 'It works both ways, trust does,' he countered reasonably. 'A wife can conceive another man's child.'

'Yes, but I wouldn't.'

'It's possible. You might be carrying some Devon gentleman's begetting.'

'Ye-es,' she conceded. 'And you might be carrying the pox.'

They stared at one another like a pair of prodded, fierce fighting cocks and then she laughed and watched the outrage seep from his handsome face.

'I won't ask again why you can't trust, Katherine, unless you want to tell me, but if you won't trust, what are you going to do about it?' She must have looked puzzled because he added, 'Take holy orders?'

'Good heavens, no, I've Cecily's future to consider.'

'Of course, and I can see that is the most important consideration of all. Shall we return to the great hall for now?'

Feeling like a gate that had been climbed over, if gates could feel, she patted the log beside her and to her surprise, he sat down.

'Is it difficult minding Ned? That's what you are doing, isn't it?'

'Yes, as his chamberlain, I am expected to be at his side most of the time and his father made me swear to always safeguard him.'

'Then perhaps you should become Archbishop of Canterbury as well. Thomas à Beckett managed both.'

'A pox on Thomas à Beckett!'

'My lord! You are cursing a saint.'

'Hell take it, madame!' he exclaimed. The endearing, harassed look was back. 'Hear me out and then you will understand.'

*Will I indeed?* The old wounds from Will's infidelity ached still. She watched him lean forward, hands clasped.

'I don't mean to make a monk of Ned. The trick is to permit him everything except that which could do him infinite harm.'

Infinite harm? Because she did not answer, he glanced sideways at her, seemingly frustrated that she did not murmur approval. It was the most perfect rationalisation for dealing with wealthy whores and biblers that she could imagine. Did he sample the adulterous wives first to see if they were clean and wholesome, inquire who else they had lain with and whether they were free of sores, warts and Heaven knew what else?

'By the Saints, my lord,' she said finally, with a deep sigh although it was tempting to scoff. 'You set yourself a labour worthy of Hercules. And I consider your concern is misguided. Ned is not a fool.'

For an instant, he looked as though she had slapped him.

'No, madame, he is highly intelligent but when as a king you can have everything you ever dreamed of, what do you do when there are no more challenges? When you are bored and sated? It seems to me, my lady, that the seeds of self-corruption that we all carry inside us could then begin to germinate.'

And had they germinated in him? Was it experience or merely self-interest for his own future that had turned this man into a royal guard dog?

She sucked in her cheeks. 'So, no Southwark wagtails for Ned.'

His eyes narrowed. 'Definitely no Southwark wagtails or any other wagtails. Who the Devil taught you that term?'

'Ned did.'

He swore beneath his breath.

'I am the same age as Ned,' she said, kicking her heels against the timber, and then springing to her feet, 'and I hardly think that in his shoes I need to have my choices made for me. We both suffer from my brother Richard's interference enough as it is.'

He strode after her. 'Ouch.'

'Yes, ouch, my lord.' The sun was gone now. She was conscious that the wind had swung east and shivered, cradling her arms. He offered her his mantle and was refused. Then without even asking, he took hold of her arm so that she was compelled to stop.

'I said all that about Ned in confidence, Lady Katherine.'

'Yes, I know.'

In a few moments they were within the gaze of the world. My Lord of Canterbury's barge was waiting at the steps to carry his grace back to his palace across the river and the water boatmen were lighting their lanterns. Perhaps they recognised the lord chamberlain was with her and this time they kept a respectful distance. With so many people in sight, Kate feared no impropriety so she was caught off guard when he swung her off the path behind a squat oak.

'You are going to marry me, Kate,' he stated, with a possessiveness that was both delicious and challenging, and he kissed her thoroughly to make sure she understood.

'I'm not,' she argued faintly, when she could breath. 'I am not marrying anyone just yet.'

'No argument.' He kissed the side of her throat. 'Sealed, signed and soon to be...' he teased her lips, 'delivered.'

'No.' Her fingers lying flat against his breast flexed against him. His right leg was pressing against her skirts and she could feel the hardness between his thighs. Oh, he wanted her and it wasn't a coupling to beget an heir but a lusty desire that was finding an answer between her own thighs.

'Why not?' His breath teased her lips and he kissed her again. His hands, sliding beneath her cloak, curled round her bottom and drew her hips against his body. 'Come back with me to my chamber now and lie in my arms.' He smiled down at her. 'God as my witness, I'll exchange vows with you here and now if that's what you want. Come with me, Kate.'

Her treacherous body arched desirously, but desperately mustering mind and strength, she pushed him back. 'No, my lord.'

'By Heaven, you contrary creature, why not?' Another kiss so seductive, she could hardly stand.

'Because...'

'Oh, Hell take it! It's not Ned you want, is it?' Now it was he who eased back, his hands settling at her waist. He looked fearfully certain and certainly hurt.

'No, that's so preposterous,' she giggled. 'We've just kissed like that and you think I want Ned. Besides he kisses too wetly.'

'What!' Laughter dimpled his cheeks and he looked down at her as Marcus Antonius might have gazed at Cleopatra if she had said the same outrageous thing about Julius Caesar. '*Ned* kisses wetly? The King of England kisses wetly?'

'He does, he does,' she laughed, sliding a playful finger up the fur lapel of his mantle.

'Then why not you and I? What was the "Because"?'

'Because you are far too handsome for me. How can I keep you? Look at me, a dowdy Devonshire —'

'Wren?' he suggested, eyes twinkling.

'Wren, yes, that will do. I was thinking sparrow actually.'

'I was thinking a lady jay.'

Kate's mouth became an 'O' of astonishment. 'Well, you are a swan, my lord. A royal swan, you belong to Ned.'

'You are not implying something disreputable, are you, my lady?'

Her skin scorched beneath his amusement. 'No, no, my lord, of course not.'

'I don't give up easily, Kate Neville.'

She felt as though she was being wrenched apart to deny him.

'Well, my lord, nor do I.'

There were ways to leave without giving offence to anyone, particularly a royal or brotherly 'anyone'. A letter, perhaps, from Grandmother Bonville, make-believe, of course, that Cecily was unwell.

'Madame, don't forget your wine.' Eleanor pushed the swaddled goblet of mulled wine into Kate's hands and knelt to prod the fire into a more cheerful mien.

'You write a reasonable hand, don't you, Eleanor?' If she and Eleanor concocted a concise letter summoning her home to Shute, then perhaps it might be enough to convince Richard and Ned to let her go…

'I believe so, my lady, thanks to you. Curse it, this wood is still green.' Eleanor frowned at the profusion of smoke refusing to keep within the chimney mantle.

'Like me.' Kate padded across to the window and opened the lights to let some air in to cleanse away the smoke. 'Oh, damnation!' The laughter and music from the great hall still tempted her like Satan's whisper, but her heart knew that if Lord Hastings drew her once more into the shadows before tomorrow, she would end up in his bed.

'Go and ask my sister's servant if there is any ink and paper at hand. You and I are about to forge a letter.'

The forgery took several attempts. Watching someone else painstakingly labouring tongue in teeth when she could have dashed it off without blots or crossings out first time played havoc with Kate's beleaguered nerves.

'Mercy, this looks as though it was written by a notary with hiccoughs,' muttered Eleanor, completing the address while her mistress softened the orange sealing wax.

'Written in haste and agitation.' Kate dribbled the wax into place and firmly squished the Harrington-Bonville seal into the orange blob.

'Your pardon, madame, but are you so very sure this is the right path? It's still my reckoning that Lord Hastings would be a good master.'

'Please do not question me, Eleanor. Do you think I do this lightly? Lord Hastings so beguiles me in his company that my common sense flies out the window. If I stay here, my brother will have me wedded and bedded before the week is out and I'm not willing to wed again, not this yea —' She broke off as voices came from beyond the door and a loud hammering shook its timber. 'If that is one of my brothers or Lord Hastings, tell him ... tell him what you will, but I'll not see him. Do it, Eleanor!'

But she wasn't prepared to see a stubbled Robert Newton leaning exhausted against the lintel. His eyes widened with warmth at seeing her standing behind Eleanor but Kate was more concerned about why he had come.

'Bid him enter! Is all not well, Master Newton? Eleanor, hook the *couver-feu* off and reheat the spiced perry we had earlier! Have you come all the way from Chewton, Master Newton? Sit, sit, I beg you!'

'From Shute, my lady.' He snatched off his hat, and bowed to her before he sank wearily onto a little bench by the hearth. 'Lady Bonville has sent you a letter, madame,' he said. Casting his sodden leather hat to the floor, he burrowed a hand into the pouch on his belt. 'My little lady was ill with fever when I left.'

'Heaven forbid!' She swiftly read the brief message with mounting disgust at herself. It was almost as though she had willed this ill-fortune on her child. Grandmother Bonville's plea that she should return home was an alarum call to sanity. All that mattered was Cecily. Without her, life was not worth living.

'You are a good man,' she said, clapping a hand on Newton's bowed shoulder in thanks. He lifted his other hand, perhaps to enclose hers, but she turned to pace the floor. 'Is there truly any danger that she might die?' she demanded, dragging a hand in distress across her lips. God be merciful! What if Cecily were already dead? She sent a desperate plea to Heaven.

'I do not know, my lady.' His face always told the truth. She read common sense there, not panic, yet something else. Surprise? Some sort of regret? before he added, 'Folk always reckon that girl children are stronger.' For a moment, it seemed like he wanted to get up and offer comfort. Good of him but uncalled for.

'We shall return with you tomorrow,' she decreed, hovering at Eleanor's heels as the girl warmed the pannikin on the embers. Her mind was already making a list.

Eleanor tipped half a cup of perry into a mazer and carried it over. 'Here, Rob, lad, the chill be off it.'

'With luck we can hire a barge to take us to Reading on the morning tide, Master Newton. In any event we'll travel light with just our horses,' Kate informed him, picking up the writing board and inkpot from the bed steps. 'Meanwhile, you, good friend, need a comfortable bed for the night.' Clipping a paper in place, she dipped the quill in the well and wrote swiftly. 'Give this to any one of my Lord Chamberlain's servants,' she said, handing the authority to him. 'They will find you repast and somewhere decent to sleep. Tell no one that we are leaving the court. I need to have the king's permission first.' And she certainly did not want her brother or Hastings to talk her out of leaving.

Newton seemed to understand but his complexion was grey with fatigue as he rose to his feet.

'Go with Master Newton, Eleanor, help him find one of the officers.'

As the latch fell closed behind her servants, she felt deep gratitude to him but then she turned her thoughts back to Cecily.

'Can you not do better than that, cousin?' Ned's dimpled grin was friendly as he lolled on a chair in his private chambers. Only his thumb, playing with the jewelled topfs buttoning his doublet, hinted that his patience was not infinite. He had been generous in granting her admittance before breakfast.

'The messenger came last night. I have to leave.' *What did Ned want her to do? Grovel?* Her indignant look achieved nothing.

'I know about every messenger.' He slung the remark politely.

'You think I am making this up, your grace?' Her gaze fell to the glittering sunnes-in-splendour on his neck chain and for the first time she truly felt the enormous power of the office her cousin carried. The sunne could warm, the sunne could burn and the sunne might decide not to shine at all.

'I think you want to escape your obligations to us.'

The greyhound at his feet sighed and turned over.

'That is unjust, your grace.' He was her own age yet treating her like an errant child. No, like a traitor! 'I pray you, read this for yourself!' She tugged Grandmother Bonville's letter from her belt. She waited as he scanned its essence. 'See, your highness, it is no lie. Let me summon the messenger if it please you.' She was almost tempted to throw herself on her knees, but this was still Ned, her cousin, even if he was the king. 'My daughter is sick and as a mother —' The royal fingers had located a small hand bell.

'We desire my lord chamberlain to attend us,' he commanded the page who came to kneel before him.

Save for the crack of the fire, the chamber was silent. He was watching her now like a great cat daring a mouse to run away. Kate kept her chin up but she swallowed nervously. He *had* to let her leave.

Startled, the slumbering dog sprang to alert as Ned thrust himself from his chair and made use of his great height to tower over her. 'I *require* you to marry again, Katherine Neville. I want you compliant.' The last word was a purr and when she still stood resolute and tiny as she looked up at him, he gave an exasperated snarl. 'I *will* have this settled! What in hell is preventing you from obeying me?'

'I have terms.'

'*Terms*!' Her royal cousin drew breath to add more. Perhaps words like shrew and vixen came readily to his lips but he did not utter them. '*What* terms?' he asked dangerously.

'I ... I should like custody of my daughter's inheritance and ... and her wardship and marriage.' That would decide if William Hastings genuinely wanted her or whether he only wanted the profits of administering Cecily's estates.

'The devil you do!' She could hear the male indignation that any mother should demand that right.

'I am quite capable.' Her voice could have been stronger. She still felt like a mouse at the mercy of his great paws. 'You gave such a right to Sir Thomas Kyriel's widow, your grace.'

'Did I now?'

'Yes, your grace.'

'God damn it, the boy she is guardian to is not heir to half the West Country.'

Only the candles lighting the January gloom flickered in the impasse between them. Kate lowered her gaze and waited. With an angry snarl, Ned strode to the casement and stood, legs astride, fists on his belt. He couldn't see out the glass panes. His back, tense beneath the velvet and satin, told her she was dungeon deep in his displeasure. Even the knock on the door did not make him turn.

'Enter!'

Lord Hastings, seeing her there with the king, halted for an instant on the threshold before he bowed. 'Your highness, my lady.'

Ned turned abruptly. 'Entertain yourselves.' He gave his friend a hard look as he passed, and left the chamber.

'I am not sure I understand.' William Hastings came further into the room, unwrapped the chaperone of his hat from his throat and tossed it onto the small table. This morning he was more plainly clad; a short doublet of tempest-blue velvet, slashed hanging sleeves lined with silver-grey taffeta. 'Katherine, what service do you wish of me?'

*Your loyalty. Your love.*

For Kate, finding words was difficult, like scooping slippery fruit from a beaker for Cecily. 'I … I have just asked his grace's leave to go home.'

Genuine concern surfaced in his face. 'Is your daughter sick?' he asked.

'Yes. A fever.' She passed him the letter from the small table by Ned's chair.

'Then you must leave.' He read it and glanced defiantly towards the door that Ned had left by as if suspecting permission had been withheld.

'Yes,' she agreed bleakly.

'The roads won't be good. It may take you thrice as long.'

'Yes, but I have no choice.'

Hastings nodded, but he seemed at a loss, like a man roughly wakened, not yet in his full wits.

'It leaves matters between us unresolved,' he said.

'I … I am in your debt, my lord, for all your kindness in making my stay here a joyful one.' Oh, she sounded so frigid but … by the Saints, this was so awkward. 'My lord, I have to set out now. My servants are waiting.'

But he did not step aside. 'Katherine?'

She felt tension cinch itself about her ribs as he looked at her. A look that blended the masculine emotions of annoyance, pride and resolve coated by the slightly worried crease of brow that she found endearing. No, he was not going to move. He wanted an answer. He deserved an answer.

She sat down rebelliously on the king's own chair, pressing her spine against its back and sliding her fingers along the carved arms as though decades of Plantagenet fingers might have left some patina of authority that might transfer to her.

'You desire to become Cecily's guardian, my lord,' she began, prodding the royal footstool with her toe.

'I *desire* Cecily's mother.' The words pleasured her as though he had touched her in forbidden places and the glint of challenge in his eyes was sufficient for her treacherous body to begin lowering the drawbridge in a shiver of obedience.

Drawing in a deep breath, she decided to be equally forthright. 'My lord, I do not deny that I desire *you* as I am sure does every housewife in London, but there are matters and matters, some which matter and some which don't, if you see what I mean?' Because he was silent, she lifted her face. He was standing with his hands behind his back.

'I have not the hell of a notion what you are talking about.'

'Well,' she began again, smoothing a crease of her robe. 'Not to mince words, my lord, it matters to me that Cecily should have a father again but it would seem important to me that he is accessible, not distant, and —'

'And what?'

'I believe it would prove very difficult for a man whose life … well, for such a man to be in two places at once.'

'Serve God and Caesar?' His tone hinted at irritation and disappointment.

'That is one way of putting it, my lord. I have seen this last week how burdensome high office can be. I could see such a man tugged in all directions as though his limbs were tethered to galloping horses. His duties, his attendance on the King's grace, those who take advantage of his time and generosity of spirit, all these would conspire to keep him away…'

'From the marriage bed?'

Heat burst into her cheeks. 'Yes.' It was spoken with a defiant lift of chin.

'You would be a demanding wife, Lady Katherine?'

'I would be extremely demanding, Lord Hastings.' An exaggeration but never mind.

'And you believe I cannot meet your demands?'

'I believe you would be torn between your duty and your family. In plain speech, my lord, I am not sure I have the stamina nor the will to explain to my daughter —'

'Children,' he corrected, with a look that seared her to her bones.

'C … children, then, why their father is never at home.'

'It depends on what *you* want.' The statement came from above folded arms. Accusation limned his voice although he did not speak with any vehemence.

315

'I should have thought it was crystal clear, my lord.'

'By Christ's Blessed body, my lady!' he exclaimed, unwinding his arms. 'Is compromise so unacceptable to a Neville? Can you and I not improvise with the cards that Fortune has dealt out to us? Have you no answer, madame? In my lacklustre, humble opinion, compromise is the spine of everything, whether body and spirit or...' he added, striding over to grab the arms of her chair, 'husband and wife!'

Ned's chair was hard against her shoulder blades. She was not aware of flinching but it was like having a magnificent, dangerous leopard inches from devouring her.

His angry breath was clean upon her face and the loving half of her wanted to reach up to draw his face closer and kiss the displeasure from that unsmiling mouth. But the other half? The thinking part of her, wounded by Will's unfaithfulness, might never fully heal. To be betrayed by this beautiful man would be a hundred times more hurtful than Will's coupling with Lovidia. Could Hastings not see how tormented she was? Maybe he did. He stepped back, his breath as uneven as hers, putting a careful distance between them.

'Katherine ... Kate...' Like jewels from a treasure chest, the words were being chosen with the finest of care. 'Kate, when you lie tonight in your bed alone, think of me, for I shall think of you, my body will grow hard at the thought of you, hard and aching with lust for you.' He glanced downwards at his body now and then back to her face, as though he expected a reprieve.

She turned her face to the side. 'My lord, in this palace I doubt *your* body's needs ever go unanswered.'

There it was, in the open at last. Distrust finally hurled at him, an insult that would soak into everything he was. Irretrievable, having being spoken. As painful to her as to him.

Hurting, she watched anger smash away the seduction in his face.

'Christ Almighty! You must pardon my stupidity, madame.' He moved away from the chair, slapping his forehead with his palm. 'I see now you have other reasons.'

She rose shakily. 'I mean no disrespect.'

'But you want perfection?'

How could she answer?

*Perfection? Happiness?* scoffed her common sense. *Go! Chase a rainbow!*

Beneath his contemptuous stare, she clapped a hand to her lips with shame. In forcing him away from her, she had smashed her fist through a future that might have been as glorious and precious as costly glass.

'Madame.' The rustle of his sleeves and the rattle of the doorhandle compelled her to turn. He was waiting for her like an indifferent servant, his fingers curled into the iron ring. 'I hope you get what you desire, my lady. Perhaps the castrato Thomas sent you would best suit your needs. Fare you well.'

The door closed behind her and she bit on her forefinger in hurt, in terrible hurt. Life should be full of laughter not tears, not battles and blood and cuckolding and betrayal but joy and togetherness and riding knee to knee and curling up in a husband's arms beneath the down-stuffed coverlet. And love.

Reeling back against the cold stone wall of the passageway, she could not stop the rush of tears. *And love.*

# 17: KATE

*15th January 1462, Salisbury Plain, Wiltshire*

The old prioress at Amesbury, Joan Benfield, warned Kate that the weather was unsettled. She could feel it in her bones, she told them, as she farewelled the party at the abbey gatehouse after their overnight stay.

Although it had not rained since they had left London by hired barge, progress from Reading the previous day had been slow and Kate had slept ill at Amesbury, fretting that it might take two or three days more to reach Shute. If she lost Cecily, the light of her world would go out.

Her other concern was that they might get lost and they had few supplies with them. This morning they would cross the southern edge of Salisbury Plain, chalky grassland that would be firm beneath the horses' hooves. However, it was a way she did not know. Normally they carried spare horse shoes and plenty of horse feed but she needed to journey swiftly and their party travelled light. The carts containing her new robes and other personal items would not leave Westminster until the roads hardened again.

The sky had been fairly clear when they had left the priory but after they had gone about two miles, the clouds to the north-west began to take on a greenish mien, and the wind had strengthened.

Newton waved to Kate to draw rein. 'My lady, there is a storm coming. We need to turn back. There will be no shelter.'

'Turn back? No, we must press on.' She saw him exchange concerned looks with Eleanor. 'We can outride it if we make haste.'

Her common sense told her they would be caught whichever way they rode. There were no copses, no hedges to shelter them from the force of the wind. Only a stone circle of the ancients eerily broke the horizon, monstrous stones, stark as bleached bones against the tempestuous sky.

'Mayhap we could shelter there, my lady?' exclaimed Eleanor, but Newton's men were having none of that.

'This be the Devil's country,' cried one of them, and they were all crossing themselves.

'We're wasting precious time. Come on!' Kate gave spur and the others followed. The horses, sensing the brooding storm and their riders' apprehension did their best, but glancing back across her shoulder, Kate saw the massive wall of rain closing in.

'Faster!' she exclaimed.

But the storm caught them, stoning their heads with pellets of hail.

'Close up!' yelled Newton, herding them into a tight huddle as fat bodkins of icy rain rammed into their backs. Her men nobly did their best to shelter her and Eleanor, but Kate's horse was terrified, trying to break away.

Her cloak was cered to withstand rain but this torrent was merciless, driving its way in where the seam between hood and cloak had not been greased thoroughly. Rivulets of water sped off the shiny surface and soaked into her riding skirt around her calves and then into her woollen hose above her riding boots. The front of her hood was dripping water down the bridge of her nose and the groves in the cloth draped across her thighs and supposed to keep her lap dry, were puddled and sodden.

As the storm, uncaring, headed remorselessly on and the rain lightened, the company broke apart.

'Jesu!' Newton tipped out the gutter of water that had been flooding over his hat brim and rubbed the moisture from his face with a sodden glove.

Eleanor was staring in dismay at the trickles of red dye, spilling like blood, from her sleeves.

'Don't grieve over it, Eleanor. You may have as much of my cloth as you please when it arrives at Shute,' Kate promised. 'Are you dry underneath?'

'Yes, my lady.'

'Good.' Lucky Eleanor. Kate herself was soaked to the skin but she did not want a fuss. 'And the rest of you?' She took their grunts for assent.

'Master Newton?' His taut face told her he was holding back a string of curses. 'Then we press on,' she affirmed.

'Aye, to the next inn for to warm ourselves,' Eleanor muttered.

But there was no next inn and it was as though the Devil indeed had snatched every dwelling from the plain. Only a huddle of beech trees greeted them where the chalk gave way to clay but what was to be gained in tarrying there?

The first signs of habitation they came upon were meagre hovels, scarcely a hamlet let alone a village and there was no inn.

'We need a goodly sized town,' grumbled Kate, trying to hide her shivers. A town that would have a choice of inns with fires and irons to heat the ale and roast meat to warm their bellies. 'How far are we from Salisbury? That's around here somewhere.' A good meal and then they could press on.

'God knows, my lady. I do not know this road. We should have brought a guide from Amesbury. We could still return there,' he added, his voice acquiring volume.

'No, we are not going back, Master Newton.'

She sensed resentment from every one of them as they rode on, but they did not have a sick child whom they loved more than all the world. She prayed for an alehouse at the least but they only encountered more God-forsaken farming hamlets that could have scarce boasted a dozen souls let alone a tavern or church where they might shelter.

Kate's feet were numb inside her boots. Oh, how she longed for a pot of hot, spiced wine. A mile on, her horse stumbled and threw her. It could have been worse. The fall shook her but mercifully nothing seemed broken. Half of her was covered with mud and just in those brief moments the heavy rain had splashed onto the exposed lining of her furred undercloak. Her saddle was wet now and gave her a damp seat as Robert and the groom helped her back onto the shaken mare.

They rode slower now, fearful of further mishap. The rain was abating at last but the wind bit like a flagellant's whip as her skin lost heat. She felt shivery and began to weary but said nothing; the more miles they put behind them, the closer they were to Shute.

'My lady, watch out!' Newton grabbed her horse's reins as the mare stumbled again. Kate tried to concentrate but the cold was numbing her mind. Her legs were like ice.

'We'll stop at the next farm,' Newton was declaring angrily. 'Upon my oath, we shall!'

Maybe that was wise. It was as much as she could do to stay in the saddle.

'My lady said we must not tarry,' Eleanor argued.

'Holy Mother of God, woman! Look at her face.' Kate caught the word 'corpse'.

'We ... we go on!' she insisted. 'D-don't worry over me. As close to Salisbury as we can.'

But she was not sure that she could. The wind was numbing her mind. Maybe that was best. She could ride without resisting, without thought.

Then she was aware of some half dozen riders overtaking them and then surrounding them and her people arguing. One of the strangers shouted at Newton then at her but she ignored him, trying to rein her horse away but then the man grabbed the lead rein and they were being herded off the road like some hapless sheep.

Kate had a vague notion of the track rising, of being urged from the saddle. Her feet, frozen for hours, collapsed under her. A man — not one of her people — tried to steady her but when she collapsed like a ragdoll, he lifted her up and carried her into a smoky darkness where there were frightened voices and harsh words. She was aware of being set down on an earthen floor and rainwater spitting down on a miserable fire. Was this Purgatory? Her mind was too torpid to panic.

Someone was giving orders but it wasn't Newton. People took her outer cloak away and a tall fiend thrust a taper into her face. She was too cold to shiver anymore. All she wanted to do was lie down and sleep forever.

'Christ Almighty!' Hands shook her. The voice was loud. It sounded like Lord Hastings but it couldn't be because they were miles from Westminster and her mind must be playing tricks. And it could not be Hell, because he said, 'Christ'... yet the Devil must blaspheme or he wouldn't be the Devil.

Eleanor — yes, Eleanor — was undoing Kate's woollen mantle and dragging off her gloves.

'Quickly, woman! Oh, out of the way!'

Stronger hands found her garters and were rolling down her stockings but there was no sensation left in her feet. Why were they undressing her when it was so cold? The fire was pitiful.

'Now her gown! Down to her bare skin. Go to it!'

'That I will not!' Eleanor's voice was terrified.

Fierce hands were hauling Kate's sodden gown over her head and a dagger edge sawed through the laces of her chemise. She struggled and found her elbows grabbed and held from behind while her clothing was peeled away. For a moment she was utterly naked and then she was wrapped afresh in fur.

'Now your clothes as well, girl! Strip! *Strip!*'

Eleanor was screaming at someone.

'Is that milk not ready yet?' cried the man's voice. 'Hell, will you scald her insides! Give it here!'

Some voice was coaxing her. Kate was vaguely aware of being eased up. The thick rim of a beaker touched her chin, then warm liquid bobbed against her lips and she opened her mouth and felt the wondrous warmth fill her mouth and sink down into her belly.

'More! Drink more!'

Then she was permitted to lie down again and turned onto her side. A woman's body, Eleanor's, nestled up to her back and legs, slender arms wrapped her waist and breath, close as a lover's, touched the icy skin of her neck. Swift hands were rolling the fur tightly about them.

*Maybe we never left Westminster or perhaps the Devil is about to bake me in an oven*, Kate thought as the world retreated and her mind sank into oblivion.

She came to her senses groggily and it took a while to comprehend she was lying in some sort of animal-skin cocoon with a woman's naked flesh tight against her back. Raising one eyelid, she could see within hand's reach a tiny wall of stones encircling a heap of glowing embers, a pair of boots, and some crudely made fire tongs. The air was smoky and she felt unpleasantly hot. It must be Purgatory, she concluded. But lying with another woman naked against her? This was a punishment beyond her comprehension. How many years was she supposed to stay like this before the Devil drove her down into his furnace? She was not ready for this, Cecily needed her. Cecily! Mother of God forgive her sins! She had failed to reach Cecily!

She panicked, stifled, struggling to escape and a startled Devon voice shrieked in her ear, '*No, madame, no!* Calm yourself!'

'Eleanor! Is that you? Christ have mercy, where are we?' Kate struggled to free herself but the girl's arms were wrapped about her. She had many a time shared a bed with her bodyservant, but not pressed together like this — this was utterly sinful. 'What has happened? Is this Hell?'

The girl's laughter vibrated against Kate's ribs. 'God save you, madame, no.' Another amused splutter. 'This was my lord's notion. It were the only way, he said. Now if you'll forgive me, I'll get out now and make myself decent, for my bladder is fair to bursting. I'll be bringing you some more warm milk soon enow. *Turn around, if you, please!*' She was giggling, making no sense as she wriggled out. Kate heard the rustle of clothing behind her and rolled over, trying to see in the darkness.

A wooden stall with the glimmer of a palliasse lay along the wall with a raggedy, rough-woven curtain tethered to a rail above it. To the left, a broad-brimmed ploughman's hat and a cowskin shared a hook upon a door of crudely hewn boards.

Eleanor reached to the latch for support as she slid on her shoes.

'Eleanor, wait! For the love of heaven, which lord?'

'This one,' said a man's voice. The pair of knee-high, spurred boots arranged before the fire suddenly moved and Kate's thawed mind realised that inhabiting them was a pair of legs clad in dark hose. The boot caps turned her way and she blinked up at the fine woollen houppelande, the richly embossed buckle on his leather belt, the collar of office and above that, the face of the king's chamberlain. Lit from below, his grin was demoniac and Kate caught her breath. As if the sumptuously clad Lord Hastings would be standing in a hovel like this.

'Katherine?' The man even sounded like Lord Hastings and now he crouched down beside her. His fingers felt surprisingly human as they tilted her face to the feeble firelight. 'Do you know me? Katherine?'

'This is the Devil's work. It … it can't be you,' she protested. 'You're at Westminster with Ned.'

'No, I'm here with you and you're a foolish hen, Kate. You nearly killed yourself.'

She gazed at him, struggling to understand. 'Then this isn't Purgatory?'

His laugh was tinged with irony and there was a sensual twist to his lips as his gaze moved across her bared shoulders. 'Only for me, I think.'

She struggled to extricate herself and then realised anew that she was not wearing a thread of clothing. 'I am going mad.' Clutching the fur roll to her breastbone with one hand, she scrambled back onto her knees and tried to make the sign against the evil eye. 'In the Name of our Lord Jesus, if you are the Devil manifesting yourself as Hastings, I abjure you, incubus! Get you gone!'

There was a silence. Then he said with amusement, 'I'm still here.' Not only that but he was trying not to roar with laughter.

'Oh,' said Kate with a mixture of disappointment and relief that was rapidly changing to hot embarrassment. She remembered riding post-haste because Cecily needed her. 'But where's my daughter, you incubus?' she exclaimed with righteous anger. 'Have you taken my daughter?'

Lord Hastings, if it truly was him, looked quite chagrined. 'You'll see her soon enough. I have sent a messenger ahead to Devonshire. Now do you think you could come to your senses? I've been called a plethora of names in my time by some of England's greatest whoresons, but *incubus* … no, my lady, that is unjust of you.'

Before Kate could answer, a draft of icy air goose-fleshed her shoulders as Eleanor came in. 'Here we are, my lady. Fresh and warm from the cow.'

'From our own horned beasts,' murmured Hastings, rising to his feet. 'We always serve it up in Purgatory to newcomers. It helps people feel at home before we start using the pincers.'

The crudely fashioned beaker was real enough; the milk, warm and true to her tongue. Kate glared up at the lordly devil over the rim, feeling even more stupid. Yes, she remembered rain, the diabolical, unrelenting rain and the ceaseless road! Her fingers touched a dag of mud still in her hair at her temple.

'Souls,' she corrected.

'Pardon?'

'Not people but souls, sirrah. You would not get people in Purgatory.'

'You tripped me up.' He sucked in his cheeks. 'How many fingers, my lady?' His right hand rose, the thumb hidden.

'Four,' answered Kate grimly. 'How many fingers, my lord?' It was the V-sign of the defiant archers at Agincourt and unladylike but it made her feel better.

'I see you are restored to your old self, Lady Harrington,' he replied dryly. 'You want answers, I suppose.' As if pinioned by her fierce stare, he added, 'We are in a poor farmhouse on the road to Salisbury.' *With him*. Now why was that?

'Excellent,' she said, 'then I can find my way. I thank you for any assistance you have rendered, Lord Hastings, but whatever coincidence of planets or machinations by the king and my brother served you up here can take you hence.'

'But, my lady, you don't understand,' interrupted Eleanor. 'My lord saved your life yesternight.' Clearly in alliance with Lord Hastings, the girl glanced up at him for endorsement.

'Not without your invaluable help, Eleanor.' The debonair smile was pasted on again. 'But maybe we should not have bothered. Your lady has warmed up into a temper or is this the last remnants of frost, do you suppose?'

Kate stared from one to the other. 'Perhaps telling me what happened might be useful, my lord.'

Eleanor answered eagerly. 'You were almost frozen to death, my lady, but my lord wrapped us up like a pair of caterpillars and you slowly warmed.' Kate remembered the fall but not being brought to this place. 'You were soaked to the skin, my lady, but there was no stopping you and the damp began to numb your mind. Truly, you were falling into some deep sleep unto death an', saving your pardon, madame, but it was seemingly no different from what some beggars do when they lie down in snow.'

So despite her servants, she had nearly died. Lord Hastings added nothing but he was watching her with concern.

'Then I owe you both my life and I thank you.'

She finished the milk, her mind sharpening by the instant. Whether Lord Hastings had come after her was of no consequence if Cecily lay grievously ill. She had to get back to Shute. 'Eleanor, inform our people that we leave within half an hour.'

'But, my lady —'

Hastings took the beaker and checked that she had drunk it all. 'What your servant is trying to tell you, *my lady*, is that firstly, it is still about three hours to daylight, secondly, mighty cold out there, and thirdly, I have no intention of letting you venture forth until you are fully recovered.'

'I feel fully recovered now,' Kate lied, although her body was still weary and her muscles stiff. 'Eleanor, we shall leave at dawn. And what is so amusing?' The girl's lips were a tight pleat in the firelight.

'You cannot travel without clothes, Lady Katherine,' Lord Hastings pointed out reasonably. Dashing her glance downwards, Kate saw where he was looking and cursed inwardly. The fur wrap was halfway down her breasts. The wretched man was loving every minute of this.

'I should like my clothes returned, my lord.' She tried to keep her tone even.

'Only when they are dry. Mind,' he murmured silkily, 'you would look fetching in one of my shirts.'

It was hard to be dignified when you felt like the centre of a pastry roll. She lapsed into a tense silence, her knuckles glimmering white as she clasped the fur tight against her. She was furious with Ned and Richard. If they had sent Hastings to bring her to obedience, they mistook their quarry.

'So why are you in Wiltshire, my lord? Conducting a new doomsday book survey or finding some rural virgins to keep the king's grace in good humour.'

'Madame!' Eleanor was looking at her in horror. Yes, she was behaving badly, Kate admitted to herself.

Hastings took a flask from the breast of his doublet and smiled at her before he took a draught. 'I am here to bed you, of course, but all in good time. I don't want a bride with less heat than a snowman.' His capable hand pushed the stopper firmly back in.

'Bed me?' Kate's stare rose. She was looking up once more into a face that echoed her own — determined and much more, for it did not take an angry fool to read the desire in his eyes or the ownership in the smile curling his mouth.

'Bed me?' she echoed, reeling beneath that devastating purpose in him. 'The hell you will, my lord! I told you I was not in a marrying mind.'

'But I am, madness though it is, and I have the permission of your brothers and the king's grace, as you know well.'

It was impossible to lash out in fury from such ludicrous confinement. 'Oh, by Heaven!' Snarling under her breath, she struggled to turn her back on him and her maidservant, and glared into the darkness with tears biting behind her eyelids.

Above her, she heard him laugh good-humouredly and felt a hand that was not Eleanor's settle with assurance on her bare shoulder. Even his touch had a power over her. 'Easy, Katherine, we'll not being doing it before this hearth like a couple of peasants.'

'I'll not be doing it at all, my lord.' A clenched teeth answer.

Her maidservant intervened. 'But, my lady, I beg you to remember that Lord Hastings saved your life.'

'You be quiet!' Kate wriggled round to challenge him. 'Have you abducted me, my lord?'

'Not yet.'

'Please you, my lord,' whispered Eleanor, as though someone had asked her to play at peace broking. 'Can this matter not be set aside until she's —'

'No.' He was laughing, damn him! 'No, anger is healthy. It will heat your lady's blood.' He leaned down, his handsome mouth compassionate, his eyes provoking her. 'You'll keep, Kate. The morning will suffice. And you, little Eleanor, should get some more sleep. There's a pallet over there.' Then he turned away and set wood to cover the embers, ignoring Kate who was still as hissy as a snake. Fuming, she curled her body away from him.

Eleanor obediently disappeared behind the curtain and save for the crackle of the new wood and the girl's deepening breath, the hovel fell silent. It was chill now without Eleanor to shield her from the draft seeping beneath the door. Kate was too tense to sleep but she closed her eyes tight and feigned slumber.

His tiresome lordship was not asleep either. She heard the creak of boot leather as he crossed to the door, and the latch lifting. The instant he was gone, she loosened her covering and shuffled across to peer out the cracks in the wooden shutter. It was still dark as pitch outside but it had stopped raining. She saw a lantern moving around the yard and heard Hastings speaking softly. Several other voices answered. How many did he have with him? It looked as though the rest of his company and her own people were in the barn alongside; a glimmer of light showed beneath its doors. She tried to make out the rest of her surroundings. Judging by the shifting shapes under the open byre, that was where the horses were tethered.

Was Hastings intent on taking her back to Westminster? Her mind slid over the alternatives open to her once dawn came. Newton and her escort were capable of helping her but even if they could get her away, she could never outride Hastings and his men, and Newton might get horsewhipped or do something gallant and futile.

Not just the lantern returning her way but the stabs of icy air through the cracks drove her back to the hearth. Sweet Mother of God, she thought, curling about the stones and vigorously rubbing her hands over her goose-fleshed arms, what a fool she had been to think she could sidestep this conspiracy of men determined to bend her to their will. Well, there was still the word 'no'. Hastings could hardly force a ring on her finger without her consent. She snuggled deep into the fur blanket and realised it had the scent of the musk he used in its folds. Then the latch lifted and she felt the cold come in with her future master. She sensed he halted, staring down at her, before she heard him poking the logs and then the rustle of wool and creak of leather as he lowered himself to the floor. Silence.

How could she reach Shute? She sent prayers for her little child heavenwards to every saint who might intercede for her but again and again her thoughts drew her back to her own future. If Hastings hauled her before a priest, would Holy Church support her refusal? She began to doubt her chances. Even in cases of noblewomen abducted and raped, the church usually urged marriage in case a child had been conceived. All that stood in Hastings' way was a jolly Benedictus and a spatter of holy water and then he could consummate his physical ownership of her. At that thought, her treasonous body began to ripen, quivering with the imagining as though his body already claimed her.

And God's mercy, there was little to stop him doing it now.

She turned over stealthily and stole a glance at the man through her lashes only to discover he was still awake. He checked her, not smiling now, and assuming she still slept resumed his solemn reverie, staring into the dulled fire, his mouth a stubborn quill slash. The nervousness tensing Kate's limbs to shaking subsided. Maybe he did not want this any more than she! And yet the way he had looked at her, the way he had been able to heat her blood and spur awake her womanly parts deep inside. God's truth, he could evoke a hunger in her, an urgent yearning to taste the danger of him, like daring the fire to burn her skin or recklessly mounting a wild stallion. Marriage with Hastings would be … would be like harnessing the light of the sun for it would hurt … chill her to the bone, whenever his gaze turned away.

The real man shifted, leaned an elbow on the ground, careful to arrange his body so that the meagre heat still reached all of her. That thoughtfulness again. Was her survival truly due to his quick thinking? Her chance of holding Cecily again within her arms due to him?

He was clever, she knew that. He even knew she was watching him for he turned his head.

'Did you know that Towton was fought in a snowstorm, my lady?'

'Is that what you were thinking about?'

A small flame was struggling in the embers. Its light danced and flickered upon his skin.

'Yes.' The word was a long sigh.

Well, at least a man remembering a bloody battle was certainly not thinking about making love.

'Today reminded you?'

Hastings nodded, still watching the feeble flame playing across the logs. 'The wind was so icy it could have cut parchment and there were so many wounded, too many. Some staggering, some screaming for help. Others were just lying there in the snow across the fields or down in the ditches, slowly freezing to death.'

Kate began to understand. She propped her chin in her hand. 'But you saved them.'

'Me, no, but we had one of the best surgeons I have ever met in my life, thank God. He could sew men back together better than any tailor. But the cold was the very devil. It took a damn long time to find some of the poor wretches. Brought in with their eyes staring, their skins white and waxy. I would have sworn some of them were dead until the surgeon made me feel for a pulse in their necks. We didn't have heated bricks but we did have the living, and do you know what he ordered us to do? He paired each frozen wretch with a man who was still whole. "Hold 'em as though they were your best beloved," he told them, and it worked for most. Truth to tell, some of them recovered better than the wounded who had been brought into the tents straightway.' He turned his head to look at her.

'That is how you knew what to do?'

'Yes. I did not think the words "goose" and "numbskull" could ever fit you, Katherine, but in your mad haste, you not only put your own life at risk but your servants' as well and that is quite unforgivable.'

'Cecily —'

'Cecily,' he cut in, 'has a doting grandmother and a houseful of servants to look after her, madame, not to mention my own physician who will reach Shute today. Besides, girl children are tough little mites. Speak the truth, Katherine. You were not running to Cecily, you were running away from me.'

He should have been voted a speech of gratitude for setting her mind at ease somewhat about her daughter but she was still feeling rebellious. 'We have already had this conversation.'

'And I am found wanting, while you are, what, perfection? Is that why Will Bonville found solace with a farmer's daughter?'

Her body trembled with fury. 'Where on earth did you hear that?'

'Oh, there are few secrets if you know how to loosen men's tongues. All I needed to do was send my servants down to the palace stables with a firkin of ale. Simple as that. Your groom and horse boys spewed out all the gossip. Let me see, what else did I discover? Ah yes, I now know your master of the horse will wed Lovidia since he can't have you.' She was too astonished, too angry, to answer. 'And I *don't* want Lovidia although I understand she is the prettiest wench in Devonshire.'

'But you do want the London widow you embraced outside the stables,' she snapped. 'The tall one with the yellow braids and the green riding cape.'

There was an uncomfortable silence. Outside, the dogs began barking again.

'My sister? I think not.'

Kate bit her lip, guilty of not having heeded Chaplain Rotherham's warning.

Hastings was laughing softly. 'Envy is a deadly sin, my lady.'

'So is lechery, my lord.' She turned her head away.

'You suffer from that as well?' he mocked. 'Then you are in goodly company for I am afflicted with it at this very moment.' His hand turned her chin towards him.

'No, I don't think —' she stammered, glancing towards Eleanor.

'You think too much and you are a goose, you know that?' he said softly. 'And if I permit myself to kiss you, damn it, I shall have those furs off in a thrice and I shall not be able to stop myself. But I do have a sense of honour despite your suspicions. Can you not trust me?'

Trust? No, she could never trust entirely ever again. Marriage with Hastings would be a compromise. Love could hurt. But not to love... Not to love him was like telling the sun not to shine and without his warmth and protection her life would be an emptiness. Besides, Cecily needed a father.

She watched Hastings' fair eyebrows lift, expecting an answer, and somehow she was able to nod.

'Good, now stop being so difficult.' His knuckles caressed her cheek like a lover. 'You have lovely eyes, you know that? You wear your soul in them.'

Will Bonville had never spoken so. She could feel the pieces of armour falling away from her, unbuckling. Even if this was flattery — and she prayed it was not — the praise was healing.

'God willing, you and I have a lifetime ahead of us to frolic, and I tell you what, Lady Harrington,' he slid a possessive hand across the fur that was drawn tight across her thighs. 'We are going to give young Cecily a whole quiverful of brothers and sisters.'

Speech was stolen from her. She watched him withdraw to the other side of the stones where he settled his shoulder against the earth.

'You were right about this being Hell,' he murmured. 'But there is still time for redemption, sweetheart.'

In the cold light of day with her clothes barely fastening, starched by road mire and stinking of wood smoke, Kate felt inglorious, beleaguered and shamed that she had put her people through such a nightmare journey. However, she knew her obligations and she requested the farmer and his family be brought before her so she might reward them for the use of their dwelling. Of course, she should have known that Lord Hastings had already given them coin to replace the firewood and the fowls that had comprised last night's supper and this morning's broth.

She found the new bane on her life submitting to his manservant's razor next to the water butt outside the barn.

'I gather you and your men intend to accompany us on to Salisbury, my lord?' she said coolly.

'Yes.' He tugged the napkin from the neck of his shirt and wiped his face with it. 'I have sent a messenger to advise the bishop, my lady. No doubt you would prefer to lodge in his palace overnight.' He paused for her to argue but she ignored the question in his eyes. 'Well,' he said, 'my people are ready to leave.'

'And mine, my lord.' She curtsied gravely and crossed the yard to where Newton waited with her mare.

'I hear you purpose to wed Lovidia, Master Newton. Why was I not informed of this?' A month ago, she would have considered it treason and condemned Newton for behaving no better than Will in betraying her trust but now she found herself speaking of the matter with utter calm. That other Kate now seemed a life long ago.

'Bastards like me cannot have what they want in life, my lady. I have not lain with her if that is what you are thinking.' For a heartbeat, his face told her everything and then he dragged his gaze away and made pretence of checking Guinivere's saddle was secure. Behind her, she sensed that Lord Hastings was watching them. 'Old Lady Bonville wants the boy to be brought up proper like. I'll be a father to him.' He cupped his hands to help her mount. 'Is all well? You know I would risk my life for you. Have you any orders for me?'

*What was he expecting?* she thought sadly. That she would order him to battle Lord Hastings and his retinue single-handed, then carry her off across his saddlebow? In fact that was the last thing she wanted now. Maybe in London she had discovered who she really was. She met Lord Hastings' assertive stare across her servant's shoulder and knew her future.

Shaking her head, she said, 'You are the loyalist of servants, Robert Newton, and a good friend and you shall have a fine wedding. There will always be a place for you in my household. Always.'

The wind had changed. An easterly was at their back as they rode westwards. Within sight of Salisbury's ramparts, Hastings drew rein and pointed with his riding crop. 'That bridlepath will take you west towards Wilton avoiding the city, my lady, or you can come a-marketing with me.'

'*A-marketing?*' That was a new coverlet of words to hide the marriage word! She had not been expecting any choice, more like his gloved hand on the leading rein of her mare and the closing in of his horsemen around her. And they were under scrutiny, their combined entourages agog to know who was really wearing the boots and spurs.

'Forgive my honesty, Lady Harrington, but it will hardly escape common notice that you are...' Lord Hastings' gloved hand strove to summon the right words from the air. He was looking pointedly at the dried mud appliqueing her blue-black riding gown and cap. '...bedraggled.'

'Then we had better go shopping, my lord,' Kate agreed tartly, kneeing her mare forward. If he was wearing a triumphant grin, she did not want to know.

Will Bonville had disliked shopping. Well, what eighteen-year-old male would? The few times they had visited Exeter together, he had abandoned Kate to his mother's company and hotfooted it down Fore Street to meet his friends at the Antelope. However, Lord Hastings, after dispatching a messenger to the Bishop's Palace and giving their retainers leave to frolic for a few hours, took Kate and Eleanor straight to Master John Halle's famous Doghalle. A housewife's heaven! It shelved everything: spices from the East, dyestuffs, woad, madder, even costly alum, wines, vinegars, tar, pails, bowstrings, Paris thread and Venice buttons, bales of all manner of cloth: russet, fustian, finest wool, linen, damasks, glowing velvets, Italian silks and brocades, and even some ready-made garments: fur cloaks and velvet mantles, caps, hats and gloves.

Not a word was whispered in the shop about my lady's appearance. Perhaps with their streets criss-crossed with streams and ditches, Salisbury merchants were used to lords and gentry sliding into the mire. John Halle himself was summoned to attend his noble customers. Together with Hastings, he helped Kate choose two caps with stitched-in veils, one of lavender blue velvet edged with pearls, the other, damson with a taffeta lining and veil of palest rose.

As for fabric for a new gown, Kate was not very good at making up her mind. She flitted round the storeroom like a joyous bee, her interest landing here and there until Hastings extracted a bale from an upright stack of other rolls — a shimmering brocade of cornflower blue, embroidered with tiny songbirds and lily flowers.

'You like this?' he asked.

'Hmm, yes I do. Can't you hear me purring?'

'No, I did hear a gurgling of hunger. How much do they need to measure out, Katherine? I am treading water here.'

She was hungry, ravenous, and suspected he was, too, yet before finding a tavern, he hastened her to a tailor recommended by the Doghalle. There she was briskly measured by three tailors while the fourth sketched a neckline for her approval. Her womanly heart was frisking with delight. The blue kirtle together with a cream silk undergown would be delivered to the bishop's palace that afternoon.

Hastings' authority amazed her. Here was no green boy but a mature handsome man squiring her and yet marriage meant bedding with him and she had lain with no man but Will. That side of things would be challenging and probably a disappointment but it was part of the bargain with making sons and heirs. Of one thing she was sure, he would safeguard her and Cecily. That alone must blow her doubts away.

He actually consulted her about where they should dine. The George Inn, where she had stayed before, was packed with liverymen from the glovers' guild celebrating the birth of someone's son and even though the landlord would have right swiftly kicked out his regular diners to accommodate my lord chamberlain and my lord of Warwick's sister, they passed it by and ate supper instead at the Rose in Minster Street.

After the meal was done, he undid the uppermost knopfs of his doublet and drew out a folded parchment. 'By the way, the king's grace asked me to give you this. It's from the Patent Rolls, a copy, of course, and hastily done, I might add.'

Puzzled, curious, she shook open its warm folds. It had been drawn up the day she left Westminster. 'By my faith,' she whispered, her eyes widening as she read. 'Do you know what's written here?'

'"A grant to the king's kinswoman, Katherine, late wife of William, Lord of Harrington, custody of all castle, lordships et cetera during the minority of Cicely" — by the way, have they spelt it wrong? — "daughter of the said lord and kinswoman and heir of William, Lord Bonville, with the marriage of the said heir" and so forth.' He smiled and drew a finger across her parted lips. 'You look very sweet but why so astonished?'

'You don't mind?'

The smile deepened. 'You mean not having the grant of custody from Ned?'

She nodded.

'Why should I mind?'

And how could she answer that?

'Have you a safe place about your person for that or shall I keep it for now?'

She glanced down at her cleavage and he laughed. 'Sweetheart, no, adorable as you are there, you are not of sufficient fish-wifely proportions.'

It was needful to search his face as she handed back the document for safekeeping. There was no dimple of insincerity, no wry twist of lip or flicker of calculation. Adorable? So he did not think her too round, too unslender, if there was such a word.

'Well, Kate, shall we be on our way?'

She could see they were expected at the bishop's palace when they finally rode into the vast walled close that embraced the cathedral. Hastings had already sent word.

It was a welcome fit for a prince. Outside on the steps of the turreted palace were several shelves of shivering clerics; canons and vicars and cathedral officials. Off to the side, a cluster of little choristers in blue gowns, hooded with lambswool, sang Kate an anthem. In the absence of Bishop Richard Beauchamp, who was away on a royal commission, the dean was pleased to formally welcome them.

She was shown up into a bedchamber that was sweet and clean. It had whitewashed walls adorned with tapestries, and the wooden panels of its ceiling were painted with nightingales and goshawks. The servants told her the bishop's bathhouse had been heated up for her and afterwards, pink, warm and clean, she stretched out within the crisp, clean sheets of the bed and slept for two hours, until she was awakened by Eleanor with the newly made gown across her arm.

Lord Hastings was waiting in the bishop's hall. He had forsaken his riding clothes for a doublet of amber velvet, black hose and clean boots. He gave her a most approving smile and offered his arm. 'Would you care to see the cathedral before supper?'

She understood. It was to be done like this — understated. Tomorrow they would ride on to Shute.

Gathering the train of her gown over her arm, she rested her hand on his wrist. Long before they reached the cathedral steps, she saw the dean just happened to be standing in the porch of the west door waiting for them.

Hastings halted, drawing her round to face him. 'You have a choice, Katherine. Step forward with me now or Brother Aloysius can take you to view the clock and King John's *Magna Carta*.'

Kate began to laugh. She laughed so much it nearly gave her a stitch in her side.

'That, William,' she declared, sleeving away her tears, 'must be the worst proposal of marriage in England's history.'

'It was not a proposal just a choice.'

She started to march towards the cathedral. 'I am doing this for you,' she called back to him over her shoulder. 'I should hate you to lose office — or face.'

He actually gave a huzzah that disturbed the pigeons and took to his heels, grabbing her hand and tugging her after him.

'Steady!' she screamed, clutching up her skirt lest she fall face down onto the cobbled path. Her cap was askew and likely to topple. 'What is the hurry?'

'In case you change your mind, Kate Neville.' But he stopped, straightened her headdress and then with his arm about her, they sedately walked forward to be married at the cathedral door.


Sharing her wedding supper in a room full of clerics was hardly the stuff of dreams. Kate sat through her wedding breakfast anxious about the bedroom sport to follow. She had no skill in such games but it must be endured from now on.

'How does the new underlinen feel?'

'Stiff. It will need a few launders to soften, I daresay.'

That slow appealing smile that hinted at a lusty allegory.

When she finally found herself alone in the bedchamber listening for her new husband's foot on the stair, she was shaking as if an ague possessed her. At least there had not been the putting to bed by a crowd slopping with wine and firing lusty jokes as there had been at Chewton.

He actually knocked. There was a courtesy to Hastings' character that made him utterly redeemable.

She did not await him like a soldier awaiting inspection but walked across and opened the door.

'I thought you might have barred it already,' he said, pushing a jug of wine and two goblets into her hands while he took the wooden beam from the corner and slid it across to keep them private.

'You would have found a ladder, I daresay. Perhaps you would have preferred it that way.' She looked up for an answer.

'*Any* way!' he said, rescuing the jug and striding across to set it on the small table. Moonlight flooded across the coverlet of the bed and outside a robin sung out the evening watch. Some thoughtful person had set posies of dried herbs upon the pillows.

Hastings took the goblets from her and poured out some spiced wine. 'To us!'

'Lord!' exclaimed Kate, coughing. She was not expecting it to be hot and so spicy. 'What has this in it? Pepper?'

'For courage. Well?' He jerked his head meaningfully towards the bed.

'Well?' she echoed.

'Well, you are the one who has been married before.'

'Yes, I am,' she giggled. The absurdity of it lessened her tension. She realised she probably should have climbed into bed with nothing on. 'The procedure is we take a run for the bed and see who gets there first,' she told him with a straight face.

He received that edict with equal composure. 'Then I'd better check.' He strode across and bent to lift the bed's petticoats.

'What on earth…?'

'Tightening the bed ropes, sweetheart. I'd hate us to crash through the ceiling and land in the middle of Bishop Beauchamp's dining board.'

Kate was still laughing as he came back to her and caught her hand, carrying it to his lips. 'Honestly, William, I wasn't being serious.'

'I know, my sweet bride, but we are going to do it nonetheless.' He let go of her and leaned forward for the race, his hands on his knees. 'Ready?'

'Ridiculous!' But with a gurgle of merriment, she snatched up her skirt and braced herself.

'Go!'

She landed with her knees on the bed, and collapsed face down with laughter, heels in the air.

'I enjoyed that!' Hastings exclaimed, dragging her up to face him. 'It should be written into the missals throughout Christendom.' He kissed her, his arms drawing her tightly in to his body. There was possession, desire and fire in that kiss and she was dry tinder for easy kindling.

'You know what I sense, Kate?' he murmured between kisses. 'I reckon Will Bonville was a selfish lout. Did he ever give you any pleasure?'

'How do you mean?'

'They call it the little death in France.'

'Well, that has whetted my appetite already,' she said dryly. 'But, oh, I rather like *that*.' His fair hair was against her breasts as he teased her nipple with his tongue.

'Tonight is for your pleasure, my dearest Kate.'

And it was. For the first time in her life, she knew the pleasure of lovemaking and afterwards as her body settled to stillness like the vibrating strings of a lute after plucking, she felt at peace, loved and secure. Even if his body would never be hers alone, there was a generosity in Hastings, not to mention skilfulness, that made her feel like a goddess.

*Your husband will be famous and much loved.*

Much loved? Yes.

'Thank you,' she murmured, leaning over to kiss the lips of her new lord, where he lay beside her. 'You were right, I was "such an innocent". But I'm not now. Can we do it again, please?'

# 18: ELYSABETH

## TWO YEARS LATER
### 29th April 1464, Grafton

Trying to explain her strategy received two astonished looks from her sons.

'We are going to run out into his path and petition him?' echoed Tom. '*The king?*'

'Dangerous, Mother,' muttered Dickon. 'Horses don't like surprises.'

'Your grandfather says the king will be riding past Pottersbury tomorrow morning after hunting in Whittlebury Woods.'

'Well, I am not going to kneel in the dirt to the king.'

Elysabeth could have shaken Tom. 'It's your inheritance. If you want to be a real beggar for the rest of your life, stay at home.'

'Isn't that what you are about to do, Mother, beg?' He slammed the book down, even though it was one of the precious few his grandmother had managed to retain from her first husband's library, and folding his arms, strode to the window.

'Tom's angry,' Dickon observed like some alchemist watching a heated powder give off vapour.

'Yes, I noticed,' Elysabeth growled.

'Grandfather says you can climb back up by marriage,' Dickon remarked.

Elysabeth took a deep breath, counted to ten and said, 'You don't realise what's involved, Dickon. It doesn't happen that way often. Other people, the nobility, don't respect you for it.'

Tom turned. 'So, instead we are going to grovel in front of the royal horse.'

'Yes, we are. We *all* are. And this is Grandfather's idea.'

Calculating where the grovelling should take place had necessitated several Woodville expeditions, a great deal of arguing and some palm greasing to be certain that Lord Hastings' master huntsman would guide the king's company along a particular bridlepath. The latter ran through a shallow valley below the fields of Pottersbury and it was agreed that the petitioning should be made at a clump of trees large enough to shelter a woman and two children as well as provide an ample view up the track. They didn't want the hunting party to spur past them.

They left their ponies at the farm on the western rise and walked down through the meadow. Elysabeth was not in good temper when they arrived at the gate onto the lane. Her hem was sopping and heavy from the dew and a wave of rain cloud was breaking on the horizon.

'What are we supposed to do, burst out from the thicket like savages?' muttered Tom.

'I still say it will frighten the horses,' Dickon pointed out.

'Over there!' Elysabeth said firmly, pointing to a clump of young oaks at the end of the hedgerow.

'It's starting to rain,' Tom complained. 'We are going to look like drowned rats.'

'Good,' snapped Elysabeth. 'Maybe he'll feel all the more sorry for us.' But she wasn't even sure what 'he' looked like. She could recognise Lord Hastings but the others? It would be embarrassing to kneel before the wrong man. At least the king would be one of the youngest and dressed more regally. Mind, King Henry had always looked as though he had bought his clothes from a slopseller.

If she could get her beloved Astley back this would be worth kneeling in the mud. They had been over three years now at her parents' hall and she desperately wanted her independence. Late last year, the Chancery case had been decided in her favour but the attainder had not been reversed. She was still the widow of a traitor.

By the time they had endured a swift but heavy shower, her veil was as soggy as her spirits, and she felt like murdering rather than grovelling. This was the most foolish scheme her imbecile parents had ever —

The sound of cheerful male banter reached her at last and she grabbed the boys' hands.

'Ow, you're hurting,' wailed Dickon.

'Nervous, Mother?' smirked Tom.

'We are doing this for you, you ingrate.' But she could see that behind the scowl, he was primed like a taut crossbow. 'They must have had a good morning. That's in our favour. Whatever happens, don't let them force you off the path.'

From the easy jingle of harness, the hunting party were ambling along, thank God!

'*Now!*' They stepped out quickly, a threesome hand in hand but spread out enough to prevent the royal progress.

The party had no choice but to draw rein.

'Oh Lord,' drawled someone. 'Not another plaguey petition!'

Elysabeth was frantically searching their faces. Not the two men at the front. Nor Lord Hastings — his eyes narrow with disapproval. She glimpsed the astonished face of the youth who had been at Kirby Muxloe. There were so many young men, all well clad. Oh, God help her!

'What is it, woman, we haven't got all day?' bawled someone.

*Woman?* She was a duchess's daughter.

'I ... I have a petition for the King's grace.' Spoken gravely, clearly.

'Ha, told you,' crowed the first voice.

She fell on her knees, tugging the children down with her and letting go their hands, she tugged the petition from her cleavage.

'Can I put my hand down there, too?' guffawed one of the youths. Lord Hastings was not entertained. He was looking angrier by the instant. 'Bring it here!' he commanded.

But, then, the tall youth from Kirby Muxloe kneed his horse forward to the front of the company. His hazel eyes took in the dark wet of her gown across her shoulders and around her neckline.

'Lady Grey?'

She nodded, uncertain how to address him. Was he a lord or a knight? Laughter rumbled through the party as he dismounted. He gave her a hand to help her up and gestured to Tom and Dickon to stand.

'And who are you?' he said to Tom.

'Thomas Grey, sir. I was Lord Ferrers but Grandmother has married again.'

One of the other young men 'ahhed' with mock sympathy.

Tom flinched. 'The petition is about my inheritance, sir. *I* didn't fight at St Albans,' he added, glaring in the direction of the mockery. 'And there was only one king when my father died.' Now he, too, was scanning the faces, seeking out the king.

'Hmm,' said the young giant, pulling a face that shared Tom's dilemma. 'And now there *are* two kings, which one would you like to serve?'

*Say the right thing, Tom*, Elysabeth prayed. Whoever this youth was, he seemed to be the only one who would intercede. Oh God, which one was the king?

'Whoever is most likely to give us peace, sir.'

'Well, that's a clever answer but you're not exactly jumping off the fence, are you?'

'I am open to advice, sir,' Tom was saying audaciously, a rare grin lighting his face. Elysabeth drew a sharp breath at his recklessness.

*This isn't the time, Tom. You don't provoke —*

'Which would you pick, sir?'

'Why, me, of course,' answered the young man. 'Give it here, Lady Grey, I'll read it, I promise you.'

*He was the king?* Her jaw slackened. Speechless, she handed the parchment over and fell to her knees totally mortified, unable to stare anywhere but at the mud and stones. God's mercy, did he believe she had known all along? What must he think of her?

'Do you live near here?' he was asking pleasantly.

'She's Sir Richard Woodville's daughter.' Hastings had dismounted to join the king. He made the information sound like a slur.

'My mother is Jacquetta, Duchess of Bedford, your grace.' She lifted her chin defiantly. 'We are staying with my parents because we have nowhere else to go.'

'Difficult, eh?' The royal humour was inappropriate and he was appraising her with the same teasing smile that he had used at Kirby Muxloe. *This is no light matter*, she wanted to exclaim. *We are penniless.*

'Yes, your grace, not easy,' she affirmed.

He was helping her to her feet again, both hands now. 'Maybe I should call on her grace. Where is it you live?'

'Grafton, your highness.'

At the corner of her vision, Lord Hastings looked as stony as the path, but his royal master appeared not to notice his disapproval.

The king tucked the petition into the breast of his hunting brigandine, ruffled Dickon's head and shook Tom's hand. One of his retinue had brought his horse alongside and he mounted and then looked down at Elysabeth with his slow lazy smile.

'Good day to you, Lady Grey.'

Tom dragged her out of the way as the company gave spur. She was still standing like Lot's wife after they vanished from sight.

'Well, that went better than I thought it would.' Tom's voice oozed with self-congratulation.

Dickon appeared to be the only one not in a state of awe. 'That man surely was not the king. Kings are old with grey whiskers and crowns on their head.'

'That's the other king, Dickon, you ass.' Tom pushed him towards the gate. 'Come on, Mother, let's go home to breakfast.'

# 19: KATE

'You're mighty quiet, Ned,' Kate observed.

The king was sprawled in a chair in the private parlour of the Rose and Crown with his boot soles to the fire. His belly might be full of venison but his head was full of something else. He was chewing his thumbnail.

Laying a sheaf of papers aside on the small table, her husband muttered, 'He's met the delectable widow Grey. The wretched woman waylaid us on the way back from the hunt this morning. How she knew we were going to ride that way concerns me, Ned. I'll have to look into that.'

Ned shrugged.

'It's a matter of your protection,' William persisted.

'I don't think Ned needs *that* kind of protection, my love,' Kate murmured. 'Have I met this beauteous paragon?'

'Well, *I* have,' William muttered across the rim of his winecup. 'Several times. All low neckline so you get an eyeful. Jacquetta, the mother, is a Burgundian and the father, Woodville, was my Lord of Bedford's steward. Fellow probably got a leg over before the old man was even in his coffin. Don't look so blank, Ned, you pardoned him and his son, Scales, after Towton. And you reappointed him to the royal council last year.'

'You mean Richard appointed him.' Ned removed his thumb and rose to his feet. 'Jacquetta was sister-in-law to Hal of Agincourt. I'd like to meet her.'

Kate held a cup of wine out to him. 'The duchess or the daughter?' she teased.

'Reconciliation,' murmured Ned silkily, sucking in his cheeks and watching her husband's face. 'Isn't that the name of the game at the moment, William, my friend? Re-con-silly-ation.'

# 20: ELYSABETH

## *29th April 1464, Grafton Hall*

With all the children present at breakfast, the older members of the family made no comment as Elysabeth told them of her meeting with the king. She recognised a gleam in her mother's eyes that boded mischief.

'He was just being polite,' her father said later, when the king's promise to visit was again mentioned in the privacy of the solar. 'The royal party have left the hunting lodge at Penley, so I'm told. He's at Stony Stratford tonight but soon to be riding north to deal with the Scots. There's commissions gone out for the king's army. We have as much hope of him calling here as finding a golden egg in the henhouse.'

The duchess snorted. 'No, I believe 'im, Richard. Mind, it eez not good that we may 'af to make a feast — and we are not talking salted 'erring — but you do not make omelettes without cracking eggs, *hein*?'

'What omelette did you have in mind, my darling?' asked Elysabeth's father, exchanging a meaningful look with her mother.

'A golden one, of course. What other colour eez there?'

When his highness did ride in with a small group that afternoon, Jacquetta refused to let Elysabeth downstairs to greet him.

'You will stay up 'ere. We need to see how hungry he eez?' She wasn't talking about supper.

'No, *Maman.* I am not going to let you use me like this. I am not some green girl.'

'*Non, non, non,* you come down and 'e will think you are a mercenary baggage. You stay here then 'e will come back again. You do this or I will lock you in. See!' she waggled the chatelaine keys on her belt.

'You are being ridiculous.'

'*Non,* clever.' She tapped the side of her nose.

It was torture to stay upstairs. Elysabeth risked looking out as King Edward mounted to leave and she caught him looking up at the windows as if seeking her and her heart turned over.

Surprisingly it was Tom who reaped some joy from the royal visit. Perhaps King Edward had restored something that had been missing for him. Manly approval? Hope?

Catching her eldest in rare good humour after the king had left, Elysabeth came to the point. 'Did his grace say anything about restoring your lands, dearest? Has he read our petition?'

'No.' Tom shrugged. 'Grandfather says we have to take it slowly. That it's really my lord of Warwick who makes those sorts of decisions.'

*Maybe Lord Hastings, too*, thought Elysabeth.

Outside she found her mother leaning on the fence of the horse paddock with her chin in her hands and her brow like a winter field of furrows.

'Has his company emptied the larder?'

'No, I am just thinking 'ow the king can you see you naked.'

'Maman!!!!'

She was about to march away but her mother caught her arm. 'Maybe 'e sees you bathing in the river.'

'What! In a river in April! Surely you want the king to marry a living woman not one who's dying from cold water and stupidity!'

Marry! Did she say marry? Jesu! Her wits were failing her. But Elysabeth had no intention of becoming a royal mistress, if that's what her mother had in mind.

''ush,' her mother commanded, laying her fingers upon Elysabeth's lips. 'If 'e sees how beautiful you are, 'e will not be able to resist. It eez not witchcraft, it's *womancraft*.'

Invited to return for supper, the king happily allowed himself to be seated at the board in her father's chair between her mother and herself. The repast was simple but the viands were accompanied by sauces that had been served in the palaces of Bruges and Paris.

'Created for Philippe le Bel, your grace,' her mother assured King Edward. 'Monseigneur, my first 'usband, 'ad a very good master cook that 'e poached from Queen Ysabeau of France. We 'ave zer recipes.' She darted Elysabeth a see-I-was-right smile.

King Edward nodded enthusiastically, his mouth full, swallowed and said, 'Very good. Very good indeed.' Then he asked, 'Did you ever see Jeanne d'Arc, your grace?'

'Once, eet was in —'

'Maman,' protested John and only a Woodville would have recognised the swift rustle and responding flinch from a kick below the board.

'You 'ave something to say, my son? Ah, you haven't, so let me finish. *Oui*, I saw la Pucelle in Rheims.' That caused another exchange of glances between her older children. 'You 'ave been to Rheims, sire?' The king shook his head. '*D'accord*, Jeanne was a young girl with her hair cut like a soldier's. Not beautiful, like my Elysabeth here, but like a boy. No breasts to speak of.'

'Do you believe she was a witch, madame?'

'*Non*, my lord, but she 'eard the voices of angels in 'er 'ead, but then so does the son of the innkeeper in Towcester and that is because he slept with 'is sister and 'e did not know because she was zer love-child of 'is father by the Stony Stratford priest's daughter and —'

'Maman!' Elysabeth risked a bruising. 'His highness doesn't need to hear all that.'

'But 'e eez the king. This is 'ow zeez things 'appen. Maybe la Pucelle's grandfather had many children outside wedlock.' A shrug. 'Sometimes princes need to bring fresh blood into the family. You be careful marrying this Bona of Savoy, sire.'

'Why?' asked the king, most amused.

'Because she is the French Queen's sister. If you marry Princess Bona, and you 'ave a beautiful daughter, it is not 'ealthy that she marry the Dauphin because that would make them first cousins and that is not good. Too close. Their child could be stupid. The French are stupid enough already.'

'There speaks a true Burgundian,' commented Elysabeth's father. 'Elysabeth tells me you are a keen fisherman, my lord.'

The conversation moved into safer waters — the River Tove and its scaly inhabitants. The king seemed hooked by the suggestion of a morning's fishing. He could afford the time. It would take a few days more for his army to gather at Leicester.

'Do you fish?' he asked Elysabeth, when he could get a word into the rapid Woodville conversation of interruptions.

'Of course she does,' exclaimed the duchess, and John swiftly endorsed the lie before Elysabeth could protest otherwise.

'Oh, you have to take Elysabeth, Father,' he quipped, 'and if it's a *Grey* day, you don't have to get up so early.'

Elysabeth's daydreams had not included worms.

'You can wear a pair of Lionel's hose and wading boots,' John suggested, as he potted the bait and prepared their equipment for next morning.

'I'm supposed to be a respectable widow. If his highness brings Hastings with him, then I am not going.'

'I'll wager ten marks he won't.'

'You haven't got ten marks.'

'Oh, I shall before long. Once I marry a wealthy widow.'

More fool her.'

Trying to tie a pair of Lionel's hose to a gypon before daybreak was easier if you were on the outside but she managed. She also took care to cram a wide winter cap with lappets well down on her braids so the local bird catchers, labourers and any other neighbours who rose early would not recognise her.

The king proved to be a wake-up-cheerful kind of fellow. He arrived with a couple of esquires and was instantly taken round the back of the house where the rods had been arranged for his selection.

Elysabeth watched him for a moment from the doorway. He did not waste time deciding. Instead, he looked round, saw her standing there as if he already knew and smiled.

'Hey, *good* morning,' he said, admiration in his voice as his gaze absorbed her male attire, the sleek-fitting boots and the belted doublet.

Her hands lifted instinctively to grasp her missing skirts for a curtsey and they laughed together as she bowed instead.

'Elysabeth!' exclaimed her father frowning, but whether he feigned his scowl or was genuinely disapproving of her clothing, she could not be certain. It was a mercy their local priest was not a fisherman. She'd be on her knees for a week, if he glimpsed her now.

But she would be punished with blisters on her heels for certain from Lionel's boots, she reckoned, as she and the boys followed the others down the lane.

The king and her father were discussing the organisation of tournaments. The king wanted to hold one at Smithfield in London and invite some of the French and Burgundian jousters to take part. Her father, a former tourney field champion, was full of helpful advice. He was also extolling Anthony's accomplishments and the king was definitely interested. Then excusing himself, his highness dropped back to join Elysabeth and Tom.

'You didn't bring Lord Hastings, then, your highness,' Elysabeth observed.

'Lord, no, doesn't want to fish at sparrow's fart. Like a dancing bear in the mornings, all growls. Needs a good prod to get him going.' She knew how that felt.

'We've met Lord Hastings, your grace,' Tom informed him, trotting at his side, no longer dazzled by the royalness but definitely keen to have attention. 'Mother asked him if he would take me as a page.'

The king gave him a friendly clout. 'Obviously refused, eh, Thomas. Why was that?'

'Because there was no profit in it, I think. I'm not criticising him for that, my lord. It was a sensible decision on his part but disappointing for Mother.'

The king gave her the smile that she remembered from Kirby Muxloe and made no answer. They walked on happily with the two boys between them.

Even kings could be single-minded. 'So what's it to be, gentlemen?' his highness asked when they reached the riverbank. 'Perch, chubb, bream, trout?'

Elysabeth sighed and left the men discussing such niceties while she delivered the usual maternal sermon on being careful not to hook their companions, themselves or her, and to take care on the muddy riverbank because it was easy to slip and the river was running fast. The Tove had deep pools where the Woodvilles bathed in summer but Dickon could not swim.

She had not fished since childhood and she shivered with the cold as she watched Tom bait her hook, wishing she had worn skirt and petticoats over the woollen hose. The water was dark and turgid but it boded well. The fish would be off their guard expecting worms and suchlike that always washed in with the spring rains.

The morning was glorious with the promise of early summer. A swallow dipped and played in the air above the river and the buds of the hawthorn and blackthorn were bursting open.

King Edward was clearly enjoying himself. For a little space, he could forget the rebels in Northumberland, the opportunism of the Scots and the continued existence of King Henry VI. That pleased her. She had only seen kindness in him and she was thankful that he had not been the enemy commander at St Albans. She could save all her resentment for Richard Neville, Earl of Warwick.

She liked Edward Plantagenet, liked him very much. People said it was the Nevilles who made all the decisions in the kingdom and that the king was just their cipher. But she did not think so. Or if that was true, it would not be for long. People warmed to him. The Woodville household from her father to the youngest swineherd were already worshippers and it wasn't because he was the king (well, maybe partly), it was because he made an effort. He wasn't high-horsed with anyone.

'Phff.' She wasn't concentrating.

The king had heard her. He set down his rod and came along to her. 'Cut yourself? Here, let me see!'

'It's nothing, my lord.'

'Come on! Didn't you know I have an Oxford doctorate in healing?' he teased. 'One of my many skills besides signing charters for horse fairs, forbidding merchants' wives to wear cloth of gold, and buttering up my lord of Warwick and the King of France.'

'No wonder they crowned you.' Laughing, she let him take her hand and turn it over.

'Need to keep it clean.' He carried her finger to his lips and sucked it. 'Best way,' he said, eyes gleaming. 'I'm sure you'd do the same for me.' The wicked charm in his eyes would have melted stone angels. 'And if being mortally wounded brought me the touch of your lips, my lady, there's no lengths to which I'd not go.' Then the flirtatious man changed once more to the earnest fisherman. 'Would you like me to cast for you? Make it go further.'

'I *can cast*, my lord.'

*Yes, but it would be a delight to put my arms about you and show you*, his face told her. What woman would or could resist?

Smiling, she nodded, allowed him to stand astride behind her and take her arm between his hands and cast.

'Hey, be at ease more and let me, whoops.' Because the float had landed too near the bank, his grace seemed compelled to keep his arms about her as he reeled in her line to try again. Oh, she could have let her head rest back against his shoulder and sighed with delight but her children were watching.

'Thank you, my lord. Perhaps I should try on my own now.'

He released her. The grin was dimpled, scurrilous. *Not on your own if I have any say*, his hazel eyes informed her but the splashing along the bank made him swing round to look and then, boys and men, they were all shouting and advising as one of the esquires reeled in a goodly sized chubb.

The king was like all men, capable of diverting his entire concentration at an instant. Now all his attention was on casting.

Elysabeth was happy to watch him. She would keep this moment of perfect brief happiness in the pages of her memory until the day she died. The joyful shouts of the men, that early swallow darting and playing above the shimmering river, sunlight, warm upon her back as she —

— screamed and fell backwards into the water with a resounding splash that had her children roaring with laughter. Her brother, apologising for barging past, a concerned father, not to mention the King of England, too, hauled her out to drip amongst the nettles on the bank.

'You clumsy —' Elysabeth bit back the words, glaring at John, as she dashed the water from her lashes. This was her mother's scheming.

'Never mind, my lady,' exclaimed King Edward. 'I'll escort you home before you take a chill. I have to be back at Stoney Stratford by ten o' the clock.'

Elysabeth took a step but her boots were aslosh. The king laughed, bade her sit down then he pulled off one boot and John pulled off the other. The hose was clinging to her body like a second skin except skins didn't threaten to slough off in an instant.

*You conniving cur*, she told John with her eyes. Nor was her father's expression as pure as new fallen snow. Had her brother been closer, a kick on the knees would have whacked him into the water. Meantime, the king was gazing down at her with a male look she remembered from her married days and it wasn't a hunger for breakfast.

'If you can get that doublet off, you can borrow my mantle,' he was offering. He and John had to tug hard at the sleeves to rid her of it. But then with Lionel's shirt clinging tightly to her breasts, she might as well have been naked from the waist up.

'You can't keep that on,' muttered John. 'There's a bush over there or we can turn our backs.'

'I'll manage,' she said, gritting her teeth.

'A moment, my lady,' the king ordered and he strode swiftly along the bank to his attendants. 'We're finished here,' she heard him say. 'I'll see you at the stables. Have my horse saddled and waiting.' Then he returned to her, grabbed Lionel's boots and held out his free hand to assist her to her feet. 'Come on, you stubborn wench. Let's get you to some dry clothes.'

He slowed his pace to match hers as they returned up the track. She picked her way along the edge to avoid the stones and the churned muddy bits. He held out his hand but she dared not take it because she needed both of hers to keep the sodden hose decently round her waist.

'I'm sorry that put an end to your fishing, your highness. My brother is a clumsy fool.'

'Hey, revenge is sweet, my lady. Tip some of the leftover worms into your brother's bed tonight or how about a large, frozen cowpat?'

She laughed, despite her shivers. 'I can tell that you don't ever do the laundry, your grace! A cowpat? That's cruel!'

'Pah, there's far worse. Had my share of falling into moats and a brother like John. We were inseparable.' He dragged a hand across his mouth. 'God keep him, he died at Wakefield beside my father.'

She looked up at him with sympathy. 'Edmund, Earl of Rutland?'

He nodded. 'By heaven, I miss the knave. Of course I've two more brothers but they are much younger. I'd like to take them fishing but they're up in Cousin Warwick's household at Middleham. Besides, there's never time. Today was an exception.' He gave a deep sigh. 'Your family is happy, Elysabeth. Be glad of it.'

The King of England had called her Elysabeth. Maybe she had just slept the night in a toadstool ring! Large, exuberant, handsome, striding along beside her as if they were old friends, dear God, her heart was full.

'Tom was so cheerful this morning,' she remarked. 'You bring out the best in him, your highness.'

He halted and they stood facing each other. 'I'll reverse the attainder somehow, Elysabeth. If it needs an act of parliament, it could take longer, but it shall be done, I promise you.'

She seized his hand and carried it to her lips, the happiest she had been since that dreadful day at Groby. 'I thank you with all my heart. Oh hell!' She quickly grabbed her ebbing hose.

He laughed. 'I'm happy for you to do that again,' he said mischievously. 'Hmm, one thing about being king, I get my hand kissed by beautiful women.'

The King of England had called her beautiful and —

For a moment she thought he might indeed embrace her but she was still oozing water and probably smelled of wet wool. 'Keep going!' He set a hand about her shoulder and urged her forward. 'Unfortunately, this matter of Thomas's lands isn't so straightforward as you might imagine.'

Ah. She braced herself for a wriggling out from his new-laid promise.

'Difficult.' He waggled his palm. 'I don't want to annoy the Bourchiers. Mind, we could be canny and do it all through Hastings. Make him Tom's guardian.'

*We?*

'My lord, he's already refused once. Do you remember, I spoke to him about it two years ago at Kirby Muxloe?'

'Oh, I thought it was only about having Thomas as a page. Well, I'll have a word with him. He's in a much stronger position than he was then. See, I'm trying to build up a loyal barony in the heart of England — Hastings especially and my brother George when he's older. Ha, a pity your father doesn't have more power.' He was looking down at her in a strange way, as though an idea had just burst open in his mind.

'What are you thinking, your grace?' she dared to ask.

'Hmm, that Thomas could become one of my Midland barons. I'll put it to Hastings that way.'

'Wouldn't my lord of Warwick object?'

'No, why would he? I am the king, after all. Hey now, what about you?' he asked, with a squeeze of her shoulder. 'Are you intending to marry again?'

'I shall have to, I daresay.'

'I should think every eligible man in Northamptonshire has lost his heart to you.'

'No, not at all, I've no riches to attract anyone.'

'That's good news because I'd not like to think of anyone but me taking you in his arms.'

'My lord.'

He stopped again and looked down at her. 'Elysabeth, if your mother invites me back to stay this night, will you come to me?'

She looked up at him in astonishment at his directness but, of course, he was only twenty-two. An older, stealthier man might have hunted in a circle before moving in with the net.

'You can't be surprised, my lovely Elysabeth. Ever since I saw you at Kirby, I haven't stopped thinking about you.'

'Nor I you, my lord,' she answered honestly.

'*Ned*. I insist you call me Ned. So what are we to do about this? Meet tonight by moonlight.'

She laughed but shook her head. Oh it was such a pleasure to laugh with him.

'Why not, Elysabeth? You and I, we would be good together and I wager you haven't —'

*Lain with a man since her husband's death?*

'No, I haven't but I'm not going to become your mistress, Ned.' *Ned*, she tasted his name. 'Besides, it's impossible to do anything here without someone in my family knowing.'

'Would they mind?'

*Is the Pope a woman?* 'I would mind, Ned.'

'Really?' He looked so disappointed. 'I could command you as your king.'

'You could try. But do men not say that in King Alfred's day a woman might walk from Cornwall to Scotland without being ravished? Wouldn't you like the chroniclers to write that about your reign, too?'

'Hey, I bet I could seduce you.'

'I'm sure you could.'

'Thomas can have his lands back.'

'Now, you are being cruel. If you can't seduce me without bribery that doesn't say much for either of our characters.'

'But there has to be a way out of this impasse, Elysabeth, my sweet. You can't have a king die of longing?'

She laughed. 'You look extremely healthy to me. No, my lord, I have to stay respectable. The nobility have always sneered at my parents. Maman is seen as a foreign woman who slept in the gutter in marrying her steward.'

'King Hal's widow married her Master of the Wardrobe.'

'Yes, to the disgust of the English. "These foreigners, you know".' She imitated Catherine Neville's dialect and the old lady's way of sucking her cheeks in and raising her eyebrows.

Ned chuckled. 'Hey, that's my Aunt Catherine.'

'Yes, yes! I'm afraid so,' she exclaimed, fingers to her mouth, embarrassed that he'd fathomed her. 'She stayed here recently.'

'Hey, you are good. You are very good. A pity I can't employ you as jester but Master Woodhouse would be insanely jealous. Can you do old Hastings?'

Elysabeth managed the lord chamberlain's concerned look. 'Excellent! Ever met his wife, Kate Neville?'

'No, I haven't.'

'Ah well, no matter.' Then he added, 'She's had a difficult time of things, like you. Lost her first husband, young Will Bonville, slain at Wakefield.'

*And her brothers' soldiers slew my beloved John.*

'But we gave her Hastings for consolation and she seems happy enough. I think you need consoling, too. I'm very good at it.'

'Perhaps when I'm feeling less like a frog. Ouch! A frog who needs horseshoes.'

Realising that he was carrying her boots, he looked sheepish.

'Only one way to deal with this, Lady Grey.' She squealed as he slid an arm behind her knees and hoisted her up. 'I'm admiring the view at the same time.'

'Put me down. I'm almost twenty-seven, dripping wet and a respectable mother of two.'

'And I'm an unrespectable father of three!'

'*Three!*'

'Well, maybe four — *and a half.*'

There had been no farewell kiss but a swift formal parting beside his horse with his attendants watching and the hour bells of the church reminding him of his duties. But her livelihood must have been foremost in his mind because to both her and her parents' astonishment, they received a message at noon brought by a royal courier to inform them that Lord and Lady Hastings would call.

It blew the household sails into a gusty but efficient spin. By the time the king's chamberlain and his wife rode in with their retinue, everyone at Grafton Hall — above and below the salt — could be seen scrubbed, shaved where relevant, pleasantly perfumed and in their best clothes, all lined up on the steps of Grafton Hall like a gaudy rosary.

Jacquetta had lethal elbows and she made use of one now. '*Voila*, zeez Katherine is not as beautiful as you, *mignonne.*'

Beauty was no matter; it was the knowledge that Lady Hastings was Warwick's sister that perturbed Elysabeth. Dismounted and more closely observed, the baroness proved to be a short young woman a decade younger than her husband. Wisps of springy sandy hair showed at the sides of her perse velvet cap, and she had intelligent blue eyes and a sprinkling of freckles. Hastings, surprisingly, had a little girl astride his saddle, a child with her mother's complexion.

'My lord, my lady, welcome!'

If her father cared to remember that he had been a prisoner after Towton when he had last encountered Lord Hastings, he made no sign of it but shook his guest's hand with a smiling face and greeted Lady Hastings with great courtesy as though everyone had been on the same side.

The formalities took a while but with all the introductions complete, Elysabeth's parents escorted their guests to the solar.

Hastings set his hat and gloves on the settle beside him and passed his child's doll to its small owner. The little girl, shy of the Woodville brood, sat upon her mother's knee until John seduced her to giggles by hiding behind the opposite settle with a fox and goose puppet on either hand. While Jacquetta sailed into safe waters with a discussion on children, conversation between the two barons was veneered with courtesy for a few minutes longer until Lord Hastings' hand found his lady's and he came to the purpose of their visit.

'Lord Rivers, your grace, you will be no doubt pleased to hear that our sovereign lord the King has decided to reverse the attainder on your grandson's father, Lord Ferrers. If parliament agrees, of course.'

'That is most gracious of the king and welcome news, my lord.' Elysabeth's father sent her a triumphant smile.

'I am much beholden to the king's grace for the restoration of my husband's honour,' she murmured, reminding Lord Hastings that it was John Grey they were talking about.

Their guest turned to address her. Reluctantly, she thought. He still seemed extremely wary of her as a seductress even though she was wearing a sober, silvery grey gown and a black cone cap. Did he think she was going to knock him to the ground and ravish him — in his wife's presence?

'In view of his grace's mercy, as you put it, Lady Grey, I am agreeable to stand as Thomas's guardian until he comes of age. In return, I shall see that his estates are efficiently managed and that he makes a suitable marriage. In fact,' Lord Hastings exchanged glances with his wife, who did not look very comfortable, 'my lady and I are agreed that our first daughter shall be considered a match for Thomas and if, Heaven forbid, he should die in the meantime, the arrangement shall stand the same for your younger son.'

Elysabeth was astounded.

'Your *daughter*, my lord?' Her gaze fell upon the little girl waggling her doll at John. This was a wondrous suggestion. Ned's doing? An heiress for Tom!

Warwick's sister raised a hand. 'With all respect, Lady Grey, please do not misunderstand us. My daughter here possesses a huge estate, all the Bonville and Harrington inheritance. The decision of her marriage must lie with the king himself.'

Hastings came immediately to support her. 'Even though you, your grace, are of high rank', he inclined his head at the duchess, 'Thomas is not of sufficient standing.'

Elysabeth's mother brushed her fingers down her lips in puzzlement. 'Your pardon, Lord 'astings, I do not know about you, Elysabeth, but, *moi*, I find myself confused.'

Warwick's sister's white skin grew rosy beneath the freckles. 'We meant that … that if God gives us a daughter.'

Elysabeth drew a breath and digested the correction with little pleasure. The proposal — a marriage alliance with the ascendant Hastings family — was astounding. Flattering but also wondrous cunning. Even if Lady Hastings bore a daughter, the girl would need to be about twelve years old or more before a marriage could move beyond betrothal. This was a long way into the future.

'You must pardon my misunderstanding,' she said, and was glad that Lady Hastings nodded graciously, so she could tactfully proceed further. 'Forgive my broaching such a delicate matter but what if you should bear only sons, my lady, and no daughter?'

At least, Lord Hastings seemed to approve of this businesslike approach. He leaned forward, answering on behalf of his wife. 'It is a possibility, of course, Lady Grey, and, consequently, Katherine and I have thought further on the matter. If we have no daughter, would you consider a daughter of my brother Ralph or my sister Anne as a substitute? I realise Anne is married to your mother-in-law's cousin but is that an obstacle?'

Worse and worse but at least Hastings as guardian to Thomas would be a fresh beginning.

'I suppose not,' Elysabeth conceded. 'What concerns me is that Tom will be eleven years or more older than any future bride. There would need to be a limit to the arrangement.'

'Shall we say, Lady Grey, that if none of my family have produced a daughter within six years and you wish to void the arrangement, you would pay a withdrawing fee of 250 marks.' What! That was a considerable sum. A whole host of reasons why she might need to break the contract rode through her mind. During the next six years, God alone knew what might come to pass.

Lord Hastings had not finished. 'In the meantime, Lady Grey, I shall pay you 500 marks which I believe is the sum you need to settle your debts.'

By Heaven, what else did he know about her affairs? How many petticoats she wore?

'That's very generous,' she answered huskily.

But this all needed Thomas's compliance. Would he welcome Lord Hastings as his guardian, the man who had already turned him down? She smoothed her skirts, taking her time to reply further. To refuse would be to insult both Lord Hastings and King Edward, and, anyway, why would she say no when she had been praying fervently to Our Lady for such a reverse in her fortune? Thomas would have to swallow his pride and be grateful. So, for that matter, would she.

Her parents' covert nods confirmed her own decision. 'Very well, Lord Hastings, Lady Hastings, I agree to your terms and I thank you with all my heart.' *Well, most of it.* 'I should also appreciate your good lordship in ensuring Thomas receives an income from the three manors held in trust for him. The case took three years to prove in Chancery.'

'Ah yes, Newbottle, Brington and —'

'Woodham Ferrers in Essex, my lord.'

'Quite.' She'd swear on the Gospels he knew as much as she. 'Consider it done, Lady Grey, providing, of course, all is proper within the law.'

'I'm sure you will find it so, my lord.' Oh God, that came out unwisely. 'I mean that the trust was set up lawfully.'

The ensuing silence was awkward and then Lady Hastings asked, 'What about you, Lady Grey? May we help you to another husband?'

'No, I thank you, my lady.'

'But you've been a widow for four years now.' Was that a reminder that she was already in her late twenties?

'To know that my son has a good future now is sufficient for me but I thank you for your concern, madame. During the troubles of '61, there must have been a time when you found yourself in similar circumstances.'

'My husband declared a traitor? Yes, Lady Grey, and more besides. The battle at Wakefield took five of my kinsmen and then my husband's grandsire was beheaded at St Albans.'

St Albans!

Was it possible to forget the dead? How could it be? Four years now but it still felt like yesterday.

Her mother fidgeted. 'Zer king is a good young man. If anyone can bring about a lasting peace, it is 'im.'

'I'm glad to hear you say that, your grace.' King Edward's unexpected presence, dry, finely apparelled and not smelling of fish, brought them all to their feet and into obeisance. Elysabeth saw his gaze, keen below the brim of his chaperon, scout all their faces before returning to hers as she rose from her curtsey.

'Is all settled then?' their cat-footed, rascal sovereign lord was asking.

'Yes, your highness.' Lord Hastings bowed. His voice held a high-ranking servant's lack of emotion. His face matched. Had his offer been only at royal command?

'And where is Thomas?' asked his highness.

'I'll send for him,' Elysabeth replied with another curtsey.

'No, you may show me where he is, Lady Grey. It pleases me to break the good news myself.' He looked to her parents. 'Madame, Lord Rivers, I think Lord and Lady Hastings would be happy to see some of the beautiful books that belonged to his grace of Bedford. Lady Grey, if you please!' He beckoned and she with a nod of deference to their other guests happily followed the king out.

She could have skipped for joy.

'Satisfied?' he asked over his shoulder. 'You owe me a debt, Elysabeth.'

At the bottom of the stairs in the shadows, she slid her arms round his neck and kissed him. 'I'm so glad I met you,' she murmured and they both laughed. She could feel the hardness of him below the skirt of his short doublet pressing against her skirt and the stone unyielding behind her back. If she let him, he would take repayment swiftly — lift her petticoats and possess her against the wall like he might any willing tapster wench. Well, she needed to enjoy the coupling as well and on her back rather than her feet or legging his waist. And, besides, she had her pride. Pride was more effective than any vow of chastity but saying the 'no' word to an ardent young king might fall on deaf ears. It was like being between a sword blade and the wall. If she denied him...

Fortunately the door above opened.

'Tomorrow is May Day,' she whispered, pulling back from the king. 'The children would be delighted if you could come a-maying with us.'

He was looking up the stairs. 'The whole brood, eh?'

'The whole brood.'

'I'll think upon it. Ah, Will.' The timbre of his voice implied, *how very inconvenient of you* to his friend but Lord Hastings was looking as impervious as duck feathers to water. Was this a frequent occurrence? Did the king's chamberlain control who had access to the royal loins as well as to the royal ear?

'Forgive me disturbing you, your highness, Lady Grey. I thought perhaps as Thomas is to be in my household —'

'Of course,' she murmured before Hastings' liege lord could argue. 'An excellent notion.'

She led the two men to the schoolroom where Thomas and the other boys were with their tutor. The poor schoolmaster nearly had a visitation from God at the sight of the King of England entering his small domain.

Elysabeth watched with joy as King Edward informed Thomas that his father's attainder would be reversed and an agreement had been made with Lord Hastings. Vindication glowed in Thomas's face and it was as though God himself lifted the burden of shame and guilt from the child's shoulders. All the king's — Ned's — doing. And, she realised blasphemously, it was like a baptism, a wondrous new beginning for all of them. She was no longer stained as a traitor's widow; John Grey's name was no longer blemished.

*Our Lady, Mary, Mother of our Lord, thank you! Your name be praised! Blessed St Jude, thank you!*

'And now, as King of England,' announced Ned, 'I decree that today's school is over and we are to have a tournament.'

'What!' Elysabeth and his grace's chamberlain spoke as one.

'Organise it, Thomas Grey! Fetch your Uncle John from the solar, and we shall need wooden swords and shields.' He was halfway out the door when Thomas exclaimed, 'But I don't fight, your highness.'

The king turned, his hazel eyes wide in surprise. Lord Hastings was staring at Elysabeth as though she had put the words in her child's mouth. Curse it, he would probably revoke his offer now.

'It's because of my father, your highness,' Tom explained, swallowing. 'I saw what the soldiers did to my father's body. I took an oath never to fight.'

The King of England, who had never lost a battle, was now lost for words, his mouth a sickle of displeasure.

'I can understand.' That admission emerged rawly, astonishingly, from the king's friend, who actually put an arm around the boy and directed a take-the-matter-slowly look at his liege lord. 'God willing, there will be no more battles, no more good men slain.'

The king's eyebrows rose. 'Ever the poxy diplomat,' he muttered. 'But we are *still* having a tournament. You two.' He pointed a regal finger at Dickon and Edward. 'Go and arm yourselves!'

'Lady Grey, might I have a word in private with you?' Lord Hastings had edged up to join her. She was standing well back

375

from the combat that was about to ensue between Dickon on the king's shoulders and her brother Edward on John's.

'My lord?' With all the yelling going on, it was a small matter to take a few steps back and withdraw through the brushwood fence into the kitchen garden. Lord Hastings was looking so grave, she wondered if there was another addendum to his earlier offer.

'Here will suffice, Lady Grey.'

There was no waste of breath commenting on the healthy bean shoots, the rows of pea sticks, the bed of gillyflowers or the clumps of sage and basilicum. Lord Hastings, taking up a stance on the path, was pleased to beat the matter into the open. 'My lady, since there is no other opportunity to advise you, I shall be brief and to the point. Your beauty has clearly won his highness's heart.'

Elysabeth drew breath to protest but he held up a gloved hand.

'Please, let me continue.'

That angered her but she managed to retort firmly, 'It is only *your* opinion, my lord, not mine, if you will not let me deny it.'

'Then for hypothesis, Lady Grey, supposing it were so.'

She plucked a bay leaf to play with between her fingers. It would help keep her temper tethered. 'Go on, my lord, if you insist.'

'As a woman of the world, my lady...' Did he mean 'older than Ned'? By heaven, she wished he'd stop looking stiff as a playing card. 'I am sure I do not need to remind you that such admiration for your person is only a passing infatuation on his grace's part and I therefore beg you not to take it seriously. He has left a trail of broken hearts from Calais to Northumberland.'

Most likely true.

Her hands rose open-palmed. 'If it is just an infatuation, then why are you warning me, my lord?' Thwat! That clonked him like a mace upon his helm, but he rallied.

'Because being a sister and a mother —' another jab at her maturity, she realised, '— you know that when a youth is lusting after a woman, he finds it hard to take "no" for an answer.'

*Oh, be careful*, she warned herself, but she could not resist saying, 'Twenty-two next month hardly makes him a youth, my lord. He is a battle-scarred commander, four years a king, and surely knows his own mind.' She would have liked to add, *and you, chamberlain, may look a comely thirty-something but you sound like Methuselah.*

'Then I must make my meaning yet plainer, Lady Grey. I say this for your own good. The king has been known to promise *anything* to coax a woman into "an arrangement".'

'*Anything?* I see. Thank you for your counsel, my lord. I appreciate the warning.'

Did he think she wanted the royal treasury to be emptied in return for favours of a carnal nature?

As if embarrassed by her direct look, he toed the nearest pebble. 'And if you do feel tempted into "an arrangement", Lady Grey, please be aware that his duties as king will not permit him to spend much time in Northamptonshire. There are many...' he paused for emphasis, as if she was one of a multitude, 'who believe that my lord of Warwick manages the day-to-day running of the realm but they are in error.' Defensive of his master. Rightly so. She liked that. Or was the message: *Ned does what I advise, let's keep it that way?*

'Be assured, Lord Hastings, that any "arrangement" is out of the question. I accept your advice wholeheartedly. I shall not become one of the king's mistresses if that is what you fear.'

Her fingers clasped the small cross she wore about her neck. 'I so swear.'

'I do not fear it, madame,' he corrected. 'I merely advise you.'

She swept ahead of him, back towards the hubbub. At the wicker gate, she turned. 'I have never nor ever will shame my family by entering into an adulterous relationship with any man. Nor did I visit you in Kirby Muxloe with such a purpose, although I imagine that was what you concluded, my lord.'

He neither denied nor confirmed that. Instead he granted her a tight smile and said, 'I am relieved to hear that you value virtue, Lady Grey. As we said before, Katherine and I are very willing to do anything in our power to help you find a husband worthy of your status.'

'As the daughter of a duchess or merely the widow of John, Lord Ferrers, who fought for Lancaster?' Ha! She snared the sudden retraction in his face before she added blithely, 'Have no fear, my lord, I shall never put such a charge upon you. And here is your lady in search of you.'

Katherine Neville stepped through with her little girl tugging at her belt tassels. 'They've finished,' she said. 'Your brothers won, Lady Grey.'

Hastings put an arm about his wife's shoulders. 'Time to be on our way then, my love. Is his grace leaving with us?'

'I don't think so. He says he is going a-maying.'

Her husband rolled his gaze heavenwards and gave Elysabeth a farewell nod. 'Remember my advice, my lady. It was offered with the best of intentions.'

'I know,' answered Elysabeth, with a bob of curtsey, careful to include his lady in a smile of thanks that she hoped would be judged sincere.

'I'll have the contract concerning your son drawn up and delivered to you tomorrow for your signature and I will receive him into my household when I return with his grace from the north. I expect he has informed you that there are supporters of the former queen who are causing much trouble in Northumberland. They must be dealt with. His grace leaves tomorrow to join his army at Leicester.'

'More battles?' She crossed herself. 'O Jesu, I thought we were at peace.'

'His grace is also meeting once more with envoys from the Scots. God willing, if he can negotiate a peace, it will leave Queen Margaret without much of her support. You look pale, madame. Are you not well?'

'I hope his grace's life will not be at risk nor yours either, Lord Hastings. And, believe me, upon my very soul, I have no love for Queen Margaret although I was once a maid-of-honour and my husband was slain in her service.'

A slight curl of lip. 'Very wise. The king can be ruthless with those who kiss his hand and then betray him. I hope your father and brothers will remember that.'

# 21: KATE

## *30th April 1464, Grafton*

Kate rode her ambler closer to her husband's stirrup once they were back on the road to Stony Stratford. Cecily was looking sleepy in his arms but they would still need to be careful in their conversation. The child could be like a little rabbit pricking her ears up.

'So, Will?'

He signalled to their retinue to fall back. 'Not much to tell, my love.'

'You mean she didn't seduce the handsome chamberlain between the sage and thyme with a trio of snails for witness?'

He grinned and shook his head. 'No, darling, not even a "come hither". Hell take it, I'm not sure what to make of the creature. I talked, she listened. I said "don't", she promised "won't". That's it, in a nutshell.'

Kate sighed. 'She's very beautiful and looks far younger than her age. I can understand why he is smitten.'

'Trouble is, love, if she's a challenge as well, that'll only egg him on. He was like that with Butler's widow but lost interest after he got her into bed.' He mouthed the last two words as his stepdaughter stirred.

'I don't think it's just her.'

'What do you mean?'

Kate searched for the right words. 'He likes being there.'

'I can't think why. I agree the duchess has some nice pieces from her first marriage but the hall is pretty damned cramped. They'd be lucky to fit thirty in there.'

'I'm not talking about the hall but *them*, Will. The family. He likes them. It's as if he can forget about being king when he's there and —'

'Arse about?'

'Yes. You heard him yesterday, going on about the way their cook served up the beef. It's everything, the food, the lack of ceremony, the Burgundian mother is very charming and exotic, and he can talk tournaments with Lord Rivers, and then there's *her.*'

'Well, he'll soon be wed to the Queen of France's sister if your brothers have their way, and she's a southerner. That might keep him out of mischief.'

Kate shrugged. They slowed their horses to let their retinue catch up. It was her own thoughts kept galloping ahead. What if Ned did not want an alliance with France like Richard did? What then? Life was uncertain. You could be sure of nothing.

# 22: ELYSABETH

## *1st May 1464, Grafton*

There were May blossoms that morning scattered over the daybed in her mother's solar, sprays of flowers pinned in the braids that coroneted Elysabeth's head and a naked dagger in his grace of England's hand. There was no one else in the house and the blade was against the skin of her throat.

'I could kill you and there would be no questions asked. I've killed men, Elysabeth, thrust my sword into them, ordered my enemies to be hanged or beheaded and much, much worse and I'm in no mood for a prick teaser. You're dealing with a king not some lovesick ploughman.'

She could feel the point sharp in the valley of her throat but she managed to say, 'And you are dealing with a woman of … of virtue.' Her hand thrust her skirts back down. Could he not read the trust and love in her eyes and have compassion for her stubbornness? 'Virtue, Ned. It's all I have left.'

'Be damned to your virtue!' There was a blatant sulky curl to his lower lip as he retreated, leaned back on his elbow. 'You kiss me with passion as though you want me and then say no.' The male eyes were speculative still, watching her as he meaningfully slid the blade slowly back into its sheaf. 'I've never had a woman refuse me.' She sat up before he touched her again. 'Of course you haven't,' she agreed, with a wistful sigh, easing her feet to the floor. 'You're young, handsome, virile and the lord of all England. And you are going to marry a princess who will give you a dozen sons and I shall hug my aching heart on the day of your wedding.'

'It sounds ruddy tedious.' He drew his finger wickedly down her spine. 'We should live for the moment and at this moment I want you more than anything on God's earth. I'm hurting, hot and hard for you.'

'Please stop tempting me.'

He knelt up to kiss the side of her neck and slid his hands down her arms to her wrists. 'Then, you do want me?'

'Yes, Ned, but I've been a wife ten years and a mother almost as long as that. I'm in love with you, not infatuated. Hastings says you have these infatuations.'

'Mercy's sake, Elysabeth, I am not infatuated and Hastings should mind his own friggin' business. *I*, Elysabeth, am a lovesick fish at the end of your line. Please, for the love of Heaven, reel me in.'

'No! My lord, no.' She twisted to look at him. 'I may not be good enough to be your queen but I am not going to become your mistress.'

'I'm in love with you.'

'And I with you, Ned.' Tears made her gaze glassy. 'By my faith, I never thought I could be in love again. It hurts, doesn't it? It hurts knowing you will marry someone else.' She felt the insistence in the fingers that had risen once more to caress her shoulder. 'Ned, everyone will be back soon and you have to leave for Leicester. There's an army waiting for you.'

'Elysabeth.'

She shook her head. 'Please go, my dear lord.'

His touch left her abruptly. There was a silence and then a rustle of sleeve.

'Very well, become my queen! How about that for an offer? Now will you lie with me?'

It had been said too easily.

*He'll promise anything.*

She looked round at him. He was lolling back now on his arm, imperious, waiting. 'Very well, my lord, prove it.'

'*Prove it?*' That put an end to the nonchalance.

She turned, resting her forearms on the cushions. 'Marry me and I'll lie with you.'

He looked at the valley between her breasts, then as though he had suddenly heard a trumpet call to battle, he sprang to his feet and paced. So she had caught him out. He strode back and forth, biting his thumbnail. And then he swung round. 'Very well,' he exclaimed, 'find a priest and two witnesses and I'll wed you.'

O Sweet Mother of God! This had gone too far.

'No, no, no,' she exclaimed, clapping a hand to her lips as she scrambled to her feet. She was uncertain whether to laugh in amazement or run from him for his own good. 'This isn't right, Ned. What about Bona of Savoy?'

'Be buggered to Bona of Savoy!'

Sensing his seriousness, she backed away towards the door, her hands patting the air. 'I'm going to leave you to think about this.'

'I have thought about it,' he said haughtily. 'Find your mother, organise a priest! Go!'


A swift, strange wedding for a king. He with no finery and she clad in a simple gown, with a chaplet of spring flowers, swiftly woven by Tamsin, adorning her unbraided hair.

Her mother, together with Tamsin and the duchess's most trusted tiring woman, both lured from dancing around the maypole in the village, would stand as the only witnesses and a little blind chorister would sing the anthem. There would be no congregation.

The chaplain, sworn to secrecy, awaited them with obvious unease at the door of the manor house chapel with the little chorister at his side All must be done before her family and the rest of their household came back from prancing in the field behind the alehouse. This was so hurried. Too hurried.

Realising she already wore a wedding ring, Elysabeth silently beseeched God to bless John Grey's immortal soul as she hurriedly slid off the gold band and handed it to her mother. That first time she had been blessed with the Queen of England's presence; this time she would have the king's. The king's because he lusted for her or because he truly had fallen in love with her?

If her questions were unspoken, the chaplain's were not. Had the banns been read? Did the bride and groom have any family members in common?

'Have done with this!' muttered her mother. 'Zey stand before you consenting. Waste no more time!'

'Just make us handfast,' Ned said with authority. 'I must leave before noon.'

'This is hasty and ill-advised then,' said the priest bravely, fingers fumbling at his throat as though he already felt the noose of punishment.

'Not so,' Ned said, smiling down at Elysabeth. 'I have given this much thought.'

But still the chaplain hesitated. Behind her, she heard her mother's impatient sigh, felt the tension in Ned's fingers as he held her hand. This was madness, folly and unbelievable.

'Lady Elysabeth?' It was at her the chaplain was pleading, the message of fear in his eyes. At last she grasped the poor man's terror. This was almost treason. If Ned changed his mind, was coerced by his counsellors into marrying Bona of Savoy or

Isabella of Castle, he could order the chaplain's death and hers as well. Warwick would probably see to it for him.

Or the Kingmaker might destroy, even kill, his royal cousin for this stupidity. Ned was taking an immense risk, too.

As if he sensed her fearful thoughts and needed to calm his own, the King of England lifted her hand to his lips and the irrepressible smile that she loved softened his face as he gazed at her.

Then so be it! God's will be done.

'Trust us,' she told the chaplain, assured now of her own truth, 'as we trust in Almighty God to bestow his wisdom and his grace upon us and to hold us in his mercy for ever more.'

'Then, so be it.' The chaplain closed his eyes for a moment before he spoke the Latin words: '*Si vero aliquis impedimentum aliquod proponere voluerit…*'


Afterwards they walked hand in hand into her parents' bedchamber. Ned was sterner now, perhaps troubled by what he had just promised or maybe his thoughts were already with his army.

'There isn't much time, sweetheart.'

'There's enough.' She knelt upon the bed, curling her arms around him and drawing his face to hers. They kissed and kissed again hungrily now, and then he was unclothing her swiftly, wrenching the shoulders of her gown down to enjoy her breasts, pushing her skirts up. Some stroking between the thighs, the intense look, a short teasing of her nipples and then he was freeing his member from the entanglement of his clothing and ready to satisfy himself within her.

'*No!*'

'No? What the hell do you mean "no"? I've just wed you, damn it.'

She wriggled back on the bed and knelt facing him. 'I mean no, not yet. You're not capturing Berwick and storming a gap in the town wall, my darling Ned, you're making love.'

'You're so beautiful, I can't help myself. Dear God, don't you want me?' Then his expression softened wickedly. 'You look as though you do.'

'I do. I'm wet, creamy with longing for you but we need to take this slowly.'

'Then —'

'Not yet!' She leaned back swiftly out of reach as he tried to grab her.

'What am I supposed to do? Chase you round the friggin' bed? None of the other women I've lain with have ever complained.'

'Did you give them a chance of fulfilment? Or did you fall asleep or ride off somewhere like you want to do now?'

'Fulfilment?' Haughty, furious, chin jutting. 'As I said, no complaints. Can't we just do this first and then —'

Some cunning was needed. 'Wouldn't you like me begging, desperate, panting for you?'

'Yes.'

'Then let us take matters a little more slowly so that we *both* enjoy this.'

'I don't know if I can. You've kept me waiting. By heaven, I have an army waiting. Hastings is waiting.'

'I want you hungry, my lord king, rrraavenous.' She bit the air like a lioness 'And I want skin to skin not a swift taking.'

'Very well,' he murmured, pulling his shirt up and flinging it to the floor. 'The King of England is not slow in learning.' He grabbed her shoulders and pushed her back against the pillows. 'I know you like *this*.' His lips and tongue swirled and teased, satisfying each breast in turn.

'I'd like this, too.' She pressed his fingers down between her thighs. 'Can you do both?'

'Not if we hold a conversation.'

His fingers instinctively knew their craft. She arched back, enjoying the pleasure of his lovemaking and then he was kissing her on the mouth again while his touch wrought its magic. Thirteen years, she thought sliding her hand about his hardness and her body was crying out with need.

Not long, not long, not —

'Now,' she gasped, guiding him into her. 'Now, now, *now*!'

In a yield of self, gazes locked, a beauteous, goodly unison of pleasure. Ned collapsed back on the pillow when he was spent, with a whistle of breath, his hand seeking hers where it lay beside him. 'Good, very good. You were right.'

'Because the act was fulfilled with love,' she whispered, leaning over to kiss him.

'Yes, you spoke true, it does make a difference.' He gathered her against his breast and for a little while they lay in silence.

Then with a deep sigh, cuddling her even closer to him he murmured, 'Know that I wed you in full knowledge of what this will mean so do not claim any more that you are not worthy. You are the daughter of a duchess, the mother of sons and the most beautiful woman in the kingdom. I honour you, my lady.' He kissed her hair. 'You will make a fine queen.'

'I don't know what to say,' she said, pulling back from him, shaking her head in wonderment.

The dimples reappeared. 'Actually, I'm lying. I just want someone to snuggle up to at night. I still miss Edmund. It gets very cold in the big bed at Westminster and it would be good to have someone I can grumble to. Ow! Stop hitting me. I can't lead an army with — Sweet Jesu! Look at the sun's height. I have to go.'

They embraced laughing and then she helped him dress.

'Take care,' she whispered, when he was ready to leave. 'Come back to me.'

'As soon as I may. You realise this may be a secret for a while.' He tucked a finger beneath her chin. 'You understand that?'

'Yes.'

'No one must know. It has to be announced at the right time?'

'I understand.'

From the window, she watched him ride away, the brim of his hat pulled down to hide his face.

It was ridiculous, unbelievable, scandalous but she was a widow no more.

# 23: KATE AND ELYSABETH

## *28th September 1464, Michaelmas Eve, Reading, Berkshire*

Across the chapter house of Reading Abbey where the royal court was gathered, Kate watched Ned's beautiful queen without envy of the woman's new status, in fact, with sympathy. Tomorrow Elysabeth Woodville would be formally announced as Ned's consort before the great altar of the abbey with his brothers and the royal council in attendance (including Richard, who was still steamed up over the matter, it was a wonder his hat hadn't blown across the chamber when the announcement was made). Ned was also talking about holding a coronation for her in the Abbey of St Peter's, Westminster, sometime next year. Determined, Kate supposed, to make everything as public and legal as possible after the scandal of his secret wedding.

Well, she hoped 'Queen' Elysabeth would never fall into Queen Margaret's vengeful hands. This woman and that impoverished family of hers were sailing into perilous waters but then the rewards undoubtedly made the gamble worthwhile. Life never ceased to amaze Kate. Nothing was certain or stable. The Lord God must be really bored sometimes, the way He let things happen. He probably said 'what if…' and moved the human chess pieces for sheer whimsy.

Beside her, Richard stood in sullen silence not at all happy. Ned was sliding out of the nursery reins and he did not like it one whit. He was muttering treasonous words like 'lunatic' and 'idiot' and 'that's the alliance with France shattered, all that cursed labour for nothing!' She and William were in the doghouse, too, for not keeping Ned under watch at all times.

Well, what's done was done, though disputing whether Ned had been right or wrong would keep the court whispering for weeks, let alone every marketplace in England. It wasn't just the secrecy of the marriage or that the woman was half-Burgundian but that she was not a virgin princess. The marriage to a woman whose maidenhead had already been breached meant a lot of English widows and mothers would be suffering the deadly sin of envy and sighing over lost opportunities. Elysabeth Woodville would be hated because her dream of fabulous riches and a princely husband had come true. Poor woman, Kate decided again. The new queen's immediate duty was to bear Ned sons — many sons, as fast as possible. If she did not give him any children, the secret marriage would provide an easy excuse for Ned to shut her in a nunnery and marry a real princess.

'Niece.' She turned to find it was Catherine Neville, clothed in hunting green with a soaring cap of gold brocade, who had touched her arm. 'Good day to you, Kate Hastings.'

'Oh, Godmama, I heard you'd arrived.'

'I wouldn't miss this for the world. Lovely, isn't she? I think we should go and be sweet to her. She cooked me a rather tasty dinner a couple of years since.'

Kate bit her lip. '*What?*'

'I could have paired her up with one of my household knights but she was clearly saving herself for something better. Come, let's try her manners.'

Old Catherine Neville, their visitor at Grafton two years ago, did not curtsey. Maybe she couldn't. A sort of stoop and deep duck of the head sufficed. Lady Hastings curtseyed beside her. *At least I recognise these people*, Elysabeth thought with relief. Part of the skill in being queen would be to make sure she remembered everyone as well as some little morsel about their interests or concerns that would make them feel singled out and valued.

'Lady Catherine, how is your tiring woman? I trust she did not suffer any further hurt from the chariot accident?'

Beside her she sensed Ned's approval.

'Ah, yes, you are already acquainted.'

'Indeed we are,' exclaimed the dowager. 'Stayed with her family overnight in a snowstorm. Now, forgive me if I ask a favour, your graces, but at my age, one doesn't sit upon one's hands. You'll be looking for husbands and wives for your queen's family, shall you not, nephew?'

'Yes.' A husbandly smile beamed down at Elysabeth. 'I suppose we shall. I'll leave you ladies to discuss the matter.' He bestowed a kiss on Elysabeth's hand, and beckoning Lord Hastings over to accompany him, strode down the hall to invade a cluster of councillors.

Elysabeth was left to deal with the dowager's request. She looked across at Lady Hastings but Warwick's sister was looking equally puzzled.

'Very well, Lady Catherine, pray feel free to ask.'

'Well, since I'm a widow, your grace, and heaven knows how little time I can expect before the Devil beckons me across his doorstep, I'm putting my order in first. If he's still available in the marriage market, I'll have *him*.'

Elysabeth followed the jab of the dowager's finger and suppressed a gasp. The only man in that corner of the chamber was her brother, John. He was busy telling some tale that had already Meg Plantagenet and Bessie Scales laughing heartily.

'*John*! You want my brother John, for a husband?'

John, who was scarce twenty years old!

'Yes, madame,' said the old dowager. 'I do! At least he won't bore me to death like some.'

'Christ's Blessed mercy, Godmother!' The jaw of the duchess's niece, Lady Hastings, almost hit the tiles. 'There would be … why, over forty years difference in your ages. That's outrageous.'

'Yes, isn't it,' chortled the sixty-five year old. 'But I'm game, if the lad agrees, that is.' She smiled wickedly at Elysabeth. 'You look as though you've been whacked on the head with a very large cudgel, your highness.'

Elysabeth bit her lip. She looked to the shocked Katherine Hastings for support but when none was forthcoming, she answered honestly. 'I don't know what to say.'

A creped-skin hand patted hers. 'Then say nothing, dear highness. We all make choices. If your brother agrees, he'll be very pampered. And England will be so shocked and busy talking about the scandalous nature of my marriage, they'll forget about the scandal of yours. Helpful, hmmm?'

That was a slap in the face.

'How very generous of you to make such a sacrifice solely for his grace the king's wellbeing, Lady Catherine,' Elysabeth retaliated with as grave a face as possible. 'I shall inform my lord king and my brother straightway.'

Lady Hastings lifted a hand to her mouth but her eyes were awash with laughter.

The old lady dipped her head, smiling, and creaked away like a storm-tossed caravel.

'Please feel free to inform your husband of this proposal, Lady Hastings,' Elysabeth said calmly. 'I think it is a matter for the royal council to deliberate upon.' If such a horrendous marriage happened without the approval of Ned's councillors, her family would suffer the opprobrium of being greedy. And she knew who would be the first to accuse them — Warwick.

Warwick's sister looked approving at the mention of the royal council but the young woman's answer did not match her face. 'With all respect, madame, it is usually the king who decides these matters.'

Another smack.

'May I inform my husband now, your highness, as you request?'

'You have leave.' Elysabeth nodded, was curtsied to and then found herself standing unattended.

'Alone, your royal highness?' Lady Ferrers made a fulsome obeisance at her elbow. Grey and a man who was probably John Bourchier bowed at her side.

Instead of bidding her erstwhile mother-in-law to rise, Elysabeth held out her hand for the woman to kiss. 'You are welcome to our court,' she said falling back on regal formality. Perhaps the only way to protect herself from mockery from now on was to hedge her person with ceremony. As queen, she might not command respect but she could enforce it. A painful unwelcome step.

'Madame, we congratulate you on your marriage.'

'Do you, Grey? How very kind.' It was tempting to remind the Greys that she had won the matter of the three manors and that Thomas was to wed an extremely wealthy heiress but that would have been small-minded and a petty revenge. Instead she said graciously, 'You are looking very well, Lady Ferrers. Marrying this young man here was a clearly a good decision.'

'Your highness has set us all an example.' A clever insult or just an ill-thought out answer?

'You have leave.' With a nod and graceful spread of fingers, she dismissed them and they had no choice but to bow once more and back away.

Kate had made her curtsey to the new queen and there would be more obeisance required at tomorrow's ceremony. She didn't particularly like Elysabeth but this new queen wasn't part of her future. There was a new babe inside her, God willing, not a girl child destined for Thomas Grey, but a boy she might safely carry to birth, and there would be more in the years to come. Happiness for her would be raising a family, busying herself with household matters. She had just spent a few weeks refurbishing Beaumont Inn, their London house, and William was talking about building a great castle at Ashby-de-la-Zouch.

'Kate.' His voice broke through her reverie. He was before her now, a goblet of Rhenish in each hand.

She smiled, well-loved and still in love. They clinked glass to glass.

'Here's to the new dynasty,' he exclaimed dryly, ranging himself beside her, his gaze flicking to the new queen. 'I like surprises but I could do without this one.'

She curled her arm through his. 'At least the mercers and tailors guilds will be celebrating. A coronation in the offing.'

'And who do you think will do the arranging, love? I'd hoped to spend more time with you and Cecily. If it's not the plaguey Scots or Margaret's rebels, it's a ruddy coronation. Secret marriage!' he growled beneath his breath. 'If he wasn't a good friend and King of England, I'd give him a bloody hard punch on the nose. Oh, Hell damn it, I'm wanted yet again.' Ned, his nose unsullied, was looking their way, a message of summons in his eyes.

William kissed her cheek. 'Back in a moment, sweetheart.'

Kate doubted that as she watched him stride over to the king. 'Moment' was her life writ large and she had resolved not to be jealous. William, because of his high offices and sense of duty, was a shared commodity and Ned had the greatest piece. And, with a queen now, there would be others. Others she did not want to think about or imagine.

*Your husband will be famous and much loved.*

Well, if William strayed, he could do it down in London out of her sight. She would give him a home to come back to, loving arms. Always.

*Jesu, I'm standing here on my own again like a leper, and people are watching,* Elysabeth realised. This is what it is going to be like. The watching. Have I the strength for this? Ned believes I have so I mustn't let him down but —

'Your highness.' Princess Meg was before her now with half a dozen of young maids-of-honour herded up behind her. Jacquetta was clearly playing sheep dog and the young girls were looking very chastened as they made obeisance.

'Lordy, I'm sorry, your highness, your mother says we are supposed to stay with you at all times. It's just we've not had a queen for four years.' Behind her, Elysabeth's mother rolled her eyes.

Elysabeth curled Meg's arm through hers. 'We'll learn together.'

Yes, people would watch her and Ned like hunters, like circling carrion.

No man could be charged with treason if criticism was unspoken. It would be covert enmity: the raise of an eyebrow, a twist of the lips, the knowing nod, the touch of an elbow. Perhaps, with time, she would acquire a protective deafness, a hardened shell.

Well no matter, her sons, her landless brothers and undowried sisters would be provided for. William Hastings would be paid his penalty fee of 250 marks and she would inform him Tom would be betrothed to the king's niece instead — as wealthy an heiress as the Bonville-Harrington child. Maybe she'd choose one of the Bourchier brothers for one of her sisters.

And she would repay those who had helped her. Roger Wigston of Leicester would receive thrice the money he had lent her, and if he hadn't sold her gillyflower pendant, she would redeem it or she would buy it back from whoever had bought it from him. It was within her power now. And perhaps she would make that flower her emblem for the coronation since it was also beloved of Our Lady and a symbol of motherly love.

Motherly love. Perfect for a queen. For a kingdom. For a king who needed sons to entrench a dynasty.

Perfect.

Behind Meg's back, she met her mother's smile.

There would be enemies and flatterers but she had her family and they would always tell her the truth. Now she knew what Ned had needed was people he could trust, who owed their loyalty to him above all others.

'Sweetheart,' Ned was at her side again. 'Come. Let's to bed. Tomorrow will be all bells and fanfares.'

That night, before she lay beside Ned, she knelt upon the prie-dieu in their bedchamber with a whole rainbow of emotions flooding through her, from fear to pride, from exultation to disbelief.

*O Sweet Mary, Mother of God, Blessed Lady, and all the holy company of heaven, I know not what the future may bring, but I thank you for the blessings of this day. Almighty God, in whom is all mercy and grace, with as good heart and mind as to me is possible, I implore you help me be a comfort to my lord husband and a goodly mistress to the people of this realm.*

*Amen*

'I'll always be here for you,' she told Ned as they lay together. 'No matter what shall come to pass. I make that promise to you.' So speaking, she carried his hand to her lips.

His large hands framed her face. 'Even if I become a penniless beggar?'

'Yes, Ned, even then. I'll always be waiting for you with love.'

After all … in truth, what other priceless gift was there to offer to a king?

# HISTORICAL NOTES

It is estimated that between 1450 and 1500, during the struggle for the crown between the Houses of York and Lancaster, sixty-two of England's lords and their heirs were slain. Of the forty-four noble ladies who were left as widows, twenty-one remarried.

This is the story of two of those women, Kate and Elysabeth, whose husbands fought on opposing sides. Kate was the sister of the earl known in history as 'Warwick the Kingmaker' and Elysabeth became very famous in her own right.

As the story begins, Kate's young husband is away in Yorkshire in the army of the rebel Duke of York, and Elysabeth's husband is a captain in the army of Queen Margaret d'Anjou, the leader of the House of Lancaster.

In London, Kate's brother, the Earl of Warwick (York's nephew), is holding King Henry VI a prisoner at the Tower of London.

# A NOTE TO THE READER

Elysabeth's son, Thomas Grey, eventually married Kate's daughter, Cecily Bonville, and she became Marquess of Dorset. Their wedding is mentioned in my previous novel *Mistress to the Crown*, which deals with the later years of King Edward IV and Lord Hastings.

Elysabeth spent her last years at Bermondsey Abbey. She died in June 1492. At her request, there was no grand funeral. In the late evening, her simple wooden coffin was placed on top of King Edward's sarcophagus in St George's Chapel, Windsor. Her will, made two months before her death still exists, and I have used some of her own phrases in her prayers in the final chapter of this novel. A copy of Kate's will, written in 1503 is in the appendix of David Baldwin's *The Kingmaker's Sisters*. Hastings was buried close by the grave of his beloved king in St George's Chapel, Windsor Castle, and Kate is buried in St Helen's Church, Ashby-de-la-Zouche. Henry Courtney never became an earl and was executed in 1469.

The tree in Northamptonshire where Elysabeth is supposed to have waylaid the king is now a burned-out stump and hardly likely to date from the 1460s anyway, but often legends have an element of truth in them. It may be still possible to view the site courtesy of the farmer who owns the land.

An archaeological dig to find the remains of Grafton manor house is long overdue. It is possible the house the Woodvilles owned was rebuilt as a palace, used by King Henry VIII and Anne Boleyn. However, any stately buildings in Grafton were blown up by the Roundheads in the Civil War. Some of the Woodville family also owned Ightham Mote in Kent at one time and Edward and Elysabeth are known to have stayed there with the king's sister, Margaret (Meg) on her visit from Burgundy in 1480.

Astley has had several castles on the same site. The current ruins are once more a hotel. The tombs of Cecily Bonville, her husband Thomas Grey, their son, Henry, and Lady Ferrers are in the parish church.

Groby, which has featured in the *Time Team* TV series, is privately owned, but you can glimpse the brick tower from the road. Bradgate Public Park is still a deer park and contains the ruined home of Kate and Elysabeth's descendant, Lady Jane Grey.

Ashby-de-la-Zouch Castle, though sadly ruined, is a tribute to the power and importance of Lord Hastings and this was Kate's home for all of her married life whereas her daughter, Cecily, seems to have preferred Shute. Kirby Muxloe is now much as it would have been the 1480s. It was being rebuilt in brick by John Cowper but the sudden execution of Lord Hastings at the Tower of London in 1483 halted the building work and Kate probably no longer had the heart to finish it. Shute Hall is now holiday accommodation. I was fortunate to have visited there when it was still open to the general public and it was fun to meet the owners.

Chewton Mendip Church has a tomb with the FitzRogers' effigies on top but it clearly does not belong to them. I haven't been able to find out where Will Bonville and his father were interred.

The Wars of the Roses has been my great interest since I was fourteen, so a lot of research over the years has contributed towards this novel. There are not a lot of primary sources that throw light on Kate and Elysabeth from 1461 to 1464 but the Feet of Fines showing the 1455 grant and the Chancery documents (C 1/27/268) *Grey* v. *Fylding* concerning Newbottle, Brington and Woodham Ferrers have survived. Elysabeth was granted the right to the income from the manors in 1463, and eventually in 1466, according to the Calendar of Patent Rolls, the king granted the manors to the Archbishop of Canterbury, Bishop Robert Stillington, Lord Rivers, Lord Scales and several others. I am very grateful to former Supreme Court Judge, John Bryson, for his help in deciphering the medieval handwriting and for explaining the intricacies of fifteenth century land ownership. I am also grateful to Elysabeth's recent biographer, historian David Baldwin, for his comments.

The grant giving Kate custody of Cecily is in the Calendar of Patent Rolls. So, also, is a confirmation on 17th February 1462 of all the grants William, Lord Hastings had received from the king and the mention of Kate as his wife confirms that they were married by then.

The 1525 Survey of seventy-nine of Cecily Bonville's holdings in the West Country by her surveyor Richard Phellyps (PROE, 315/385) provides a marvellous source of information on the tenants who lived at Shute. I also delved into M.F. Bridies' *The Story of Shute*, *The Itinerary of John Leland*, D.A. Ramsay's series on *Bradgate and its villages* and Charles James Billson's *Medieval Leicester* for local information. *British History Online* is a wonderful resource especially as it now has digital copies of the Victoria County History volumes.

For readers who would like to read more about these historical people, here are some secondary sources: *Warwick the Kingmaker*, Michael Hicks; *The Kingmaker's Sisters*, David Baldwin; *Elizabeth Woodville*, David Baldwin; and *Edward IV*, Charles Ross. There are also many useful articles in the *The Ricardian*, journal of the Richard III Society, and on specialist internet sites.

If you enjoyed this novel, it would be lovely if you can give it a thumbs up on **Amazon** and **Goodreads** and word of mouth is terrific too. I hope you will try some of my other novels too, and I'm grateful to Sapere Books for bringing them out again for a new generation of readers. You can find out more about me **on my website**.

Thank you again for giving some of your precious time to reading *The Golden Widows*..

Isolde Martyn

**Sapere Books** is an exciting new publisher of brilliant fiction and popular history.

To find out more about our latest releases and our monthly bargain books visit our website: **saperebooks.com**

Printed in Great Britain
by Amazon

41890858R00225